the STRANGE

the
STRANGE

A Novel

RON BASE

West-End
Books

Library and Archives Canada Cataloguing in Publication

Base, Ron, 1948-
    The Strange / Ron Base.

ISBN 978-0-9736955-1-9

    I. Title.

PS8553.A784S76 2009   C813'.54   C2009-902201-X

West-End Books
80 Front St. East, Suite 605
Toronto, Ontario
Canada M5E 1T4

Cover Design: Caroline Versteeg
Text design: Ric Base
Electronic formatting: Ric Base

First Edition

For Jean and Hana
les femmes incroyables

It may have happened, it may not have happened: but it could have happened.
- Mark Twain

I wonder what will be thought of our generation if, in some future riot, we do not unbolt this tall, skinny pyramid of iron ladders, this giant and disgraceful skeleton ....
- Guy de Maupassant

Hypocrisy is the homage that vice pays to virtue.
- Francois de La Rochefoucauld

PROLOGUE

The falcon could talk. I swear.

At the seniors' residence in the small Canadian town where I have ended up, that's the part everyone has trouble with. Not my age necessarily, even though it is well over a hundred and counting—or my childhood adventures in Paris, London, and Vienna at the turn of the century.

It is that talking falcon.

They sit respectfully enough when I talk about the power of the Strange and how it both cursed and blessed my young life. They are riveted by my tales of the cunning and beautiful Mrs. Nevermore. They do not look dubious when I tell them that she was a sorcière and confidence woman who could persuade anybody of just about anything—she could even convince the next King of England that the Eiffel Tower was for sale. How do you sell the Eiffel Tower to the King of England? they demand to know. Ah, that's the story, isn't it? The tale that has to be told.

But when I bring up the falcon, that's when doubtful glances start to fly. I can't blame people, really. I'm a pretty ordinary fellow these days. I sit in the Great Room at the residence and, like most of the others, I fall asleep during the so-called Happy Hour. I join in the grumbling about the food even though the last thing I'm interested in is eating. Along with so many other things I have lost my sense of taste. I can still move around pretty well, but, like just about everyone here, with the aid of a walker.

Someone comes in each morning to help me dress, a good-natured Jamaican woman named Esther possessed of a deep, rolling laugh that erupts when I start up my fantastical yarns. I don't think Esther believes a word I say, but her eyes sparkle when I talk in the way good listeners can make you think they are hanging on every word.

Except for its most unexpected gift—longevity—age robbed me of the Strange some time ago. I awoke one morning and its power just wasn't there any more, like my appetite or my ability to move freely. Maybe it wasn't the Strange I lost. Perhaps it was imagination. Without imagination how could those events out of my past possibly have transpired—the gargoyles that sprang to life from the Other World, the evil Corbeau who wanted to kill me, the one-eyed Natalia who tried to seduce me to her side?

The falcon was part of all that, but no one wants to believe it. That doesn't change basic truths, though: the bird could talk, the gargoyles could fly, the Eiffel Tower could be sold, and a fourteen-year-old boy could become transfixed by a transfixing woman. He could come to learn the curious ways of the Strange, and at the same time discover resources within himself that would serve him the rest of his long life.

That is the story I have to tell, of Paris at a remarkable time, of magic, and of a transforming iron tower. These days I tell it to anyone willing to listen. After all, why keep anything a secret at this point? There is no one left to be harmed by anything I have to say, and it wiles away the time and focuses the attention of my fellow travelers through the twilight land that is old age. Is it true? they ask. Of course it is, I say. After all, like Mrs. Nevermore, I am in the business of making people believe things they would otherwise never believe. I have been in that business for a long time.

So what follows is a truthful chronicle, right down to the talking bird. I'm certain it is. How could it be anything else? How could I possibly make it up?

Part I

The Mystery of the Strange

ONE

We begin at a cemetery, me shivering in the rain, staring numbly at my murdered father's coffin.

The coffin was poised above a hole adjacent to a graveled roadway on the highest part of Père-Lachaise. The Paris of 1899 was spread out below, the Seine an inky line against the gloom. A misshapen creature the color of ash lurked behind a nearby crypt.

I blinked and refocused on the crypt. The creature faded into the drizzle. Was I imagining things? Given my present state, what other explanation could there be? An old priest in a faded cassock approached. With his sour pudding face and puffy bags beneath watery eyes, the priest seemed perfectly constructed for funerals. You wouldn't want some rosy-faced cheery soul presiding over an occasion such as this, would you? No, it was a time for dreary skies and glum preachers—and perhaps monsters skulking around tombs.

"Arnheim," he breathed in my face. A breath laced with gin. "Are you a Jew?"

"I am an American," I said.

"The eternal aliens," said the priest sadly. "Cursed to wander the world yet always outside the world."

"The Americans or the Jews?" I asked.

The priest gave me a look that was a mixture of sympathy and scorn—a little more scorn than sympathy I would have said—and wandered off. That's when I spotted the falcon in the mist. It fluttered onto a nearby tree limb, nestling tapered wings against a blue-gray back. The bird cocked its imperious black head and appeared to stare at me. Not that there was a great deal to look at, I'm afraid.

In addition to being an American and possibly a Jew in the bargain, there is something else I must tell you straight away because it may further affect your view of me. Fourteen years ago, I murdered my mother.

I did not mean to kill her. If there was anything I could have done to prevent her death, I would have done it, believe me. I was young at the time, just out of the womb. Someone suggested that bad things happened to me because I was a Jew and terrible things just naturally happened to Jews. But was I? And what was a Jew as opposed to anything else? Most importantly, did Jews generally kill their mothers at birth? Unanswered questions this morning at Père-Lachaise.

I kept my eyes on the falcon as the priest commenced to mumble curious Latin words. Jew or Catholic, or American for that matter, what was the point? Was the priest talking to his Latin-speaking Jesus, preparing the way for my father? Did the priest even know my father? I doubted it. I didn't know him. How could the priest? Even my father's name was something of a mystery.

How could Felix Xavier Arnheim, known to everyone as Flix, possibly be Jewish with a middle name like Xavier? Was that not a good Catholic name? That would explain the priest, I suppose. But how could you be anything with a Jewish last name and a Catholic middle name? Or perhaps that wasn't his real name at all. Could it be that he was not part American (on his father's side) and part French (mother from Lyon) as I had heard? And if he was not any of those things, who was I?

The priest raised his voice suddenly, as though to interrupt the unsavory thoughts of a rude boy thoughtless enough to allow his mind to meander on the day of his own father's burial. He slurred his meaningless, joyless, comfortless Latin words. How did he get here anyway? I'd never seen him in my life. The school must have sent him.

I currently attended the Lonsdale School for Boys just outside Paris. Not for much longer, though. With my father dead, who was to pay for a little Jew bugger like myself? That's what I overheard one of the proctors call me. "A malicious, sharp-tongued little Jew bugger, that one."

From that I deduced they did not like me at Lonsdale. They said I was strange and distant, a boy keeping to himself and his books. When the adults did approach I tended to doubt the absolute truths with which they assaulted me. And I "talked back."

That was a common complaint at the schools I attended. Adults would talk to me and that would inspire me to "talk back," a major failing on my part, I discovered. Adults could talk to a child, apparently. But good children did not answer back. I was not counted among the "good" children, thus I would "come to no good at this rate." I wondered at what rate one would have to operate in order to come to good. No one ever discussed this. Children were never on their way to Good. They were always headed for No Good.

Being constantly reminded that I was on the wrong course only made me more determined than ever to fool everyone. The way to defeat rock bottom expectations was to be a good student, and indeed that's exactly what I was —bright you might say, diligent in my studies, about to earn my baccalauréat. It was my dream to attend the École Polytechnique, the fountain from which had flowed many of the great scientific innovations of the past century.

But now my dream abruptly was no more than that. What was I to do? At the ripe old age of fourteen, here I was an orphan, and penniless to boot. I choked back tears, cold and wet, trying not to feel sorry for myself as I stared at that dark mahogany coffin, glistening with raindrops and hung above the open grave like a box of secrets.

* * *

The clopping of horse hooves interrupted my gloomy reverie and drew the attention of the falcon. I turned to see a great white horse weaving through the tombstones and crypts, so bright it shone in the misty rain. Its rider wore a long black coat and a wide-brimmed black hat pulled down over his eyes. The black of him contrasted vividly with the white of the horse.

When the rider was twenty-five yards or so away, he drew his mount to a stop. The horse threw back its head, emitting an impressive snort that produced great funnels of air.

The man jumped nimbly off—a tall, lanky gent floating through the drizzle with an easy, confident gait. Evil walked with the same sort of throwaway nonchalance, I imagined, and evil had the same thick mustache and unreadable cobalt blue eyes. Closer, those eyes glowed like coals lit from a furnace in hell. A long white scar slashed down the side of his nose and along a gaunt cheek.

At his approach, I instinctively backed off, feeling like a fool for reacting so fearfully. I should have been pleased there was finally another mourner present, an old friend of my father's perhaps, not evil at all but a consoling presence to ease my ordeal. He jerked his head toward the coffin. "You sure that's him in there?" he demanded in a rough voice.

"Who?" was all I could think of to say.

"Flix, of course. Is it Flix in there?"

"I suppose it is," I said. "I don't know who else would be in there. I doubt there's room for more than one person, but it's hard for me to say since I don't know about these things."

The man then did a most amazing thing. Stepping smartly forward, past the priest, he rapped a knuckle against the side of the coffin. He turned his head, as though listening for a response. When none was forthcoming, he returned to study me with those fiery eyes.

"You the son?"

"I am," I said, immediately regretting the answer. I probably should not admit to anything. But if I was not the son, what would I be doing here?

"Then you're the fellow to talk to, aren't you—the lad who can return it to me?"

"Return? Return what?"

The thin line of his mouth turned into what passed for a smile on that pale, wounded face. Skulls contained more merriment. "If Flix is in that box, and I have my doubts, then he would have handed it off to his flesh and blood. That would be you. Ned is it not?" He did not wait for me to answer. "All right, Ned. That's what I'm here for, understand? Best tell me where it is. Tell me quick so I can be on my way, and both of us will be better for it."

"What is it you want?" I said, trying to keep my voice from shaking. What failure. It shook like a tuning fork.

"Don't play with me, lad. You play with Edmond Corbeau and that's the mistake of a lifetime. Believe it. Now let's get to the end. Tell me where it is."

When I did not immediately answer, he lunged for me. I flinched away. Too late. Corbeau's fingers closed around my jacket and yanked me toward him.

"That's quite enough, Edmond," a voice called out.

TWO

Corbeau's iron fingers reluctantly gave up their grip. On the roadway was a black brougham, complete with the white cockade of the Orléanistes. I had not heard or seen its arrival, and neither had Corbeau.

The bearded coachman, a malevolent pirate shrouded in shiny rain garments, jumped to the ground. Producing an umbrella, he proceeded to throw open the carriage door.

An elegant woman in mourning noir stepped out and snapped the umbrella away from the coachman. Umbrella held high, she proceeded to the gravesite, a graceful ship's prow cutting through the rain.

She was not as pale as you might have heard or quite as red headed, but tall, if not taller than expected, and with lips more full than had been advertised, highlighting the face of a deceitful angel barely visible beneath a funeral veil—a work of art making great demands on one's curiosity, an admirer noted.

As the woman approached, the falcon rose off its perch and ascended into the air. I could see Corbeau's body stiffen, his face darkening. "Get away from here," he called out to her. "This is none of your concern."

"It most certainly is, Edmond." She made the announcement in the same strong, certain voice she used to call out from the carriage. No tuning fork quivering for her. "The boy is not your business. Leave him alone."

"Get back into your coach and be off. And don't think for a moment of bringing that thug of yours back there into play."

As he said this, he jerked his head in the direction of the malevolent-looking coachman. The woman stepped closer and I saw something in her upraised hand, gleaming through the mist.

A derringer. Pointed straight at Edmond Corbeau.

Corbeau tried a smile on his awful face that did not quite work. "Would you use that, madame?"

"Would I, indeed."

He turned his terrible glare back to me. "Don't think you are safe with this woman. Better to deal with me than her. I am only human. But this damnable woman—a sorcière if there ever was one. That's what you've got to deal with. You'll soon see for yourself."

"A sorcière with a gun," she said. "Now be off."

"Remember I warned you, lad," Corbeau said to me.

Abruptly, he swirled away and climbed back on the great white horse. He yanked at the reins. The horse rose on its hind legs and the next thing Corbeau was urging him away at a gallop along the roadway. The misty rain swallowed him up.

* * *

Seemingly unperturbed and without a glance in my direction, the woman with the derringer—although now that had disappeared—continued to the gravesite. The falcon resettled on the tree branch.

"He sleeps with Molière." Her voice, so firm and resolute a moment before, choked with emotion. An amadou-gloved hand touched a handkerchief quickly to what I presumed were moistening eyes beneath that funeral veil. Water dripped from her umbrella.

"Would you have shot that fellow?"

She glanced at me, and even with the veil I could see the flash of steely emerald eyes. Eyes no longer clouded by tears, I noticed. Or I thought I noticed. Maybe I was imagining things, the way one came to imagine so many things around her.

"Why are you shaking like that?"

"I am cold and fearful," I said.

"What is there to be afraid of?"

"Threatening, scar-faced men. Women with guns. I also saw something lurking around a crypt I didn't like the look of. There is a world of things when you are my age."

"Well, you must not be afraid of anything," she said. "Or you must not seem to be afraid of anything, which I suppose is the same thing."

"But would you have shot him?" I persisted.

"I might have," she said nonchalantly.

"What are you doing with a gun in the first place?"

"Well, it would be impossible to shoot a man like Corbeau unless one had a gun, would it not?"

"I suppose it would," I said. "Although I have never seen a gun before, let alone a woman with a gun."

"The other possibility as to why I would have a gun—perhaps I need it in order to protect you."

"Do I need protection?"

"A few moments ago it looked as though you might."

"Who are you, anyway? Is it true? Are you a witch, a sorcière?"

"Who am I? Why I am Mrs. Nevermore, of course. Who else would I be?"

I stared at her blankly. I had no idea.

"What of the sorcière part?"

"There are no such things as witches," she said.

"There are women with guns, it turns out, and I wouldn't have imagined that. So who knows about witches."

She threw a sharp look in the direction of the priest. He had begun to mumble in Latin again. "Whatever is that man saying? Is he drunk?"

"I believe he is, and whatever he's saying, he's saying it in Latin," I said.

"Not a language one should speak after drinking spirits. Or maybe it is exactly that."

"He's worried that my father is a Jew," I said. "Do you know whether he is or not?"

Those emerald eyes studied me again, narrowing, as though to take the measure of me.

"You are a strange boy, Ned."

"Because my father is a Jew?"

"Oh, dear. I suspected as much. You are feeling sorry for yourself."

"What is the price to be paid for that? You shoot me? Turn me into a mouse?"

"I will not shoot you, but I am considering the mouse."

"I am not feeling sorry for myself," I asserted.

"Understandable under the circumstances, I suppose. Feeling sorry for one's self. But you must stop as soon as possible. After all, we can make too much of childhood, can't we?"

"I don't know," I said. "Can we?"

"Childhoods are, when all is said and done, only that and we must get on with life itself, and somehow put away our youthfully endured miseries."

Put away misery? How was I supposed to do that, being at once a youth and someone enduring misery? However, I chose not to argue the point, but instead asked, "What is it you want from me?"

"Co-operation for a start."

"And after you have that?"

"Providing you do not turn out to be the trouble you so far threaten to become, you will be pleased to help me do what it is I do."

"And what do you do?" I asked.

"I provide the confidence that allows one to believe."

"What good is that?"

"If you can show off a puddle and convince someone it's the River Nile, then it is of a great deal of benefit."

"I don't want anything to do with such a thing," I stated archly.

"Don't be ridiculous. I offer you a life of adventure and you offer me clichés about right and wrong."

"I never said a thing about right and wrong," I protested.

"You will. No sooner do I arrive than you assault me with dull pro-testations about what you will and will not do. Can right and wrong be far away?"

She waved her hand to and fro as though brushing away something particularly unpleasant. "I have no time for such delineations, so don't bother me with them."

Mrs. Nevermore paused to take a breath. "Still and for all, you are not for regular society, and that's to the good."

"It is?"

"It suits my purposes. I am an outsider as well. I just know how to put a better mask on it. Well, I can teach you how to wear the mask, Ned. Don't worry about that."

"Why should I wish to wear a mask?"

"Because if you are no one thing, then you can be any thing, and that opens up all sorts of interesting possibilities."

She glanced around impatiently. "We are wasting words and time standing about here. Let's be off."

I looked at her in astonishment. "Off? Off where? I have no place to go."

"Of course you do. I am now in charge of your care."

"How did that come to pass?"

"It came to pass because I am all you have in the world. Otherwise, you are prey to men like Corbeau."

She had a point. The thought of having to deal with Corbeau by myself was not appealing. Still, his words echoed: *I am only human. Her, well, a sorcière if there ever was one. That's what you've got to deal with. You'll soon see for yourself.*

But if I did not go with her, even though she might be a sorcière, then where was I to go?

"I suppose you will put me in another school," I said.

"Why should I do that?"

"Because it will be best for me."

"Will it? Who says that?"

"Everyone at all the schools I've attended. Besides, I'm close to my baccalauréat."

"Science is it not?"

"That's right," I said.

She made an unpleasant face. "I'm afraid there is far too much reality in science for my liking."

She craned her neck around and motioned to the coachman, standing in the rain near the carriage. He did not move. She frowned. "Honestly, that man."

She threw me a challenging look. "What about it, Ned? Are you coming with me or not? Better decide quickly."

She turned and marched away, holding the umbrella high. The coachman held open the door, deftly plucking the umbrella from her as she entered. The priest stopped his drunken Latin mutterings. The rain fell harder, obscuring the view of Paris below the hill.

Lightning ignited the sky. The falcon rose off the tree and began to circle. Thunder rumbled like a warning drum. I turned back to the roadway. The brougham had not moved. I debated what to do. The rain fell even harder.

Seemingly from nowhere, gravediggers appeared and went to work lowering my father's coffin into the ground. I watched it disappear as more lightning creased the ever-darkening sky.

I turned and started toward the brougham. A hand gripped my shoulder. The priest's rain-drenched face was inches from mine. I could smell the stale liquor on his breath. "This will all end badly," he said.

I tore away from that gripping hand. The priest laughed and twirled round, a clumsy pirouette performed by a drunk—then he was gone. I peered through the rain. No sign of him.

I stumbled toward the brougham. The coachman blocked my path. He possessed large, sweeping features as though God were an artist determined to make bold strokes with a mouth as long as a river, a foothill of a nose, and eyebrows like curling black snakes. The boldness made the man's face seem as impenetrable as the side of a cliff. High up on that cliff, like small warning lights, eyes gleaming with suspicion as they inspected me.

"Did you see that?" I said to him.

"See what?" he said in a gruff voice.

"That priest. He just vanished into thin air."

"I see no priest."

"That's the point. How could you? He disappeared."

"I am Prince Gamelle," he said. "Make sure you don't give me any trouble."

"A prince?"

"I have been in exile in Lausanne, but now have returned to reclaim my rightful place on the French throne."

"But there is no French throne," I protested. "And if you are a prince, why are you driving a carriage?"

"There. I knew it. You have a big mouth. You are trouble. Young rascals like you are always trouble."

Prince Gamelle held the coach door open so that I could climb inside. I heard the ominous squawk of the falcon circling overhead. The rain poured down. My future was as bleak as death.

THREE

The carriage containing my sullen self and the oblivious Mrs. Nevermore continued to number 52 rue des Saints-Pères in the St-Germain-des-Prés.

I felt overwhelmed by this overwhelming woman, so certain of her next step while I, despite my show of combative arrogance, remained so uncertain of mine. The sense of my own vulnerability did not help matters. I had lost my father, attracted a dark customer named Corbeau who might or might not murder me, and was left with no one in the world except this mysterious and enigmatic woman. Who knew what she had in store for me?

Number 52 turned out to be an imposing house all but lost behind a high wall replete with a mass of clinging vines and a dramatically arched entranceway. I followed Mrs. Nevermore through the entrance and across the narrow courtyard. Weeds pushed up between the cobblestones near a broken down carriage shrouded in cobwebs and dust, shoved into a corner of the crumbling stone wall near a gnarled old tree. A falcon with a black head sat on one of the thick branches. I swore it was the same bird from the cemetery.

"The falcon," I said to Mrs. Nevermore.

"What about it?"

"Is it yours?"

"Mine? How could it possibly be mine? Falcons don't belong to anyone."

"They don't?"

"Of course not. How could they?"

She fumbled in her purse for the iron key that unlocked the massive front door and we proceeded into the gloomy vestibule. The staircase was voluminously cobwebbed, its marble tiles scuffed and broken.

The eight rooms on the main level were traditionally French, naturally, with their ten-foot ceilings and their intricate wedding cake scrolls, but the walls of those rooms were faded and cracked with age and neglect. The toilet leaked—and wasn't it something of a triumph that there was a toilet in even a fashionable Paris house at the turn of the century? The toilet, however fashionable, caused the walls in the drawing room to buckle and stain. French doors badly in need of paint opened proudly onto balconies with wrought iron grillwork by Hector Guimard. However, one dared not step onto those balconies to inspect Monsieur Guimard's artistry for fear they might collapse. What's more, there were no servants, not even a chambermaid to attend to Mrs. Nevermore's needs. In such a house at such a time in Paris, this was unthinkable.

"They are a waste of time," pronounced Mrs. Nevermore.

"Anything that does not suit you appears to be a waste of time," I noted.

"Anything that does not suit me is."

At mid-afternoon the funeral gloom had given way to a sun that found its way above the wall, seeping through the tall windows, casting the salon in the light shafts floating in swirls of dust. Bad paintings adorned the walls. *La peau laiteuse* of a nude reclining woman surrounded by Roman centurions about to do god knows what, gleamed out of the gloom. Tiny figures stood before a vast Romanesque ruin. Naked wood nymphs frolicking in a forest glade near a bubbling stream ignored a tanned but quite bored Christ—the erotic vision of a long forgotten Italian painter Mrs. Nevermore apparently befriended in Florence. The nymphs were beginning to crack and peel on the canvas. Jesus, however, remained intact and unmoved.

A black rococo sofa was flanked by armchairs covered in embossed red velvet long since faded pink. Globe-shaded lamps were set upon brass end tables from North Africa (as it turned out). No books disturbed the dust on the shelves, as Mrs. Nevermore, despite the intellectual appearances she loved to cultivate, could not sit still long enough to read anything more complicated than the most popular daily papers.

A long kitchen, its cupboards and counters made of cherry wood, clusters of copper pots and pans intricately dangling above a flagstone floor, stretched across the rear of the house. Spice boxes sat upon countertops. A magnificent cast iron, coal-fired Eagle kitchen range of British manufacture dominated one side of the room. Swathed incongruously in a white apron, the coachman cum bodyguard and general Jack-of-all-trades, Prince Gamelle, stood guard over simmering, steaming pots atop the hotplate. His vast features quickly reformed themselves into a frown aimed in my direction, a frown I was to see often in the coming days.

"You rise every morning at six," he commanded. "You will come down to the kitchen, retrieve the coal from the bin in the back and start the fire in the stove. It is fitted with patent reversing dampers so that the ovens can be heated at either the top or the bottom. But to accomplish this, we must have coal first thing—by six thirty at the latest. That is when I arrive to prepare breakfast."

"Ned will do just fine," said Mrs. Nevermore in that airy manner of hers that seemed designed to put an end to further conversation on the matter. Gamelle did not say anything but the way he looked at me said everything about what he thought of my capabilities. The Lonsdale School for Boys began to seem like a shining, welcoming oasis of joy.

* * *

Late that afternoon, having just that morning watched my father dropped into the cold ground, I was put to work helping Gamelle prepare dinner. He shoved meats into the oven, roasted mushrooms and potatoes in frying pans, sliced vegetables all accompanied by various grunts and growls as though he was a stalking animal on the hunt for food at sunset. There was no conversation, even when I tried to provoke it.

"How long have you worked for Mrs. Nevermore?"

This was answered by the banging of a pot on the hotplate.

"I mean, you do work for her, do you not?"

He concentrated on roasting onions in a pan over the coal fire.

"Or is there something more to your relationship that I should know about?"

The oven door banged open.

"After all, I am going to be living here, aren't I? So these are the things I should know. Don't you agree?"

He turned from the stove. His florid face gleamed with perspiration. He held a large pan containing the sizzling roast with oven mitts the size of a blacksmith's bellows. I thought he was going to throw the roast at me. "Shut up," he ordered. "You have no sooner arrived and already I am sick of you!"

Dinner was served in a large dining room overhung with a crystal chandelier. Mrs. Nevermore sat at one end of a long table, I at the other.

Gamelle poured red wine from a decanter for her. For me, he offered his customary scowl. Mrs. Nevermore did not feel particularly compelled to engage in conversation, either. I felt quite compelled.

"I have been thinking about Gamelle," I said.

"What of him?"

"He says he is a prince."

"Gamelle is indeed a prince," asserted Mrs. Nevermore. "He is from Lausanne." As though that was the end of the argument right there. "When the monarchy returns to France it is quite possible he will be king."

"How soon do you think that will happen?"

"I have no idea."

"The future king of France driving your coach and preparing your meals, that is very impressive," I said.

Mrs. Nevermore made no comment.

Since Gamelle was from Lausanne, was I correct in concluding that is where she had met him? She paused and then advised she had never been to Lausanne.

He was her servant? Not a servant, she replied. A partner in various business ventures.

That was their relationship? It was. What would happen once Gamelle became king? Surely he could not continue to work for her and run France at the same time? Mrs. Nevermore concentrated on her food. Had she heard me?

She lifted her head and said, "I have it on the best authority that the Comte de Chambrun, the dashing cavalry officer all Paris is talking about, will put himself up for election to the chamber."

"Do you know what happened to my father?" I asked.

"Apparently, the comte is a royalist," Mrs. Nevermore continued, undeterred by my attempt to shift the conversation. "I have no doubt he will support Gamelle in his quest for the throne of France. I must arrange a meeting between the two of them. I'm sure they will find much common ground. I'm a bit of a royalist as well, the more I think about it. This whole idea of a republic makes me slightly suspicious. The restoration of the House of France might not be such a bad idea, and it's not just the aristocrats who think like this. Much of the fashionable monde with whom I'm acquainted is intrigued by the notion. And of course they love Gamelle."

"I asked you about my father," I said. "I want to know what happened to him."

She carefully placed her fork down on the plate before she said, "He died."

"The police told me he met with foul play. That he died as a result of meeting with foul play."

"Whatever that means."

"At this meeting with Monsieur Foul Play, he was apparently murdered."

"The police should not have told you that," she said quietly.

"They said he was stabbed with a knife. A number of times."

She picked up her fork and used it to pin a piece of the roast before lifting it delicately to her mouth.

"They are fools, the police. It would be a waste of time to listen to anything they had to say."

"Edmond Corbeau," I said.

"What about him?"

"He says my father owed him money."

"He's a liar. Your father owed him nothing."

"Could he have killed my father?"

"How would I know?" she said in a dismissive voice. "How would I know what Edmond Corbeau would or would not do?"

"This morning you were ready to shoot him."

"And so?"

"So if this man is dangerous enough that you would do that, perhaps he is dangerous enough to murder my father because my father would not pay him money."

She paused at length before she said, "That's enough. I must go out. Help Gamelle clean up the dishes."

She rose from her chair and swept from the room, imperious, the great sleek ship that was Mrs. Nevermore sailing into the night.

FOUR

I retreated to a tiny attic room up a narrow flight of back stairs at the top of the house. All my things had been taken from the Lonsdale School for Boys, packed into a steamer trunk and moved into this room. Everything included my sketch books and pencils. I found them jammed near the bottom of the trunk, along with my sketches of the Eiffel Tower. This was my hobby you see, my passion you might say, drawing the tower.

I tried to sleep, but couldn't. I lay on my back, studying the swirling shadows crisscrossing the cantilevered ceiling, visions of my father's rain-splattered coffin hovering like an unanswered question above his grave. I contemplated my aloneness in a cruel and uncaring world. Eventually, I got up and went to the narrow windows that overlooked the courtyard and the street beyond the wall. The windows were glazed with diamond-shaped panes and they opened outward, on hinges, like doors.

There, caught in the light from a nearly full moon, stood a figure in black. He shifted around and the shadows swallowed him. Then he reappeared, the moonlight catching at his arm and shoulder, but leaving his face in darkness. Corbeau? It was hard to tell. Whoever it was, he was not moving from his position on the street.

I sat there by the window, concentrating, clearing my mind completely for what I had to do next. I opened the window and eased out onto the ledge. The ground lay perhaps forty feet below. I let myself fall about ten feet, before bringing myself to a stop and pausing in mid-air.

Something I failed to inform you of previously.

To say I am able to fly would be exaggerating what I can do. Better to say I hover, and it takes a great deal of concentration to do that, so I do it as little as possible. Also, it's not something I want people to see; they already think me curious enough as it is.

Another confession: without too much concentration I can move small-ish objects around. I'm able to push a pen across a table, for instance, or direct a ball of thread across the room. Parlor tricks, really. No more than that. Sleight of hand without the sleight of hand. How I came into possession of these powers, I don't know. I've had them for as long as I can remember. Maybe I got them in exchange for my mother's life. I would have gladly taken my mother instead, but I had no say in the bargain that was struck, if that's indeed what it was.

I touched down on the ground—it had taken me a while to be able to do that properly after many crashes and sprawls in the dirt—paused to get my bearings, and then hurried over to the stone wall surrounding the courtyard. I lifted myself to the balustrade running along the top of the wall. I gripped it, and peered over so that I could see down onto the street.

Corbeau was nowhere in sight.

An instant later, a humped creature sprang onto the balustrade beside me. It possessed pinprick yellow eyes and pointed ears, its spine erupting out a curved back, pulling tight a sickly gray film of skin.

A second thing appeared. The two of them balanced on the wall on either side of me, twisting their awful heads, baring sharply protruding fangs. The one on my left reached out a misshapen claw and struck me on the shoulder. So surprised was I that I lost my concentration and that, coupled with the force of the blow, sent me flying away from the wall.

I landed on the cobblestones with a thump, stifling a cry. I lay there gasping, trying to get the wind back inside of me. I looked up at the top of the wall, expecting these terrible creatures to pounce on me.

Instead, a flap of wings marked the arrival of the falcon, seemingly coming out of nowhere at a tremendous rate of speed. It hit one of the creatures, sending him spiraling back over the wall. The second creature cried out in alarm and then quickly disappeared. The falcon fluttered down and landed close to where I lay sprawled.

"Are you all right, Ned?"

I stared up at the bird. "What did you just say?"

"I asked if you were all right."

"But how can you do that?"

"You are lying on the ground after falling off a wall in the middle of the night," the falcon stated equably. "I would think it the most natural thing in the world to inquire as to the state of your health."

"But you are a bird."

"I am a falcon. Peregrine by name."

"But falcons can't talk."

"They can't? If that is the case, they failed to tell me."

"And how do you know my name?"

"How should I not know your name? I saw you at the cemetery, did I not?"

"But why talk to me, thus making me doubt my sanity? I'm only a child after all. This is the last thing I need right now."

"Well, don't blame me for what's happened. It is the world you are in Ned, where the power of the Strange exists, the unreal is real, and the falcons occasionally have something to say for themselves."

"The power of the Strange? I don't understand what you're talking about. What's that?"

"It's what you appear to possess, although, if I do say so, you're not much good with it."

"I have no such thing."

"Tell that to the two gargoyles who showed up tonight."

"Is that what they were? Gargoyles?"

"You've never seen them before?"

"No," I said firmly.

"You have now—which tells me that you have entered into the Other World."

"The Other World?"

"There is the one world you occupy. And then there is the other world that occasionally occupies you. Not a safe place, if you want my opinion."

"Why is it not safe?"

"Who knows? I suppose that's why it's the Other World. But it's full of nasty creatures and dreadful things normal people don't see. Alas, I'm afraid you can see them."

I got to my feet, checking to make sure I was still in one piece. "Well, whatever world I'm in I'm tired and want to go to bed."

"Good night, Ned. But as you go along this next while, go carefully and remember one thing."

"What's that?"

"Gargoyles are afraid of bridges."

"That's the most ridiculous thing I have ever heard."

"Nevertheless, it is true," said Peregrine.

Wings shaped like scimitars lifted him gracefully up into the tree where he settled on one of the upper branches, barely visible, unmoving.

I couldn't have spoken to him. I couldn't. None of this was actually happening, I decided. It was a product of my fevered late night imaginings.

Talking birds. How ridiculous.

Sorry. Falcons.

FIVE

Paris was indeed filled with goblins and monsters and other bizarre flying creatures in those days, although they kept mostly to the sewers and the shadows of the city—in the Other World Peregrine talked about.

Their existence was immortalized on the ramparts of Notre Dame Cathedral, man-beasts, carved into stone. Nominally, these stone carvings acted as spouts carrying rain water away from the cathedral. That's why they were known as gargoyles, after the Latin word meaning drain.

However, suspicions abounded that their real purpose had nothing to do with dispersing rain water. They adorned Notre Dame to scare off their real life brethren.

I had never seen any gargoyles before the previous night and as time went on I saw no more and thus doubted whether I had seen anything at all. The bird—falcon—said I possessed the power of the Strange. Well, I certainly was possessed of something, but was that it?

I dared not say anything to Mrs. Nevermore since that would force me to explain what I was doing outside my room clinging to a wall late at night talking to falcons and harassed by gargoyles. Tell her that and surely I would end up in one of those dark places where they keep crazy orphan children.

So I kept quiet and my new life at number 52 rue des Saints-Pères fell more or less into dull routine. Arising each morning, I washed and dressed before going down to the kitchen where I cleaned the stove, brought in coal from the back and got the fire started.

Prince Gamelle would arrive at his usual time without a word of greeting —save for a menacing grunt—and prepare coffee. He served Mrs. Nevermore café au lait in a large bowl when she arrived in the kitchen at seven thirty. She wore a morning peignoir either of ivory muslin trimmed with bows and lace or pale lavender nainsook with trimmed ruffles.

"Apparently she was married to a naval officer," she was saying to Gamelle when I came in one morning. "He bored her and so she filed for divorce last week. Yesterday the naval officer registered his disapproval of such things by firing two bullets into her thigh."

"This was the talk of the bois yesterday afternoon?"

"At Longchamps. Everyone was talking about it."

Another morning Mrs. Nevermore was saying, "He has written a show at the Folies Bergères for her."

"Surely it could not have been performed," said Gamelle.

"Most certainly it could. Last evening. *L'Araignée d'Or*. She played a golden spider draped in a few wisps of metallic lace."

"And what did she do?"

"She writhed prettily."

It went like this each morning. She sat with her coffee while Gamelle prepared a cigar, Cuban, Romeo y Julieta. He used a penknife to cut off the cap. A vesta or wax match was struck to light the cigar. Gamelle took care to ensure that the flame did not directly touch its end. Mrs. Nevermore then sat back inhaling luxuriously on the cigar, slowly releasing the smoke into the air. Gamelle discreetly opened the window above the sink.

This daily ritual amazed me. Not so much the gossip. It was everywhere in Paris like the garbage in the streets. But I had never seen a woman smoke a cigar before. It had never crossed my mind that such a thing was possible. Now here I was living with a woman who smoked every morning as though it were the most natural thing in the world.

By eight o'clock Mrs. Nevermore had finished her coffee and the cigar, exhausted her cache of gossip and disappeared into her bedroom. Exactly one hour later she emerged, meticulously groomed in her day dress, with little jewelry save for a discreet silver bracelet (jewelry being frowned upon until evening). The rigid rules of fashion prohibited the display of any décolletage and frowned upon ample skirts during daylight hours. Mrs. Nevermore, who would break many rules in her lifetime, would never crease, let alone break, the rules of fashion. Break the law and you could get away with it. Defy the dress codes of the day and you exposed your rank in society, and that Mrs. Nevermore could ill afford to do.

Clothing was not a matter of merely dressing, it was a daily science. There was the proper morning gown, the right luncheon gown, the dress for visiting and the dress for walking, the appropriate gown for dinner, the correct gala dress for the theater.

* * *

At nine thirty on the dot, Mrs. Nevermore went to work at a handsome Chippendale secretaire that stood in a corner by the window in her study. At one o'clock sharp, if she was staying in, Gamelle summoned us for lunch. She would close and lock the desk and then adjourn to the dining room where I would join her. At lunch, there was no gossip. Conversation took the form of a lecture aimed at me.

"Society invented good manners for the purpose of sorting people out, Ned," she said. "Your manners immediately define you to others. If you are a churlish bore then you will not survive in society, and thus are of little use to me. That is why you must display good manners at all times. Remember a single word wrongly placed can betray your origins or mark you as an individual with a dubious past."

"Do I have a dubious past? Is that what you are trying to hide?" I asked.

"We hide nothing," she said. "Speak properly, wear the right clothes, and show up in the right places and you will never have to hide. People will simply assume you are whom you purport to be."

"And that is useful?"

"It is the essence of our business," she said.

"Except I am uncertain as to exactly what your business is," I said.

A fleeting look of impatience. "I have told you before, Ned. We are in the business of making people believe."

"What do you make them believe?"

"You give them something they want to believe," she said.

"But I want to be an engineer," I protested.

"There. You see? We are in the same business after all. What is the essence of an engineer? Is it not to make people believe in what is not there?"

"I suppose it is," I had to admit.

"There you are, then," she said with a trace of satisfaction in her voice. "We are kindred spirits."

Well, I wondered about that since I seemed to be excluded from everything. Doors closed, documents disappeared quickly from view, conversations hushed or stopped altogether as soon as I appeared. Neither of them seemed comfortable in my presence. Once I thought I saw Mrs. Nevermore hide her derringer beneath sofa cushions. When I went back later to check, there was no derringer. Was I imagining things? No, I had already seen her with it. Or had I? Perhaps I was not imagining enough.

When all was said and done—although little was said and whatever was done was done out of my sight—I knew every detail of her daily routine but nothing about her or her business. She would disappear for days at a time without explanation. When I asked Gamelle where she had gone, he grunted and ordered me to bring more coal for the stove. On her return, she merely smiled away my inquiries. Once when she came back, I heard Gamelle's voice raised from the study. "Well, you had better come up with something!" he exclaimed.

Come up with what? And what would happen to us if they did not come up with this nameless thing? I wanted answers and when they were not forthcoming, I began to plot the ways I could attain them.

My attention focused on that Chippendale secretaire. I came to believe that the truth of Mrs. Nevermore lay inside that desk.

SIX

One night I watched as Mrs. Nevermore finished her work and, as usual, closed and locked the secretaire before rising. She went along the corridor to a closet next to the kitchen, opened the door and carefully placed the key on a hook at the back.

After that, I kept an eye on the key, opening the closet every so often to ensure it was still there. But I never gathered enough nerve to remove the key from its hook and unlock that desk.

Finally, there came an evening when Mrs. Nevermore had an appointment requiring Gamelle to act as her coachman. This was the opportunity I had been waiting for.

As soon as I heard them leave, I slipped down the stairs, opened the door, and stepped into the courtyard. There was no sign of the coach, but Gamelle had taken the time to relock the front gate. That meant that when they returned, Gamelle would have to stop and unlock the gate, thus giving me the warning I needed.

I started back across the courtyard and that's when I spotted Peregrine in his tree. I had seen him on occasion since the first night we met, but when I tried to talk to him, he just cocked his head and stared unblinking at me. Truly I was mad, believing I had actually talked to a bird. What a fool!

"What are you up to, Ned?"

I stopped and peered up at the tree. Peregrine sat in shadow. "You are not talking to me," I said.

"No? Then why are you talking to me?"

"I just want to make that clear."

"It could not be clearer. You are not talking to me, but permit me to talk to you."

"Why tonight all of a sudden? I've tried to talk to you on previous occasions and you said nothing."

"Falcons are known for their ability to sit very still for long periods of time and to say nothing."

"Then why are you talking now?"

"Despite the fact that you don't want to talk to me?"

"Exactly," I said.

"I believe I am talking because I have something to say."

"Which is what, exactly?"

"That puts us right back where we started: What are you up to, Ned?"

"None of your business."

"I fear you are up to no good, sneaking about just as Mrs. Nevermore departs the premises."

"I merely want to ensure the front gate is properly locked. You never know. Corbeau could be in the neighborhood. Or those gargoyles from the Other World you go on about."

"You're not poking that nose of yours where you shouldn't, are you?"

I was of course, not that I was about to admit anything to him. It irritated me that he had guessed my plans.

"I'm going inside," I said.

"Be careful, Ned. If I were you, I would not do what you are about to do."

"I'm not doing anything," I said defensively.

"Everything will be revealed in due course," Peregrine said.

"Everything will be revealed in due course? What kind of nonsense is that? What is to be revealed in due course, and how would you know anything about it?"

"You just have to be patient—like a falcon."

"I have no more time for talking birds."

"Falcon," Peregrine amended.

"Particularly talking birds who have no idea what they are talking about."

Angrily, I stepped back into the house, closed and locked the door before going up the stairs. I took a deep breath, calming myself. I was all alone at number 52. The keeper of the secrets was gone.

A shivery thrill shook my body as I went along the corridor to the closet. I grasped the doorknob and turned it. The door opened. My nostrils filled with musty odors of forgotten overcoats and discarded gloves. Hat boxes crammed a shelf. Mud encrusted riding boots crowded the floor. My fingers brushed the little brass hook and the dull black iron of the key that dangled from it.

Taking the key, I hurried back into the study and sat at the secretaire, fitting the key into the lock. The tumblers clicked away and I flung open the top to reveal—

Nothing.

A patina of dust clogged the pigeonholes. Drawers were empty, not even a stray paper clip. The duplicitous Mrs. Nevermore, always a step ahead. Or perhaps the desk had always been empty, part of an elaborate ongoing trick: maintaining secretiveness without actually holding onto something as potentially damaging as a secret.

"What do you think you're doing?"

I swirled around to find Mrs. Nevermore standing in the doorway, stunning in head to foot noir. The color matched the churning darkness in her eyes. I stood staring in the horror only someone caught red-handed can experience. My mouth opened but nothing came out. How the blazes did she get in here? I hadn't heard a sound.

"You were going through my things," she pronounced.

"No, I wasn't," was all I could, stupidly, manage.

"On top of that, you lack the wit to tell me anything but an obvious lie. I catch you in the act and you can't even figure the way out. What kind of little fool are you, anyway?"

Tears unexpectedly flooded down my cheeks. The last thing in the world I wanted was to cry in front of this woman. Besides, that only seemed to enrage her more. "Now you cry? You betray my trust after I bring you into my house. And you cry!"

She was shouting, her face twisted in a fury like nothing I had seen before, advancing toward me, her hand shooting out. Suddenly I found myself flying across the room.

I hit the far wall and bounced to the floor, dazed, the room swirling. Her slim hand fluttered again. This time I was picked up and thrown up to the ceiling. I hit it and was plummeting back down when I came to my senses enough to halt my descent, hovering inches off the floor. No more tears. Now I was in a fury of my own. I sent a footstool skittering across the carpet. It struck her legs, knocking her off balance. Giving off a cry of alarm, she tumbled to the floor.

The next thing, a nearby lamp came whizzing past my head, narrowly missing me before crashing against the wall. I parried weakly with a Dresden china shepherdess mounted on an end table. She easily deflected that, and sent it spinning into another wall. I got the end table into the air, but not very far and it didn't have much speed. The table bounced across the carpet, finally running out of steam a couple of feet from her.

In return she sent a cascade of books tumbling from the surrounding shelves, spinning toward me, hardback missiles fired with such force that they sent me diving for cover beneath the secretaire.

The door to the study burst open and there stood a pop-eyed Prince Gamelle. What a view he had: Mrs. Nevermore sprawled on the carpet, her skirt up to her knees; me cowering beneath the secretaire, the room around us in a shambles.

"What are you doing in here? What's going on?"

Mrs. Nevermore pulled at her skirt. Already her face was rearranging itself into its former cool serenity. "It's all right, Gamelle. Ned and I were in the process of coming to certain realizations about each other, that's all."

"You are beginning to understand the boy is cursed and not to be trusted," Gamelle said.

He threw a pile of my Eiffel Tower sketches onto the floor in front of her. "What's more he is a lazy, cursed boy who does nothing but draw the Eiffel Tower," he said scornfully. "What do we need with such a person as this?"

"You were searching my room." I made the statement sound as indignant as I could. "You toss me about while this terrible man goes searching through my room."

"Let me put the little brat into the street, and we're done with him," offered Gamelle.

Mrs. Nevermore stood and smoothed her hair, looking around as though realizing for the first time what havoc we both had created. "Gamelle," she said in a steady voice, "why don't you let me talk to Ned alone?"

Gamelle did not like that one bit. He aimed a final scowl in my direction before he said, "I'll be outside if you need me," and left.

Mrs. Nevermore bent down and retrieved the sketches.

"Put them down," I ordered. "Those are mine. They have nothing to do with you."

"And the inside of my desk has nothing to do with you," she said as she flipped through the sketches. "However, that failed to stop you."

She looked at me. "These aren't bad."

"What do you know about it?" I said sullenly. I crawled out from my redoubt beneath the secretaire and stood eyeing her uneasily, not wanting to be flattered by her words, but flattered nonetheless.

She bit at her lower lip as she lifted up another of the sketches.

"Why do you draw the Eiffel Tower so much?"

Why, indeed.

Over the course of a long life I have found that what is most true is what endures. I say this as a very old man who survived a depression and two World Wars and has seen more than his fair share of things, and not as the boy about whom I write in this chronicle.

The truest things find the deepest roots in the landscape of our souls. They cannot be swayed by time or fashion or cries of outrage against them. True is true and it lasts beyond anything.

Monsieur Gustave Eiffel's achievement was the embodiment for me of what was most true and therefore most enduring. Real truth becomes part of nature, its lines simple and pure melding seamlessly with the universe. So it was with the tower. It was my centre of gravity, the high, iron-strutted demonstration of man's ability to do better than he ever imagined.

There was also something else. This might sound ridiculous but since I've already introduced gargoyles and talking falcons, how much less can you think of me for stating the following: the tower was essential to my well being. Without its life-giving energy I could not exist. At least that's what I had come to believe. If I did not visit the tower regularly, I felt myself weakening, my powers draining away. Of course I never told anyone about this. How could I? Who would believe it? I hardly believed it myself.

So I said simply, "I draw the Eiffel Tower because I love it."

"You love the Eiffel Tower?"

"Not everyone does," I added in an attempt to represent myself as a neutral observer, capable of understanding there was another point of view. "At the beginning it was criticized as a 'dizzying, ridiculous tower,' and a gigantic factory chimney. The writer Guy de Maupassant calls it 'a tormenting nightmare.' There was even thought of tearing it down."

Mrs. Nevermore glanced up sharply. "Thought of what?"

"Tearing it down," I said. "In fact that was the plan. Were it not for the tireless efforts of Monsieur Eiffel himself, they would do just that."

"Even now?"

"Very much now," I stated. "My poor tower has many enemies and it is in need of repairs—expensive work, I'm told—so that has revived calls in many quarters for its destruction."

Mrs. Nevermore considered this at length, fingers drumming the surface of my drawings. Then she put them aside and came over to me. The fierce, scary glow of those jade eyes had been quelled, replaced by something far more sympathetic, hard to resist, at least for me, lonely and miserable and unsure of this woman and her intentions.

"I know you are confused about certain things, Ned," she said in a serene voice. "But if we have assured each other of nothing else this evening, it is that we are different. We both possess the power of the Strange."

"The power of the Strange?"

"Exactly."

"I've heard the phrase before," I said, thinking of Peregrine.

"It's what makes us different."

"I don't want to be different."

"Unfortunately, that's not likely to change anything. What you want and what you have, I'm afraid they are more often than not two very dissimilar things."

"I have heard that because of who we are, we are part of the Other World, and therefore are prey to monsters and gargoyles. Do you know anything about that?"

"Who filled your head with such nonsense?"

"Peregrine."

"And who is Peregrine?"

"The falcon outside in the tree."

"Birds cannot talk."

"Falcon. He's a falcon. And he talks."

"I understand you have a lot to deal with right now, Ned, but please don't let your imagination run away with you. This will not help us."

"It's true. I swear it is. The falcon can indeed talk."

"Well, he had no business talking to you." She waved a dismissive hand and then turned and headed for the door. "Now come along. We must be off."

"Off? Off to where?

"The Champs de Mars, of course."

SEVEN

"At nine hundred eighty-four feet it is the world's tallest structure," I announced as we came through the fairgrounds at the Champ de Mars the following afternoon. "Seven thousand tons of iron stands on four massive masonry piers running one hundred forty-two yards each way."

The air lay heavy around the Eiffel Tower and the rising spires and domes of the soon-to-open l'Exposition Universelle, reducing the Trocadero Palace to a hazy outline beyond the arch of the tower's girders. A great globe twisted on its axis near the three-hundred-fifty-foot-high Ferris wheel framed by chimney stacks spewing soft puffs of smoke across a cloudless sky.

"The girders that constitute those seven thousand tons are hollowed and made up of twelve thousand parts held together by two million five hundred thousand rivets. Two million five hundred thousand rivets! Quite impressive, I would say."

Mrs. Nevermore did not seem impressed.

"The tower is painted with a special reddish brown paint called Barbados Bronze," I continued, undaunted. "Its tone is quite dark on the lower piers, but as it gets higher, Monsieur Eiffel ordered the tower to be painted in lighter shades so that as you reach the top, it is nearly pale yellow."

"Why would he do that?" demanded Gamelle who was acting as coachman.

"This adds to the impression of height," I said in my most authoritative voice.

We joined the cavalcade of luxury vehicles and fine saddle horses already on parade through the park. What with the imminent arrival of the exposition, the Champ de Mars was becoming more popular than the Bois as the place for *le gratin*, the Upper Crust, to see and be seen. The actress Réjane passed by in a Victoria hitched to a pair of perfectly matched white mules. "A present from the king of Serbia," Mrs. Nevermore confided.

"What's the king of Serbia doing with white mules?" I wondered aloud.

"Kings have such things," she said. "That's why they are kings."

Then I said, "How is it you come to be the way you are? To have this power of the Strange, I mean."

Mrs. Nevermore's attention was diverted to a landau pulled by horses outfitted with bridle chains of pure sterling silver, the driver and footmen in gold-embroidered liveries. An old man in a frock coat hunched low in the carriage. "Dr. Péan, the eminent surgeon," announced Mrs. Nevermore with unnerving authority. "He has grown rich removing appendixes. When he is operating, he wears a black frock coat. His hands are encased in white gloves. Such is his dexterity with a scalpel that when he has finished an operation there is not a single drop of blood on him."

"Did you hear what I said?"

"Of course I heard what you said. How could I not? After all I am sitting right beside you."

"How did you acquire the powers you have?" I said.

"I could ask you the same question, could I not? How is it that you are the way you are?"

"I have no idea."

"I would answer the same. We are the Strange, and, as I told you, that gives us the power."

She looked at me and I do believe I saw a trace of sympathy in her eyes. Just a trace. Gone in an instant. "If it's any consolation, there are others. Paris is full of people like us."

"With this same power of the Strange? Do you think so?"

"I know it to be a fact."

I certainly did not know it. Until last night I would have said there was no one else like me, although on reflection that seemed highly improbable. Why would God make only one like me? The answer was, according to Mrs. Nevermore, He didn't.

"Not that it does any of us the least bit good," she continued. "What is it to move objects from here to there? Not much of anything. No, one must move men and to do that one must have a head on one's shoulders. Otherwise you are simply another freak at the carnival. That's where most of us end up, doing silly tricks that the audience believes are sleight of hand, but of course there is no sleight of hand at all. That's not for me, and I trust it's not for you either, Ned."

"No, of course not. I don't want to be in a carnival. I am destined to be an engineer."

"Then you had best stay with me, and avoid the petty squabbling we allowed ourselves to indulge in last night. We are for much better things."

"What better things are we for?"

Instead of answering, Mrs. Nevermore leaned forward and told Gamelle to stop, and then immediately bounded out of the brougham. She waited until a troop of cavalry from the elite Chasseurs à Cheval thundered past on gray half-bred Arab horses, their uniforms bright with shiny buttons and silver braid, the light blue of their jackets giving fine contrast to their red trousers.

She ploughed ahead, ignoring a couple on bicycles. A youthful clerkish fellow was aboard a Steel Fairy while his prim-looking lady friend in a tiny hat secured by a chenille-dotted veil, maneuvered the Little Queen.

I joined Mrs. Nevermore beneath the girders. A surge of energy jolted through my body. I felt instantly stronger.

"What's wrong?" Mrs. Nevermore demanded. "What are you doing?"

"I believe it is the radiant energy emanating from the tower," I said. "It's the only explanation I can come up with."

"What does it do for you?"

"It keeps me alive, I think."

She gave me a dubious look, and then shrugged. "Come along. Let's go to the top."

"That would be very interesting indeed," I said. "At the tower's summit there is a beacon with a range of nearly one hundred and twenty miles. Thus the tower can be seen as far away as Chartres and Orléans. The light is electric, of course, and it is encased by a cylinder containing France's national colors of red, white, and blue."

Mrs. Nevermore proceeded toward the elevators taking passengers up to the first level. I remained where I was. When she realized I was not at her side, she stopped and called to me. "Ned, don't stand there blathering away with that idiotic expression on your face. We don't have all day."

"Many people believe the tower to be frivolous and without value," I continued. "But that is not the case at all. Monsieur Eiffel has said that it could be used as a lookout if there is another war or a siege. You could see the enemy forty-five miles away. This is an invaluable advantage."

"Ned, what's wrong?"

"Why, if the tower had been here when the Germans advanced on the city in 1870, who knows what the outcome might have been? The Germans could well have been defeated and France spared a terrible agony."

Mrs. Nevermore returned to the spot where I stood riveted.

"Also for astronomical observations, the tower is perfect—the purity of the air at that height, the absence of mists."

She gave me a perplexed look.

"What's more, there are all sorts of scientific observations that can be made. The fall of bodies through the air, for example."

"Ned."

"You might not think anyone cares about such things, but many scientists do," I maintained stoutly.

She stamped her foot impatiently. "Ned!"

"I cannot go up to the top!" I angrily blurted. "That is plain enough, isn't it?"

Damn her anyway, but this was the second time in less than a day she had reduced me to tears. This time, though, instead of anger, her face softened, the impatience gone.

"Do you know what it is?"

"I'm not certain," I said. "I believe it's the radiant energy. At the top of the tower it increases. What gives me life down here destroys me up there."

She considered this revelation in the same serious manner she previously considered my sketches. "It's not necessary anyway," she concluded with a shrug. "Getting to the top will not help us."

I looked at her in a new way: Help us?

"What do you mean?"

She started away. "Come along, Ned. No use lingering here staring at bolts and struts."

We went back to the carriage where Gamelle waited. "Well?" he demanded. "What do you think?"

"It just might work," she said.

Gamelle stared up at the tower. "I don't know."

"What might work? What are you talking about?" Neither of them paid the least attention to me.

"I don't want to have anything to do with whatever it is you're planning," I announced. "I am a child. I should be in school."

Mrs. Nevermore looked thoughtful. "It's important to understand that we cannot do this alone. We will need assistance."

"We cannot do what alone?"

A flush bruised her pale cheeks. Her voice discarded its customary neutrality and took on an excited tone. "We will require the best help available. Nothing less will do."

"We will get no one," said Gamelle. "No one will have anything to do with us."

"Don't be ridiculous, Gamelle," said Mrs. Nevermore airily. "I already have the person in mind."

Gamelle frowned. "I trust you are not thinking what I believe you to be thinking."

"How can you know what I am thinking? How can anyone know? It is impossible. A great deal of the time I have no idea myself, until I have thought of it, of course."

"I know what you are thinking," Gamelle insisted, "and I do not like it."

"We need the best, that's all. And thus we will have the best."

"Madness," groaned Gamelle. "Absolute madness."

I had not the remotest idea of what either of them was talking about. But I did not like the sound of it.

EIGHT

The great pavilions of Les Halles stood greenish-gray in the night beneath endless roofs suspended by multitudes of columns.

Around us, a rising tide of farmers and merchants, tradesmen, and *fortes femmes* flowed into the marketplace, their carts and wagons brimming with produce, everyone impatient and anxious to be rid of their goods in preparation for the morning market.

A potter eased himself stiffly off his cart, shouting to a couple of louts offloading cabbages and bundles of spinach with the soil still clinging to their exposed roots. The louts came over and began to unload the clay pots piled on the back of the potter's cart, carrying them into one of the stalls lining the square.

Beyond the stalls crammed with mountains of cabbage, bundles of sorrel, clusters of artichokes, piles of carrots, and mounds of lettuce tied with straws, stood a tavern called l'Astuce. Gas jets cast the interior in a sickly yellow glow, as though a particularly ugly monster was dying, the life seeping out, accompanied by raucous music and a great deal of shouting and laughter. Mrs. Nevermore marched toward the yellow monster, weaving around sides of beef strung up on hooks hung from iron bars.

When I saw where she was headed, I stopped and announced, "I cannot go in there."

That failed to stop her. She disappeared into the monster's crooked mouth.

I was being totally corrupted by this woman! I took a deep breath and plunged in after her.

* * *

A pall of smoke clogged the interior, so thick it was difficult to make out anyone, and when you did get a view of the clientele, you immediately regretted it. Later, when the more fashionable Montmartre bars closed, the society dandies desperate for one more drink would add much-needed luster to this place. For now a ragged band of one-armed, one-legged, milky-eyed devils idled away the time before their coach left for hell. No one gave me a second glance as I entered. Why should they? I was one of them. I fit right in.

I spotted Mrs. Nevermore weaving artfully through the crowd, headed toward the end of the bar. The individual lounging there was worthy of a second glance. While everyone else seemed to have gone directly to seed, he appeared to have stopped in a better neighborhood first before descending into his present circumstances.

Tall and lanky, the remnants of youthfully chiseled beauty somehow intact despite red blotches like little flares erupting along the surface of his skin, the hair curly still but shot through with hints of gray, his haunted blue eyes gleaming with a combination of worldwide weariness and soul-shaking sadness.

Here then was Smiling Jack Dozen—for that is what they called him, Smiling Jack—in a creased, ill-fitting suit of some dreadful ginger color. He was like a beautiful building crumbling from neglect, but still lovely, particularly when he chose to flash that smile of his. No one produced a smile quite like Jack Dozen. With a smile like that, you could only like him. But threadbare poverty overwhelmed his humor and dulled the merry glint he tried to keep burning in those troubled blue eyes. There was no disguising the sense of a life wasted—the tragedy of a failed man clung to him like a sickly sweet smell.

"See, I'm at the bar in the Crillion Hotel, when I spot this bloke," Jack was saying. "As likely a mark as you're going to encounter. American. Manufactures farm machinery in one of those gawd awful American places, Missouri, something like that. Perfect. So I arrange to have his wallet flinched. Easy as pie. Poor bugger has no idea it's even gone."

"Why you want to steal his wallet?" demanded a codger with a beet-red dome and a toothless grin. "You being the brilliant international con man and everything."

"I lifted his wallet, you ass, so I could give it back to him. I've recovered his missing wallet in Paris, so I'm his best friend in the world. He wants to see the sights, and I'm not talking about the Louvre here.

"So 'round to the Folies Bergères we go, in the company of two comely *dégrafées*, properly primed for the evening. Dazzled is our boy. Overwhelmed at the prospect of so many bare legs, so much perfume-scented sin. He's practically giddy!

"Well, between nibbles on the American gent's corn-fed ear, one of our *dégrafées* lets it slip that the owners are discreetly looking for more investment in order to expand the business. They are being very careful since putting money in the Folies—what with the coming of l'Exposition Universelle bound to draw hundreds of thousands of visitors—well, it's like investing in a gold mine, only better, because you get to sleep with pretty girls with charming accents.

"The next thing, the Folies director himself appears at our table. He's no sooner seated than the American is on him, demanding to invest in his business. Won't take no for an answer. I try my best to talk him out of it—a gamble, not a sure thing. But he won't hear of it. He wants in! Desperate. Wants this more than life itself. He's putting cash on the table, making a terrible scene. Finally, the director gives in. Very well, he says, Monsieur can invest one hundred thousand francs. No more. Not another centime. Under any circumstances. Thirty-four thousand advanced before leaving Paris will serve as a demonstration of good intentions. The remainder delivered only after proper, formal contracts are signed."

"And he did this?" the codger asked incredulously.

"Turned over the cash the next day. Not even the blink of an eye. Enthusiastic. A gent happy to give his money away. Does one's heart a world of good."

"But what about the contracts?" someone sputtered.

Jack gave the man a look suggesting he had suffered an unfathomable depth of dementia.

"There are no contracts, are there Jack?" Mrs. Nevermore insinuated herself against the bar. "There never are any contracts. You take the money and run. By the time your American realizes he has been taken for the thirty-four thousand, he is back home in Missouri or wherever, feeling like a fool, and counting himself lucky that he didn't lose more."

Jack turned and looked at her with the blankness of a man drunk or surprised or both. "Mrs. Nevermore, I believe you are the last person in the world I wish to talk to."

"Then let's not talk, Jack. I don't wish to interrupt tales of your brilliance. Look where it's got you, after all. Allow me to buy you another absinthe. The green goddess remains your drink of choice, I see."

"The queen of poisons. Like you, dear Mrs. Nevermore." He saw me standing there staring up at him.

"Who's the squirt?"

"Ned Arnheim, a young man who loves a good story, and an orphan," Mrs. Nevermore said.

"A story-loving orphan, you say?"

"I did not like your story," I asserted.

"A critic," pronounced Jack.

"I am not supposed to be here," I said.

"None of us is, lad. None of us is." Jack finished off what remained of his absinthe.

Mrs. Nevermore called to the barman, a muscular brute with a pockmarked face and an impressive handlebar mustache. "Monsieur, a brandy and water. Also, another absinthe if you will for my friend Jack."

Curiously, this made Jack angry. "Who the hell do you think you are?"

"You object to me buying you a drink? Goodness, times have changed."

"I never wanted you buying me drinks."

"Sorry. I must have had another Jack Dozen in mind. Still, why not let me buy for your devoted friends?"

"Ah, but I have no friends."

"You do indeed," said the codger with the toothless grin. "Finally, a reason to endure this bugger and his endless stories that always have him so successfully fleecing the rich and stupid."

The codger addressed his companions. "Gentlemen, raise a glass to a young woman from a better life, done made a wrong turn to arrive here with money to buy us thirsty oafs a much appreciated libation."

A murmur of gratitude went up as the barman arrived with Mrs. Nevermore's brandy. He was not anxious to linger, knowing this was not exactly the paying end of the bar. Twenty francs transformed him into Mrs. Nevermore's best friend.

"They drink until it's gone," she said.

The barman grinned. He was missing two front teeth. The other patrons looked pleased as could be, except Jack. He leaned into her and said, "So what are you up to then?"

"A job."

"You don't need me, lady."

She nodded toward the twenty-franc note. "There's more if you help me."

"How much more?"

"Two hundred francs—and the ticket to a fortune."

"Go straight to hell. There are no tickets. Only the marks of this world believe such talk. You played me once. You'll not to do it again."

"What do you want from me, Jack? Great love? Undying passion? I don't have those things for you, sorry. What I do have is a second chance—and need."

The barman placed a fresh absinthe in front of him. He stared at it for a long minute and then raised it in his hand so that the light turned its liquid to shimmering jade. "They say it causes sudden delirium," he said. "I am still waiting." He drained it down and when he saw me watching him, snapped, "What the devil you looking at squirt?"

"At you, monsieur, wondering what we've come to if you are our best hope."

That elicited a shaky laugh from Smiling Jack. "Am I your best hope? You really are in trouble."

"That would be my conclusion, but Mrs. Nevermore refuses to confirm it."

Jack spoke to me, but he stared at her. "Admitting to trouble was never in the cards for our Mrs. Nevermore, even when she was in the thick of it."

"No trouble, Jack," Mrs. Nevermore replied smoothly. "Just business."

"Don't believe you, not for a minute." His voice was slurry now. That last absinthe made his words run together, so that there was no real end to the one, no beginning to another. "You're in trouble. The worst kind if I'm the best you can do."

He gave her what was supposed to be a knowing look, but it just came out bleary and unfocused. Then the color drained out of his face; that glorious face that had seen everything and everything had rendered it melancholy, convinced of the world's folly yet determined to beat against it, anyway. Except that the beating would have to take place tomorrow. For now Smiling Jack Dozen collapsed in a ginger-suited heap on the floor amid cheers from his free-drinking pals.

NINE

A blue mist clung to the ground as Mrs. Nevermore led a trio of Jack's drunken acquaintances carrying him through the twisting labyrinth of narrow streets surrounding Les Halles. The night air reeked of stinking gaslight and rotting vegetables, the pungent smell of onion soup and horse droppings and human sweat. A grimy flare of light marked a small cafe, its patrons huddled at tiny tables, solemnly drinking colored liquids.

A Cyclops with a fat lip and a scraggly beard marked our passage while nearby a harridan, her wild nest of wiry hair exploding around three chins, leaned against a wall, exposing a sagging breast before she threw up.

The streets grew darker still. It was as though we had fallen from the real world into its murky underside —the Other World Peregrine talked about. I expected goblins and gargoyles. They might be lurking in the nearby eating houses, the ones that transformed themselves after midnight into hostels where for a few sous the homeless could sleep at crude wooden tables, their heads buried in their arms.

From behind open windows came howls of unnamed rage. A baby cried. A lone dog barked in the distance.

I shuddered with fear. So this is where you could end up if you were an orphan, particularly a careless waif such as me who freely consorted with the likes of Mrs. Nevermore and her friends. This evening served as a loud warning, a reminder of the folly of going against the rules—of being different, if you will. You ended up drunk at places like l'Astuce and navigating endless cobblestone streets all leading the miscreant—me—straight into the hovels of hell.

We turned another corner, and abruptly the street narrowed even more and we found ourselves in a cul-de-sac.

Jack's three friends lowered him to the paving stones. Jack groaned his disapproval. That didn't seem to matter to the trio. They turned to face Mrs. Nevermore and myself and they did not look nearly so friendly.

"What is it?" said Mrs. Nevermore.

"I think they want your purse, madame," a voice behind us announced.

I turned to find the barman from the tavern standing there. In this light, mustaches bristling, he seemed twice as big as before. "Give us that and there will be no problem."

"There is indeed a problem, monsieur," Mrs. Nevermore said in a calm, firm voice, "in that I am not about to give you anything."

"Then we will take it from you," said the barman.

"You should give him what he wants," I said to her.

"I will do no such thing."

The barman produced a thick wooden club. A scrawny little devil with a wispy beard abruptly had a knife in his hand. The other two apparently would make do with their fists. Jack snored away on the street.

The four men began circling in on us. Mrs. Nevermore's eyes darted from one assailant to another, but she did not move. I was more than ready to make a run for it.

One of the louts lunged. Mrs. Nevermore's hand shot up palm out and the next thing the lout was airborne, rocketing upward and then coming straight down again, his head striking the pavement with a terrible crack. I had a vision of an egg broken against the side of a porcelain bowl.

The others, stunned, stared at the body in amazement. "God almighty," someone said in a low, disbelieving voice.

Mrs. Nevermore spun on the barman. The club flew from his hand and into hers. She stepped forward and struck the barman in his ugly, pock-marked face. His nose exploded in blood. He screamed and fell back.

Mrs. Nevermore attacked again, this time whacking the side of his head. The blow drew a second scream from the barman before he crashed to the pavement. Meanwhile, the scrawny little fellow with the knife grabbed Mrs. Nevermore from behind. His arm snaked around her throat holding the knife to her face.

"I'll cut you! Swear I'll cut you," he shouted. "Give me the purse!"

For a small eternity no one moved. The night silence was broken only by the moans of the barman and intermittent snores from Jack.

"Give it to him!" I called desperately to her.

"No."

I concentrated hard. To my relieved surprise, the knife went flying out of the scrawny fellow's hand. Dumbfounded by the sudden loss of his weapon, he loosened his grip on Mrs. Nevermore, and then with an anxious yelp turned and ran away down the street. The barman lay still on the paving stones near the fellow with the broken head.

"Ned," Mrs. Nevermore called to me. When I did not immediately respond, her voice rose and became sharper. "Ned! Go to Jack. Get him up. We must get out of here. Now."

Jack looked at me groggily. "Got a drink, squirt?"

I helped him to his feet.

TEN

Mrs. Nevermore led the way while I dragged Jack along, stinking of booze and the smoke clouds of l'Astuce. He mumbled incomprehensibly to himself, contented mumblings from the sounds of things, a man happy in his semi-comatose state. How I envied him.

We turned along an alley that soon opened into a courtyard. Several carts were stacked in a corner near the dark hulk of an abandoned wagon tipped on its axle.

With Jack more or less in tow, I followed Mrs. Nevermore up a stairway beneath a wooden overhang. A corridor opened onto the yard below. The air stank of boiled cabbage.

I propped Jack against the wall. He muttered some more as Mrs. Nevermore went through his pockets until she found a large key and then inserted it into the rusting lock of a nearby door.

"Wait here," she said, ducking inside. Soon enough a light ignited the darkness. Mrs. Nevermore reappeared in the doorway holding a lit candle.

"Bring him in," she ordered.

I wrestled Jack into a tiny room containing a cot, a washstand, a chest of drawers, and a large makeup desk dominated by a triptych mirror. Pots of facial paint, bits and pieces of costumes as well as wigs, and wisps of false beards and mustaches crowded the desktop.

Books were piled everywhere, along with faded playbills. The walls were plastered with tattered theater posters, sad testaments to the Drury Lane and Covent Garden productions Jack Dozen headlined: sullen youthfulness for *Hamlet*, adorable romanticism for *Arms and the Man*.

His roguish appeal in the original production of F.C. Sansom's *Sal and Methuselam* briefly made him a star. Jack was Methuselam in the melodrama of a lovelorn young couple whose chance at happiness is wrecked by Sal's mother. She believes her daughter too good for Methuselam because he is a sausage man whose product may or may not come from dead cats. The old lady forbids the relationship whereupon Methuselam throws aside his unsavory trade and runs away to become a soldier. He is killed and Sal, overwhelmed with grief, commits suicide by swallowing an oyster, shell and all. That seemed a trifle far-fetched to me. Who could possibly love so much they would swallow an entire oyster?

I got him on the cot. Mrs. Nevermore shut the door. Jack struggled to sit up.

"What was that all about back there?" he demanded in a slurry voice.

"I'm afraid you're going to have to find another place to drink," she went on. "If I were you, I wouldn't go back to l'Astuce any time soon."

Jack looked blearily at her. "Get out of here. Take the squirt with you."

"I'm not leaving until I talk some sense into that liquor-soaked head."

"Sense is staying away from you, lady. Sense is having nothing to do with another of your bloody fool schemes."

Mrs. Nevermore dropped a hundred-franc note onto the table. "Sense is getting off that bed, taking the badly needed half, and agreeing to work with me."

He managed a laugh. "That is no sense at all. Get out. Get out of my pathetic little hovel. Get out of my miserable excuse for a life. I do much better without you."

She did not move. "I'm not going to lie to you, Jack. I'm in trouble. I need the best to pull out of a bad jam, and you are the best. That's why I'm here."

"Gawd, you are something, I will give you that. You're standing on the gallows, the noose around your neck, and you'll calmly try to lie your way out."

"It's a good role, Jack. Not Shakespeare or Shaw, but better than *Methuselam*, I'll wager, a fine part that will make us both rich if you perform the way I think you can."

"That's not the problem. You're the problem."

"Get off that bed, Jack. Come and get the money. Then we go to work."

He looked over at me, and said, "You. Bottom drawer of that bureau over there. Open it."

Mrs. Nevermore nodded. "Get it for him, Ned. But don't move from where you are."

"I don't want to do that," I said.

"Do it."

I turned to face the bureau and concentrated on the bottom drawer. It opened slowly. A bottle of cheap brandy lifted out and hovered in the air.

"Put it on the table, Ned," she ordered.

I directed the bottle across the room, bringing it down smartly on the table beside the hundred francs.

Jack looked at Mrs. Nevermore. "So he's one of you is he?"

"One of us, Jack? One of the freaks?"

"I need a drink," he said.

"It's over here."

He laughed again, mirthless laughter, and in that flickering light from the candle he took on a ghoulish hue, an exhausted ghost haunting the black depths of Paris desperate for a drink. Was it my imagination or, by contrast, did the hard light and the dankness of this awful place somehow make Mrs. Nevermore more enticing than ever? Did she thrive in the dark hellish holes like some exotic mushroom? I believe she did. The sorcière at home in the abyss.

Jack motioned to me. "Squirt. Help me off the goddamn bed."

I looked again at Mrs. Nevermore. "Give him a hand, Ned."

I went over and helped the best I could as he heaved himself to his feet.

"It just doesn't make a great deal of sense to me," I said.

"What's that?"

"Killing yourself with an oyster."

"That's why you go to the theater, lad. It's there you meet the women willing to kill themselves for love. Alas, they are largely absent from life. Instead, they kill you. Just ask Mrs. Nevermore over there."

"How were you on stage?" I wondered.

He appeared to seriously consider the question before he answered. "As Methuselam, not so bad. Romantic and shallow but that's what the part required. For just about anything else, I lacked the greatness. Shakespeare wasn't my forte. Never could properly catch the old boy's rhythms. God, I saw Henry Irving's *Hamlet* at the Lyceum and that's when I knew the jig was up. I wasn't a patch on that performance. But I'd a sweet sullen face, and I could remember the lines, hit the mark, and sail on charm."

I steered him across the room. Mrs. Nevermore seemed an ocean away.

"What happened?"

"I got old. The audience grew tired. Or I grew tired, the audience old. I'm not sure which. A drink or two might also have been involved. And a woman. I vaguely recall a woman or two."

He reached the table, letting loose a blast of absinthe-scented air.

Shaky white fingers gripped the bottle, uncorked it, and then lifted it to his lips for a deep, restorative swig. He slammed the bottle down again, and leaned on the table, breathing hard, as though he'd run a long race. His eyes were on that money. "So what is it then, Mrs. Nevermore? What have you in mind?"

"The sale of some property."

"And what kind of property would that be?"

"The Eiffel Tower."

"Fancy that. Didn't know it was for sale."

"Tell me what isn't."

Jack stared at her, and then took another deep swig of brandy. I could hardly believe what I was hearing. Sell the Eiffel Tower? Preposterous. Impossible. Jack certainly would react the same way. He was a drunk, but a drunk with a head on his shoulders. But instead of immediately laughing and dismissing the idea, he offered a gentle smile aimed in my direction. "You and the squirt here, is it?"

Mrs. Nevermore said, "Gamelle, too."

Jack frowned. "That bastard? As likely to slit my throat as work with me."

"He won't slit your throat. However, Corbeau might."

That briefly silenced Jack. "He's around?"

"Apparently."

"No wonder you couldn't get anyone else, and ended up at my door."

"That's not it, Jack. I came to you first."

Jack raised his eyebrows in my direction. "What about the squirt here? Where does he fit into this? Going to levitate the Eiffel Tower, is he?"

"Ned will work with us and do what is necessary."

"I will not do anything illegal," I announced sternly.

"A good squirt, then. Just what we need, a law-abiding citizen." Jack said this with a widening grin, the charmer emerging. I wasn't sure how to respond, doubtful that either a good squirt or a law-abiding citizen was much appreciated in this crowd. He put the bottle down, and looked directly at Mrs. Nevermore. She returned his gaze without flinching.

"The Eiffel Tower, eh? That's the grift?"

"Are you up for it?"

"I am not up to much of anything. Certainly not the kind of serious play you've in mind." He nodded toward the money. "And even if I was, one hundred francs won't cover it."

"That's just the beginning. There's more."

He shook out another peal of mirthless laughter. "Don't con the con man, dearie."

"No con, Jack. Straight goods."

"Don't believe you. Sorry. The word is that you'd fallen on hard times. Lost your touch. That Argentina thing. Corbeau. All messed up badly. Thanks to that bastard Flix."

"It wasn't Flix," said Mrs. Nevermore.

"You would have a hard time convincing Corbeau of that. Or me for that matter."

"I know full well who was responsible, and so do you."

"You can't blame her for everything, Laura." A surprisingly gentle tone to his voice. Blame who, for everything? I wondered.

"Blame her for that, Jack. Certainly blame her for that."

"He was my father," I announced. Jack gave me a vaguely surprised look. "Flix Arnheim was my father." The statement sounded defensive, as though I was trying to convince myself.

"That a fact?"

"Yes it is," I said.

Jack reached for the brandy bottle. "Didn't know Flix had a kid. Let alone a warlock kid."

"Well, he did. And I am not a warlock."

"Flix with a warlock." There was a nasty edge to Jack's voice. "That must have done wonders for his ego."

I started to say something but the words choked in my throat.

"That's enough, Jack," said Mrs. Nevermore in an admonishing voice.

"Yes, maybe it is at that." Jack looked at me. Was it my imagination or were his rheumy eyes searching for forgiveness? "Do yourself and this lady here a favor squirt, and get out before I say more of the nasty things I'm only going to regret later."

"Forget Flix, forget Argentina, forget everything," Mrs. Nevermore said. "None of it makes any difference. We've both tumbled a bit since then but I doubt either of us has lost the touch. All we need is the right opportunity to get back into it. Here it is."

He laughed and shook his head. "The Eiffel Tower. Well, well. A comeback, is it?"

"The biggest score either one of us will ever see," said Mrs. Nevermore with impressive confidence.

He looked at her again, his face a mixture of great sadness and shining hope. "Ah, Mrs. Nevermore. The remarkable Mrs. Nevermore. How have I sinned so badly that the deities would summon you back to ruin my life?"

"Or save it," she said. "Are you in or not?"

"For what it's worth, I was in love with you," he said.

"In or out, Jack?"

"Maybe I still am, for all I bloody know."

"Jack."

He smiled—Smiling Jack in flower—and lifted the money off the table.

Part II

The Working of the Strange

ELEVEN

Have you heard about Father Hyacinthe?" Mrs. Nevermore sat at the kitchen table as usual in her peignoir with her coffee and cigar. "He's the delightful monk at Notre Dame. Everyone who meets him immediately converts to Catholicism, it is said."

"You cannot sell the Eiffel Tower," I announced. I had thought about this most of the night, the words I would say and how I would say them. Plain and strong. That's what I had decided. I could not be part of such a terrible thing. It was unthinkable.

"Of course I never converted, but then I am impervious to the demands and strictures of formal religion. The idea of God as a grumpy old geezer demanding that we daily get down on our knees and say nice things about him, well, I find that an impossible concept."

"You are not listening to me. This is not right. I will not have anything to do with this."

"Still, I do like Father Hyacinthe," she went on. "However, I now understand he has thrown away his cassock and decided to marry a young American widow. She came to him through a friend. Seeking spiritual comfort of all things. From the look of it, he was able to accommodate her. Apparently she is a Baptist. Whatever that is.

"Everyone is in shock, of course. Only an American widow, a so-called Baptist at that, would even dream of marrying a French priest. Who else would be so presumptuous? A Belgian, perhaps. Otherwise, I can't think of anyone."

"You cannot ignore me," I continued vehemently. "You took my drawings and then used them to decide to sell the Eiffel Tower. I won't allow it!"

My voice had risen to angry desperation. For the first time she actually seemed to hear me.

"Whatever are you babbling about, Ned? Honestly, I do wonder about you sometimes."

"The Eiffel Tower does not belong to you," I said.

"What kind of fool do you take me for? Of course it doesn't belong to me. Why ever would I think otherwise?"

"Then how can you even think of selling it? It would be impossible"

"Nothing is impossible, Ned. Only improbable. And it is with the improbable that you succeed."

Before I could argue the point, the back door opened and Smiling Jack Dozen stepped into the kitchen. He didn't look so bad this morning, shaved, wearing a bowler hat (or *chapeau melon* as they called it in France) and a black suit, a little shiny and threadbare around the cuffs, but otherwise presentable enough. Not quite a gent, but hardly the vagabond drunk of Les Halles, either.

"There you are, Jack," said Mrs. Nevermore as though he showed up every morning around this time. "I was just about to tell Ned here about marks."

"You were not," I groaned.

"Very important," said Jack, removing his bowler and seating himself at the table, as though this too was a ritual in which he participated regularly. "Without the mark, you got nothing."

He sniffed at Mrs. Nevermore's coffee bowl. "What's that? Coffee is it?"

"Ned, get Jack some coffee, will you?"

"There's a good lad," said Jack with a pleasant smile. "Now you take my cousin Sydney, who actually got me into this business. A master at choosing the mark, our Sydney, although, I must say he had it easy thanks to his Rumanian box."

Despite myself, my curiosity was piqued. "What's a Rumanian box?"

"Simple enough, lad. It's an elegant mahogany box about twelve inches by twelve inches. A cabinetmaker in Budapest hand carved them for Cousin Sydney."

"And what does this box do?"

"It makes money," said Jack, as though everyone should know that about a Rumanian box.

"You mean you earn money with it."

"No, no. I mean it actually manufactures money. The box contains a series of highly polished brass knobs and dials. You place a bill in one end, adjust the knobs and dials, and out comes a bill just like it on the other end."

I looked at him incredulously. "But that is impossible. No such machine exists."

Smiling Jack Dozen threw his head back and laughed. "Well, you know, and I know. And certainly Mrs. Nevermore knows. However, luckily for my Cousin Sydney, those marks I was telling you about? The suckers of Palm Beach in America, they didn't know."

I asked him how much his cousin sold these machines for.

"Twenty-five thousand a piece, give or take."

"But none of this makes sense," I cried. "Who would ever think you could buy a machine that manufactures all the money you would ever need for twenty-five thousand dollars?"

Jack just laughed some more. "Of course, it doesn't make sense, squirt. If it made sense Mrs. Nevermore and I would be out of business. As it is, my cousin never had any difficulty getting rid of his lovely Rumanian boxes."

"I believe the police in Palm Beach finally put a stop to Sydney's enterprise, did they not?"

"There's the point," replied Jack. "That was the one time—and Sydney will tell you this himself—the one time he was careless when choosing the mark."

"I believe he failed to notice the mark was an undercover policeman."

"That's why the right mark is vital. Particularly for a job like this one."

I set coffee in front of him. "Why this one in particular?"

Jack used both hands to lift the bowl to his lips. I noticed they shook a bit.

"For this we need a special mark, a gent with the kind of money that would allow him to seriously consider the Eiffel Tower. Big money such as we're discussing is good because it provides a fat payday that makes all the trouble worthwhile. One big score is worth a dozen small ones, and you reduce your risk."

"How is that?"

"Remember Cousin Sydney, squirt. Always helpful in such exercises. Every time he sold one of his Rumanian boxes, he risked getting caught. You sell one big Rumanian box—the Eiffel Tower—and you pull it off proper, well then, you don't have to sell any more Rumanian boxes, do you? Much more likely you get caught twelve times than you are getting caught the once.

"Makes sense, I suppose."

"However, the big money can also work against you. The gents with that sort of capital tend not to be so greedy, and therefore not so gullible, and a good deal more suspicious—disinclined to believe that a mahogany box can print all the money in the world."

"Or that the Eiffel Tower is for sale," I added.

"Precisely."

"Thus we need someone who is very wealthy and at the same time greedy and susceptible," said Mrs. Nevermore.

"Yeah, well, that's the trick isn't it?"

Gamelle came in, glowering. The tiny black dots on the cliff face blazed with hatred. "What is this man doing in my kitchen?"

"And a good morning to you, Prince Gamelle, France's once and future king," said Jack. "The quest for the throne keeps you as cheerful as ever, I see."

"This man is a fool and a drunk," snarled Gamelle. "I cannot work with him."

"A drunk? Possibly true," said Jack calmly. "But at least I'm not a delusional homicidal maniac like some I know."

Gamelle lunged like a cat. Jack did not move from the table, did not even seem perturbed.

"Gamelle!" The sharpness of Mrs. Nevermore's voice stopped him in mid stride. "That's enough."

Gamelle turned on her. "This is madness. What you do is complete madness!"

"Nonetheless, Jack will be working with us," Mrs. Nevermore stated quietly. "We will all work together. We will all get along. Is that understood?"

Gamelle did not move. Every muscle in his body tensed. "This man will bring us only disaster. I cannot work with this man."

"Then we will move ahead without you, and that will be the end of it. You will continue your journey to France's throne alone."

Gamelle drew a deep breath that briefly seemed to shake his entire body. "How can you put the future of France so casually at risk?"

"It's a difficult decision," agreed Mrs. Nevermore. "But considering the circumstances in which we find ourselves, it's one I am prepared to make."

Gamelle threw one final glare around the room and then turned and stalked from the kitchen. Jack picked up his bowl. I noticed his hands no longer shook. "This is good coffee," he said.

"It will be all right," Mrs. Nevermore said.

"Gamelle or the coffee?"

Mrs. Nevermore doused what was left of her cigar. "All right Jack, down to business. I want you to get a new suit today, and a frock coat as well. Very conservative, something a bureaucrat would wear. The Bon Marché should have what you need."

"The Bon Marché it is," said Jack.

"Once you're properly outfitted, go over to the Ministère des postes et télégraphes and have a look around. Keep an eye out for a suitable office, something we might be able to make use of when the time comes."

"I'll go this afternoon or first thing in the morning, depending on how soon they can have a suit for me."

Mrs. Nevermore pushed back her chair and rose to her feet. "Meanwhile, Ned and I will set about the task of finding our mark."

"Me? Why do you need me for this?"

"A woman alone in Paris with a poor orphan child to raise. What could induce more sympathy—or less suspicion?"

"I refuse to help you."

"Please, Ned. I don't have time for your tedious protestations of morality."

"I have not said a word about morality."

"You're just about to, I'm sure. I want you to be with me and no arguments. Eyes open. Mind working. Mouth shut."

* * *

In the evening, I drifted into the courtyard to take the air, my mind spinning with what I had heard upstairs. I leaned against the remains of the cart propped by the wall.

Presently, Peregrine joined me, descending from his tree to alight atop a rusting wheel rim.

"What do you want?" I demanded in a surly voice. "I suppose you're not going to talk again."

"Why would I not talk?" said Peregrine.

"You see? Just when I am expecting one thing, I get another. I can't trust anyone, not even a falcon."

"In fact, falcons are most trustworthy and loyal," he said. "What's more we are very good when it comes to listening. This evening, if I may say so, you don't look very happy, Ned."

"I'm not," I said.

"Truth be told, you never look happy."

"It's because I am forced to do things I don't want to do, by people I am not at all certain about."

"You should be a falcon," Peregrine said. "We don't do anything we don't want to do."

"I am very tired of doing what she wants and nothing of what I want."

"What does she want you to do?"

"Help her sell the Eiffel Tower."

"I see. And why don't you want to do that?"

"Why don't I want to do it? Well, it's illegal for one thing. For another, I love the tower and don't want any harm to come to it."

"I don't see how she can harm the Eiffel Tower."

"I don't know. But I fear she can. She's a witch, you know. A sorcière."

"Are there such things?"

"If birds talk, and gargoyles attack, I would say witches are certainly a possibility."

"I suppose you're right," agreed Peregrine.

"Further, don't you think that if she is a sorcière she could hurt the tower?"

"I guess she could," said Peregrine.

"I am doomed," I groaned. "I am an orphan, alone in the world. What choice do I have but to follow this terrible woman?"

"My goodness, you do continue to feel sorry for yourself, Ned."

"Can you possibly blame me?"

"I know you keep saying that, and I suppose you are right, but you do have choices. You don't necessarily have to do something just because someone tells you to. I know that sounds simplistic. But it's true."

"With Mrs. Nevermore that's easier said than done. She can be very persuasive."

"Yes, I know."

"I wonder at times if she hasn't cast a spell over me." I stopped and looked at him. "What do you mean, 'you know'? You know Mrs. Nevermore?"

"Of course I do. How could I not? I'm sitting out here in her tree, after all."

"But how do you know her?"

"I'm not absolutely sure of this," said Peregrine, "but I believe it's because of her I am able to talk."

Before I could pursue this further, the lady in question, the accused sor-cière herself, swept into the courtyard. She stopped and peered around in the dimming evening light until she spotted me.

"Ned, whatever are you doing?"

"I'm talking to this falcon," I said.

"We don't have time for that. Come along."

"He says he can talk because of you."

"Ned, I've told you before. Falcons can't talk. Let me take a look at you." She studied me up and down before reaching out and adjusting my tie.

"Honestly, that tie. There. That's better. And you might consider comb-ing your hair from time to time."

"Where are we going?"

"To find our perfect mark."

"How will you do that?" I asked.

"We will go to the place where the finest marks in Paris are to be found," she said, starting away. "And we enlist the aid of the one man who knows those marks better than any other."

Reluctantly, I followed after her. "Who is this person?"

"A Swiss peasant," she said.

TWELVE

A rotund gentleman passed through the austere, stuccoed hall that was the Ritz lobby carrying a small dog dressed in evening clothes, complete with a stiff white collar and black satin socks.

"Did you see that?" I said excitedly. "A dog dressed in a tuxedo!"

"It's the Ritz, you expect nothing less," said Mrs. Nevermore as though every day she encountered small dogs dressed in evening clothes.

Her hair swept into a rich crimson pile so as to better demonstrate the perfection of her features, she glided by the carved Louis XVI paneling of the reception desk, and up the main staircase with its wrought iron balusters. With me trying to keep up, she hurried along the Braquenié carpet, past liveried footmen serving patrons seated on Tassinari silk-covered chairs, through arched floor-to-ceiling French doors, and into the Ritz Espadon, the garden restaurant.

César Ritz, the Swiss peasant in question, as perfectly appointed as one of his rooms, huddled with a lean, sinister fellow upon whose hawk nose perched a gleaming monocle. I would soon learn this was Olivier Dabescat, Ritz's maître d'hôtel.

The year before, Monsieur Ritz, together with his partner, the chef Auguste Escoffier, had purchased a mansion at number 15 in the place Vendôme recently occupied by a bank, the Crédit-Mobilier. Backed by a syndicate of wealthy investors that included an Armenian oil magnate and a South African multi-millionaire, Escoffier and Ritz, with help from the renowned architect Charles Mewès, transformed the mansion into a hotel that was, Ritz insisted, the last word in elegance, luxury, efficiency, and hygiene.

"We have run out of live rabbits for the Marchesa Casati's boa constrictor," I overheard Olivier announce to his employer.

"Get more rabbits," ordered Ritz.

"Also Monsieur James Gordon Bennett was in here earlier this evening. He'd had a great deal to drink, as usual."

"The owner of *The New York Herald Tribune* and a terrible bore. What did you do with him?"

"What one does with bores. I sent him to Maxim's."

"Very good."

Ritz spied Mrs. Nevermore and launched himself toward us like a small and frighteningly accurate missile aimed at bussing Mrs. Nevermore on both cheeks. She was his irreplaceable and deeply cherished friend. There was no one else in the world but her. Absolutely no one! Except he did spare a moment to cluck admiringly over me, the orphan child. Saved from unimaginable harm! How fortunate was I! How lucky to have a guardian such as Mrs. Nevermore! Surely, I must be the most thankful boy in all Paris!

I gritted my teeth. Mrs. Nevermore smiled serenely.

While Olivier swept away, presumably in search of rabbits for the marchesa's snake, Ritz guided us to a corner table where three others were already seated. Ritz introduced a pale, sickly looking gentleman by the name of Marcel Proust. Next to him was an enthusiastic young Brazilian with dark curly hair, Alberto Santos Dumont.

Beside Santos Dumont sat a bristling, blunt-spoken American, Anthony Drexel, a partner of the financier J.P. Morgan. Barrel-chested, loud talking, with a thick mane of coppery hair swept back from a ruddy face, Drexel gave off the impression of absolute certainty about the world and his prominent place in it.

"Permit us to present the remarkable Mrs. Nevermore!" Ritz announced. "We are so very fortunate to have her with us this evening. And also, Monsieur Ned Arnheim."

No one, it seemed, believed they were quite so fortunate to have me present. They demonstrated this by completely ignoring me. I sat next to Marcel Proust.

"A clever boy," said Proust.

"I beg your pardon."

"You appear to be a clever boy. Is that the case?"

"And supposing it is?"

"It will get you into nothing but trouble. I know. I was a clever boy at your age. That caused me great difficulty. That and my homosexuality. Are you a homosexual?"

"I'm not sure," I said. "Up till now I haven't had much to do with women. But that has more to do with circumstances than it does with preference. So no, I don't think so."

"You do not think about your sexuality, young man, you live in it. If you have to think about it, then what is the point?" Proust's eyes glazed with lack of interest.

He turned his head away as Mrs. Nevermore, seated beside Anthony Drexel, allowed him to brush his lips against her knuckles. His eyes gleamed. I would see that gleam many times in many different men over the years, and it always was inspired by one of two things: lust or greed.

Tonight, my money would be riding on lust.

"It's all so boring, really," Proust announced. "We posture. We pretend. We deceive. And for what? The aristocracy is in decline, decimated by the Dreyfus case and by the rise of the middle classes. The grace and beauty that accompanies wealth and privilege is disappearing and, anyway, it all ends too soon and we are dead. All that will be left is Paris." He gave a wan smile. "And the Ritz, of course. The Ritz will live forever."

"As will great novels," interrupted Ritz. "The world will be left with brilliant novels by the great Proust."

"And what great novels have you written, Monsieur Proust?" Mrs. Nevermore inquired.

He looked surprised. "Why, I have not written any."

"Then the acknowledgment of you as a great novelist is all the more impressive."

"Marcel, when will you understand? You are the one who is boring, not the world," said Santos Dumont in a weary voice, as though the act of denouncing his companion had become too much. "The world is a fascinating place. But you, my God. You talk and talk about a Paris that doesn't exist, a novel you never write while you are not working at a job you do not have."

"I have a job," huffed Proust. "The Bibliothèque Mazarine. It is the oldest library in France."

"And what do you do there?"

"I am currently on a leave of absence," said Proust.

"You have been on leave since you arrived. I hear you never worked there a single day."

"I am sickly, they understand that. At least I am French and not Brazilian, your curse, Santos Dumont."

"I am a sportsman of the air, Marcel, while you are merely a fraud."

He addressed Anthony Drexel. "You see, monsieur, I came to Paris to experiment with balloons. Most fascinating. It is my ambition to fly a balloon around the Eiffel Tower."

Drexel looked at him abashed. "What the hell kind of ambition is that?"

"It is the ambition of a gentleman, monsieur," Santos asserted.

"The pastime of a fool," amended Proust.

Mrs. Nevermore aimed a glowing smile at Drexel and said, "How is Monsieur Morgan? I had the pleasure of meeting him in New York several years ago."

"J.P. never said a thing about meeting such a beautiful woman. But then J.P. is only interested in Wall Street, railroads, and banks."

"And you, Mr. Drexel?"

"I am interested in Wall Street, railroads, banks, and beautiful women."

Mrs. Nevermore laughed gaily. He touched at her arm. "Never mind painting or writing or dance or any of that nonsense, the art of the new century will be the business deal."

"My God," groaned Proust. "You really are an American."

Drexel looked pleased. "You got that right, friend. American, through and through. What's wrong with that? The next century? The American Century. You can bet on it. You know why? Americans are always looking for the next deal, something the other guy doesn't have, that's why.

"Paris is the place to be, yes indeed," he went on. "The end of the century and here is the center of the world. Gotta take the world view now, that's what I keep telling J. P. You can't look in at yourself any more, gotta look out. And Paris is the best vantage point from which to view the world, to pursue this new art form that is the deal."

"That sentiment apparently saturates American life these days," sniffed Proust.

"Americans love Paris," agreed Drexel.

"Unfortunately, Americans are not content merely to love Paris. This love drives them to actually visit. Thus Paris is full of Americans and that is catastrophic for Paris."

"What's wrong with Americans?" demanded Drexel, now a trifle put out by this turn in the conversation.

"They make horrible demands," said Proust. "They want baths and ice in their water. Iced water? Why it is the ruination of everything that is French!"

Just as I was sure Drexel and Proust would come to blows, with the sickly Proust almost certainly coming out the worst, Auguste Escoffier made his entrance. Small in stature with a large mustache, he reminded me of a fellow permanently worried that he had left his house keys somewhere but was not sure where exactly. Decked out in a formal coat, trailing the delicious aromas of his kitchen, he anxiously smoothed his hair, a gesture that only caused him to look more harried.

It was hard to say whether Ritz had created Escoffier or if Escoffier had given birth to Ritz. Certainly before the two met in Lucerne at the Grand Hotel National, Ritz was a struggling hotelier unable to find anyone who could fulfill his dream of a lodging house offering the finest cuisine imaginable. But then no one paid much attention to a fussy little cook who insisted on such revolutionary ideas for the time as simple cooking, a decently organized kitchen and fresh food.

They had in the end found each other at exactly the right time and formed one another in equal measure in a London overflowing with wealthy, free-spending visitors needing a luxurious place to stay.

Aided by Ritz's long-time patron, Lady de Grey, and his good friend, Edward the Prince of Wales, they had transformed the Savoy Hotel and become the toast of London society. They had quickly gained a similar foothold in Paris, a city as anxious as London to luxuriously house its newly acquired armies of wealthy international visitors, although why the two abruptly deserted the British capital at the height of their success remained the subject of much gossip and speculation.

"Auguste! There you are! Just in time!" cried César Ritz, jumping to his feet. "I believe you know everyone here with the exception of Mrs. Nevermore."

The chef gave her a formal bow. "Madame," he said.

"Monsieur, it's a pleasure to make the acquaintance of the man who changes the way the world eats."

"You are too kind," said Escoffier.

Mrs. Nevermore then introduced me. Escoffier barely nodded in my direction.

"Inflame us with news of the magic you have created for this evening, dear Auguste," Ritz urged.

"We begin with blini and caviar," Escoffier announced. "Then, a cream of carrot soup. After that, sole in white wine sauce followed by partridge and noodles with foie gras, then lamb noisettes with artichoke hearts and peas.

We finish with a light dessert, a champagne sorbet."

Everyone enthusiastically applauded these selections, particularly César Ritz who cried, "Bravo! Bravo!"

Escoffier acknowledged the applause with another quick bow before disappearing back into his kitchen. Waiters poured wine into glasses. A rosy informal glow descended upon the table, interesting people amid lovely surroundings consuming good wine, awaiting the arrival of a spectacular meal. Even I found myself relaxing into this atmosphere, content to take in the purr of the conversation around me.

THIRTEEN

Monsieur Drexel had just finished an amusing story having to do with persuading J.P. Morgan to eat snails in Paris the year before, when I looked up to see a pudgy, rascally character, rather unkempt and badly dressed, decidedly out of place in these privileged surroundings.

Once again, César Ritz bounded to his feet, the unwavering champion of bonhomie, unperturbed by the uncouth appearance of this new arrival. "Georges, there you are! Finally! We had given up all hope."

"My apologies, César. I had a story to complete for tomorrow's editions."

Ritz's eyes danced. "You must tell us everything, Georges." He turned to the group. "This is the famous Paris reporter, Georges Duroy."

Duroy dropped into an empty chair. Immediately, a waiter sprang forward splashing wine into his glass, filling it to the brim. Duroy gulped it down without spilling a drop. The waiter refilled his glass. Duroy took two more hearty gulps, his already reddened eyes watering with the joy of a man endlessly pleased to quench his thirst.

"The latest news, Georges, quick! Before we all burst!"

Duroy placed the glass on the table before allowing himself a shrug. "The latest news tells you who spoke at the assembly today. You do not want news my dear César. It's gossip you're after."

"We could care less who spoke at the assembly," Ritz agreed.

"Then how about gossip's oldest friend—scandal?" Duroy stated this with the authority of a man who knew he had command of everyone's attention.

"And what sort of scandal do you have for us?"

"The only kind there is," said Duroy, sitting back to allow the waiter to once again refill his glass. "The kind that involves a woman."

Duroy launched an attack on his newly filled glass.

"Indeed," agreed Ritz. "So tell us Duroy, who is involved?"

"I know one of the parties involved."

"The male or the female?" inquired Proust.

"Alas, only the male of the species, thus far."

"The least interesting part of the story," observed Ritz.

"Ah, but you underestimate the power of a name, dear César."

"Then provide a name and prove us wrong."

Duroy's eyes sparkled, the veteran gambler about to unveil his winning hand. "Try this one on for size: Sir Robert Chiltern."

Ritz's eyebrows shot up. "One of Salisbury's Souls. The brightest of the bright young men! The future prime minister of Britain!"

Even Anthony Drexel who had begun to look sleepy-eyed when Duroy arrived, perked up.

"The pillar upon whom the virtues of British decency and honor are most often built these days," agreed Duroy, sweeping the glass into his protective fist.

"Pray tell us more, Georges," demanded Ritz excitedly.

Duroy peered at his wine as though its texture might hold the secret to what he would say next. He decided it did not. With a melodramatic sigh, he delivered the glass back to the table.

"I'm still in the process of tracking down all the particulars, but I have it on good authority Sir Robert is secretly in the city, besotted by a young woman of such extraordinary beauty that he is willing to desert his family and abdicate his future for her."

"Why that could be you, Mrs. Nevermore!" exclaimed Ritz. She allowed the fragrant hint of a cool smile. "Breathes there a man in this city who would not desert his wife and family if you so much as crooked your little finger?"

Mrs. Nevermore raised her little finger and made a show of crooking it in Ritz's direction.

He clapped his hands together and burst out laughing. "I would be tempted, no doubt. But alas my wife wouldn't permit it."

"Certainly no beautiful woman in Paris is beyond suspicion until I get to the bottom of this," said Duroy, the gleam replaced by a sheen of sadness as he inspected yet another empty glass.

"So you have no idea who this woman is?" Mrs. Nevermore said to the reporter.

He brightened. "Not yet, although"—and here he allowed his voice to drop to a conspiratorial whisper—"they were seen huddled intimately together at Les Deux Magots."

"Les Deux Magots?" Ritz sounded disappointed enough that the waiter, about to recharge Duroy's glass, abruptly backed off. "They might as well stand naked in the middle of the Champs Élysées. A good scandal does not start at Deux Magots. It is far too public."

"Ah, but consider the benefits of hiding in public," allowed Duroy in a voice pleading for more of the attention that was fast slipping away. "If everyone can see you, perhaps they see nothing at all."

"But that location does open the possibility the meeting between Sir Robert and this woman was in all innocence," said Ritz.

"There is no such thing as innocence," said Proust. "Not in Paris."

"I could not agree more, Monsieur Proust," said Duroy agreeably. "Sir Robert was not even supposed to be here. A call to his office late this afternoon elicited the information that he had never left London. They are lying. He is in Paris. I have it on the best authority."

Further discussion of Sir Robert's amorous deceits was cut off by a descending brigade of waiters bearing blini and caviar shimmering upon gleaming Cristofle silver serving trays. Tonight, Monsieur Escoffier served his guests à la russe. That is to say each item on the menu was presented in the order he had announced it, rather than in the traditional manner of service à la française which decreed that everything be served at once. Each course was interrupted by a tart wine to clear the palate.

None of this appeared to make the least bit of difference to Mrs. Nevermore. She barely glanced at her caviar but rather occupied herself gazing at Anthony Drexel. He leaned over and whispered into her ear. Her smile could have lighted a French village.

Another contingent of waiters arrived bearing the cream of carrot soup. Mrs. Nevermore ignored the soup and gently placed her hand on Drexel's arm. He beamed. The sole in white wine sauce followed. Superb. I could not get enough. Mrs. Nevermore barely touched it. Bedazzled by Monsieur Drexel's hushed eloquence, she did not take her eyes off him.

The waiters regrouped before attacking again, this time armed with the partridge and the noodles with fois gras. Delicious! I'd never tasted anything like it in my young life. Food could not possibly be this good. I saw Mrs. Nevermore use her fork to push the fois gras from one side of her plate to the other.

Finally, exquisitely, came the lamb noisettes with the artichoke hearts. Everyone tasted and applauded. Ritz could not have looked happier had the Lord Jesus reserved a table for the Last Supper. Monsieur Drexel, oblivious, leaned even closer to Mrs. Nevermore, his lips moving inches from her ear. She barely touched her lamb.

The waiter army cleared the table to make way for the light champagne sorbet served in hollowed out clementines on doily-lined saucers, garnished with mint leaves. Exhausted now by the delirium of delicious flavors they had so recently savored, it was all the dinner guests, myself included, could do to force silver spoons dripping with sorbet into their mouths.

Mrs. Nevermore devoured hers with a speed that left everyone staring. She delicately placed her spoon on the saucer and turned to Anthony Drexel. She looked directly into his eyes.

"Monsieur, I see that it is growing late," she said. "Poor little Ned. He must get his sleep. I wonder if you might be so kind as to escort us to a carriage."

FOURTEEN

If you lived in Britain in those days, it was impossible not to have heard Sir Robert Chiltern's name or to have read it in the newspapers.

Sir Robert prospered in the glow of a British empire that loved him for his purity of character and integrity of spirit. Government provided him not with material gain—a member of parliament received no salary—but with distinction. That was what he was after, his place in the sun as an honest man, unaffected by what Lord Salisbury, the prime minister, called "the taint of sordid greed."

As César Ritz had pointed out, he was also one of the 'Souls' who worshipped at the intellectual altar provided by Arthur Balfour, nephew of Lord Salisbury. This tiny tribe was known to be literate, clever, and endlessly self-admiring, its members constantly holding a mirror up to themselves, adoring the reflection. If Sir Robert turned out to be less literate or clever, that was overlooked. A rapturous London press variously described him as "noble," and "pure," a "man of high character," and perhaps most dangerous, at least in Mrs. Nevermore's estimation, "faultless." No one was more talked about as a likely successor to Salisbury at number 10 Downing Street.

This then was the political demigod who had arrived in Paris the day before, the shining young man the reporter Georges Duroy said was here to conduct an illicit affair. And this was the man whose name Mrs. Nevermore tabled at a meeting with Prince Gamelle and Jack Dozen over tea in the kitchen at number 52.

"I don't believe this is a good idea," said Jack.

"And why do you say that?" demanded Mrs. Nevermore.

"Apparently, it went well at the Ritz last night. This American chap, Drexel."

"He saw me to my carriage," Mrs. Nevermore said.

"He wants to see you again?"

"So he says."

"So you've dangled the hook, Mrs. Nevermore. Let's see if our boy goes for the bait. He sounds perfect. With Drexel, you would not have to bring emotion into it."

"Emotion? Who is bringing emotion? Certainly not I."

Jack spoke slowly, measuring his words. "You're talking to Jack, remember? I was involved in that canal thing. Our last grift together."

"It makes no difference."

"I'm sorry, Laura. But I believe it does. Sir Robert defeated you—"

Gamelle flared. "Shut your mouth, Jack! You are a drunken fool!"

Jack reddened. "And you're a blood-thirsty bastard as likely to rip a throat out as take a mark —a goddamn danger to all of us."

"How would you like it if I condemn you to death now, Jack Dozen? I warn you, as soon as I am king, you will go under the guillotine's blade. A public execution! Do not think impassioned pleas for your life will have the least affect."

"Good God in heaven," Jack said, shaking his head. "What sort of insanity have I made myself part of?"

"That's enough," said Mrs. Nevermore, keeping her voice icy calm. "Both of you. Stop this."

Jack touched Mrs. Nevermore's arm. "You would like nothing better than revenge. I understand the impulse, but we are after something bigger here. Your feelings for Sir Robert puts that into jeopardy."

Gamelle sighed. "It pains me greatly to say this but I must agree with Jack. The American Drexel appears a much better prospect."

Mrs. Nevermore shook her head. "One wrong move with Drexel and he comes roaring back at us. You think I want revenge? Wait until you have to deal with an angry American robber baron deciding he's been made a fool of by foreigners in Paris—and a woman, to add insult to the injury. With Sir Robert, we know he cannot do anything. Because of who he is and what he represents, he will have to keep quiet, and pray we do the same."

Jack again, more intense this time: "Listen to reason, Laura. You've already burned Sir Robert. He sees you coming through the door and he knows something's up. Drexel sounds ripe for the picking. I say we take him."

Mrs. Nevermore seemed to spend some time weighing this argument. Then she shrugged and said, "Let us see what happens this evening."

"This evening?" I said. "What is to happen this evening?"

"Quiet, boy!" yelled Gamelle. "You will do as you're told and speak when you are spoken to!"

No one suggested this was anything but the right course of action for me.

FIFTEEN

When Les Deux Magots was a little shop for something or other, no one paid the least attention. Now that it had been turned into a café, everyone in Paris flocked there. So much was changing so quickly, it was hard to keep up. Thus a stop at Les Deux Magots was necessary in order to hear the latest gossip. Of course, one's presence at the café could also fuel the very gossip one was hearing—which made it even more curious that Sir Robert Chiltern would choose this place for a rendezvous.

But sure enough, from our vantage point in the black brougham across the street, Mrs. Nevermore and I could see him seated outside near the wall, legs crossed, leaning on his walking stick for a better view of the passing parade. Even at this distance I could see he was a true Englishman, unmistakably so, a gentleman adrift on the continent, complete with top hat and tailcoat, closely cropped brown hair, neatly trimmed mustache, his shirt collar rising stiffly to a chin that Mrs. Nevermore declared disappointing.

"A weak chin," she noted. "I view a man's chin or lack thereof, as a major impediment to intelligence."

"This man across the street is advertised as the next leader of the British Empire, but because of his chin you mark him an idiot?"

"The idiots run things, Ned. Why do you think it is things don't run well?"

"What then of my chin?"

"You have a very strong chin."

"That's a relief, I suppose."

"Thus there should be no major impediment to intelligence," she said. "Save and except for the fact you are a man."

"That is an impediment?"

"A great impediment. Practically insurmountable. I shall have to spend a lifetime helping you overcome it."

I didn't like the sound of that.

Sir Robert arose, dropped some coins on the table, pulled discreetly at his left gloved hand, adjusted his walking stick, and then strode to the curb where he hailed a carriage. Whatever he had planned for the evening, it was not about to play out at Deux Magots. Mrs. Nevermore rapped on the window. A grunt of disapproval exploded out of Gamelle, once again in the role of coachman. He urged his horses forward and we set out after our quarry.

"Well, well," said Mrs. Nevermore with a chuckle, "imagine that."

"What is it?" I demanded.

"Unless I miss my guess, Britain's pillar of virtue is headed for the Madeleine."

"And that is where?"

"That is where good men go to be bad."

* * *

We came along boulevard de la Madeleine, joining a ceaseless line of carriages jammed up and down the tree-lined street, their lanterns shimmering through the darkness. Many good people appeared intent on being bad this evening.

Mrs. Nevermore ordered the carriage to stop in the very shadow of the L'église de la Madeleine and we climbed out. I found myself excited at the prospect of being so close to so much sin. I had really only heard of sin during the various school services I was forced to attend. As far as I knew, I'd never been exposed to any of it, so being where it actually transpired was an unimaginable delight. It hovered in the air, on the sidewalks, lit by gaslight, fueled by imagination. Sin! Of course I would not actually indulge in it. I would only observe so that I knew what it was and could act accordingly. My breath came in little gulps and curious rasps.

"My goodness, Ned," Mrs. Nevermore said. "The last time I saw you like this, you were refusing to climb the Eiffel Tower."

"I am fine," I said.

"Then come along, and try not to look as though you're about to faint."

"I am not about to faint," I protested, my legs wobbly, feeling as though I might do precisely that.

Crowds jammed the boulevard. For the time being, everyone appeared to behave themselves. Very disappointing.

I spotted Jack Dozen in the crowd outside the Café de Paris, smart in his new suit and adorned with an admirable top hat. He gave a slight shrug as we passed to indicate he had not seen Sir Robert.

There was no sign of him among the beer drinkers next door at Tortoni's or at Maison Dorée or the café Riche.

Finally, Mrs. Nevermore spied him in front of Frascati's on the corner of rue Richelieu and the boulevard Montmartre. We watched as he started through the crowds, strolling toward the Café de Paris, ramrod straight, shoulders back, his walking stick striking the pavement as though keeping time, the preening dandy out for a night on the town.

A graceful swan of a woman abruptly darted into view and fell into step with him. Nearly six feet in height, crimson-tinged golden hair visible beneath a small hat cocked at an enticing angle, she possessed a single glittering blue eye. Her other eye was hidden by a black patch. The eye patch had the effect of lending an extraordinary sensuality to her. Jaded *boulevardiers* paused for a closer look. I glanced over at Mrs. Nevermore. She was frozen to the spot. You could see from the pale tautness of her face that the appearance of this magical young woman had unsettled her.

Jack Dozen stepped past us, and he knew it, too. He said, "Natalia."

Mrs. Nevermore responded by turning away.

Something was terribly wrong. How did they know this woman? Who was Natalia?

Meanwhile Natalia tugged at Sir Robert's sleeve, a full red mouth turning in a coquettish smile, forgiving all his trespasses. She took Sir Robert's arm in a manner that suggested she had taken it before as they continued along the street. We followed, my mind filling with all sorts of questions about this one-eyed woman who could at once so entrance a future British prime minister and upset Mrs. Nevermore.

They reached the Café de Paris, paused, talking together, as though debating whether to go inside. Finally, Sir Robert led her through the tables into the café's interior. Abruptly, Mrs. Nevermore materialized at my elbow, a certain tension playing at the corners of her mouth. "Go inside," she said. "Then report back on what they are up to."

"I cannot go into such a place," I said in alarm.

"It's only a café, not a den of iniquity. Now do as you are told."

I decided it best not to argue. Besides, I desperately wanted another look at this curious, one-eyed beauty.

I scurried inside.

Sir Robert and Natalia were seated at the back of one of the salons among the usual array of poseurs arguing loudly and attempting to speak wittily over the casseroled veal, the house specialty. Natalia looked up and for an instant that mesmerizing blue eye stared straight at me. I gulped and backed quickly away, filled with a terrible sense that I had been spotted and now she knew who I was and what I was up to. A waiter approached and demanded to know if I was waiting for someone. A bit unnerved, I slipped back outside to where Mrs. Nevermore and Jack waited.

"What are they doing?" she demanded.

"They are eating," I replied.

"Aha!" cried Jack.

Mrs. Nevermore gave him a frozen stare and walked away. Jack looked at me sheepishly—and winked. "Not a happy turn of events, lad," he said. "Not a happy turn of events at all."

"Who is this person, this Natalia?" I demanded.

"Boyer. Natalia Boyer," Jack said. "Mrs. Nevermore's worst enemy. Arch nemesis. All that stuff."

"I had no idea she had an arch nemesis," I said.

"Well, lad, now you do."

                                        * * *

Sir Robert and Natalia reappeared on the street an hour or so later. She smiled sweetly into his eyes, and again pulled at his coat sleeve. Sir Robert seemed not at all offended by this attention, the happy suitor emerging after a delightful meal with his love. With a last squeeze of hands, they parted company. Sir Robert walked off one way along the boulevard while Natalia Boyer went in the opposite direction.

"Now what?" said Jack.

Mrs. Nevermore debated with herself and then turned to me. "Ned, I want you to follow her."

"Me?"

"See where she goes, and what she does. And Jack, you're onto Sir Robert. We meet back at Deux Magots."

I wanted to tell her that this was not right, that following people about and prying into their personal lives was not something with which I was comfortable. But there was no time for such arguments.

Besides, I was consumed by a fascination with Natalia Boyer, who had succeeded in making an imperturbable woman plainly perturbed.

SIXTEEN

In my previous safe, cocooned life before I encountered Mrs. Nevermore, mysterious one-eyed beauties, schemes to sell the Eiffel Tower, evil men named Corbeau, not to mention homicidal princes who thought they should be king of France, I could never have imagined following anyone.

But here I was darting through the nighttime throngs, Natalia's swanlike figure moving ahead of me, not at all difficult to keep in view as she hurried along, deftly avoiding the gleam-eyed *flaneurs* practically devouring her as she passed.

She turned off the boulevard on to the rue de la Paix, and went through the place Vendôme. She passed rue St. Honoré at the point where rue de la Paix became Castiglione on her way to the rue de Rivoli opposite the Jardin des Tuileries.

The crowd here was less like a predatory animal stalking the night, more middle class and respectable. Nearby, luxurious mansions were backed by formal gardens and fronted with cobblestoned entrance courts. Natalia slowed, glancing about as though on the lookout for someone.

Presently, a small, wiry man joined her. It was none other than Auguste Escoffier, the renowned chef from the Hotel Ritz. She gave a welcoming smile when she saw him, and quickly took his arm as though in this dreadful sea of humanity here was safety.

They continued along together, the swan towering above the stovepipe. She giggled merrily at something he whispered in her ear, and held him even more closely as he led her to one of the outdoor cafés. They were greeted effusively by the mâitre d' who seated them at a prominent table near the front. A waiter approached. Escoffier issued terse orders and the waiter went away.

Natalia promptly produced a handkerchief from the sleeve of her dress and began to sniffle. Escoffier leaned toward her solicitously. Natalia buried her lovely head more deeply into the handkerchief. Escoffier placed his hand on hers. The waiter returned with a stein of beer and a glass of wine for the sobbing Natalia. She took a sip before resuming her weeping. Escoffier never touched his beer but kept his eyes fixed on his companion.

This went on for a half hour or so before Natalia stood abruptly, her face flushed with anger. Then she turned and flounced out of the café. Escoffier sat very still, as though trying to collect himself. Then he tossed franc notes down on the table, and hurried after her.

I watched Natalia hail a carriage while Escoffier hopped from one foot to the other, trying to persuade her to do something she had no intention of doing. When a carriage arrived, Natalia called out to the driver, "Forty-five avenue de la Grande Armée."

Escoffier reluctantly held the door for her. She climbed inside, the door closed, and the carriage was gone in the night.

He stood in the street, his head bowed, looking disconsolate. Then he pulled himself together and marched miserably off along the boulevard, the lover unloved. It was a look I would see many times over the years—experience myself on occasion. But it was something I saw for the first time that night.

I was turning to leave when something slammed into me. Fighting to keep my balance, I tripped over a curb and fell to the pavement. I looked up to see Edmond Corbeau. Was it my imagination or did that white line of scar tissue glow like mercury in the darkness? I believe it did. He wore a black homburg this evening, a cape that fell to his knees, and formal white gloves. A gentleman killer, our Monsieur Corbeau.

The next thing he lifted me up and unceremoniously propelled me into a nearby alleyway. He dropped me down onto the damp cobblestones.

"You are following my wife. Why?"

"She's your wife?" By now I had managed to sit up, tiny stars bursting around my eyes.

He jerked me to my feet, this time choosing a nearby wall to throw me against. More stars. "I ask you again, monsieur. Why do you follow her?"

"I didn't know she was your wife."

"Answer me!" he shouted impatiently.

"It's none of my business, but if she is your wife, what is she doing out alone at night in the company of other men?"

In response Corbeau hammered me against the wall a number of times.

"Listen to me, Monsieur Ned Arnheim, son of the late bastard and cheat, Flix Arnheim, your father caused me to lose a fortune."

"Is that why you killed him?" I demanded groggily.

"I killed him?" He looked dumbfounded. "You will return my money. Or monsieur I most definitely will kill you. In the meantime, stop following my wife!"

"So you are saying you did not kill him?"

"You young fool. You have to look no further for your father's killer than the occupants at number 52 Rue des Saints-Pères."

A tally-ho stagecoach full of late night revelers burst into view, clattering down the alley, lanterns waving wildly on either side of the coach. I couldn't believe it was in the alley, there being barely enough room to accommodate it. But here was the coach bearing down upon us and no room to get out of its way.

I rose into the air. The coach thundered on. I got a bird's eye view of the flaring red nostrils of one of the two black horses heaving toward me. I willed myself higher, coming abreast of the driver, his eyes bulging as he saw this boy fly up in front of him.

He was going to hit me, I was certain of it. I willed myself to go up— and up I went, gathering unexpected speed. I saw the startled, rouged face of one of the female passengers atop the coach as it shot past me. My foot struck her bare shoulder.

And then the coach was gone from the alley. A silence followed as though all the noise of the world had shut down. I lowered myself to the ground, expecting to find the mangled remains of Edmond Corbeau, not so lucky as I to escape the coach.

But there was no sign of a body. The alley was empty.

SEVENTEEN

Mrs. Nevermore was already seated when I arrived at Les Deux Magots an hour later. Corbeau's words continued to ring in my ears:

You have to look no further for your father's killer than the occupants at number 52 Rue des Saints-Pères.

Could Mrs. Nevermore have killed my father? Tears had been briefly shed at his graveside—had they not? But since then she barely mentioned him. I had no idea why she would kill him, but then I had no idea why she wouldn't, either. She was, after all, a witch, a sorcière mad enough to believe she could sell the Eiffel Tower. That made just about anything possible.

"You look pale, Ned. Would you like something to drink?"

"No thank you."

"Are you all right?"

"It is late and I am tired and instead of attending to my education I am forced to follow women around the streets of Paris."

"In this city following women is an avidly pursued pastime. What did you discover?"

"After she left you, she met someone else at the Tuileries."

"A man."

"Yes."

A flash of impatience. "All right, a man. Did you recognize him?"

"It was Auguste Escoffier."

She looked briefly surprised and then occupied herself sipping at a café noir. "You're certain it was Escoffier?"

I nodded. "Who is this woman, anyway?"

Mrs. Nevermore carefully placed her cup on the table. "Suffice to say she is an enemy."

"Not my enemy," I said.

"Ah, but she is mine, and therefore a danger to you."

"Is she connected to Edmond Corbeau?"

She gave me a curious look. "Why ever would you say something like that?"

"Previously, Edmond Corbeau was a great danger. Now this woman is also dangerous. It would stand to reason that two such dangerous people might be associated."

"I've told you before Ned, you mustn't talk back. It's an ugly habit, one that can land you in all sorts of difficulty."

"I believe I am already in a great deal of difficulty, and what's more, I don't believe it has anything to do with me talking back."

Before the argument could go any further—when in fact it was going nowhere at all—Jack Dozen arrived looking flushed and out of breath. He slumped into a chair and ordered an absinthe.

"Back to his hotel, tucked in for a good night's sleep is our Sir Robert." He glanced at me. "Natalia?"

"She met Escoffier," said Mrs. Nevermore.

Jack also looked surprised. His absinthe arrived. He downed it in a single, impressive gulp. He ordered another. "Let's leave this alone."

Mrs. Nevermore tapped her nail against the side of her demitasse and let out a long sigh.

"We have the mark," Jack went on. "Mr. Anthony Drexel of New York. Very rich and heaving at the bit. Use him and be done with it."

"Maybe I prefer Sir Robert."

"You cannot be serious. Not after what we saw tonight."

"I can be very serious indeed," replied Mrs. Nevermore.

Jack looked beside himself.

"Natalia is back in Paris and working a grift that involves Sir Robert and perhaps Escoffier, too," Mrs. Nevermore continued. "We save poor Sir Robert from her clutches, make ourselves heroes, and then we turn him to our advantage."

"Natalia will not stand idly by and let this happen," Jack said. "We buy much more trouble than it's worth."

"Don't tell me she scares you, Jack."

"Don't mind admitting that one bit. The woman is a witch, and we're well advised to stay as far away from her as possible."

"Haven't you heard? There are no such things as witches."

"When Natalia's about, I'm not so sure that's true."

Mrs. Nevermore looked at me. "What happened once she left Escoffier?"

"She took a carriage," I said.

"To where?"

I hesitated. If I told her no more, then she could do little more, and it might save us all. She looked impatient again. "Ned, this is not a good time to start lying to me."

But did she not lie to me? People in her sort of business must lie to each other all the time. How could they not? Adults in general spent inordinate amounts of time deceiving one another. You would think it simpler just to tell the truth. But it never was.

I said, "She gave the driver an address. Forty-five avenue de la Grande Armée."

"Good for you. You've done excellent work this evening."

Jack looked less pleased. "What's the plan, then?"

"Go home and get a good night's sleep," Mrs. Nevermore announced. She placed franc notes on the table and then stood. "Come along, Ned. It's past your bedtime."

"Yes, I'm just a child after all," I said caustically. "Hard to remember at times."

"That's why I am here to remind you," said Mrs. Nevermore, without a hint of irony.

Jack disappeared. We joined the crowd that even at this time of night thronged the street, Mrs. Nevermore moving through like a great, lovely ship determined to get to port. I struggled to catch up to her.

"Why didn't you tell me you encountered Corbeau?" She said this without looking at me.

"What makes you think I encountered him?" was all I could think of to reply.

"Ned, don't lie to me."

The woman could read my mind! I swear she could.

"So they are together."

"What did they say to you?"

"He says he is married to Natalia, is that true?"

Mrs. Nevermore did not immediately answer. "It is said they are married. Whether it is true or not, who can say. Anything else?"

"He continues to insist I pay him the money my father owed him."

"Your father owed him nothing, you will pay him nothing."

She came to a stop at the intersection of boulevard Saint-Germain and rue des Saints-Pères.

"They are deformed creatures Ned, she with her one eye, he with his scarred face. Their deformities have made them both mad. Pay no attention to anything either one says, but always keep your wits about you. They are very dangerous."

"Therefore, we should stay as far away from them as possible—find another mark, like Jack says."

"I didn't say that."

"But shouldn't that be what you are saying?"

Instead of answering she started away along rue des Saints-Pères.

I called after her. "We stay away from them, right?"

There was no answer.

EIGHTEEN

Bright and early next morning, Mrs. Nevermore and I turned off the Étoile onto avenue de la Grand Armée. In those days, the days of my youth, Paris was much smaller and the Champs Élysées lay at the edge of town. One ventured as far as Étoile with a heady sense of adventure. The great avenues Napoleon laid out from Étoile, including the newly named avenue Victor Hugo, soon ran past chicken coops and pigsties and into orchards.

The same was true of the avenue de la Grande Armée. Near Étoile, the avenue was flanked by imposing gray blocks of monolithic apartment buildings constructed for the rich from all over the world. Soon enough, though, it dwindled off into pastures and grazing cows. Rural France, an area with which I was totally unfamiliar, was a tantalizingly fresh breath away.

The avenue at this early hour was almost empty as our carriage drew adjacent to Natalia's address at number 45. Mrs. Nevermore ordered the driver to pull ahead.

Neither of us was in a good mood. She barely spoke over a breakfast free of chatty gossip or her usual cigar. That irritated me. It was one thing for me to be miserable, but how dare she so completely take the territory I staked out for myself? If she was responsible for my father's death, why had she taken me in? Perhaps she felt guilty, leaving a poor orphan homeless. Thus the impulsive act of generosity on her part. Any day now, she would tire of me, and the next thing I would be dead, too, singing with the angels alongside my father—or perhaps more accurately, shoveling coal with him in hell.

"Why aren't you talking?" I demanded crossly as she sailed along the avenue and, as usual, I hurried to keep up.

"Because there is nothing to say," she replied.

"What will you want of me today?"

"Today? Today, I want of you what I want each and every day, and that is for you to do as you are told."

"I don't know why I should listen to you," I said in a sullen voice.

"Because I am the person in charge of your well-being."

"There are those who might question how successful you have been in looking after that well-being."

"My goodness, don't tell me you're to be one of those rebellious creatures one reads about in the daily newspapers."

"I don't know," I said. "I have no idea what the rebellious creatures one reads about are like, therefore I cannot say if I am one of them."

"I fear that you are, and that is not a good thing for our relationship."

"How does this rebellion manifest itself?"

"It begins when it becomes apparent that one has entirely too much to say for himself."

* * *

We approached a tiny dress shop, its facade painted a rich chocolate brown. A sign in discreet yellow letters announced that we had reached Chez Marie-Jeanne. The little brown shop with its yellow sign stood at right angles across the street from number 45.

Inside, the narrow interior was empty save for the owner, Madame Marie-Jeanne Phellion, a trim woman in a gorgeous autumnal gown. Her dark brown hair mounted into an elaborate pile, Madame Phellion smelled fresh and lovely, as though she had just climbed from her bath to greet the day's first customer. The shop, like its owner, gave off a seductive air as enticing as anything that could be found in the *grand magasins* that currently bewitched the fashionable women of Paris.

Mrs. Nevermore took in the large window looking onto the street, affording a clear view of Natalia's building.

"Good morning," Madame Phellion announced in a lilting voice. Surprisingly pudgy fingers touched lightly at the back of her exposed neck. The widest hazel eyes imaginable lent her a startled quality, as though she was constantly amazed by the world and unsure of what to make of it.

"I have the ready-to-wear frocks, all the rage now," said Madame Phellion. "However, I see you are wearing a day dress by Monsieur Jacques Doucet."

"What a keen eye you have," said Mrs. Nevermore admiringly.

Madame Phellion actually blushed. "So for a discerning client such as yourself, not swept up in the current fashion for the ready-made, I have a brilliant tailor who can perform miracles."

"What I would like is a cup of tea," Mrs. Nevermore said.

That caused Madame Phellion to pause. "Well, that's a problem. I don't sell tea. It's dresses, I'm afraid."

"And some water for the boy," added Mrs. Nevermore.

"I'm not thirsty."

"As well as a comfortable chair by the window so that I can keep an eye on the street."

Madame Phellion's wide hazel eyes had grown to positively saucer-like proportions. "The boy does not wish to sit?"

"I demand to sit," I said.

"Now in return for this," said Mrs. Nevermore, "I will pay you ten francs. Half now, half when I leave. Is that acceptable?"

"It is."

Madame Phellion's eyes had ceased spinning and narrowed speculatively. Mrs. Nevermore handed her six francs. "A little more than the half. A show of good faith."

"You can have two cups of tea," said Madame Phellion.

She produced an imitation Louis XIV rosewood chair with delicate flowers woven into its fabric, not particularly comfortable, or designed to encourage long sits, I noticed. I was ushered off to a bench in the corner, out of the way of the adults—my lot in life.

Mrs. Nevermore finished her tea. Madame Phellion did not offer another cup. Outside, the street gradually came to life with barouches and broughams as well as double-decker omnibuses, their horses pacing steadily.

An intense young woman in a straw hat wheeled past on a bicycle, leading a brigade of conservatively dressed, grim-faced males, jabbing walking sticks at the pavement as though wishing to punish it. I couldn't help but notice the blackened shirt cuffs on many of the supposedly well-dressed gentlemen.

Across the street, a second story window opened and a servant casually emptied garbage into the gutter. Passersby calmly stepped over the refuse falling around them. As always, I was amazed at the filth of everything in a city that purported to be so cosmopolitan.

Each time the door to Madame Phellion's shop opened it brought in the stench of the morning air, a putrid combination of rotting garbage, unwashed bodies, and horse dung (each of the city's reported two hundred thousand horses was said to drop six to seven tons annually onto the streets).

A few customers came and went, women, alone or in pairs, strolling distractedly through the shop, running fingers daintily over the racks of clothing.

"The hobble skirts in the fashion of those designed by Jeanne Paquin?" inquired one voluminous lady.

"I can give you such a skirt, but with pleats so that you are better able to walk in them."

"Pleats?" The woman looked horrified. "You will never catch me in a pleated skirt, you can count on that."

And she hurried from the shop, leaving Madame Phellion to push those pudgy fingers against the back of her hair, and wonder at the vagaries of her clients.

The morning wore on. A middle-aged woman after great deliberation purchased a shawl. A client who did not bathe regularly and therefore smelled badly, advised Madame Phellion in a conspiratorial voice. She suspected the woman washed her hair with eggs no more than once a month.

Nearing midday, I began to get bored. What had started out as an adventure, a spy mission to find out things we weren't supposed to know, had deteriorated into a dull exercise in sitting and waiting. Mrs. Nevermore noticed me fidgeting and announced that it was time for lunch. Thank goodness.

That's when I saw Natalia Boyer pass by the window. Mrs. Nevermore saw me start and turned to look.

"Follow her," she said.

"Right now?"

"No, dear boy, I want you to wait an hour or so and then follow her."

"Where shall I meet you?"

"Back at the house."

"Then I shall need some money."

She pushed coins into my fist. "Hurry," she said.

NINETEEN

A balloon, launched from the nearby Tuileries Gardens, floated in the cloudless sky above Étoile, soaring amid flocks of sparrows—or *les moineaux de Paris* as they were known—attracted by the horse dung that littered the street.

Black wagons weighted down by heavy barrels pulled by huge white horses forced a horse-drawn trolley to a quick stop amid the angry clatter of bells. A motorcar, still a curious sight on these streets, blared its horn. Women paraded past in long skirts, wearing blouses with lots of lace and frills, little hats perched on their pretty heads, parasols open in order to shade their lovely faces from the afternoon sun.

Natalia without a parasol stood out from her contemporaries, floating through the mob at least a head taller than anyone on the street, easy to keep in view.

I could hardly contain my excitement—and relief—at being freed from the perfumed boredom of Madame Phellion's dress shop. Anything was better than another hour of that particular agony. Now here I was once again the spy on the avenue de la Grand Armée following a beautiful woman. Who knew where she might take me on a sun-drenched afternoon full of floating balloons and swirling sparrows? Still, I had to be careful, and keep an eye out for the evil Edmond Corbeau, who certainly would not like the idea of me once again following his wife.

I was busily thinking this while trying to keep Natalia in sight. Thus it was a while before I noticed the bird floating in the air above me. I jumped in surprise.

"Hold out your arm," ordered Peregrine.

"Why should I do that?"

"Just hold out your arm."

I did and he settled onto it. I could feel his talons digging in as he gained purchase. "That's better," he said. "Now you are a real falconer."

"What are you doing here?"

"Did you not hear me? I just gave you a compliment."

"I do not want to be a falconer," I said. "I don't want to have anything to do with you. Talking to a bird will only get me into trouble. Why do you keep bothering me?"

"I happened to be passing by when I saw you and thought I would drop in for a visit."

"I don't believe it," I said, trying to keep my arm up and Natalia in sight. "I think you are following me."

"What are you doing, anyway?"

"It is none of your business."

"You're following that tall woman up ahead. Is that it? Perhaps I can help."

"I don't need your help. In fact, I was doing just fine until you came along."

By now people were beginning to notice me traveling along at high speed with a falcon attached to my arm. Not something you see every day on the streets of Paris. I began to get nervous.

"You can't stay here," I said.

"Why not?"

"Because I require the use of my arm and you're on it," I said.

Immediately he hopped onto my shoulder. "There. Is that better?"

Passersby were stopping to gape at me with this bird on my shoulder. Here I was supposed to be anonymous in the crowd so I could follow Natalia Boyer. Instead I was quickly becoming a major object of attention. It was a matter of time before Natalia noticed all the fuss going on behind her.

"Be off with you," I hissed. I rolled my shoulder around to try to make him leave. Instead, Peregrine just dug in deeper.

A stout woman scowled at me. "What are you doing to that bird?"

"He's not a bird, he's a falcon."

"Here, here," said an elderly man leaning on a cane. "You shouldn't hurt the bird."

"I'm not hurting him," I said. "I am trying to get him off my shoulder."

"Why should you do that?" demanded the stout woman. "Is that not your bird?"

"It is not," I maintained. "I am a poor lad, walking along peacefully minding my own business when this bird landed on me. Now it won't leave."

"They're very fast, these falcons," said the old man in an authoritative voice. A small crowd had gathered. I lost sight of Natalia.

"Perhaps the fastest species known to man," the elderly gentleman continued. "Speeds of over one hundred miles an hour, I understand."

"A hundred miles an hour?" The stout woman sounded dubious. "I don't believe it."

"That's what I understand," said the old man.

As though to demonstrate this truth, Peregrine rose off my shoulder and shot into the air at approximately the advertised speed. It was something to see, I must admit. You couldn't help but be impressed. The crowd gasped in unison. Everyone lifted their faces to watch Peregrine disappear over the Arc de Triomphe.

That's when I spotted Natalia crossing Étoile.

TWENTY

Natalia descended onto the Champs Élysées and ducked inside the most extravagantly outrageous of the dance halls lining the street. The Étoile Palace was an ornate Arabian Nights fun house with a great glass canopy covering the entrance.

Called the theater of the poor, these dance halls were the current rage. There were more than three hundred in the Paris area alone. I had never been inside such a place, knew of them only as part of schoolboy mythology wherein any number of wildly imagined offenses were mindlessly committed.

Taking a deep breath, and summoning what little courage I possessed, I pushed through the brass-plated double doors. A bulbous attendant in a blue jacket with polished buttons and gold braid cheerfully took my two francs without so much as batting an eye.

I entered into a vast hall with a vault ceiling beneath which those staples of local entertainment, the cancan dancers, occupied the floor in a blur of lifted skirts and waving legs—or perhaps it was waving skirts and lifted legs.

I should not sound too blasé about this. In an age when women did not even wear drawers, I had never seen so much as a raised skirt, let alone a lifted leg. Just as my mind was about to reel out of control at the confusion of erotic possibilities swirling before me, the cancan dancers abruptly disappeared, replaced by a dull mime, followed by lackluster acrobats, all very uninspiring and causing the audience, myself included, to stir impatiently.

The orchestra in the pit below the stage, having gone silent to mark the sad end to the dancers, now regained its enthusiasm and struck up a fanfare that blew a tuxedoed gentleman with glossy hair out from behind the curtains to announce at the top of a hoarse, strained voice, the arrival of "Natalia the

Magnificent!"

A roar went up from the crowd, an enthusiasm that not even the cancan dancers could match. This could not be my Natalia, could it?

The curtain parted to reveal a stage bare except for a single cherry wood end table daintily perched on three legs. Sure enough, just as the announcer promised, here suddenly was the object of my stalking desire, dressed in a shimmering white gown, the virgin goddess in the afternoon amid raining applause. She stepped to the edge of the stage and addressed the crowd.

"Good afternoon, ladies and gentlemen." She peered into the audience, that blue eye glinting mischievously. "Well, I should say gentlemen. There is only one lady present."

That brought a burst of laughter and a surge of musical energy from the orchestra as Natalia moved back across the stage bowing gracefully to her audience.

She said, "I will need a gentleman with a handkerchief—unused of course."

Hands shot up immediately. No one seemed the least hesitant to get on a stage with Natalia. No one but me. She seemed in no hurry to choose her victim as she came down off the stage and glided through the mob of up-raised hands and eager faces. Then she made an unexpected turn and came over to where I stood.

"Here's a young fellow," she announced. "You look as though you might be proper enough to have a handkerchief I could borrow."

"I—I do indeed," I managed to stammer.

I handed over my handkerchief. "Shouldn't you be home with your mother?"

"I'm an orphan," I said. That inspired groans and hoots.

Natalia seemed unperturbed. "Even the orphans are welcome here!" Cheers and laughter.

The handkerchief trailing from her uplifted hand, Natalia remounted the stage where now stood a tall, slim gent in a silk brocade coat and a jewel-encrusted turban. If it wasn't for that shiny white scar I might not have recognized Edmond Corbeau, the last person in the world I wished to encounter this afternoon. However, he paid me no attention, but busied himself laying out three objects on the table: an apple, a pear, and an egg.

The orchestra fell to an ominous hum. Natalia rolled the handkerchief into a ball and placed it beside the other objects. Corbeau, his sinister face a regal mask, swept the table with an elegant hand. Natalia stepped forward, picked up my handkerchief, and tossed it into the air where it disappeared.

"Where did it go?" She picked up the egg, holding it between her thumb and forefinger. "Could it be in here?"

Shouts of "No!" and "Impossible!" She grinned and began to roll the egg in her cupped hands until it too disappeared. Natalia looked chagrined. "That was not supposed to happen. Where did it go?" She asked.

With a sly smile she pointed to the pear. "Could it be inside that pear?"

That inspired more shouting. Natalia heaved the pear into the air, followed by the apple. Before our collective and astonished eyes the pear disappeared—or seemed to disappear—inside the apple!

Natalia held the apple before her rapt audience. Abruptly her hands closed over the fruit, crushing it in her fingers. As she did this the remnants of the apple turned to white dust. She then poured the dust on the table in a small pile and struck a match, touching its flaring end to the white powder.

Flames shot high in the air, and as they did, they transformed themselves into a small tree. The flames quickly died away leaving the tree on the table. Corbeau, standing poker-faced at the back of the stage, moved forward and handed Natalia a silver wand. She waved it over the tree and—well, magically —it began to sprout leaves and then white flowers and finally, apples.

Natalia picked one of the apples, and motioned for me to come forward. Hesitantly, I mounted the stage, half expecting Corbeau to lunge at me. But he never moved, and those deep blue eyes did not so much as shift in my direction. She handed me the apple. "Think of me as Eve in the garden." Her voice was a seductive purr. "Take a bite."

The audience roared.

I bit. The audience gasped. It was an apple, no doubt about that. She flicked the wand again and as I held it, the apple opened and out popped my handkerchief.

Amid thundering applause, Natalia leaned forward so that her face was close to mine. "We both know what it is to suffer through life, don't we, Neddie?" She touched the wand briefly to her cheek just below that eye patch.

Two doves emerged from the tree, descending upon the handkerchief, lifting up its corners before rising with it until they—and the handkerchief —vanished into the blackness above the stage.

"We are kindred spirits my love. Never forget that."

The orchestra reached a tumult of heroic fanfare. Natalia bent closer and kissed me on the cheek. "So be careful, Neddie," she said into my ear. "She is evil. You are in great danger."

Her hands fluttered gracefully in the air and when they descended again they contained my handkerchief. She handed it back with a dramatic flourish. I allowed her to usher me off the stage. When I was safely away, Natalia turned to the audience, bowing deeply, basking in a deep roar of approval. Nearby, Corbeau was not looking at her or the audience.

He was glaring at me.

TWENTY-ONE

Where have you been?" demanded Mrs. Nevermore when I finally made my appearance at number 52 rue des Saints-Pères. She waited for me in the drawing room, not looking particularly evil, I thought. But who could say? Perhaps I was indeed in great danger as not only Corbeau but now my new acquaintance, Natalia Boyer, warned.

"I was doing what I was told to do," I answered. "Following Natalia."

She issued a dramatic sigh. "What did you find out?"

"Natalia can turn flames into apple trees and make handkerchiefs disappear."

"She can do much worse than that if you are not careful."

"The audience at the Étoile Palace loved her."

"That's where she performs in Paris?"

"And it is quite a performance."

Mrs. Nevermore clearly did not like that. It gave me no end of satisfaction.

"What she does on stage, is it real? Or sleight of hand?"

"What happened after the performance?"

"Is she like us, Mrs. Nevermore? Different? Does she have the power of the Strange?"

"Ned, answer my question."

"Nothing," I said. "I came back here. Now answer mine."

She rose abruptly from her chair and in a flash was across the room. Those emerald eyes bore into me; her small white hands gripped my arms.

"What are you up to?"

"You are the sorcière, Mrs. Nevermore. You tell me. What am I up to? Or am I just asking a question?"

In reply, she gripped my arms even more tightly. "Let me remind you of what I told you before: she is evil, a mad woman who will stop at nothing to get what she wants. Never forget that, Ned. Otherwise, you endanger my life as well as your own."

The vehemence of her words caught me off guard. I thought of saying something clever, something that showed her I was not willing to back down. But the look on her face did not encourage that.

She turned and started to march away. I summoned the courage to call after her. "Perhaps you are the danger, Mrs. Nevermore."

She stopped and turned to look at me.

"Could it be you are more of a threat than either Natalia or Corbeau?"

"Come along, Ned," she said. "We don't have a great deal of time."

"Time for what?"

"To make ready for our gentleman caller."

* * *

Anthony Drexel bearing a bouquet of impressive white lilies arrived at eight-thirty swathed in luxurious scents. His face shone. His hair glistened. He was a gentleman in command of the world tonight, every fiber of his body calibrated to impress a lady.

In order to achieve that goal he was even willing to briefly acknowledge the lady's young ward. I let him in the door and he merrily pumped my hand until it hurt.

I led him up the stairs and into the drawing room. He could not take his eyes off Jesus among the wood nymphs.

"Is that the Lord Jesus?" he inquired.

"From the Bible story about the naked wood nymphs," I said.

He looked at me. "I was not aware there was a story in the Bible dealing with wood nymphs."

"There isn't? Are you sure? Well, what do you know? Would you like to sit down?"

"Very kind of you," said Drexel, finally tearing himself away from the painting to perch on a chair. He held the lilies between his legs as though using them to protect his groin. For all his radiating masculine energy, he appeared nervous, which surprised me. What did the rich have to be nervous about, after all?

"I would offer you something to drink," I said. "Except I'm not certain there is anything to drink. And if there is something I'm equally uncertain what it might be. Do you want a drink? Maybe you don't."

"That's all right." He looked me up and down the way adults look at children they must endure, measuring them for the future, trying to ascertain at a glance if they are ready for life's hardships.

He said, "So then, how are your studies going?"

"They are not going well."

He seemed vaguely surprised. "No?"

"In that I am not studying anything. Orphans do not attend school."

"They don't?"

"We're much too emotionally distraught."

"Are you? I didn't know that about orphans."

"Yes. We are quite fragile."

"I see."

Drexel stared, his mouth slightly open, those flowers still positioned to protect his groin. Mrs. Nevermore made her entrance also swathed in rich odors. A battle of competing smells ensued. Drexel stumbled to his feet, waving the flowers around as though they were the white flag of surrender.

Mrs. Nevermore laughed merrily and plucked the bouquet from him, exclaiming her delight. He could not have looked more pleased. She looked different, I would have to say, somehow softer and—what was that?—more alluring? Yes, definitely more alluring, although she had not changed her dress or really done anything I could put my finger on. Maybe the eyes, something sparkly about them, moistened with the anticipation of spending time with the delightful Monsieur Drexel. Drenched in her scent, he could only be smitten.

"Ned, take these lovely flowers and put them in a vase, won't you?" She thrust the bouquet into my uncomprehending hands. "Don't you have studies to complete?"

Drexel looked confused. "Studies?"

"Why yes, studies, the boy has his studies," Mrs. Nevermore stoutly maintained.

"I thought he said he wasn't in school."

"School?"said Mrs. Nevermore with a butterscotch smile accompanying the hand steering the flowers and me from the room. "Of course the boy's in school. Honestly, Ned can be such a scoundrel at times."

Drexel frowned at me. I was not about to amount to much trying to fool the wealthy and powerful. I went back to the kitchen and stood there wondering what to do with the flowers. Below, someone rang the doorbell. I tossed the flowers into the sink and went back to the drawing room.

"Now who could that be at this time of night?" said Mrs. Nevermore.

She returned moments later with Jack Dozen, resplendent in his new Bon Marché suit, his hair slicked back to show off an anxious expression.

"Sorry to bother you, Laura," Jack announced sorrowfully, "but I'm so upset, I didn't know what else to do."

"It's all right, Arnaud." She turned to Drexel. "Monsieur Drexel, I would like to introduce you to my brother-in-law, Monsieur Arnaud Poisson. Arnaud is the deputy director general of the Ministère des postes et télégraphes. Arnaud, this is my American friend, Mr. Anthony Drexel."

Jack looked appropriately chagrined. "I apologize, monsieur, for barging in like this."

"There is nothing to apologize for," said Drexel in a jovial voice, shaking Jack's hand. "Come, why don't we all sit down? Mrs. Nevermore, is it possible to have wine? Of course it is. I am in Paris, after all. Our friend here looks as though he could use a drink."

I was dispatched to the kitchen to bring wine and glasses. When I returned, balancing a bottle on a silver tray with three glasses, they were already seated, Jack leaning forward on the sofa, his head hung in despair. Mrs. Nevermore, in the role of the concerned sister-in-law, laid a reassuring hand on his knee. Drexel slumped in a nearby chair, the picture of relaxed confidence. He sat up as I put the wine tray down on the ottoman in front of him.

"There we go. Here's what we need, all right."

Jack made a show of wringing his hands. "This is not something I should even think about in public, let alone discuss."

"Don't be ridiculous, Arnaud," Mrs. Nevermore said in a quietly reassuring voice. "Mr. Drexel is a friend and therefore can be relied on for complete discretion."

"Absolutely," agreed Drexel. He glanced at me and I took that as my cue to reach for the bottle and begin to pour. Jack grabbed at his glass as soon as it was filled and without waiting for the others took a deep swallow. In the midst of play-acting a distraught *fonctionnaire*, he was not about to pass up a drink. His eyes watered. He looked more anguished than ever.

"Really, I should not say anything. It was a mistake to come here."

"Arnaud, please calm down. This is not like you."

Jack proceeded to make an impressive show of running his hands through his hair before issuing yet another tortured gasp. "The government this evening made its decision and, my God, what a monumental decision it is—bound to change the very face of Paris."

"Decision?" Drexel was sitting up straight, the hunting dog abruptly scenting prey.

"Arnaud, please, do not feel compelled to tell us anything," Mrs. Nevermore interjected. "I know you are sworn to secrecy when it comes to these matters."

Drexel said nothing. His wine glass was untouched. He appeared to be holding his breath.

Jack also stayed silent. Then he blurted, "They will do it, Laura. It will happen—just as I predicted."

I stared at Jack. So did Drexel. The hunting dog lunged. "What will happen?"

"Please, Arnaud," admonished Mrs. Nevermore. "It's best for everyone you don't say anything else."

Drexel looked as though he was about to cry out, "Say it, blast you! Say it!" But he managed to restrain himself.

Jack looked ready to divulge everything. "If you trust Monsieur Drexel, then I see no reason . . ."

"No!" Mrs. Nevermore cried. "If this information should ever fall into the wrong hands it would be devastating."

She turned to Drexel. "Monsieur, I'm so sorry, but obviously you can see we have a bit of a crisis. Would you mind terribly if we continued our conversation at another date?"

Drexel rallied a smile. "No, no, of course not."

He rose uncertainly to his feet.

"Really, there is no need to go on my account," Jack said. That note of desperation in his voice had nothing to do with play-acting.

Mrs. Nevermore clasped Drexel's hands in hers. "I do appreciate this, Anthony. Please, you must allow me to make it up to you as soon as possible."

"I look forward to it," Drexel said as she moved him toward the door. He did not bother to conceal either his confusion or his disappointment. As he left I got a look at his eyes. They glittered with something I knew little of at the time, but about which I have since learned a great deal.

Greed.

* * *

"What the bloody hell was that about?" demanded Jack as soon as Mrs. Nevermore returned from seeing a flustered Anthony Drexel out the door. "We had him and you let him go!"

Gamelle materialized from the back, looking mystified. "What happened? Where did he go?"

"Ushered out the door by our brilliant Mrs. Nevermore," said Jack angrily.

Mrs. Nevermore did not say anything. Looking preoccupied, she went to the window and watched as Drexel crossed the courtyard and went through the entrance to the street. He stood there for a minute or so before a cab came along. He hailed it and climbed in the back. Mrs. Nevermore turned from the window.

"Laura, are you listening to me?" demanded Jack.

Mrs. Nevermore brushed away the question with a familiar wave. "We need more information about Monsieur Drexel before we tell him anything."

"Because?"

"Because something is not right."

"Right? What wasn't right? He was practically eating out of your hand."

"Maybe that's it, Jack. Anthony Drexel, the tough, uncompromising partner to the great J.P. Morgan, and he's so easily seduced?"

"You're a woman. He's a man. That's what happens between men and women."

"I didn't have the right feeling about it."

"Madness," declared Jack. "Absolute madness. He's a good mark, Laura. As good as I've seen, and you push him out the door."

"Be quiet!" Gamelle thundered in that voice that always raised the hairs on the back of my neck. "If Mrs. Nevermore says he is no good, then he is no good. And that's the end of it!"

"Honestly, Gamelle, she says 'jump' and you get down on your bloody knees and beg to know how high."

"I'm not saying he's no good," interjected Mrs. Nevermore. "I'm just saying I'm feeling uneasy. We need to know more about him."

Jack glared at her. "How do you propose we do that?"

Mrs. Nevermore's gaze fell upon me. I did not like that look one bit.

TWENTY-TWO

"No! I won't do it!" Did I sound hysterical? Possibly I did. I was fourteen after all, and given to hysterics on occasion.

"Why would you not want to perform a simple, helpful task?" inquired Mrs. Nevermore.

"Because it is illegal!"

"Since when is visiting a hotel illegal? Honestly, Ned, you are impossible."

"It is illegal to break into a man's room," I shot back.

"You will not be breaking in anywhere. I would never allow you to do such a thing. You will have a key. All you have to do is walk in, take a look around, and walk out again. Nothing could be easier."

Once again we were gathered in the kitchen. I was at the table with Mrs. Nevermore. Jack Dozen paced the floor somewhere behind me. Gamelle glared out from his customary perch against the counter, arms crossed over his white apron.

"Why can't you do it?" I demanded to know.

"For the simple reason that I will be with Anthony Drexel. That's what will enable you to enter his room at the Ritz."

"What about Jack? He would be much better at this than me."

Jack immediately stopped pacing. "No you don't. Don't get me involved in this."

"Besides, Drexel should not see Jack wandering around the Ritz, it could ruin everything. As for Gamelle, we need him standing by in case of trouble."

"Then you expect trouble."

"I expect nothing," insisted Mrs. Nevermore. "Gamelle is our insurance, that's all."

"I am an orphan child," I stated bleakly. "I should not be made to do such things."

"Don't allow yourself to sound so hard done by, Ned. Honestly, it grows tiresome after a while."

"I don't want to do it," I repeated.

"Damn it, boy!" Gamelle came away from the counter at full roar. "You will do as you are told or you will be out on the street with the rest of the unappreciative orphans!"

"Gamelle, that's enough. No one's being thrown onto the street. Instead, we will all work together to achieve our goals. Ned, you will be part of that. There will be no more arguing."

What else was there to say? At the end of it, I didn't have much choice, did I? Crude as he was, Gamelle was right. I either went along or risked being tossed out. As much as I suspected her, even feared her, I did not want that. I did not want to be left alone.

* * *

Gamelle unceremoniously ushered me down the back stairs to the courtyard. No sign of Peregrine on his usual tree branch. We went out onto rue des Saints-Pères and along to boulevard Saint-Germain where Gamelle hailed a cab. We took it over to the place Vendôme.

"Quit shaking, for God's sake," he ordered as we walked toward the Ritz.

"I am not shaking," I said. "Possibly shuddering a bit, but not shaking."

"Pull yourself together! Otherwise you will spoil everything."

"The name of the hallman I'm looking for."

"Remy, for God's sake. Remy. How can you not remember a simple name such as that?"

"Remy," I repeated.

"He will be waiting for you near the front desk. He will have the key. You return it to him on the way out."

"What am I looking for in Monsieur Drexel's room?"

"God, boy, I don't know. Look! Go through his luggage, his drawers. See what you find. But no more than five minutes. Then you leave, no matter what. Is that understood?"

"How will I know when the five minutes are up?"

"You look at your watch, you young fool!"

"I don't have a watch," I said meekly.

Gamelle groaned and shook his head in despair. He reached into his vest, unhooked his own pocket watch from its chain, and presented it to me. "If you lose this, I will kill you."

I doubted it would take the loss of his pocket watch for him to do that.

"I still don't understand what I'm looking for," I said.

He responded by grabbing the scruff of my neck and heaving me forward. "Get going!"

I calmed my nerves enough to enter the hotel. The doorman held open the door for me, grinning and saluting, as though I was just another valued guest. That welcoming smile made me feel better as I stepped down the three marble steps leading into the lobby.

A formally dressed couple strolled past going toward the dining room. A chubby, red-faced hallman lingered near the front desk. This had to be my contact, Remy. He looked as shifty-eyed as they come.

"Don't stop!" he hissed as I approached. I slowed but kept walking. "You're Ned, are you?"

"I am."

A white gloved hand shot out. It contained a gold key. I grabbed it and he said, "Room 405. Be quick about it. That bastard Olivier's about this evening, keeping an eye on everything. Five minutes. No more. Got that? Five minutes!"

Not daring to try what little courage I had left with a ride on the elevator, I nodded and kept walking toward the staircase. Five minutes, I reminded myself. I have only five minutes!

Clutching the key in my fist, I began shaking all over again, fearing the cobra-eyed Olivier would jump out and demand to know what I was doing in his hotel. But no one interrupted my progress. I mounted the stairs, taking them two at a time until I reached the fourth floor.

A hall in shades of pale green loomed. My footsteps fell soundlessly against the luxurious carpet. I glided along to 405. The key fit easily into the lock. I turned it, the tumblers clicked, and I stepped inside the suite of that great American entrepreneur and businessman, Anthony Drexel.

I checked my watch.

I had already used a minute of my allotment just getting up here. This was ridiculous. Five minutes was not enough time to do anything. Why had I ever agreed to such a foolish arrangement?

The room stank of cigar smoke. Plum-colored walls and white muslin window curtains were suffused in gold light emanating from electric wall lamps hidden behind pleated shades. A pair of trousers was thrown across the floor. White shirts had been tossed into a corner while inelegant men's underpants lay atop the bureau keeping company with a pair of garters.

Socks, not stockings—Monsieur Drexel was nothing if not modern—formed a foothill atop a flannel vest. The remains of expensive cigars were crushed into various cut glass ashtrays around the room. An empty bottle of champagne leaned out of an ice bucket. Copies of the latest Paris papers littered a high brass bed that did not appear to have been slept in.

How was I to find anything in this mess? What was I to report? Multi-millionaire Americans do not tidy up after themselves? But then perhaps they were not supposed to. After all, this was the Ritz. Here they picked up for you, did they not? Wasn't that one of the reasons you became rich? So you could drop your trousers on the floor and someone would pick them up for you? The maids would earn their pay cleaning this suite.

I edged further into the room, not quite sure what to do. Once again I checked my watch, thrilled to have a watch, even if it was only for a few minutes and even if it did belong to Gamelle who would kill me if I lost it.

Only three minutes left. I tried not to panic.

Gingerly, I picked up one of his shirts and noticed that, as with so many men, the cuffs and collar were black. Monogrammed initials were vaguely discernable through the grime of the cuffs: J.J.G. Not the initials, I thought, of a man named Anthony Drexel. A mistake? Had the hotel laundry returned the wrong shirt? How could that be in Monsieur Ritz's hotel, where perfection was not only prized but demanded?

I carefully placed the shirt back on the floor where I found it, and opened the fitted cupboards. They were empty save for a carefully folded man's corset, evidence that our Monsieur Drexel was engaged in fierce combat with his ego and his pot belly.

I admired the zinc tub in the bathroom before turning to the counter around a sink that featured a golden swan, its long neck bent gracefully forward, doing double duty as a water spout.

Various toiletries were strewn about, including a shaving brush and a straight razor, edged with soap. A worn leather toiletry bag from Hermès gaped at me.

I peered inside and saw a folded piece of paper. I plucked it out. A bill from Harrods in London. For laudanum, of all things. The great Drexel apparently needed to calm his nerves from time to time. However, the bill was made out not to Anthony Drexel but to one Joseph J. Ganning.

J.J.G.

I glanced at Gamelle's watch. Two minutes left!

From the other room, I heard the sudden rattle of a key in the door. I dropped the bill back in the case and hurried into the other room. The sharp click of a turning key; indistinct voices in the hallway—someone was coming into the room! I had no choice but to get down on my knees and slide under the brass bed.

No sooner had I squirmed into my hiding place than the door opened and in stepped two pairs of shoes; one pair of glazed black, followed by brown boots, scruffy from wear.

"I have an appointment this evening." The American voice of Anthony Drexel. The door closed.

"There are more pressing matters to deal with tonight." The second voice, low and guttural. It sounded familiar, but I could not place it. I did not like the sound of that voice at all.

"To you, maybe," said Drexel. "But this is a lady, a beautiful lady at that. She knows important government types. I could be on to something big."

The feet moved further into the room.

"Ten thirty at the Gare de l'Est station. That's all that counts. This is about to come to its end, and here you are hanging about the Ritz under his nose, pretending to be someone you quite obviously are not."

Where had I heard that voice before?

The feet now moved around the bottom of the bed. The man with Drexel was sticking close.

"No one here is the wiser. They all believe I am a rich American. It's a grift I've pulled off several times in the past few years, here, in Monte Carlo, and in London."

"You don't seem to understand, my friend, you are supposed to be working for us, not going off on your own. I thought Natalia made that clear."

Natalia?

"Don't push at me, Corbeau. I've a good thing going here, it's not interfering with you or what you've got planned tonight. That's the end of it as far as I'm concerned. Out of my way. I'm very late for this appointment."

So now I knew who was in the room with the man turning out not to be Anthony Drexel. I was petrified with terror.

Corbeau snarled, "The end of it for you, Ganning, but not for us."

"Look, I've had enough of this. You've got business elsewhere, why don't you get about it?"

"Yes, I suppose you're right. You're not worth wasting more time over."

Silence, and then Drexel said in a strangled voice, "What are you doing with that?"

Abruptly the two pairs of shoes were very close. The two men might have been dancing together.

Except that was not what they were doing.

Desperate movement followed. Clothing brushed against clothing. The muted thump of bodies struggling. The man now known as Ganning cried out, a cry quickly cut off. Then came an awful gurgling sound, a choking and gulping as though someone was trying to get air into his throat. The glossy black shoes backed away from the scuffed brown boots.

Something dropped to the floor not far from where I lay. It was the straight razor I'd seen in the bathroom. What would either man want with a razor at this time of night? Then I noticed something else.

The soap along the blade's edge had turned red.

Ganning's large head crashed against the carpet. His body lay inches from the end of my nose, one green eye staring sightlessly at me. Blood spurted from his throat and I knew exactly how the straight razor had been employed, and that it was Edmond Corbeau who had employed it.

I could hear water running in the bathroom sink. The water shut off, and the glossy shoes returned to the bedroom. My heart raced. I dared not breathe. All Corbeau had to do was bend down to retrieve the razor and I would be discovered and that would be the end of it.

But he never bent down. Instead, he strode purposely to the door, opened it, and walked out, carefully shutting it behind him.

Silence.

I lay there with Ganning inches from me, his blood pumping across the carpet, streaming ever closer, a red tide about to wash over me. I scrambled out from the bed.

The room was exactly as I had left it except that now amid the clutter there was a dead body. I eased around the end of the bed, unable to take my eyes off Ganning, as though I expected him to sit up and demand to know what I was doing in his room.

That did not happen.

I got to the door, opened it, and slipped into the hall. I felt suddenly weak. My knees buckled beneath me. I banged against the wall, taking deep gulping breaths. Strength began to return to my legs and I was able to stumble along the corridor to the staircase.

Remy the hallman was not in the lobby. How long had I been upstairs? Hard to say. Everything was a blur of dead bodies in rivers of blood. The doorman grinned and bade me goodnight as he held open the door to the Ritz. The cold air of the place Vendôme hit me. I searched around for Gamelle. There was no sign of him. Did he get nervous and leave without me? What time was it, anyway? I felt in my pockets. They were empty.

I had lost Gamelle's watch.

TWENTY-THREE

I stood there in the place Vendôme not sure what to do next. My breath came in short, panicky gasps. I tried to get my mind to focus. All I could see in front of me was the corpse of Joe Ganning—and Peregrine.

Peregrine?

He hovered in the air a moment and then dropped to my shoulder. "Ned, you can't stay here," he said.

"Where's Gamelle?"

"I don't know, but you can't stand there like that. Come with me."

"I can't leave without Gamelle."

"Ned," he said in the sort of commanding voice I had not heard from him before. "We have to go." He spread his wings and lifted off my shoulder.

"There's a dead man upstairs," I said dully. "I saw him get killed."

"All the more reason to leave before someone sees you," Peregrine said.

"Corbeau killed him."

"Follow me." He rose from my shoulder, his wings flapping in a lazy rhythm that propelled him out of the square. Numbly I trailed after him, not knowing what else to do.

We went through dark streets that led along the Seine and then we crossed a bridge, me in a daze, not particularly aware of where I was going, just dumbly following after the silent Peregrine. Thus my surprise when we rounded a corner and I found myself on the rue des Saints-Pères.

"Are you all right, Ned?" Peregrine asked once we entered the courtyard.

"Is this the Other World, Peregrine? Is that where I am now? Full of blood and death?"

"You're not far from it, I'm afraid. That's why it's important you keep your wits about you."

He flew up and perched in the tree. "Go inside, Ned," he called down. "Everything will be better once you're inside."

I went up the stairs into the drawing room. Mrs. Nevermore, resplendent in one of her morning gowns, sat in a chair, as though expecting admirers. It was late. What was she doing in a morning gown? A fashion faux pas from a woman who would not be caught dead in an inappropriate frock!

She was on her feet, face tense, hurrying toward me, and I thought she would embrace me. She seemed to sense that's what I had in mind and came to an abrupt halt. We stood awkwardly confronting one another.

I had a sense of Jack Dozen somewhere in the background. My legs went wobbly again and the blurriness was back. I felt her slim, cool hands steadying me. I longed to fall into her arms.

"I lost his watch," I blurted. "He's going to kill me."

"Whose watch, Ned?"

"It belongs to Gamelle. He said he would kill me if I lost it."

"He's not with you?"

I looked at her blankly. "He didn't wait for me at the hotel. I thought he came back here."

"What happened, Ned?" Her voice was gentle, insistent. "What happened at the hotel?"

"Corbeau killed him," I said. "He did it with a razor. He cut his throat with a razor."

She looked at me as though I spoke in some ancient tongue she could not comprehend. "Who? Who did Corbeau kill?"

"Anthony Drexel. Only he is not Anthony Drexel. I believe he is Joe Ganning."

I spent the next few minutes babbling out the story in short, excited bursts, straightening out certain confusions and contradictions under gentle prodding from the preternaturally calm Mrs. Nevermore. "How did you know?" I asked. "How did you know there was something wrong with Drexel?"

"His nails," she said.

I looked at her quizzically. "His nails? What about them?"

"They weren't manicured. When I was in New York last year, Mr. J.P. Morgan commented on his partner's beautifully manicured nails. He couldn't believe a man would—or should—spend time on such things."

"Where's Gamelle, then?" Jack demanded. "God knows I never thought the day would come when I worried about the bastard, but don't tell me Corbeau didn't find him lurking outside the hotel and took care of him. He's coming for us next, I'll wager anything."

I looked to Mrs. Nevermore for confirmation of this terrible possibility. She merely fixed her cold emerald eyes on me. "You heard them talk about the Gare de l'Est station at ten thirty. Was that it, Ned?"

"Yes," I said. "Something will finish up then."

"But they didn't say what?"

"No. Do you think Gamelle is dead?"

"I don't know. I do know Gamelle doesn't kill easily, but right now we have other things with which to concern ourselves. Gamelle would understand that. He knows a good deal about doing what is necessary under unfortunate circumstances."

"And what is necessary for us?"

"For us it is necessary to get to the Gare de l'Est," said Mrs. Nevermore.

Jack looked shocked. "You must be joking. We're walking right into the hands of Edmond Corbeau!"

"We walk into no one's hands, Jack. Instead we will keep our wits about us and do the last thing they expect."

"We get ourselves killed," Jack said gloomily.

"I have come close enough to getting killed for one night," I said. "He is a terrible creature, Corbeau."

"He is a man," pronounced Mrs. Nevermore. "And men can be defeated. Now come along, Ned. We are going to be late."

The cool hands which had been holding me until now released their grip. I longed for her touch.

But I was disappointed.

TWENTY-FOUR

The prostitutes, tarts, *les grands horizontals, lorettes, cocottes, dégrafées*—whatever one cared to call them and the profusion of names surely was unique to the French—gathered in the shadows outside the Gare de l'Est, painted exotic birds of the night with crimson mouths, faces rouged, hungry eyes kohl- rimmed, their hair built into elaborate nests, earrings rattling over mountains of décolletage, inspecting me with a dead-eyed hunger as bogus as it was desperate.

Bending to show off breasts as they raised their skirts, accompanied by uncertain smiles of invitation, they seemed not at all concerned about my age. What was I after all but one more nocturnal client? Age was of no consequence or impediment to these ladies. How they wanted me and yet at the same time did not want me at all. They would love with all their might, and hate with a bottomless fury, I suspected; such were the contradictions inherent in selling one's body.

Not that I knew a great deal about the body-selling business one way or the other.

The whole notion of women selling themselves and men wandering around making purchases at once confused and intrigued me. If you had a wife, what were you doing paying other woman for what presumably could be had at home? Or could it? Perhaps being married meant you could not have sex with your wife. But if that was the case, how did wives and husbands produce children?

For a young man such as myself, though, I imagined a *cocotte* could be of use. What woman otherwise was likely to fall into bed with me? On the evidence provided thus far, not many—none, in fact. However, if I paid, I suspected the likelihood would increase exponentially.

Alas, I had no money with which to discover the truth or otherwise of my theory. But even so, just being propositioned by all these women was a curiously satisfying sensation. Most adults either ignored me or paid only fleeting attention—a pinch of the cheek here, a tousle of hair there, no more than a patronizing moment before moving on. These particular adults acted as though they were glad to see me, that my age was of no consequence, and I was just needy enough, I suppose, to be impressed by the vehemence of their subterfuge.

"Ned!"

Mrs. Nevermore materialized from the darkness, startling beauty emerging out of a nightmare, viper black replacing unimpeachable white; a woman of night and shadow. As always I was surprised at how easily she appeared to fit onto life's darker landscapes. She anxiously surveyed my face as though to ensure I had not been corrupted by the temptations around me. "You are supposed to be keeping watch."

"Which I am doing."

"You are far too interested in your surroundings."

"I was considering the possibility of obtaining the services of one of these women," I said.

She looked at me with a surprised expression. "Young men should be out seducing women not hiring them off the streets."

"I wondered about that," I said. "But supposing no proper woman is interested, would one of these women not be simpler?"

"You are not the most handsome fellow, Ned, but with a little training in the art of charm and seduction you should do well enough for yourself without resorting to prostitutes. Besides which, you do not wish to risk the scandal that a dalliance with these women might entail."

We crossed the street beneath the station's neo-Corinthian façade. The tarts by now had lost their smiles, replaced them with jealous sneers directed at Mrs. Nevermore before fading away, bowing to a rival with whom they could not possibly compete.

"So then I must wait until I marry before I can be in a bed with a woman?"

"Why does bedding women suddenly interest you?"

"I would not say the interest is sudden," I amended.

"Women adore a man who adores women, so keep that in mind," said Mrs. Nevermore. "That way you will not have to worry about bedding women, as you put it, either before or after you are married."

"But surely I won't be going to bed with other women after I am married."

"Why ever not?"

"Because I will be married, and love my wife, and not wish to do anything to offend her."

"That is the most ridiculous thing I have ever heard, Ned. Where do you get these ideas?"

She came to a stop in the station's cavernous interior, nearly empty at this time of night. "Listen carefully. When you are married, you will be expected to have a mistress. Your wife may even take a lover, as long as no one finds out. Everything is permissible, as long as one is discreet, and is not so foolish as to divorce. One must never do that if one wishes to avoid becoming a social outcast."

"I am not so sure of this mistress business," I said. "Would you want your husband to take a mistress?"

"My husband?" She said the word as though she had just found it in a pile of excrement. "I would never be so foolish as to take a husband."

"Then how can you be *Mrs.* Nevermore? And why would I take a wife?"

"Because that is what men do. They marry. As to why I am Mrs. Nevermore, one could say I find it helpful. I would not find it at all helpful to actually be married."

"Supposing I am not in love? I wouldn't marry then, would I?"

Mrs. Nevermore waved her hand dismissively. "Love has nothing whatsoever to do with it. My goodness, you are a naïve young man. Right now, I cannot be concerned with naïve young men. Enough of this!"

She breezed on, leaving me feeling even more confused than before. Suppose my wife and I were so much in love we only wanted to be with each other? I doubted I would like the idea of her with another lover, and I hoped she would not want me to have a mistress.

Did that make me so totally naïve? I suppose it did.

* * *

I fell into step with Mrs. Nevermore. Our footsteps echoed like hollow drumbeats beneath the station's massive glass roof. Talk of love and marriage and mistresses was forgotten. The gloomy atmosphere added to the tension I abruptly felt as Mrs. Nevermore led the way along the Doric colonnade.

"What are you expecting?" I asked.

Mrs. Nevermore just shook her head.

A burly porter huffed past dragging an empty luggage cart. A conductor in a rumpled black suit removed his cap and rubbed at his eyes. A small intense man burst into view, all but lost amid the vastness of the station. Auguste Escoffier did not see us as he hurried past, lugging a large Louis Vuitton bag.

Mrs. Nevermore brought me to a stop and together we watched as Escoffier disappeared toward Platform number 4. It was here that the *Orient Express* was due to arrive on time from Strasbourg.

Soon enough the cry of a train's whistle, a high keening echo, reverberated through the station. Mrs. Nevermore tensed and then stepped briskly onto the platform. I followed.

A locomotive's headlight broke the gloom. Porters listlessly shifted luggage wagons around and started down the platform. A tiny knot of people dressed in shabby finery, befitting the sort of persons waiting for a train at this time of night, turned anxiously toward the oncoming headlight. Escoffier waited stiffly near the edge of the platform, gripping the Louis Vuitton bag.

Amid belching clouds of black smoke, the gasp of brakes and explosions of steam, the Deauville, the great iron monster that was the pride of the French rail system, slid into view, bringing behind it a series of Pullman cars that constituted the *Orient Express* in all its burnished glass and ashwood marquetry magnificence.

The next thing I saw the blur of Edmond Corbeau stride into view. He wore a black cape over a suit beautifully cut to fit his slim frame. I could not take my eyes off those glossy black shoes I'd viewed so closely as he ran a razor across the late Joe Ganning's throat.

I wondered if he'd had a chance to clean the blood off them.

TWENTY-FIVE

Corbeau trailed Escoffier through the steam and smoke thrown off by the train. I longed to cry out, to warn him that the shadow of death itself was closing in. Mrs. Nevermore seemed to sense what I was about to do and put out a restraining hand. "Stay quiet, Ned," she ordered in a low voice.

"It's Corbeau," I said.

"I know who it is."

A swarm of disheveled, sleepy-eyed passengers discmbarking from the Pullman cars with heavy bags and cranky children engulfed Escoffier. It was then that Corbeau stepped smoothly up. I didn't quite see what happened next, but when Corbeau turned away, Escoffier was left standing there empty-handed. I caught a glimpse of Corbeau with the bag disappearing amid billows of steam and the ghostly shapes of escaping passengers.

"Follow him," curtly ordered Mrs. Nevermore.

"I am tired and up past my bedtime," I protested.

"Ned, stop acting like a child and do as you are told." She pushed franc notes into my hand, a sure sign that marching orders had been given and must be obeyed.

* * *

I followed Corbeau down an ill-lit bricked passageway that led onto the street. He ignored the anxious offers from the waiting prostitutes, continuing along, his stride quick enough, but unhurried. Whatever was in that bag, he obviously did not fear that Escoffier would come after it. He hailed a carriage. I ran to the curb and waved down a second cab. "I want you to go after that carriage," I said, pointing to Corbeau's departing coach.

"Young lad like yourself, you should be in bed this time of night, not ordering cab drivers around," said the coachman in a surly voice.

I showed him some of Mrs. Nevermore's franc notes. "Hop in," he said.

The carriage started off with an unpleasant jolt. I sat back in the shadows, feeling tired and drained. I could not fall asleep, I told myself. Too much was happening. I was following a man who could easily kill me. I must keep my wits about me. Still, there was nothing wrong with closing my eyes. A minute's rest. That's all I needed. Then I would be fine.

* * *

I awoke with a start just as the carriage turned through Guillaume Coustou's les Chevaux de Marly, the rearing marble horses restrained by their naked grooms marking the entrance to the Champs Élysées. I stretched in the shadowy cabin, trying to shake myself awake.

The night descended around, satiny blue, broken by blazes of light from the lamps of the carriages streaming up and down the boulevard. A full moon fought through thickening clouds to illuminate the chestnut trees lining either side of a roadway that transformed itself into a silver pane lifting us toward the distant gleam of the Arc de Triomphe. The driver slowed and called down in an anxious voice, "The other gentleman has stopped. What do you want me to do?"

I looked out the window. Corbeau's carriage stood in front of the Étoile Palace. I disembarked up the boulevard a bit. In the meantime, Corbeau disappeared into an alley running alongside the theater.

I followed him.

The narrow, damp alley stank of urine. I reached a doorway and tried the handle. It opened and I stepped inside to find myself facing a gas-lit corridor leading to a staircase. Up the stairs, a balcony filled with various pulleys and ropes overlooked the stage upon which Natalia Boyer had so recently performed. A single gaslight cast a yellowish haze. Beyond lay the gloom of the silent hall. Edmond Corbeau stood at a table with the Louis Vuitton bag.

Natalia stepped into view. To my amazement I saw that she wore only a corset and stockings.

"Any problems?" I heard her say.

Corbeau shook his head. "He barely knew I was there."

"And Drexel?"

"Taken care of."

"All in all, nicely done."

Her fingers drifted across the top of the bag. They looked at each other, and something unspoken went between them. She pulled him out of sight into shadows behind the stage.

The bag sat upon that table, an invitation. The temptation was irresistible.

I focused on the valise and to my delight it rose off the table. I concentrated harder and the bag ascended through the air. For an instant, I lost my concentration and it plummeted toward the stage. I managed to refocus, stop the bag's descent, and then bring it up to the balustrade.

From somewhere below in the darkness, a high-pitched cry made me jump. The cry was followed by a jumble of insistent words I couldn't quite make out. Natalia? What was wrong with her? She sounded in terrible pain. Then it struck me what was going on back there in those deep shadows. The breathless reward for a job well done, I surmised.

Perhaps they celebrated too soon.

I took the valise and started back down the stairs. Behind me, I heard Natalia calling out. Her plaintive cry was followed by a low, animal-like grunt. Edmond Corbeau in compliance.

Did all adults sound like this when they made love? I wondered. Did one make different sounds with one's mistress than with one's wife? I presumed that mistresses might well be more demonstrative because, after all, they were mistresses and thus had more time to cultivate wildness, would they not? Logic seemed to presume they would. At least this was my assumption.

The next thing I was out on the wide boulevard of the Champs Élysées. I dived into the welcoming gloom of a side street and kept running.

TWENTY-SIX

Above the bleak masses of apartment blocks, scudding clouds played cat and mouse with a full moon so that on occasion as I ran, the streets seemed flooded with a curious iridescent light. When the light failed, the streets descended into darkness and in that darkness things shifted and whispered.

A humped shape caught in flickering lamplight, a tail disappearing into an alleyway, a shadow untangling itself from other shadows to shoot up a nearby wall. A trio of bat-like creatures swooped past. The denizens of the Other World were about tonight. The world I did not wish to see I could see more clearly than ever. I was running through my own nightmare.

Something dropped down in front of me—a gargoyle crouched on his haunches, sickly gray in the uncertain light, yellow eyes glittering, jaws opening and closing mechanically. I came to a stop. The creature swiveled his head, emitting one of those guttural shrieks that raised the hairs on the back of my neck.

I could see a bridge ahead of me and restarted for it, remembering something Peregrine told me the first time we met—gargoyles are afraid of bridges. I thought it ridiculous at the time. Now I fervently prayed it was true.

Another gargoyle thumped into view. I picked up speed. A third, bigger than the others, sprang out of nowhere and smashed into me, knocking me to the street. The others closed in and then reared back as I abruptly elevated myself. Airborne, I headed for the bridge, everything inside me straining with the effort it took to keep moving.

The big gargoyle flew up to intercept me, wing-like protuberances spread. Sinking back to the ground in order to avoid him, I stumbled on the uneven paving stones. That allowed the gargoyle to get in front of me. If I moved, he moved with me, not attacking, but not letting me go, either. He was playing with me. His tiny eyes showed no emotion and thus were all the more frightening—a playful monster in the night taking his time killing me.

Terror grew inside me and it produced a malignant energy I had not experienced. I shot off the ground again, fueled this time by fear, and, curiously enough, all the stronger for it. The bridge lay dead ahead. I glanced behind and saw the gargoyles, caught off guard by my quick action. They recovered soon enough and whipped after me. A moment later, I found myself out over the river.

I dropped beneath the span of the bridge, hoping to lose myself in its darkened recesses, but they were right behind me. One of them reached out to seize me. I managed to spurt away, coming out the other side of the bridge. I rose up toward the balustrade. My foot touched the ledge.

That big gargoyle pounced. I felt the tremendous weight of its body, sinewy arms embracing me. The terrible smell of the thing clogged my nostrils. I lost all concentration. Gravity drew me back to earth. The thing refused to give up its grip and thus we plummeted down together, crashing onto the bridge. I rolled away. The gargoyle sprawled on his back, writhing in the nest formed by its broken wings. It tried to sit up, screaming.

Then it began shaking violently.

Flames burst around its haunches and shot up that swelling torso. In agony, it tried to rise off the bridge, but those shattered wings refused to work and soon they burst into flames. The gargoyle lurched forward, engulfed in fire. It fell over the balustrade, tumbling down, lost in the blackness of the river below.

Everything grew very quiet. There was no sign of the others. I got up slowly, my whole body shaking. So Peregrine had been right. Gargoyles did not like bridges. I looked around and to my relief saw the valise lying a few feet away. I went over and picked it up.

I was on the Pont Alexandre III, named for the Russian czar and newly completed to celebrate an alliance between the French and the Russians, a triumph of the baroque with its exhausting confusion of nymphs, lamps, cherubs, and winged horses. No wonder the gargoyles didn't like it. Perhaps they had more taste than I imagined.

I stood there catching my breath, feeling a stinging pain in my hand. Somehow I had scraped it during my encounter with the gargoyles. My hurting hand nonetheless clutched the Louis Vuitton bag. I realized I had gone to all this trouble to retrieve it and I had no idea what was inside. I bent to unfasten the latch and open it up.

Wads of bank notes spilled out.

I stared wide-eyed. What was Escoffier doing with so much money at the train station? And why did he allow Corbeau to take it? More to the point, what was I to do with this newly discovered fortune?

No one knew I had it. What if I just walked off the bridge and disappeared? Would anyone be the wiser? I could not believe I was thinking like this. It was all wrong. But there it was, the bad Ned with the devious thought: Take the money. Run!

I bent down and closed the bag and lifted it up. Yes, why not? It was my way out of the trap I found myself in, was it not? I heard something and glanced up in time to glimpse Peregrine flash past me.

And then he was gone.

For a moment I couldn't see him. But then Peregrine whipped back towards me as though shot from a cannon. The world's fastest creature! Who could dispute the claim?

I called to him, frantically ducking away as he swooped in. Those talons of his were a blur, clamping the edges of the valise, yanking it from my grasp.

He sped upward, headed for the moon, clutching the valise. Instead of the moon, though, Peregrine altered those beautifully tapered wings ever so slightly and glided away along the Seine.

I watched him arching over the river until he was lost in velvety blackness. I expected him to come back. He had to come back. This was some ridiculous joke he was playing. He did not really intend to steal the valise from me.

He did not return.

TWENTY-SEVEN

It was nearly dawn before I got back to number 52 rue des Saints-Pères, tired, my hand hurting, feeling like a complete failure. How could Peregrine do this to me? What's more, how was I ever going to explain what happened?

I retrieved the valise all right, but then a talking bird stole it from me. I could just imagine the look on Mrs. Nevermore's face as I told her that.

Entering the courtyard, I hoped against hope that Peregrine would be there with the valise. But he wasn't. I thought of running away, but it was late and I was dead tired, and besides, where was I going to run to?

I found Mrs. Nevermore up and seated in the drawing room wearing the same morning dressing gown, the opaque light pouring through the windows rendering her ghostlike. In that light, the ghost looked tired and anxious. The optimist might believe she was actually worried. Age has worked its magic and today I would read that fleeting, anxious expression for what it was.

But back then I was fourteen and carrying around a few scars and no scarred fourteen-year-old is an optimist. Mrs. Nevermore did not help matters. As always when she spoke, it was in that matter-of-fact voice that did not permit demonstrations of emotion or shows of concern.

"You do insist on trying me, Ned."

"You persist in sending me into the night," I said.

"I did not send you out to disappear until dawn."

"I didn't realize there was a time limit."

Gamelle, in his shirtsleeves, came in carrying the Louis Vuitton bag. I stared at him in astonishment. "How did you get here—and where did you get that?" I demanded.

"Where would you expect me to be?"

"Outside the hotel. Waiting."

"I am a prince of royal blood. I can only wait so long. Five minutes in fact."

I couldn't take my eyes off the bag as I said, "If not waiting, then dead. Your throat cut by the evil Corbeau."

"No one cuts my throat. I gave you a watch, did I not? So that you would know when five minutes was up. Did you not look at it?"

"I left your watch at the hotel."

He pulled an object from his pocket. "You mean this watch?"

"How did you get it back?"

"How does anyone retrieve his property? When you did not present yourself, I went up to the room and found it."

He put the valise down on the floor in front of Mrs. Nevermore.

"Peregrine," I said with a groan. "I should have known. He's working for you."

"The boy ought to be flogged," Gamelle pronounced. "That's what's needed here. He runs away from the hotel. He allows a bird to steal from him. What good is he? A good flogging."

"Not so fast, Gamelle." Mrs. Nevermore turned her gaze to me. A rather gentle gaze, I thought. Not unsympathetic.

"So then Ned, perhaps you can tell us what happened after you left the station tonight, and where you ended up."

I sat on a chair and as briefly as I could, I told them what had happened, leaving out the part about the gargoyles. No need to push too hard at the bounds of my credibility.

When I finished, Mrs. Nevermore said, "You hurt your hand, Ned."

"I scraped it when I fell."

"We must do something about it. Is that the bag in question?"

"Peregrine came along and snatched it from me," I said. "It's full of money."

"You see? A bird!" pronounced Gamelle in a disdainful voice. "Flog him, I say."

"A falcon," I amended. "I thought he was a friend. I didn't think he would do such a thing. But then everyone lies, don't they?"

"Don't be so melodramatic Ned," said Mrs. Nevermore evenly. "No one is lying to you."

I fell into sullen silence. As far as I was concerned, everyone was lying. But I was too tired to argue with her.

Gamelle left the room but soon returned with a tea tray. The scowl had disappeared from his face.

"The thing is," I said, "why would Monsieur Escoffier hand over a bag of money to Edmond Corbeau at the Gare de l'Est in the middle of the night?"

"Perhaps Monsieur Escoffier is a generous man anxious to help others."

"Yes," said Gamelle with a mirthless laugh, "that must be it."

Mrs. Nevermore arose and took the bag, setting it on a nearby table. Gamelle did not move but his eyes avidly followed her. She opened it, peered inside, and then said to Gamelle, "Perhaps you'd be so kind as to count it."

"My pleasure," he said and promptly began to remove wads of bank notes and lay them on the table.

Meanwhile, Mrs. Nevermore went over to the tea set. "Would you like some tea, Ned?"

"I'm starving," I said.

"Of course you are. It's been a long night. Let's go into the kitchen and see if we can find you something to eat, and see to that hand."

* * *

Mrs. Nevermore bathed my hand, and then applied iodine and bandages; Nurse Nevermore, I thought. She smiled at me, a soft reassuring smile that I couldn't help but react to.

A croissant, uneaten from breakfast, was placed on a saucer and put in front of me. I took a bite. It was a bit stale but tasty nonetheless.

Mrs. Nevermore dumped the water and put away the bandages and iodine and then sat across the kitchen table and said, "You did well tonight."

In spite of myself I was thrilled. I had managed to please the hard-to-please Mrs. Nevermore.

"Perhaps some day I will impress you in ways that do not involve stealing money," I said.

"Perhaps you will indeed, but try to keep in mind as you seek to achieve this, that you have not stolen any money."

"No? Then what have I done?"

"You have retrieved stolen property. In the way you think of things, you have done good."

"And in the way you think?"

She blessed the question with another smile. "I am pleased that you are so bright and resourceful." She said this in the sort of neutral tone that made one wonder if she was pleased at all.

"Now, you must get some sleep. We have a busy day ahead of us."

"Wait a minute," I said.

She looked at me inquiringly.

"Tell me what you think, Mrs. Nevermore. I'm only a child you see, and I don't understand what has happened."

She studied me intently. "I do wonder about you and childhood, Ned. It seems to be quickly deserting you."

"No small thanks to the situation you have put me in. So tell me."

"Very well," she said with a sigh. "We have stumbled across Natalia in the midst of running a double grift. The first grift was mounted against Monsieur Escoffier. Somehow, the unfortunate Joe Ganning, our Monsieur Drexel, got his nose stuck in it. From what you tell me, he was operating his own grift at the Ritz by impersonating Anthony Drexel. Corbeau got wind of what he was doing. You saw what Corbeau does to people he thinks are in the way."

"But why was Monsieur Escoffier paying all that money?"

"We don't know yet. We will soon enough."

"And their other grift?"

"In its early stages, I believe. It involves Sir Robert Chiltern and perhaps others. It may be the biggest grift Natalia and Corbeau have ever tried to run."

"So then what is to become of our grift?"

"The Eiffel Tower? Why should anything change?"

"It required Monsieur Drexel, and now there is no Monsieur Drexel. Thus we are without a mark and therefore without a grift. Is that correct?"

"That is not correct at all."

"So you have not given up on the tower?"

She grinned. "By now you should know me well enough, Ned. I never give up."

Gamelle, beaming for a change, entered with the bag.

"One hundred thousand francs," he announced happily.

I could hardly believe such an amount of money existed. Mrs. Nevermore seemed unimpressed. "Ned, would you care for another croissant?"

"Did you hear what I said?" Gamelle's face darkened, the happy boy, never present for long, beating a retreat.

"Indeed I did, Gamelle," Mrs. Nevermore acknowledged.

"One hundred thousand francs makes this a very successful enterprise."

Mrs. Nevermore shook her head. "It makes the enterprise no such thing. This is a pittance compared to what we will achieve if we do things properly."

"What are you suggesting?"

"I am suggesting nothing," said Mrs. Nevermore. "I am saying that later this morning after he has rested, Ned and I will return the money to Monsieur Escoffier."

A black scowl swallowed the happy Gamelle. "I cannot believe you are saying this."

"I know you can't," Mrs. Nevermore replied calmly. "That is because you fail to think these things through. You see a tree and want to cut it down, forgetting there is a much larger forest. You will rule a country some day, Gamelle. You should keep that in mind."

"When I am on the throne, I will gladly recall your words," countered Gamelle. "However, while you stare at the forests, we go broke. One hundred thousand francs is right here. That pays a lot of unpaid bills."

She strode over and took the bag from him. "Thank you, Gamelle. That will be all for now."

Gamelle looked even angrier—and a lot more dangerous than I had ever seen him, the rival to Edmond Corbeau in the fearsomeness department. But he said nothing, and more to the point, did nothing except turn on his heel and skulk from the kitchen.

TWENTY-EIGHT

A yellow-eyed gargoyle with skin the color of smoke ripped the flesh from my face while Edmond Corbeau cut off my arm with his straight razor. The gargoyle leaned forward and with its beak-like snout began to peck at my eye.

Tap. Tap. Tap.

That woke me smartly enough. But no one was tearing at my eye. Instead, someone tapped on my window. I got up from the bed and went over and there was Peregrine perched on the window sill.

I opened the window. "I don't want to talk to you," I said.

He poked his black head inside. "Now what have I done?"

"What have you done? You stole my bag on the Pont Neuf, that's what you did."

"It wasn't your bag," he said.

"It wasn't yours, either."

"I wanted to ensure it got back here safely."

"I would have done that."

"Sometimes I do wonder about you, Ned. I wonder what you are thinking and whether what you are thinking is completely honest."

Could he possibly know what I had in fact been considering just before he swooped in? After all, he was only a bird, even if he was a talking bird. He couldn't possibly read my mind. Could he?"

"I thought you were a friend," I said.

"I am indeed a friend."

"You lied to me."

"I did no such thing."

"You certainly failed to tell me that you do Mrs. Nevermore's bidding."

"Bidding?" Peregrine sounded affronted. "I do no one's bidding. I am a falcon, after all, and we are the kings of the air."

"I don't have time for this," I said in a cross voice. "I have to get dressed."

"You are a good fellow, Ned, truly you are. I just want to make sure you stay that way."

"Goodbye, Peregrine."

I closed the window on him. He cocked his head as though not sure what I was doing. He sat there on the sill for a time before he lifted off and flew away.

Still angry and feeling betrayed, I bathed and dressed. Gamelle waited in the kitchen, complete with morning glower. He demanded to know why I had not brought the coal. I was tempted to say that I brought him a bagful of money instead, but I had not really done that, thanks to a certain bird.

To my surprise, Gamelle rewarded my silence with café au lait and freshly baked bread. Hope for humanity flared briefly.

Mrs. Nevermore, dressed to go out for the day, finally arrived with the Louis Vuitton valise. No gossip or cigar this morning. I still had a mouthful of bread and the coffee only half drunk as she pushed the bag into my hand and ushered me out to a waiting carriage.

* * *

A police wagon was parked on the far side of the place Vendôme. I wondered if detectives might be waiting for me inside the hotel, Remy the hallman screaming, "There he is! He's got the key! He's got the key!" But the Ritz lobby remained elegantly quiet; far too early for the rich to be up and beating about. There was no sign of Remy, either, which was a relief. We went into the dining room to be greeted with solemn authority by Olivier, the maitre d' hotel. He gave no sign that anything at all unusual, a murder, for example, had recently taken place in his establishment.

"Is Monsieur Escoffier about this morning, Olivier?" inquired Mrs. Nevermore.

"He is, madame."

"Then could you please tell him Mrs. Nevermore is here and wishes to have a word with him."

"Yes, madame."

He led us to a corner table and held the chair for her while she seated herself. A large, middle-aged woman entered, carrying a falcon. Kin to Peregrine, but much better behaved. Olivier seemed unperturbed by the bird's presence in his dining room. "Good morning, Madame McLean," he said.

"Good morning, Olivier," said Madame McLean. "I'm afraid we are running low on pigeons."

"I will see to it, immediately."

He led her to a table on the other side of the room. The falcon gave a haughty blink as though being in the Ritz dining room was beneath its dignity.

"Do you suppose that falcon can talk, too?" I inquired of Mrs. Nevermore.

"Falcons can't talk," she said.

A miserable English couple who could not bring themselves to look at each other sat nearby. Perhaps they would have been happier had they owned a pigeon-eating falcon. A very small man with a very long waxed moustache sipped his coffee in a corner, hiding from the world.

"One of the Russian grand dukes," announced Mrs. Nevermore, nodding toward the small man with the waxed moustache.

"But which one?"

"Vladimir."

"Any grand duke could be named Vladimir," I said. "Besides, he does not look so grand to me."

"These grand dukes can be quite deceiving," she acknowledged. "Particularly the ones named Vladimir."

An anxious squad of liveried waiters descended. One of the waiters poured coffee, while another unfurled a freshly ironed linen napkin and draped it across my lap.

Tea arrived, followed shortly by an agitated and haggard-looking Auguste Escoffier. "How may I be of service, madame?"

"You can explain to me, monsieur, how it is you came to be associated with the international adventuress Natalia Boyer."

There was little enough color in Escoffier's face, but whatever was left immediately drained away. "You are sticking your nose into business that is of no concern to you," he sputtered. "Is that understood?"

She carefully replaced the fine English bone china cup upon its fine English bone china saucer. "I am impressed that in a French hotel you serve on English china."

This only made Escoffier more agitated. "I propose that you leave this hotel."

"Don't be ridiculous. If you wish to serve on English china, that's up to you."

"I want you out of here!" he thundered. Across the room, the falcon fixed his unblinking gaze upon us. His owner seemed oblivious to the small drama unfolding. However, the English couple, presumably bored with their own lives, had become avid spectators.

Mrs. Nevermore pulled the bag from under the table so that Escoffier could see it. He went even whiter, the anger draining off his face. "How did you get this?"

"Perhaps, monsieur, we should discuss this somewhere more private."

Olivier, looking uncharacteristically anxious, materialized at Escoffier's elbow. "Is everything all right?"

Escoffier made an effort to pull himself together. "Yes, yes of course, Olivier." He looked at Mrs. Nevermore. "Will you come along with me?"

"I'd be delighted," she said. "Ned, perhaps you would be so kind as to carry the bag."

I stood and picked it up. Under the watching eyes of Olivier, the English couple, and the falcon, we followed a considerably deflated Escoffier back to the kitchen.

Even at this early hour, the heat from the kitchen's great cast iron cooking stove, with its splayed feet and ornate top plate, saturated the air. Intense young men in toques and white aprons already had broken into a sweat as they busily chopped and cut, toiling beneath a tangle of pots and pans.

Other equally intense fellows in black coats, aprons tied about their waists, scurried back and forth carrying trays laden with the delicacies that today hopefully would enchant the better classes of Paris. The *garde-manger*, working at a large table as far away from the blast furnace stove heat as possible, oversaw the creation of an asparagus salad while the *entremettier* dropped endive into the pot he was using to prepare the luncheon soup. Nearby, the *rôtisseur* prepared chickens.

The conductor of this large and unruly orchestra paid it scant attention as he ushered us into his glass-enclosed office and shut the door. The sounds and the heat of the kitchen vanished. Escoffier cleared his throat and nervously smoothed his hair.

"We have a terrible situation this morning," he said. "A maid found a body in one of the rooms."

"Presumably a dead body," said Mrs. Nevermore.

"Indeed," acknowledged Escoffier. "I believe you met the gentleman. Monsieur Anthony Drexel of New York."

"Oh, dear."

"Except it appears this man was not Monsieur Drexel at all, but an imposter."

"Goodness," said Mrs. Nevermore. "An imposter at the Ritz. Who could imagine such a thing?"

"César is with the police to ensure they handle the situation as discreetly as possible. But of course this is the last thing we need right now."

"Well, as you grapple with one crisis, monsieur, perhaps we can help you with another."

She took the bag from me and placed it on a desk. He stared at it for a long, tense moment before he said, "I will not press you as to how you came in possession of this. However, it goes without saying that I owe you an apology for the way I carried on in the dining room just now. This has been a trying time. I have not been at my best."

"I understand."

"I presume you know what's in the bag."

"I do," Mrs. Nevermore said.

"You have earned a generous reward."

"I do not want a reward, monsieur."

Another look of disbelief crossed his pale features. "You don't?"

"It's information I'm after."

"Information?"

"About your relationship with Natalia."

Escoffier looked more pained than ever. "Why would she be connected with this affair?"

"The man who relieved you of the valise last night, I know him to be Edmond Corbeau. We followed Corbeau to a place where he met up with Natalia. It's at that point we were able to retrieve the valise."

"And why would you be involved in these matters?" Escoffier summoned what remnants of superiority he still had in him.

"You need help. I believe I am able to provide you with the assistance you require, but you must be honest with me."

He gave a sigh and slumped into a nearby chair. For a moment, I thought he would not say anything. But then he began to speak in a low monotone I had to strain to hear. He met Natalia Boyer as he was about to leave London. A few weeks after his arrival in Paris, he encountered her again at Les Deux

Magots. They began an affair shortly after that.

Those were the happiest times of his unhappy life, he said, a life otherwise spent avoiding a sickly wife waiting gloomily in Monte Carlo. Here was
entrancing Natalia in his arms, the hotel of his dreams a reality, the miserable
wife all but forgotten.

Then Natalia met him late one night with a tearful confession: she worked
for a syndicate in possession of certain documents that outlined criminal behavior on the part of Escoffier and Ritz. It was her job to make use of these
documents and demand payment for them. She had participated in other
schemes of a similar nature. But this was different, she said. She had grown
extremely fond of Escoffier and did not wish to continue with this group.
If he would only agree to pay off the syndicate, she would arrange for the
return of the incriminating papers. The syndicate could not bother him further and it would have no more claim to her services. Thus they could finally
be together. The price: one hundred thousand francs. Presented at Gare de
l'Est.

"Well, you saw what happened," said Escoffier sorrowfully. "They took
the money but gave me nothing in return. Natalia lied at the beginning and
she lied at the end."

"Be assured, monsieur, she will keep right on lying," said Mrs. Nevermore. "There is no syndicate. There is only Natalia and her husband, this
man Corbeau."

Escoffier looked more defeated than ever. "Husband? She's married to
him?"

"A particularly dangerous and nasty individual."

I noticed she said nothing about Corbeau's involvement with the corpse
upstairs.

"They have held onto the documents because they plan to use them
against you again and again," she said.

"Yes, well, at this point that shouldn't surprise me, should it?"

"You must tell me what is contained in these papers that make them so
damning to you and Monsieur Ritz, and thus so valuable to Natalia."

Escoffier gave a wary glance in my direction before leaping off the chair
and throwing up his hands. "This is so horrible! A terrible, terrible embarrassment."

He heaved a sigh. "But I suppose you will have to know. While I was
at the Savoy in London, certain . . . improprieties occurred. There is no use
pointing fingers at this juncture, but it's fair to say I knew little of what was

going on until the management of the Savoy confronted César and myself with evidence that nearly five thousand pounds worth of various wines and spirits were missing from the hotel. They threatened to bring charges that almost certainly would have resulted in scandal and perhaps even prison. However, they were as anxious as we to avoid difficulties."

"So a deal was struck."

"In exchange for our resignations, they agreed to drop all charges."

"Which is why the two of you left London so quickly and came to Paris."

He nodded. "I thought it was all behind us. So did César. But then Natalia appeared with a copy of the report from the Savoy management."

"And the one hundred thousand francs was the price for it?"

"The price for the report was merely an expense, what it would take for us to stay in business. The price for love, well, I considered that to be nothing at all, a fine investment." His words dripped with self-loathing. "What a fool I was."

His fingers angrily massaged his temples. "I must have that report. Otherwise, César and I are both ruined."

"Monsieur, you manage to leave the impression that there is still something you are not telling me."

He cast another worried look at me as though I might run screaming through the lobby with the news of his secret.

"I could kill César, I really could," he continued. "Not only was he involved in these illegal activities but so was His Highness, Edward the Prince of Wales."

"The Prince of Wales? The heir to the English throne was involved in stealing wine?" Even Mrs. Nevermore, who was surprised by nothing, appeared taken aback by this revelation.

"You don't know him, I'm afraid. He is lazy, indolent, cruel, and broke."

"Forgive me, but a monarch in waiting without money seems highly improbable," said Mrs. Nevermore.

"Not so improbable if you know the circumstances. His mother intensely disapproves of the prince's lifestyle, particularly after he was involved in a gambling scandal several years ago. She made him give up baccarat, his favored game of chance, and severely reduced his allowance. Every farthing he receives from her is closely monitored. As a result, he is desperate for money—will do anything in order to maintain his lifestyle and not give in to his mother. It is only because of Edward's involvement that the Savoy chose not to pursue their case against us."

"There being concern that if your case came to trial, a scandal involving the Prince of Wales might become public."

"That's right."

"Tell me this. Did you introduce Natalia to Sir Robert Chiltern?"

He hesitated before he said, "Sir Robert was a guest of the hotel."

"And so Natalia met him here."

"I assure you she was not the least bit interested in him."

"But he is extremely close to the prince, is he not?"

"Well, yes, that's true. Sir Robert and the Prince of Wales are good friends. It is my understanding that the prince now heavily relies not only on Sir Robert to finance his various schemes, but also Sir Robert's friend, Lord Goring."

"I see," said Mrs. Nevermore.

Escoffier studied Mrs. Nevermore anxiously. "You say you are able to provide assistance, Mrs. Nevermore."

"Yes."

"Then I presume the rumors swirling about you have a certain truth. You do not come without a certain . . . reputation."

"Ah, a reputation," said Mrs. Nevermore. "The curse of women everywhere."

"Not in this case, I would say," Escoffier said. "An ability to deal with unpleasant realities is desperately needed."

"I would have to agree with you."

"It would seem you are our only hope for salvation from this mess. César and I would be forever in your debt, a debt to which you could attach any price you wished."

"What of the Prince of Wales?"

Escoffier paused before he said, "While I cannot speak for His Highness, I believe that under the circumstances he would be most appreciative."

Mrs. Nevermore allowed the kind of smile that one might find on a spider spinning a particularly successful web. Whatever she was up to it now involved the future King of England.

Part III

The Secret of the Strange

TWENTY-NINE

The wax candles of the great chandelier dominating Sir Robert Chiltern's house in Grosvenor Square illuminated the rather ludicrous—ludicrous at any rate to my critical eye—18th century tapestry dedicated to the triumph of love that hung from the staircase wall.

"Paris, what is Paris?" thundered Lord Caversham, K.G. from his stooped vantage point beneath that tapestry. "Beautiful, but nothing more! Vienna? What? The burial ground for the Hapsburgs, and enough of them, I say! But London! What? There's the city for you! Not just a city, the *imperial* city, capital of the world! What? Why? Because the British Empire is the world, and here is the heart of that world!"

Mrs. Nevermore, elegantly turned out in a smart afternoon dress, bobbed her head appreciatively. Among her many abilities, I would learn, was the one that allowed her to look interested in the most dim-witted conversations imaginable. She performed this feat now for the benefit of Lord Caversham, that crumbling pillar of the British establishment and father of Lord Goring, the much discussed man-about-town and close friend not only to Sir Robert but the Prince of Wales.

Mrs. Nevermore inquired about Lord Caversham's fondness for ratting, that fascinating sport of gentlemen requiring one's dog to kill more rats in a limited time period than the dog owned by one's opponent.

"Of course I'm still involved! Nothing wrong with it, a fine sport, despite the sneering and huffing that goes on," declared His Lordship.

Mrs. Nevermore arranged a sympathetic expression. "You probably miss the public hangings at Newgate Prison, My Lord."

"Damned right I do. Country's become far too civilized you want my opinion. Coddling criminals and all that!"

"What then should I make of all this I've been hearing about Sir Robert?"

"Next prime minister, mark my words!" Lord Caversham continued at full happy throttle. "Salisbury, bless his heart, is old, all but finished. New blood to resuscitate dying Westminster, that's what we need! Sir Robert's the man for it. Nothing can stop him, I wager."

The old fool leaned heavily upon his cane, as ancient and gnarled as one of those Roman gargoyles in another city that doubtless would never measure up to the imperial delights of London. He noticed me standing dutifully at Mrs. Nevermore's side. "What, hey! Who's this young snipe in our midst?"

"That's young Ned Arnheim."

"Arnheim?" The old lord's thick eyebrows curled above eyes filling with suspicion. "A Jew, then?"

"An orphan. I have taken the boy under my wing, hoping to expose him to the better things in life."

"London's the place, no doubt of that!" bellowed His Lordship. "The best things in life for a young man are all here. Have you considered a career in the military for him?"

I stared in astonishment. *The military?*

"He is a child prodigy," I heard Mrs. Nevermore say. "The piano. The boy's a genius."

A revelation to me.

"I brought young Ned along in hopes he might entertain Lady Chiltern's guests this afternoon."

"Piano player! What? No bloody piano in the house," announced His Lordship.

I was relieved. Mrs. Nevermore looked crestfallen. "What a pity."

Lord Caversham threw a final glance in my direction, and announced "Military!" in the same manner anyone else would cry "Waiter!" Leaning even more heavily on his cane, he hobbled away, child prodigies not headed for a career in uniform apparently of scant interest.

"How can you say I am a prodigy?" I demanded.

"Who's to say you are not?"

"Until I sit at a piano. Then it may become more apparent."

"I thought you could play the piano," she said vaguely.

"Well, I cannot."

"Just as well then they have no piano," said Mrs. Nevermore.

* * *

We had arrived at Victoria station the day before and checked into Claridge's, the Mayfair hotel renovated and re-opened the previous year by its new owner, Richard D'Oyly Carte.

After refreshing ourselves in the en-suite bathroom and experiencing the delights of the electrical lights—electricity being a novelty I'd not encountered before—we set out for Mrs. Nevermore's friend Lady Markby. She was the white-haired society doyen who famously said of London society at this time of year, "No one stays at home unless they are dying." Mrs. Nevermore had pressed her into service a number of times over the years in order to facilitate entrance into places where the moneyed and titled convened— the private dinner tables with a footman stationed behind each chair; the Royal Box at the opera, the soprano Nellie Melba providing background for the gossip of the day; the drawing rooms of Berkeley and Belgrave Square; at the Albert Gate in Hyde Park; and, most important, in the Grosvenor Square mansion occupied by Sir Robert and Lady Chiltern.

"I can't take you back there, I can't!" Lady Markby howled when we came through the Adam doorway at her Mayfair house. She glared at me. "And with a child no less!"

"The boy is an orphan," announced Mrs. Nevermore, as though it was well known orphans couldn't be left alone.

Lady Markby was not reassured. "I don't know what happened the last time I took you there, but it was awful, dreadful!"

However, once the wailing ceased, Her Ladyship was left to face certain realities. She was a widow possessed of a title and entrée into society but no money. Mrs. Nevermore, while something of a social pariah in London, was nonetheless in possession of working capital thanks to Auguste Escoffier, funds she was willing to share with the needy. Lady Markby being entirely needy—and a little greedy to boot, which never hurt—had no choice but to acquiesce.

But so vast was her discomfort at again being cast as Mrs. Nevermore's sponsor that she ordered her driver to stop at Harrods so she might purchase the packets of heroin currently the rage among the women of London.

Last year everyone took laudanum, that potent mixture of opium and alcohol. But this year heroin was the calming drug of every lady's choice. Society women particularly liked the way Harrods did the drug up in those attractive little packets.

Mrs. Nevermore, I was relieved to see, declined Lady Markby's offer to share her purchase.

"You don't take anything?" Lady Markby sounded incredulous.

"One of my numerous shortcomings. I insist on seeing the world without the rosy colors."

"I need something for this evening," said Lady Markby. "I can't get through without one of these little packets, don't you know. I just can't do it."

And thus with a chemically becalmed Lady Markby in tow, we found ourselves in Sir Robert's octagonal room, trading stiff pleasantries with Lady Chiltern, a woman with stars in her elaborately piled hair and tulle at her shoulders, of grave beauty it was said, and who, if anything, appeared more doped up than Lady Markby.

"And I understand you are now a mother," said Mrs. Nevermore.

"Twice over," said Lady Chiltern, glancing quickly around to see if any of her other guests might rescue her. Only Lord Caversham was in sight, and that would be no rescue at all.

"A boy and a girl, I understand."

"Indeed. Little darlings, both."

"Then motherhood suits you?"

"Does it not suit any woman?"

"I don't know about any woman. Certainly, I don't think it would suit me."

Lady's Chiltern's artificially bright gaze fell upon me. "What then of this young man?"

"I have taken him under my wing," said Mrs. Nevermore.

"Then motherhood of sorts has arrived," said Lady Chiltern.

"We are discussing a career in the military for him," said Mrs. Nevermore. "Lord Caversham has offered to be his mentor."

Lady Chiltern's gaze again fell upon me. It did not like what it saw. "The boy appears ill-equipped for a life in uniform."

"I am," I agreed.

"But I understand he's a prodigy of some sort," added Lady Chiltern with unexpected charity, desperate for the bright side of this conversation.

"The piano," said Mrs. Nevermore.

"My goodness." Lady Chiltern said.

"I had hoped Ned might play for us."

"Alas, we have no piano," said Lady Chiltern.

"I want to be an engineer," I said.

"Trains are so noisy," Lady Chiltern said.

Her eyes once again danced desperately around and then exploded with the light of salvation. "Ah, there's Mrs. Marchmont, just arriving. Would you excuse me?"

"Is Sir Robert to be with us this evening?"

"Shortly," said Lady Chiltern, all but running to greet Mrs. Marchmont.

Lady Markby waved a fan in front of her flushed face. "That was perfectly dreadful," she groaned. "I shall never be invited here again. I once had a small shred of a decent reputation, don't you know. Now even that is gone."

"Nonsense, they love you and are willing to forgive you anything, even me." Mrs. Nevermore looked around. "Will the Prince of Wales be here?"

Lady Markby's eyes widened in renewed horror. "Lady Chiltern would never hear of it, don't you know! Bertie's bunch don't run in this set, I can tell you. They are so vulgar! That dreadful man! Such a scandal! No one in our circle will have a thing to do with him."

"He is to be the next King," said Mrs. Nevermore.

"You are supposing the Queen will die, and I have it on the best authority that she is immortal. Sixty some years and counting, don't you know."

"Queen Victoria may be many things, but I doubt immortal is one of them," said Mrs. Nevermore.

"Who's to say? I mean no one ever sees her, do they? Who knows what sort of state she's in? But I suppose if anyone could kill her off, it would be her son whom she absolutely loathes, don't you know. It is said she leaves the room when he appears."

Lady Markby lowered her voice and waved her fan in front of her mouth, presumably so no one could read the movement of her thin, moist lips. "The Queen never forgave him for the death of Albert, her adored husband, haven't you heard? She believes the scandals involving her son drove Albert to an early grave, and who's to say they didn't? The man is shameless! I mean did you hear about him and that dreadful hussy Lady Mordaunt? They say she is mad. Mad!"

"In general? Or just where the prince is concerned?"

"Then there is that Mrs. Alice Keppel he has recently taken up with. I understand"—and here she lowered her voice even more—"there is *Greek* blood in her veins!"

She paused to allow us to take in the severity of this accusation.

"I can't imagine what his poor wife, Princess Alexandra, must think," prattled on Lady Markby, waving her fan even more furiously. "But I suppose it's because the man is bored. He has absolutely nothing to do with himself since his mother won't let him do anything. I hear he spends all his time in Paris when he is not with Mrs. Keppel, chasing around after tarts. However, I have it on the best authority he soon enough must end that sort of behavior."

"Oh? Why is that?"

"Haven't you heard? They say Bertie's broke. Penniless! Why he's even had to give up baccarat, and Bertie loves baccarat more than anything."

"You don't say," Mrs. Nevermore said distractedly, looking over my shoulder. I turned to see Sir Robert Chiltern finally make his entrance.

THIRTY

Sir Robert went blank with surprise when he saw Mrs. Nevermore. He recovered quickly, even managing a fair approximation of a welcoming smile.

"What's more you have brought with you the remarkable Mrs. Nevermore," he exclaimed to Lady Markby. "What a surprise." Not a *pleasant* surprise, mind, just a surprise.

"It's so good to see you again, Sir Robert," Mrs. Nevermore said. "I've been hoping our paths might cross here in London."

"And who have we here?" His gaze fell on me. Mrs. Nevermore made introductions. "A prodigy, you say?"

"The piano," Mrs. Nevermore said.

"Impressive." He focused surprisingly kindly eyes upon me.

Up close, one tended to be more forgiving of Sir Robert's chin, its shortcomings tempered by the glitter of his smile and the warmth in his eyes. Here was a good man radiating the trust and confidence of a born leader, a gentleman who could lead a great empire and still take the time to understand the problems of the common man. Little wonder the British people were so enamored of him. Of course, they hadn't seen him sneaking around the flesh pots of Paris with a woman not his wife as I had. That might have shaded their view somewhat.

Sir Robert returned his attentions to Mrs. Nevermore. There was no longer so much warmth in his eyes. "You and the boy reside in Paris?"

"Where I must say, Sir Robert, the natives are endlessly fascinated by your every move."

Sir Robert became so pale that even Lady Markby noticed and ceased the waving of her fan.

Again, he made a quick recovery, the color flooding back into his cheeks as fast as it departed. "Indeed? Isn't that fascinating? I can't imagine the French would have the slightest interest in my comings and goings."

"To the contrary," she said. "They can talk about nothing else when it comes to the man they consider Britain's next prime minister."

"What a pity then that the French cannot vote in an English election."

"Ah, but they can influence it. Can they not?"

"Forgive me Mrs. Nevermore, but I think you overestimate the French."

"Better not to underestimate anything at this point, don't you think?"

Sir Robert gave her another blank look before turning to greet Lady Chiltern who had reappeared with her jaw set, as though about to undergo invasive surgery, her beauty not so much grave now as funereal.

"Look darling, what a surprise," Sir Robert announced in tones of false exuberance. "Our Mrs. Nevermore has come back to us, from Paris of all places, and with a young man who is a prodigy, no less."

Lady Chiltern produced a smile that would not have looked out of place on a skull. "Yes, and we have Lady Markby to thank."

The skull-like grin beamed in the direction of the offending Lady Markby who looked as though she had been sentenced to death—which in a way, perhaps, she had.

"Mrs. Nevermore hasn't seen the renovations we've done on the library since last she visited," Sir Robert said. "I was just about to show them to her."

"Yes," said Lady Chiltern. "Why don't you do that, Robert, while I see to our other guests? Don't be too long, though. Everyone wants to talk to my world-famous husband."

She stated this last as though testifying in court. Divorce court? Sir Robert pecked his wife on the cheek in a way that suggested the virtues espoused in the triumph of love tapestry were no longer being celebrated in the Chiltern household. Lady Chiltern looked as though she had not been so much kissed as insulted. What was going on? I wondered as I watched Sir Robert lead Mrs. Nevermore away. I knew little of what a marriage was supposed to be, but this did not seem to be it.

I was left alone with Lady Markby who fluttered about presenting me with nervous glances suggesting the last thing in the world she wanted was to be stranded here with an orphaned child prodigy about to join the military. I could hardly blame her.

Lady Markby sailed off in search of more sympathetic companions. I drifted around the edges of the room, saw that no one paid me the least attention, and sauntered down the corridor along which Sir Robert had disappeared with Mrs. Nevermore.

The door to the library was closed tight. I could hear the murmur of voices behind it, but nothing distinct. Above the door was a leaded fanlight. I looked about, saw no one, and, taking the chance, lifted myself off the floor up to the window.

I peered into the sort of book-lined room that I would come to understand wealthy young men build for themselves upon deciding to go into politics. If only they would read these volumes, I would eventually conclude, then their time would be filled productively, and they would not be out getting themselves into trouble with enticing young women.

I could see Sir Robert pacing about before a seated Mrs. Nevermore. More important, I could just hear his voice through the thin glass: "Then tell me please, what the devil are you doing here?"

"Believe it or not, Sir Robert, I've come to help you," said Mrs. Nevermore.

He stopped pacing and confronted her. "You would be of greatest help if you would leave this house and stay out of my life."

"We would be better advised not to waste time and instead get to the discussion of Natalia Boyer."

That produced a silence heavy with tension. Sir Robert turned away from her, clasping and unclasping his hands.

"I have no idea who or what you are talking about, madam," he said.

"I think you do," Mrs. Nevermore countered. "You are intimately involved with Natalia, Sir Robert. Perhaps that is not who she is calling herself for your benefit. But that is most definitely her name."

Sir Robert stormed over to where Mrs. Nevermore sat. "I do not wish to hear any more on this matter!"

Mrs. Nevermore did not move. "Listen to me: Natalia Boyer only pretends to be your friend. She is in fact a confidence woman who recently orchestrated a blackmail scheme involving César Ritz and his partner, Auguste Escoffier."

"That cook and the hotelier who were run out of London?"

"Natalia relieved them of one hundred thousand francs."

"This is utterly preposterous!" howled Sir Robert.

"I believe she now has set her sights on the Prince of Wales and is using her affair with you to get to him."

Below me Sir Robert puffed himself up to the full height of his regal being. "I have heard enough of these slanderous lies. Stop now. You must allow me to call a carriage for you."

Mrs. Nevermore rose to her feet. "You should know Natalia has documents implicating not only Escoffier and Ritz, but also the Prince of Wales in connection with certain adventures at the Savoy Hotel. If you do not wish to protect your own reputation, you might consider that of the man who is soon to be King. I am at Claridge's should you change your mind."

"My God!" he exclaimed. "How did you ever get into my life?"

I heard a sound and shot back to the floor just as Lady Markby rounded the corner. She looked taken aback and I wondered if she had seen me airborne.

"There you are," she said in her fluttery voice. "Whatever are you up to, young man?"

"I was flying through the air," I said.

"Well, you must stop at once. That is no way for a gentleman to behave."

Just then Mrs. Nevermore stepped out of the library. Lady Markby turned to her. "This young man is not behaving appropriately," she announced, and then flounced off along the hall.

"You mustn't upset Lady Markby, Ned," Mrs. Nevermore said. "She is simply not herself this evening."

"I'm sorry."

Rather than being in a state of agitation, as I expected, Mrs. Nevermore smiled serenely.

"What happened in there?"

"I'm afraid love has made Sir Robert deaf to anything resembling common sense."

"What will we do now?"

"We will take our leave, and then we will wait patiently. Sir Robert has been forced to hear the worst, and the worst has a way over time of sinking in and settling into one's consciousness where it cannot be so easily ignored. Let's see how long it takes Sir Robert."

THIRTY-ONE

It did not take long at all.

When Mrs. Nevermore answered the knock on the door of her rooms at Claridge's first thing the next morning, she was expecting a porter with tea. Instead a messenger handed her a note. She read it quickly and then ordered me to dress.

I gave her my best sour face and put on my coat. "What was in the note?"

"An invitation," she said.

"What sort of invitation?"

"The sort that arrives when powerful men are worried about their skins," she said. "My favorite kind."

Outside the hotel, Mrs. Nevermore hailed a Hansom cab and pushed me inside. She ordered the driver around to 45 Curzon Street in Mayfair.

"Why are we going there?"

"That is where Lord Goring resides."

Saying the name caused her mouth to tighten. She shifted around and stared out of the carriage as we came onto New Bond Street. A hawker at the corner was trying to persuade a tiny crowd to purchase one of his toast racks.

"You seem tense," I said.

"I am no such thing."

"You are tense because of Lord Goring?"

"A cad and a scoundrel," she pronounced. "A man supremely certain of his own world and sorry for anyone who is not in it. In short, a blind fool, and a wastrel to boot. There is nothing more to say of him—other than to point out that his father, Lord Caversham, would heartily agree with me."

By now we were rounding Berkeley Square. A newsboy held papers above his head and cried out, "'Orrible murder! "'Orrible murder!" He did not specify what murder.

We crossed Fitzmaurice Place and the Hansom cab turned right onto Curzon Street. Mrs. Nevermore became even tenser. She frowned and exhaled a long breath.

Then, one of those unexpected insights available only to untried youth: "You were in love with him."

An uncomfortable pause followed before she said, "I have no idea what love is. Do you?"

"Perhaps it has something to do with not wanting a mistress. But then I am only a child, and so I don't know much of anything. You are a fully grown adult and thus should know more."

"The older I become, the less I know about that particular subject." More uncomfortable silence. And then she said, "As far as I know, I was not in love with Lord Goring."

She did not sound convincing.

"What about Jack Dozen?"

She gave me a startled glance. "What a curious question. What about him?"

"Did you not love him since he loves you?"

"Only a very foolish woman would be foolish enough to fall in love with Jack Dozen, and I am not a foolish woman. Well, after Lord Goring I am no longer a foolish woman."

The carriage came to a stop in front of number 45. The coachman climbed down and opened the door for us. "Here we are ma'am," he said.

Lord Goring's butler answered the door when Mrs. Nevermore rang the bell.

"Hello, Phipps."

Gray-haired, firm-jawed, impassively elegant, Phipps did not so much as raise an eyebrow. "Madam, Lord Goring is waiting for you."

He stepped back smartly to allow us inside.

"How have you been, Phipps?"

"Never better, madam. And yourself?"

"Surprised to be back here."

"I can imagine," Phipps said drily.

He led the way along a short hall to the library. He knocked once and then opened the door and again stepped back so that we could enter.

The architect Robert Adam, a Scotsman who, alas, had been to Rome, originally designed the interior. Thus one entered into a book-lined reproduction of the Coliseum, rising two stories to a dramatic skylight. Those spaces not filled by books were adorned with various paintings of frigates and battleships at full sail—a curious interest of Lord Goring's. Curtains of hand-woven silk featuring a floral pattern against a light green background cut off the morning brightness.

A trio of George III giltwood torcheres uncertainly illuminated the gentlemen who now struggled to their feet. There was Lord Goring, of course, still the personification of the London "swell", a man of extreme elegance and splendor, a flawless dandy into his late thirties, but these days a rather chubby flawless dandy, a burgeoning swell, if you will.

With Lord Goring was Sir Robert, no longer the reassuringly powerful figure he struck so effectively the evening before. This morning he resembled a discarded rag—an exhausted rag at that, his hair uncombed, his skin curiously pale and molted in the light from the torcheres. He stumbled into an upright position, all kindness gone from his eyes, replaced by an angry suspicion underscored by dark circles; a man distrustful of everyone, staring into the depths of hell.

The third gentleman present smelled of cigars, sported a short, gray beard, carefully trimmed, and apparently dined at the same restaurants as Lord Goring for he too possessed a girth that could only be termed expansive. The pupils of his merry eyes were not rimmed with black circles but shot through with red. This was a gentleman who stayed up too late and drank too much, and did so without apology. Someone once said of him that he was not so interested in making money, only spending it. The previous night, by the look of things, he had been out spending it.

"You've arrived on time as always Laura, and as always accompanied by a surprise," Lord Goring said. "This morning it is this young gentleman. You must tell me who he is."

"This is Ned Arnheim. An orphan."

"An orphan you say." Lord Goring looked amused by the allegation. "Is that the same as being an Anglican, I wonder."

"Worse," said I.

"Well put," said Lord Goring with a genuine laugh. He gripped my hand. I liked him immediately. "Welcome young Ned, orphan and early morning wit. Would you care for some coffee?"

"No, thank you, sir."

"Then let me introduce you to our guests, Ned. Sir Robert, you perhaps already know."

"What the devil is this going to accomplish?" Sir Robert's angry words were directed not at me but to the room in general.

Lord Goring turned to the room's third occupant. "Mrs. Nevermore and Ned, I don't think you've met my dear friend, Edward."

"The Prince of Wales," Mrs. Nevermore said.

"We were at the Grand Hotel in Cimiez last year. My mother was there for six weeks. Don't know how she put up with it. Service just wasn't up to snuff. Didn't we meet? Queen Wilhelmina of Holland came by for afternoon tea. Were you there? They served those delightful cucumber sandwiches."

"I'm afraid it wasn't me, Your Highness."

"Could have sworn," he said.

The prince wore an ascot tie anchored by a gold pin with a single turquoise and a double-breasted frock coat. What surprised me was the bright red waistcoat he adopted for the morning; the rogue was out, even at this early hour. It struck me that, despite his waistcoat, this portly soul would hardly set feminine hearts aflutter. But he did possess a certain regal bearing which I suppose came from knowing that some day, somehow, he would rule an empire.

Maybe that was it, the intoxicating effect royalty could have on the opposite sex. As I have stated several times throughout this narrative, I was young and naïve when the events I chronicle occurred. I have since learned that men of wealth and power do not need the added value provided by looks. Being men of wealth and power is usually quite enough to get them exactly what they want, women included.

His Highness gravely shook Mrs. Nevermore's hand. I thought I detected a speculative twinkle in his pale blue-gray eyes, as befitted a gentleman with a notorious interest in members of the opposite sex.

"Cimiez is so hot in the summer, don't you find?"

"Stifling," agreed Mrs. Nevermore.

"Although it is close to Nice and the casino, which is fine."

Lord Goring addressed Mrs. Nevermore. "Laura, first of all I should say that whatever happened in the past is in the past, and forgotten. We must focus on the current situation we all find ourselves in."

"I concur, Lord Goring. No one has approached you?"

"Not as yet, no."

"Then I suspect they will not come so directly, but through Sir Robert."

The man in question chose not to tear his eyes away from one of the more impressive renderings of a frigate in full sail at nightfall, its twenty-eight-pound guns dramatically lighting a choppy sea.

"They have some sort of report, is that it?" growled the Prince of Wales.

"From investigators at the Savoy Hotel. A fraud involving César Ritz and Auguste Escoffier."

"And I am named in this report?"

"You are," said Mrs. Nevermore.

The prince said nothing, but it was evident from the look on his face this was not good news.

"What do you want from me?" cried Sir Robert suddenly. He leapt from his seat to confront the others. "My resignation from the government? You may have it forthwith."

For such a bear of a man, the Prince of Wales moved with surprising agility over to where Sir Robert stood.

"I don't require your resignation, sir. Neither does the prime minister. However, I do want you to pull yourself together and take some responsibility here! My God! You strut about, your little gang of Souls, and you think yourself so much better than the rest of us."

"That is not true," said Sir Robert in a faltering voice.

"Then show some backbone!"

"She loves me," he gulped. "I am certain of that—more certain than anything in my life. But—"

"But what, man!" exploded the prince.

"Well, we spoke last night."

"Natalia is here? She's in town?" Mrs. Nevermore could not hide her surprise.

Sir Robert nodded forlornly. "She has confessed her involvement with certain disreputable people, professionals at this sort of thing. Natalia swears her love for me and doesn't want to be part of their blackmail scheme, but feels trapped by these villains."

"Natalia told Auguste Escoffier much the same thing only days ago," Mrs. Nevermore said. "I'm sorry, Sir Robert, but I know Natalia only too well. She has no feelings for you."

"Then you don't know her at all!" came Sir Robert's angry retort.

Mrs. Nevermore turned to Lord Goring and the prince. "There are no 'people,' no villains forcing Natalia to do anything. There is only Natalia and her husband, a nasty piece of work named Edmond Corbeau."

"He is not her husband!" Sir Robert shouted angrily. "She would never lie to me. It is not possible!"

"She will use her affair with Sir Robert against him in short order as well as the documents that incriminate you, Your Highness."

"That I have already discerned," said the prince. "What I need to know now is what can be done about it."

"If I know Natalia, she will wait a few days before arranging another meeting with Sir Robert. She will be terribly sorry, but the only way out is to make a large cash payment to her people. The documents incriminating His Highness will be part of the deal. Except that you will not receive them and there will not be one cash payment but many. Once this begins, it does not end."

"Then it must not begin," said the prince.

"Can you do something about this, Laura?" asked Lord Goring.

"I can put a stop to Natalia's scheme."

"You can do that?"

"I can," she replied.

"She has left London," Sir Robert blurted.

"For where?" demanded the prince.

Another loud exhaling of air. "Vienna. Early this morning. She is a magician by trade. She has contracted to do a show there."

"All the better for us that she is away from London," Mrs. Nevermore said.

"Can you go to Vienna?" asked the prince.

"Immediately. Providing we reach a satisfactory arrangement, Your Highness."

Lord Goring looked shocked. "Do you have any idea to whom you are talking?"

The Prince of Wales gave a delighted laugh. "It's all right, Goring. Mrs. Nevermore makes perfect sense. For services such as only she can provide, one wants to pay, indeed one insists upon it. That way, one can be assured of discretion. Is that not so, Mrs. Nevermore?"

"Total discretion, Your Highness."

"What would you like?"

"Dinner with you at the Ritz in Paris when this is over."

Goring and the prince fixed her with incredulous stares. "That's all?" said Lord Goring.

"That would be quite enough. What about it, Your Highness?"

"If that is the price," said the prince with a grin, "then I would be only too happy to pay it."

"I leave for Vienna forthwith," said Mrs. Nevermore.

Lord Goring looked relieved. The prince stepped closer, his bearded face abruptly sagging with solemnity.

"This is a good thing you do for us, Mrs. Nevermore. The empire sits at its apex. The typical Englishman lives well and in great prosperity. The world is largely British and the better for it. This is a very good age in which we live and it is all thanks to men like Salisbury, our prime minister, and his lieutenants, gentlemen such as Lord Goring here and Sir Robert, and, if I daresay, myself; leaders who have helped make this country what it is today. But we are, alas, only human, and being human subject to the usual foibles in an age that does not tolerate them. Thus good men who have given their lives to govern must hide certain things for the benefit of all. In helping us stop these villains who tear away the beating heart of this nation, you also do a grateful country a great service."

The Prince of Wales signaled the end to his call to arms by dramatically bending to kiss Mrs. Nevermore's hand. If I'd had a flag, I would have waved it.

"Well, England will be saved not from London but from Vienna," announced Mrs. Nevermore in the sort of no-nonsense voice one uses when setting out to save empires. "So the sooner Ned and I are on our way, the better."

She beamed her most irresistible smile at the prince. "Perhaps you would be so kind as to see me to my carriage."

The prince, being very much the man he was, beamed right back. He took Mrs. Nevermore's arm. I noticed the look on Lord Goring's face. Wistfulness? Or was that a hint of jealousy? Hard to say.

Outside, the Prince of Wales opened the carriage door for Mrs. Nevermore.

"My mother will not cross the Channel on a Friday," he said. "Peculiar, don't you think?"

"I look forward to seeing you in Paris, Your Highness," she said.

"What's more, she always travels under an assumed name in France. Madame la Comtesse de Balmoral. Silly, really. Everyone knows who she is, after all."

The prince kissed Mrs. Nevermore's hand before helping her inside. She could not have looked more thrilled.

* * *

"The hypocrisy of the aristocratic British male," Mrs. Nevermore announced as the carriage bore us away from Curzon Street.

"I'm afraid I don't understand," I said.

"Of course you don't, Ned, for you are the worst of all possible things, a man."

"You make it sound like a handicap," I said.

"It is a terrible handicap," she asserted.

"Yet one has only to look around to see that the male appears dominant over the female in this life."

"Nature's most dreadful mistake," Mrs. Nevermore asserted. "And nature has been particularly careless when it comes to the aristocratic British gentleman."

"How is that?"

"Be he a knight or a duke, marquess or lord or prince of the realm, it makes no difference, this sort of high born individual demands a world wrapped in a rigid moral code that works very well as long as everyone but himself has to live by it. Caught breaking the rules he created, the morally superior British aristocrat will move heaven and earth to hide the fact. You heard the prince. It is for the good of the country! What silliness! How weak they are, these men, how easy it is to despise them and take advantage of their hypocrisy. Thank goodness for morality and stupid men such as the Prince of Wales. They go hand in hand and because they do, an ambitious woman comes out much the better."

THIRTY-TWO

No sooner were we back in our rooms at Claridge's than Mrs. Nevermore seated herself at a satinwood writing desk, pen in hand, hotel stationery in front of her. "Ned, I want you to take this down to the front desk, and have them send it as soon as possible."

She finished writing and handed me the sheet of paper. "Go quickly. Meanwhile, I'll see to our luggage. We leave for Waterloo Station this afternoon."

I looked at the paper. She had composed the following message in large capital letters: "LEAVING FOR VIENNA STOP WILL BE IN TOUCH STOP." It was addressed to Gamelle.

"So Gamelle will not meet us in Vienna?"

"Why ever should Gamelle come to Vienna? Gamelle doesn't even like Vienna. Frankly, I can't say I blame him."

"Without Gamelle, I would say our task is hopeless, particularly when it comes to defeating the fearsome Edmond Corbeau."

"Corbeau is not all that fearsome."

"Jack is afraid of him," I said.

"If we avoided everything Jack is afraid of we would never leave the house at number 52. Frankly, I don't think poor Gamelle will be anything but a bull in a Viennese china shop, and therefore of little help defeating anyone. The two of us are more than enough to take care of Natalia and get those documents back."

"What's more," I went on, "Corbeau possesses the power of the Strange. I suspect Natalia does, too. That makes them even more formidable."

As I suspected it would, that made her glance up sharply at me. "What makes you think Corbeau has any such power?"

"I just know," I mumbled in a sullen voice. "That's why I don't think we are any match for the two of them."

"Then, as usual, you underestimate us. Now stop arguing. Go downstairs and deliver the telegram."

There was no use pursuing the matter further. Besides, I was more anxious to ride up and down the lift, the hotel's elevator device being an entirely new experience for me. I leapt onto the rattling iron contraption, went up three floors, and then came down again.

I considered repeating the process but other guests were waiting, and so I exited and crossed the lobby to the front desk, gave the clerk my room number and handed over Mrs. Nevermore's telegram. He said he would send it off immediately and gave me a receipt.

I carefully folded it and put it in my pocket and returned to the lift. Seeing that it was deserted once again, I thought I would take a couple more rides before returning to Mrs. Nevermore and the unappealing prospect of Vienna.

Someone touched my shoulder. I swung around to find two men in dark suits and bowler hats. One of the men, a heavy set, clean-shaven blond character, gave me a smile that would not have looked out of place on Father Christmas. "Are you Master Ned Arnheim, then?" An English accent, more working class, not like the plumed and polished Mayfair tones I'd been hearing that morning.

I felt my stomach tighten. "Who might be asking?"

"Monsieur, you would be well advised to answer my colleague's question." The second fellow was much slimmer with hooded cobra's eyes I didn't like. He had darker hair, a mustache, and a French accent.

"And what if I were this Ned Arnheim?"

"Then we would wish to have words with you, young sir," said the Englishman.

"Words on what subject?"

"Are you Ned Arnheim or not?" The Frenchman impatient, as Frenchmen tend to be.

"I am a young man taught not to speak to strangers," I replied.

I tried to bluff my way past them, but the Englishman blocked my path, discreetly flashing a badge. "There now, Ned. I'm Detective Inspector Cecil Ribblesdale of the London Metropolitan Police Service. This gentleman here is Monsieur Anton Ganimard of La Sûreté Nationale in Paris. Let's not have any more problems or we will continue this encounter at New Scotland Yard with its wonderful view of the Thames."

* * *

They escorted me down a short corridor into a sitting room full of leather furniture and green-shaded desk lights. Ganimard shut the door so that the three of us were alone.

They sat me on one of the sofas. Inspector Ribblesdale pushed his bowler back on his forehead, pulled up a straight back chair and dropped into it, slapping his knees as he settled, hunched forward, facing me. Ganimard kept his bowler in place and remained standing in the background. He did not look happy, befitting a Frenchman not in France.

Ribblesdale, in contrast, had taken on a much more cheerful air now that he had dangerous Ned Arnheim in his clutches.

"Lad, we've been in touch with the authorities at your school."

"You talked to Lonsdale?"

"Lonsdale School for Boys, that's right. They tell us you're a fine young man, a tendency to talk back at times to those in authority, but a pretty good fellow all in all. So I suppose what we're attempting to do here today is ensure that your current status doesn't change."

"Why should it change?"

"It might change because of the company you've been keeping."

"For your information," I said archly. "I have just come from a meeting with the Prince of Wales."

"We know all about where you've been, Ned. We've been following you ever since you arrived in London. In fact, Anton here, he came in on the train with you."

"From Paris? Why would he do that?"

"Because he is investigating the murder of your father." Inspector Ribblesdale twisted around. "Isn't that so, Anton?"

"Flix Arnheim, American scoundrel and international confidence man who more than once has come afoul of the law, dead from stab wounds administered by an unknown assailant."

"So that's where we are, lad." Ribblesdale turned back to me. "An unsolved murder brings Anton to London. A dangerous, deceitful woman puts the two of us onto you."

"I know of no women either dangerous or deceitful."

Well, I suppose I knew one.

"Come along lad, you know full well I'm talking about Mrs. Laura Nevermore, not her real name, incidentally. Or did I mention that already?"

"You did not mention it. What is her real name?"

"She's got a number of them does our Mrs. Nevermore, hard to tell what's real and what's not. Whatever her name, I'm bound to arrest her in connection with a fraudulent scheme having to do with a supposed South American canal. Our Mrs. Nevermore was involved as well as the late Flix and a number of others, including a failed British thespian by the name of Jack Dozen."

"They were going to build a canal in South America?"

"That's the point, lad. There was no canal."

"You believe my father was involved in this?"

"We do not *believe* anything," said Ganimard, stepping forward. "We *know* he was the mastermind of the attempt to defraud the citizens of Great Britain."

"Anton and me, we think that's why Flix got himself killed. Someone was pretty upset with him."

Ribblesdale again slapped his hands against his knees, and hunched forward even further. "You're the innocent in all this, Ned lad, I truly believe that. The thing is, though, you're in danger of getting caught up in the same mess as the others if you're not careful. Best to throw in your lot with the forces of law and order as personified by Anton and myself."

"How should I do that?"

"Tell us what she's up to, our Mrs. Nevermore. Any idea? From what Anton can see from Paris, and what I deduce since she arrived in London, she's about to hatch a scheme that involves Sir Robert Chiltern and the Prince of Wales. Fill us in, Ned, so we can stop her before she does even more harm than she's already done. You can trust us, lad. Sure as anything, you can."

I didn't trust them at all. But of course I was not about to say anything. Instead, I did what any child overawed by the adults swirling around him was expected to do—I nodded.

Ribblesdale cocked his head as though expecting more and not wanting to miss it. When I failed to meet his expectation, he sat back and once again thumped hands against knees. "What's wrong, lad? Surely you got something to say for yourself."

I said, "As far as I know Mrs. Nevermore came to London to visit her friend Lady Markby and to take in a number of social events, including a reception at the home of Sir Robert Chiltern. She then visited another old friend this morning, Lord Goring. As it happened, Lord Goring was entertaining the Prince of Wales when we arrived."

"Let me tell you something." Ribblesdale's working class English voice had lost its jocular quality. "Lord Goring is no friend of Mrs. Nevermore. The only reason your Mrs. Nevermore is not on her way to Scotland Yard this minute is because of the presence of the Prince of Wales. The last thing we want is to publicly embarrass His Highness."

Ganimard stepped forward again. "Do yourself a great favor, Monsieur Ned. Save yourself from a prison sentence—co-operate with us."

"I just told you everything I know," I said insistently.

"All right. I accept that," said Ribblesdale, traces of his former good nature returning. "But from here on in, you keep your eyes and your ears open. You see something lad, you let us know. An honest boy, you'll be in the clear when the rest go off to jail. That's a promise."

"Eyes and ears open," I said carefully.

"You got it, Ned. Eyes and ears."

I paused before I said, "I will do my best, sir."

Ribblesdale brightened. "That's the spirit! That's the kind of co-operation we're after. Right, Anton?"

Ganimard just stared at me and didn't say anything.

Ribblesdale quickly filled the silence. "You're returning to Paris this afternoon, are you?"

"No," I said. "Vienna."

Ribblesdale and Ganimard traded glances. "Vienna? What the devil's going on in Vienna?"

"I don't know," I lied. Well, it wasn't that much of a lie. I didn't really know what Mrs. Nevermore had up her sleeve.

Ribblesdale was on his feet, slapping hands against knees one last time. "You'll be all right, Ned. Trust me on this. Just go carefully from here on out. This is a dangerous woman, not be trifled with. We'll be close by. There when you need us. Not to worry."

Numb, my mind reeling, I lurched back to the lift and took it up to our rooms. Mrs. Nevermore waited impatiently, decked out in elegant travel clothes as an ancient porter gathered our luggage.

"Ned, wherever have you been? Honestly! A simple thing like sending a telegram. I suppose you were on that lift. Now come along. We're off to Vienna!"

THIRTY-THREE

The owners of the *Orient Express* liked to boast that in the year of 1899 with new tracks laid across the continent, they could move a passenger from Paris to Constantinople in just sixty-seven hours. But who wanted to spend sixty-seven hours on a train? Not me, thanks very much.

By the time we arrived in Westbahnhof train station's great hall with its impressive iron-beamed awning, traveling from Paris to Strasbourg and from Strasbourg overland to Vienna, I was frankly relieved to be on firm ground again. Perhaps I was not cut out to be a traveler.

Mrs. Nevermore, however, seemed as fresh as ever as she shot out the arched entranceway and down the steps trailed by three porters grappling with our luggage, summoning the horse-drawn Faiker that would take us into the city.

Ah, Vienna! The capital of the Austrian empire captured in a creamy swirl of fin-de-siècle, one hundred and five square miles (the rival to London in total area) bursting with art and intellect, wrapped in the architecture of Josef Hoffmann and Otto Wagner, caressed by the music of Beethoven, Schubert, Brahms, and of course, Strauss, who alas, had expired that very year.

Rings spread out from the River Danube like a lovely open fan. The grandest of these rings, not to mention the newest, was the Ringstrasse, a monument to Emperor Franz Joseph's desire for greatness. Built upon the ruins of the fortifications that once extended for three miles around the city, the Ringstrasse was a *via triumphalis* one hundred and eighty-seven feet wide, within whose confines could be found stately edifices, gothic cathedrals, imperial palaces and fine parks.

The Ringstrasse served as an informal demarcation line, keeping artists anxious to change the world away from suburban bureaucrats determined to keep that world much as it always had been. Coffee houses filled with revolutionaries reading newspapers, playing chess, and consuming endless amounts of coffee and schnapps—polite revolutionaries it should be said for here in Vienna, changing the world was one thing, but good manners were everything.

* * *

The hotel Sacher Wien stood opposite the State Opera. Edward Sacher founded the hotel, but it was his plump wife, the former Anna Fuchs, a butcher's daughter, who made it a success. Frau Sacher had a very small hand, everyone said, but it showed up everywhere. Mrs. Nevermore and I found her in her office working away at the damask tablecloth she embroidered during what little time she was able to take away from her hotel duties.

"You see, everyone who stays here who is anybody—and everyone here is somebody—writes their name upon my tablecloth," she stated, without looking up. "Later, I stitch the autograph with thread. All the famous names of Vienna are represented."

"I don't see the emperor's name," Mrs. Nevermore said.

A frown marred Frau Sacher's plump, smooth features. "He will soon sign it." But now she stopped sewing and looked up at the two of us.

"César Ritz suggested I get in touch with you," said Mrs. Nevermore.

"He has surfaced in Paris, I see."

"He has taken Paris by storm."

"I wonder about these storms," said Frau Sacher. "Didn't César also take London by storm? Then the storm abated, and he hurried away in the night amid a flurry of interesting rumors. At least, this is what one hears in remote Vienna."

"He speaks highly of you," Mrs. Nevermore said, seating herself so that she faced Frau Sacher.

"No, he doesn't," Frau Sacher replied firmly. "I doubt if he speaks of me at all. Even so, I can hardly chastise him. After all, he sends to me the remarkable Mrs. Nevermore."

"So you know who I am."

"You might even say I know who everyone is. But possibly that is too much, since I do not know this fine young man."

"Ned Arnheim," said Mrs. Nevermore. "An orphan."

"I dislike waltzes," I said.

Frau Sacher smiled patiently. "I am not certain whether Vienna is ready for a waltz-hating orphan. We shall see."

From her valise, Mrs. Nevermore withdrew a box of cigars and offered its contents to Anna Sacher.

Her blue eyes grew large as she surveyed this unexpected prize. "Romeo y Julieta," she said. "Some say it is too mild and believe the Partagas has a stronger flavor. But I prefer these."

Eagerly Frau Sacher plucked a cigar from the box, and then produced a penknife, adroitly cutting off the cap. At the same time, Mrs. Nevermore removed a Vesta matchbox from her purse. Opening it, she chose one of the wax matches inside.

Mrs. Nevermore struck the pink head along the ridge at the bottom of the matchbox and then lit Frau Sacher's cigar. She inhaled luxuriously.

"A perfect draw," she commented after slowly exhaling. "You will join me, of course." Her eyes contained the suggestion of a challenge: What are you made of, Mrs. Nevermore?

Withdrawing another cigar, she said, "I too prefer the Romeo y Julieta."

The two women proceeded to smoke in silence. Reluctantly Frau Sacher removed the cigar from her mouth. "Sitting here each day I hear many secrets, but then again I hear nothing at all," she said. "This is why I am successful, you understand. I hear but I do not hear. I see but I don't see. I am that most rare of things, discreet. Also, I have a good nose for cigars—and problems."

Frau Sacher waved her cigar and smiled brightly. "Are you to be a problem for me, Mrs. Nevermore?"

"I see your cigar has gone out," Mrs. Nevermore said.

She stared at the box of Vestas. It slid open. Presently one of the matches lifted into the air, its head making a hissing sound as the wax ignited. The match moved like a tiny tailing comet over to Frau Sacher. Unperturbed, Frau Sacher leaned forward and relit the end of the cigar against the hovering flame.

She sat back, contemplating Mrs. Nevermore. Then she snapped her fingers and the match erupted in a phosphorescent glow before disappearing.

Mrs. Nevermore focused on the cigar box. Its lid closed with a soft snap and it became airborne.

"The Countess Misa Wydenbruck-Esterházy."

"One of the city's foremost hostesses."

Frau Sacher calmly watched the levitating cigar box as it shot through the air towards her.

"I understand Countess Misa hosts a garden party this afternoon to which all Vienna is invited and at which the famed Natalia Boyer will perform her much-acclaimed magic tricks."

"That is my understanding as well."

"I would like to be there," said Mrs. Nevermore. "So I can expose young Ned to the various aspects of Viennese society."

The cigar box came to a stop not far from the end of Frau Sacher's nose. She smiled. "I believe Countess Misa would be delighted to know that such a personage as yourself is staying with us. She would think me remiss if I failed to inform her of your presence—and of course, the presence of our young gentleman here."

"That would be most appreciated."

Frau Sacher shifted her head. The box lid popped open, allowing the cigars to fly out. They danced on air, like puppets pulled by invisible strings.

"I take you at your word you are not trouble. There are those, alas, who would argue the point, particularly when Natalia Boyer is involved."

"I cannot imagine who would say such things," said Mrs. Nevermore.

She focused on the hanging cigars. They flew back into the box. The lid snapped closed again. The cigar box dropped down onto the side table beside Frau Sacher's chair.

She looked at the box with satisfaction and then laughed good-naturedly.

"I am smoking a fine cigar in gracious company and it is a lovely day in the capital of the world, so I will pay no attention to such idle talk. Still, a word of advice before you take your leave: do nothing to disappoint me."

"I would rather die first," Mrs. Nevermore said.

THIRTY-FOUR

A butler fed wood into the fireplace in our rooms via a trapdoor that opened onto the hall.

I scanned the local newspapers, noting that the anti-Semitic press, which was to say most of the journals in Vienna, had launched another attack against Gustav Mahler, the newly appointed director of the Vienna opera, unable to come to terms with the fact that a Jew, the son of a mere tavern keeper, had taken on such an important position. Karl Luger, the mayor as well as the city's leading anti-Semite, expressed his horror. How could such a terrible thing have happened?

Once the room was bathed in light from the fire, the butlers vanished. Mrs. Nevermore emerged from her bath, swathed in one of the hotel's robes, her face scrubbed clean, reducing it to startling innocence.

I put the newspapers to one side. "So Frau Sacher is one of us," I said.

"She is indeed."

"Then the power of the Strange is not possessed only by people in Paris."

"Of course not," said Mrs. Nevermore. "People are different everywhere. Despite the best efforts of those who are not different to stamp them out, they manage to survive."

"But how did you know about Frau Sacher?"

"You know these things, that's all."

"I didn't know," I said.

"You will."

She seated herself at the table beside me.

"This afternoon, Ned, I will be making use of your unique talents as well as your resourcefulness, in ways I have not used them until now."

"I don't want to do this."

"I know you don't. But allow me to make you aware of certain things. Perhaps then you will understand why it's necessary for you to help out."

I did not want to hear tales designed only to get me to do what every fiber in my body told me I should not do. But I could not resist. I wanted to know more and here was the opportunity. "All right," I said.

"As you know, I have grave doubts about the species that is man. But your father was different."

"He had the power of the Strange?"

"Flix was unlike any man I've ever met. And because he was, I loved him in a way that I never thought possible to love anyone."

"So you do know something of love," I said.

"Something. But not everything. Not nearly enough, I suppose. But I do believe Flix loved me, although he had the same suspicion of love as I did. For us, love was always the mark's weakness, the thing you used, the power you wielded. Now here we were victims of the one confidence game no one ever wins."

* * *

According to Mrs. Nevermore, Flix Arnheim became involved with a syndicate of British and French investors led by an international scoundrel named Edmond Corbeau.

The syndicate was set up to build a canal through Argentina. The French had tried it across the Isthmus of Panama in 1878 but that collapsed in 1892 amid ruin and scandal.

Still, the prospect of a watery ditch running between the Atlantic and the Pacific remained an irresistible dream. The Argentine Canal Project was but the latest attempt to make that dream a reality. The project was to be massive; the profits enormous. The French were ambivalent after the Panama fiasco and so Corbeau turned to the British government.

Here there was more interest, but the experience of the French remained fresh in everyone's mind and thus the government hesitated to become involved. The whole issue was due to come before parliament where it would be voted on.

Weeks before the vote, Edmond Corbeau dispatched Flix and a hand-picked team to London in order to persuade cabinet members the Argentine Canal Project was in Britain's best interest. The team included Mrs. Nevermore; a ruined actor, Jack Dozen; and a mysterious young magician with one eye, Natalia Boyer.

In the weeks that followed, the team uncovered secret after secret—the inamorata of a certain duke taken to strong drink; the right honorable gentleman with the unpaid bar bill at Boodle's; the admiral attempting to conceal the Jewish blood running through his fiancée's veins; the prominent barrister and family man besotted by London's most notorious prostitute, not to be confused with the Church of England bishop in love with the town's prettiest boys.

The price to keep these secrets? Simple—support the marvelous canal that would only enrich and enhance the Empire. So successful were they that it looked as though the proposal would easily pass parliament.

Then Sir Robert Chiltern emerged as a singularly effective opponent, an effectiveness heightened by Flix's inability to detect any trace of scandal in Sir Robert's pristine life.

All seemed lost until Flix stumbled upon a young marquess desperate to hide the fact that he had impregnated a beloved cousin. The marquess had recently returned from South Africa where another Boer war was brewing and where his father's company had been trying to break the so-called dynamite monopoly that effectively shut the British out of the country's hugely profitable mining industry.

One British company, however, was having no such problems. The company imported indentured Chinese workmen, virtual slaves forced to toil away in chains. The South African mines could not get enough of these Chinese and thus the British company flourished in what was known as the Pigtail Business. The marquess revealed that the company's chief investor was that great humanitarian Sir Robert Chiltern. That was how he had made his fortune.

Flix discovered a letter to Lord Salisbury from Sir Robert, imploring the prime minister to approve a plan that would allow similarly indentured Chinese to work in England, "at vast savings to the British mining industry."

In a country full of working class men who feared losing their jobs at the hands of foreign workers, not to mention an aristocracy that at least gave lip service to its horror of the South African mining situation, the news of Sir Robert's involvement would have meant ruin.

On the eve of his speech to the Commons denouncing the canal plan, the evidence of Sir Robert's South African duplicity was presented to him.

"And who presented this letter?"

Mrs. Nevermore said, "I did."

"Why you?"

"I was involved with Lord Goring, Sir Robert's closest personal friend, and thus had easy access to him."

"But something went wrong."

Mrs. Nevermore acknowledged this with a nod. Natalia had fallen in love with Flix. Corbeau, in love with Natalia, had Flix arrested on trumped-up fraud charges. Mrs. Nevermore went to Lord Goring. In exchange for Flix's release, she would give up the letter incriminating Sir Robert. Lord Goring quickly agreed.

The police dropped the charges against Flix. Sir Robert recovered the letter, and delivered a speech in the House of Commons denouncing the Argentine Canal Project, bringing it to a swift, ignominious end.

Soon after, Sir Robert divested himself of his South African mining interests, and gave up any idea of importing workers into Britain. By then, Corbeau's investors had lost thousands. Corbeau blamed Flix and Mrs. Nevermore and swore revenge.

"So Edmond Corbeau killed my father," I said.

Mrs. Nevermore vehemently shook her head. "I believe it was a person consumed with jealousy, desperate to rob me of the one thing of real value in my life, someone who would stop at nothing."

I breathed the word: "Natalia."

"Now you know why we are in Vienna. Business, of course, but we also aim to settle accounts."

"Supposing I have no desire to settle?"

"This is for your father, Ned. This is something you should want for him. You have the power of the Strange. Now you can put it to good use."

"I don't know," I said. "How should I settle accounts on a man I barely knew, and who had precious little interest in his own son?"

"I'm sorry you feel that way, Ned, truly I am." She did not sound sorry at all.

"There's one other thing," I said.

"What is that?"

"There was no Argentine canal. My father, you, Corbeau, and Natalia, none of you had any intention of building a canal across Argentina. It was all a fraud, wasn't it?

"Come along, Ned," said Mrs. Nevermore. "We don't want to be late for the countess's party."

THIRTY-FIVE

Countess Misa Wydenbruck-Esterházy lived at number 53 Lange Gasse in the Josefstadt district behind the Ringstrasse, one of those impressive mid-18th century houses shaded by lovely elm trees for which the city was famous.

Frisky marble cherubs entwined above the gates ignoring the carriages coming and going. Mrs. Nevermore and I insinuated ourselves among the arrivals sweeping up the perron steps, taking in the buzz of the latest gossip.

"Hans says he won't go there again," said an aging lovely clad in autumn green.

"The emperor calls, Hans will be there in a flash, as would we," said her husband, a stovepipe like most of the men present. No matter where you went, it was, sadly, a world of stovepipes.

"No, no. He says that you can't even eat at the palace. The food is awful, and the emperor is served first of course, and he eats so fast that he is finished his meal before anyone else is even served."

"And that means what?" demanded her husband.

"It means that the guests don't get to eat because protocol doesn't allow anyone to be served once the emperor is finished. You leave the palace positively starving!"

We came through an entranceway flanked by Tuscan capitals, along an ornate arcade and onto a wide terrace overlooking lavish gardens. In the midst of the gardens a small black stage, like a funeral shroud, had been set for the afternoon's performance.

Guests on the terrace pointed and gestured and indulged in the all-consuming art of Viennese gossip, interrupted from time to time so the participants could lunge at passing waiters laden with trays of hors d'oeuvres.

Within seconds the trays were stripped of their creamy, pastry-shrouded delicacies leaving the waiters to stagger away as though retreating from a battle lost.

"What do you suppose they are talking about?" I asked.

"I don't have to suppose," replied Mrs. Nevermore. "I know they discuss Emperor Franz Joseph."

"What do they say?"

"They do not say so much as they speculate—and complain. There is endless conjecture about the emperor's wife, murdered in Switzerland; the son who committed suicide; his brother's untimely death in Mexico; the tragedy of his life and how he endures."

"And the complaints?"

"What a bore it is at court, how dreadful the food, how conventional the hosts, how awful the manners. They hate it, of course, but in this society not to be at court is to invite disaster."

"So all the grumbling and complaining isn't serious?"

"Oh, but it is. Despite the tragedies of his life, or maybe because of them, the emperor is Europe's dullest monarch. He is a military man and so pursues the frugal life of a soldier. He lives in two small rooms, sleeps on an iron cot, and gets up at four each morning. He does not go out at night, eats plain food, and hardly drinks."

Down in the garden a dumpling of a woman in a burgundy dress stepped out from behind the stage curtain and announced, "Ladies and gentleman, I am Countess Misa Wydenbruck-Esterházy."

The announcement was greeted with applause. I grew tense. The show was about to begin. On the stage, the countess blushed.

"I have a wonderful surprise," she went on. "An entertainment like nothing you have ever seen. Magic, I say. Real magic, dark and very, very mysterious."

The countess's thin voice raised to a high squeal: "I give you incomparable Natalia!"

The curtain swung open and Natalia stepped out onto the stage, shimmering in shades of lemon, a pale goddess of magic, gathering the crowd around her, everyone deserting gossip and the terrace to crowd the foot of the stage. If magic was to be played out then so too were tricks, because that's all magic was in the end, was it not, a trick, sleight of hand? So everyone wanted to be close enough to catch the deception. Except by now, I knew differently. The trick was, there was no trick.

Without preamble, Natalia flicked her slim hands in the air and produced of all things, a simple needle like the one used with thread. She held the needle between her thumb and forefinger so everyone could see it clearly. Then she popped it into her mouth and swallowed it.

That elicited gasps from her audience, including, I have to admit, myself. Natalia produced more needles and swallowed them. The gasps grew louder as the numbers of needles increased. I had never seen anything like it. Her audience was transfixed.

Finally, instead of a needle, Natalia's twinkling fingers conjured a length of white thread. This too she swallowed. She paused, her face becoming solemn. The crowd went silent.

With a clap of her hands that startled us all, Natalia reached into her mouth and pulled out a needle, now attached to the white thread. She continued to pull at the thread and out came another needle and then another and another, until, as she backed across the stage, dozens of needles gleamed in the air, the thread strung through them. Only when she had reached the far side of the stage and could go no further did the final needle emerge.

No sooner did we all break into astonished applause, than Natalia snapped her fingers and the line of needles suspended in air disappeared in a blaze of light and a puff of smoke.

Amid the applause and cheers, Edmond Corbeau, carrying an array of ropes and handcuffs, and wearing a coat of red silk and gold brocade, pushed a large upright trunk onstage.

Natalia moved to the edge of the stage. Intrigued, the crowd pressed closer.

"I require some assistance," Natalia announced.

Her hand shot out, pointing at me. "That handsome young man right there. Monsieur, would you be so kind as to join me?"

I looked over at Mrs. Nevermore. Her gaze did not meet mine. I was on my own.

"It's all right, I won't bite you, I promise," said Natalia from the stage.

"But perhaps you will make me disappear," I said in a tremulous voice, knowing full well she might well be capable of doing exactly that.

"I won't make you disappear for long."

More laughter accompanied my ascent to the stage. Natalia took my hand in hers. "I'm going to ask this young gentleman to do something I would ask of no other man—I am going to ask him to tie me up." Everyone roared.

She handed me two thin ropes and then placed her hands behind her back, wrists together. "Tie me tight as you can, please. Use all your strength."

I did as I was instructed, sweating nervously binding the ropes around her wrists. Natalia grimaced playfully as I tightened the knots, causing the audience to laugh and me to sweat more. I noticed Mrs. Nevermore, grim among the laughing faces.

"That's very good," Natalia announced when I finished. She turned to the audience, trying to yank her wrists apart, unable to do it. "As you can see ladies and gentlemen, the first man ever to tie me up has made an extraordinary job of it."

Corbeau reappeared and that made me jump. He carried a large cloth sack. He kept his eyes fixed on Natalia. She pirouetted elegantly, despite her bound wrists. Suddenly the skirt of her lemony dress was gone, revealing a corset and black tights.

Corbeau unceremoniously seized her and proceeded to stuff her into the sack. As soon as this was done, he threw open the door to the trunk. Then he hauled the sack over and hung it inside before closing and locking the trunk.

With a clap of his hands, he signaled the curtain to close so that now the audience could not see the trunk or me.

That's when Corbeau thrust a cloth into my mouth. I struggled, choking on the rag, unable to breathe. My nostrils filled with a dreadful odor.

I got a fleeting glimpse of a stone-face Corbeau as the back of the trunk sprang open and I was propelled into it. The universe became distorted, as though someone had twisted it at odd angles. I heard rather than saw the door behind me close.

Everything went black.

THIRTY-SIX

I ran down an endless gilt-edged corridor, Edmond Corbeau hot on my
heels. A fuzzy consciousness asserted itself. My head throbbed and my
mouth was dry, as though I had not had anything to drink for days. I opened
my eyes and found myself not running but slumped on a seat inside a grand
auditorium.

On the stage, a circle of light threw into dim outline a knot of exhaust-
ed-looking men and women. An intense wire-thin fellow in shirtsleeves and
spectacles, his black hair in wild disarray, abruptly grabbed a rotund man
around the waist and lifted him bodily off his feet. The two men, locked in
unwieldy embrace, staggered across the stage.

"There!" he cried, planting the rotund man down. "That is where I want
you in this very large opera house! This precise spot in our beloved Staats-
soper. Nowhere else. Right there!"

Flush-faced with embarrassment, the rotund man nodded in dumb shock
as his attacker wheeled and stalked across the stage. The others reared back as
though an unfathomable horror approached.

"I am appalled by the laziness and sloppiness I see," he yelled. "Appalled!
I thought I had escaped this sort of mediocrity when I came here, but apparently not. It grows and festers like some terrible disease. Well, I will not stand
for it! You will be better than you ever imagined. You know how you will do
that? By doing exactly as I say!"

He lunged at the group and everyone cringed as though the monster was
about to devour them.

"The first time an audience hears Wagner's music they should be shaken
to the depth of their souls—swept away by its force and its chaotic complex-
ity."

He abruptly turned to the orchestra pit and raising a previously unseen baton, called out, "We start the introduction."

From the dark recesses below the stage where the musicians were stationed, roared the opening notes of *Tristan and Isolde*. Tristan's name meant sadness and was given to him after his mother died in childbirth, thus I felt a certain kinship with Wagner's tragic hero. Was I not also tragic? And heroic? In my drugged state of misery, I liked to think I was.

"Listen!" The maestro screeched over the music. "Wagner is like Prometheus. There is fire here, and it has to sear and destroy. You must help make that happen. At the end, I want the audience on its feet, stunned and silent. Then and only then will we have served Wagner the way he truly must be served."

With a curt jab of his baton, the hidden orchestra was cut to silence. Nobody on stage moved. The maestro wheeled around and that's when he spotted Natalia in the aisle below the stage. I saw her, too, through the mist that still shrouded the world, no longer in lemony afternoon creams but stark nighttime black.

He hurried down to her. "I thought you weren't interested in me."

The others, sensing salvation had arrived, began to scurry away, heads low, the convicts escaping their prison.

Natalia turned and smiled at me. "Gustav, do you know my friend Neddie Arnheim?"

He peered into the darkness. By now I had managed to rise to my feet, uncertainly mounted on rubbery legs.

"Neddie, I'd like you to meet my dear friend, Herr Gustav Mahler. Gustav is the conductor of the Staatsoper orchestra. If one reads the papers, he has ruined the opera entirely."

"The anti-Jewish newspapers say those things," Mahler said. He adjusted his wire-rimmed glasses, trying to get a better look at me.

"Herr Mahler, I am honored to meet you," I said. "I had the pleasure of hearing your Symphonic Poem at school."

Mahler threw up his hands in a helpless gesture. "The piece was not well-received. I have revised it several times since. I do not know about it, though. I just don't know about anything, any more."

He adjusted his glasses and addressed Natalia. "I should tell you, my life is really fouled up right now. You shouldn't be anywhere near me, and I should not be around you."

"I need a place where Ned and I can talk alone, Gustav, a few minutes that's all. Then I am all yours."

From the look on Mahler's face this was not an invitation he was about to turn down. "Bring him up to my rooms."

Natalia called to me in a voice as sweet as life. "Come along, Neddie. You're all right now."

Was I?

* * *

We trailed Mahler backstage. His voice echoed eerily. "Just before this opera house opened in 1869, one of the architects committed suicide because the Viennese made cruel jokes about his work, and he heard the emperor did not like what had been done. Shortly after it opened, the other architect died of a heart attack. The Viennese are said to kill off those who serve them in the cause of music. I am beginning to believe it's true.

"Naturally the entire company hates my guts. They think I ride them too hard. Perhaps I do. But it's for the music. Everything is for the music. Nothing else exists. They must realize that."

We went up into a tiny baroque apartment, consisting of a parlor and a bedroom visible through an open door. Mahler turned to Natalia. "My wife and I are seeing a doctor, a fellow named Freud."

"The alienist?"

"Here they call him a soul healer. But I don't know. It's babble, really. A lot of conversation about things it is far too late to change." He shrugged. "My wife believes he can help so I go along and I confess nonsense."

Natalia kissed his lips. "I should speak to Neddie, dear."

"It's my music," he said. "That's what no one understands. It all comes down to that, nothing else. If there was more acceptance of my music I would be happier, and perhaps not so crazy."

Natalia's fingers caressed his face. "Give us a few minutes alone, my love."

"I will be outside if you need me."

I felt very tired again. Natalia led me over to a settee and sat me down. I heard the door to the apartment open and close. Mahler was gone. We were alone. Was this what Mrs. Nevermore imagined? Should I put into play my resourcefulness? I did not feel like being resourceful. I did not feel like much of anything.

Natalia sat beside me, the good nurse with her patient, stroking my cheek the same way she stroked Mahler's. It felt wonderful. I realized suddenly how starved I was for affection. It had been so long since I felt anyone's touch. A boy's lifetime.

Her voice floated in the air, as warm and inviting as her touch.

"We must talk while we have a chance," she said. "There are things you don't know, but should. Realities you can't understand, but must."

"You kidnapped me," I said. "Is that not the reality?"

"Or perhaps I rescued you, Neddie."

"What else?" I would listen to anything in exchange for the stroke of that hand.

"I know she sent you. This is what she wanted, what she planned. Neddie my love, she is using you—and me too. Preying on my enduring love for your father."

The floating voice reported that Natalia had met Flix Arnheim years before here in Vienna, when she was a young novice magician just starting out.

Natalia had fallen for the charismatic Flix. And he was in love with her. But they needed money. Love conquered most things, my father told her. But money conquered all things. Thus they parted, each going off to pursue the various and complicated ways of the world, to discover, Natalia said, that neither of them could love anyone but the other.

In London, they met up again and their love burned brighter than ever. Any money problems soon would be resolved thanks to Flix's plan to build a canal through Argentina. The canal, when finished, would revolutionize world trade. However, it first required the approval of the British government in order to proceed. Opposition soon mounted, led by an aggressive young politician named Sir Robert Chiltern. Somehow, he would have to be stopped.

By accident Flix came into possession of a letter containing evidence that Sir Robert had grown rich through various schemes involving gold mines and indentured slaves in South Africa. If the letter became public, it would ruin the young politician and put an end to a promising career.

Flix needed someone to present the letter, a person who moved easily through London society and could comfortably reach out to Sir Robert. That person was the mysterious, enigmatic international adventuress, Laura Nevermore.

Flix, against all Natalia's instincts, enlisted her services.

Soon, however, it was evident that Laura Nevermore had fallen in love with Flix. "He pretended to take no notice, even made light of it," Natalia said. "But finally it could not be ignored and he confronted her. Do you know what he told her, Neddie?"

"He told her there was no canal, that it was all a swindle."

She looked taken aback. "No, no. Of course he didn't tell her that. Why would he tell her such a thing?"

"Perhaps it would have been true," I said.

"He told her that he loved me, that he would always love me. Laura could not handle that. She went to his apartment and that's where she did it, Neddie. That's where she stabbed him and stabbed him, and took everything from him, and everything from me, too."

A tear rolled down her cheek from that single eye. She dabbed at it with a handkerchief.

"I was to be your mother, Neddie. Flix wanted us all to be together. We were to start a new life. We would be a family."

She gulped back more tears. "So there you have it, my darling. Laura destroyed what we both loved. The day of your father's funeral?"

"I didn't see you there," I said.

"I couldn't bring myself to go. Too painful. I sent Edmond to ensure your safety until I reached you. But she got there and, well, you saw what happened. She drew a pistol on poor Edmond."

The handkerchief disappeared. Natalia sat ramrod straight, as though determined to fight against the wind.

"Now she conspires to destroy me, Neddie, and the terrible irony is that she uses you to bring about that destruction. Well, I'm not going to allow it to happen, I love you too much."

Love?

THIRTY-SEVEN

I sat up.

"I know you did not steal that money on your own," Natalia said. "She put you up to it. That is what she is about. Who you are, and what you are about, dear Neddie, that is something else entirely. I believe it has nothing to do with her. You are an honest boy and I admire that. You have been forced into things against your will. Well, it won't happen any more. Here is what we will do. We retrieve the money she stole from me. We will do it together, you and I."

"How would we do that?" I asked.

She produced an ivory-colored envelope and placed it on the seat between us.

"This is what she wants, isn't it Neddie? What she sent you for? The Savoy documents? Well, then, here they are."

I gaped at the envelope. Mrs. Nevermore was right. I was indeed resourceful. I glowed with self-importance, my previous fear tucked away.

She resumed stroking my face.

"You see, my darling boy, we use these documents as the bait that will draw her in. Once that is done, and she is defeated, we escape together. I can still be your mother, just like Flix wanted."

Natalia Boyer as my new mother, an interesting prospect. Not entirely unwelcome for a boy badly in need of a mother, I must admit.

"All I have to know is where that money is."

Ah, yes. The money. Of course. It would be the money, wouldn't it?

I eased away from that marvelous hand to give myself distance so I could see the wider view of the universe.

"Is anything wrong, Neddie?"

"Do you suppose I might have some water?" I said in voice calm as a stream at dawn. A deceiving voice; the voice I was quickly perfecting. "I'm afraid I'm feeling quite light headed again. I mean you did drug me, didn't you?"

"It's only chloroform, but it has that effect, I'm afraid. I'm so sorry about all this subterfuge, but it was the only way to get you away from her."

"It's made me very thirsty," I said.

"I'll find water and come right back."

"You're very kind," I said.

She pecked my cheek and was gone. I got to my feet unsteadily, staring at the packet lying on the settee. Oh, I was the tricky one, wasn't I? As full of trickery as any adult. Mrs. Nevermore said I had a talent for this. I said she was wrong, but perhaps not.

The envelope was in my hands. I opened it. The distinctive letterhead of the Savoy Hotel blazed atop the half dozen pages of correspondence.

I shoved the envelope into my pocket and looked around. Across the room a casement window opened into a hall. I intended to lift myself up and go sailing through. But when I tried, to my horror, I found I had no strength. The dulling effects of the chloroform had left me powerless.

I made my way over to the window, climbed onto the ledge, and then dropped down perhaps ten feet into a long passage with huge chandeliers suspended from its vault ceiling and occupied by a startled Edmond Corbeau.

He quickly recovered.

"The deceitful young Ned, son of the father, and just like him. I tried to warn her."

He reached for me. I managed to elude him, but still I could not get myself airborne. Discovering unanticipated strength in my legs, I dashed toward the staircase. Corbeau shouted and I expected him to fly up and immediately pounce upon me.

But all he could manage was a foot—he shot it out with lightning speed so that I lost my balance. I felt the weight of Corbeau on me and the next thing we were locked together, rolling down the staircase.

We thudded onto a mirrored landing. I managed to get free. I caught a glimpse of Corbeau struggling to his feet. Why was he not using his powers to stop me? No time to think about that right now as I leapt down a second set of marble stairs.

Reaching another corridor, my legs feeling stronger, I hurried blindly along, crashing through more doors until I found myself in the shadows back stage.

I stopped to catch my breath. A warren of dressing rooms and rehearsal halls lay to my right. To the left gleamed an elaborate cluster of levers and wheels, the hulking machinery for the fly tower that raised and lowered scenery. Medieval swords and daggers were set out on a nearby trestle table in anticipation of a performance of *Tristan and Isolde.*

I grabbed a sword, filled with a vague notion of defending myself against the oncoming Corbeau, and then headed onto the stage. It stretched into the enveloping darkness of the theater's gilded and tiered crater. I could just make out stairs running down past the orchestra pit on the far side.

I started across. Part of the floor fell away. I tottered on the lip of a black cavity. Another step and I would have dropped down into the bowls of the theater. Regaining my balance, I once again tried to lift myself up—and still could not do it.

Behind me, another section of the stage floor silently disappeared. I turned to see Corbeau by the machinery, working the levers that operated the trap doors built into the stage. Frozen in place, wondering which way to turn, I heard a sound and swung around just as a wall of scenery descended.

I jumped away but not fast enough to avoid being clipped by something heavy and blunt.

I tried to keep my balance, couldn't, and fell to my knees. Inches away, another part of the floor disappeared. Frantically, I fought to regain my feet, struggling to hold on to consciousness.

Corbeau loomed above me, his face curiously at peace, as though he had just said his bedtime prayers and all was right with the world.

He reached down and I was sure he would smash me with his fist. Instead, he fumbled inside my coat to get at the envelope containing the Savoy documents. Distracted, trying to lift the envelope out of my pocket, he did not notice the sword lying nearby.

But I did.

With all my strength I focused on that weapon. It rose off the floor. The blade point sliced into Corbeau's right thigh.

He howled, and snapped away from me, dropping the envelope. Staggering back, blood sputtering from his leg, cursing loudly—and then he was gone, down the rabbit hole of the open trapdoor. The magic of the theater; a murderous villain could disappear in the blink of an eye.

I stood up, feeling stronger, warrior-like; I could give Tristan himself competition. Quickly retrieving the envelope, I staggered to the stairs at the end of the stage. I hurried up the aisle past the stalls, making my way to the back of the theater.

Someone called out. Turning, I saw a lone figure outlined in uncertain light all but lost amid the stage's vastness. Natalia was Isolde, calling to her departing knight. I half expected her to break into song. I certainly expected her to turn me into an apple or make me think flying creatures were after me, some sort of magic that would stop me dead in my tracks.

Instead, she merely called out in a plaintive voice, "Neddie!"

That was all of it? *Neddie?* Nothing else? Where was the power of the Strange? It struck me like a blow: Natalia and Corbeau didn't use magic against me because they did not have any.

They did not possess the power of the Strange.

* * *

Outside the opera house, moonlight splashed cobbled streets and outlined gothic spires. I darted in and out of silent streets and squares, not trusting Corbeau's descent into that darkness or really believing that Natalia lacked the power to stop me, that her sleight of hand was no more than that.

Finally, winded, I came to a stop at the edge of the Stephansplatz. Before me rose the great towers of the Stephansdom, the cathedral that according to some was the very soul of Vienna.

Here lay sanctuary and safety. Here a body could rest and contemplate the needs of his soul, and come to some conclusions as to whether that body had just shown great strength or destroying weakness.

I crossed the square and found what I was supposed to find, an open side gate—the Singer Gate, as advertised. Above the gate, St. Paul the Apostle stared happily down, delighted to see me, a restless wicked heart.

My footsteps echoed like trailing ghosts in the vaulted nave. A gothic pulpit rose like a beacon a few yards away. I took a deep breath and went back along the length of the nave and into the transept.

The high altar was a smudge of shifting light, St. Stephen appearing to float in that light, frowning down on me, not nearly as welcoming as St. Paul. But then St. Stephen was a martyr and perhaps more difficult to fool than St. Paul when confronted with a boy so full of trickery and deceit.

Had I run away from danger? Or was I merely headed back toward it? My young head ached with the confusion of it all.

"Come along, Ned. You're late again."

Mrs. Nevermore rose from a nearby pew, a great lovely bird of prey.

"They couldn't stop me," I said.

"Of course they couldn't. You are a resourceful young man. That's why I sent you along in the first place."

"It had nothing to do with that. Natalia doesn't have the power of the Strange. Neither does Corbeau."

"We must hurry," she said.

"It's you. You have it. You conjured the creatures that attacked me. You control Peregrine. You, Mrs. Nevermore."

"Don't be ridiculous, Ned. Now come along. Otherwise we will miss our train to Paris."

THIRTY-EIGHT

I want to know more about you," I said once we were on board the *Orient Express* bound for Paris.

We sat in a dining car adorned with ashwood marquetry, picking at the Sole Normand, the tinkle of silverware and the hushed voices of our fellow passengers forming a background.

She saw the steely determination in my eyes and knew that something had lately changed. A young man sent out to steal money and lift envelopes does not come back the same.

"Do you now?" She seemed somewhat amused by the idea.

"The truth."

"The truth." She tasted the word before taking a sip of her wine as though to wash away such a foreign sound. "You are young, Ned. You have yet to learn there is no such thing as 'truth.' There are in fact as many truths as there are tellers of truths."

"I will be satisfied with your version," I said.

"And what do I get in return for all this truth?"

"The satisfaction that comes from knowing you relieved the concerns of an anguished young man."

She managed a smile. "A harder bargain would require more than mere satisfaction."

"Let's hear the truth first and then there could be other things as well."

She frowned. "I don't like this attitude of yours, Ned. You are developing an independent sense far beyond your years."

"You have no one to blame but yourself."

"I am responsible for you? Oh, dear. Then I have had a salutary effect on your personality and that is all to the good."

"Is it? I wonder when you so cheerfully use me as a pawn in your game against Natalia Boyer."

"I repeat: I did not use you. I employed you as a partner."

"Except you failed to tell me what you were up to."

"If you knew, Natalia might suspect. And if she suspected she would not have taken you, and we would not be where we are tonight."

"With you about to tell me the truth."

I wondered if truth might include a murder confession. And if it did, where would it leave me?

She sat back with a long sigh and reached into her handbag and extracted a cracked and dog-eared photograph. "I have never shown this to anyone," she said before passing it to me.

A pretty woman with sad eyes peered sullenly into the camera. The woman's name was Madeleine Wick, Mrs. Nevermore said. The photograph was taken in Birmingham after police there arrested her.

"This is my mother," she reported. The worn little photo shook in her fingers.

"Mother had the true power of the Strange, although, like the rest of us, she had no idea where it came from. It was always there, like breathing. Branded as a sorcière, a witch, she eventually found work doing a magic act with a traveling circus, a down-at-the-heels affair, barely scrapping by, playing industrial town after industrial town in the north of England."

The circus set up outside Birmingham. That's when the local police, apparently responding to a complaint, made the arrest. "She had done nothing wrong, but it did not matter. She was different and therefore a threat."

A tarnished white knight came to the rescue: Robert Baron of London and New York and various places in between, known to everyone simply as the Baron.

The Baron recently departed London where he operated a successful scam convincing creditors that he was worth millions. The creditors fell over themselves to lend him money. This enabled the Baron to purchase various estates outside the city. The estates were then stripped of their assets and resold. Somehow though, the creditors never got their money back.

Eventually, however, the London creditors ran out of patience and became suspicious. The Baron made a hasty departure for the hinterlands, landing in Birmingham where he heard reports of a real live witch held in police custody.

Curious, he arranged bail. It didn't hurt that the Baron found Madeleine

Wick unexpectedly intelligent and attractive; beauty and intelligence being necessary assets in his line of work. His newly acquired witch might prove to be useful.

The Baron whisked Madeleine off to Budapest. In the birthplace of the modern world—the Hungarian claim—the Baron, accompanied by his newly anointed baroness, caused a stir. They were a handsome, well-to-do young couple, absolutely charming, moving in the best social circles. The Baron showed his new friends the millions of francs worth of bearer bonds he carried with him in a strong box. Unfortunately, the bonds were tied up in a court battle with his deceased wife's family.

Hungarian creditors were no different than their counterparts in London, New York, and Monte Carlo. Visions of great profits dancing in their thick heads, they were only too anxious to lend the Baron and his baroness thousands of forints against the value of the bonds.

Of course, the bonds were forgeries and the court battles involving a non-existent dead wife's non-existent family would go on for years. That was fine with the Baron. So comfortable in Budapest was he that he made his baroness pregnant. He was not, it soon became clear, a man for whom impending fatherhood came as joyful news.

"I often wondered if the Baron blamed me and therefore never quite forgave me," Mrs. Nevermore said reflectively. She shrugged. "Who knows about these things? As I told you earlier Ned, we can make too much of our childhoods."

"Or maybe we can't make enough," I said.

On top of everything else, the daughter was no sooner born than Hungarian creditors, like their peers elsewhere, began to run out of patience. Impatience caused them to investigate, and the investigating created facts, and facts are the second worst enemy of the confidence artist, the first being common sense. No con man or woman can overcome either common sense or the facts.

The Baron and the baroness and their infant daughter departed Budapest by carriage in the dead of night, bound for Vienna. By now there was yet another obstacle to the Baron's ability to conduct business. The baroness had become ill. Once in Vienna, a doctor there diagnosed her with tuberculosis.

A few weeks later she succumbed to the disease.

Before a lonely daughter could fully comprehend the reality of her mother's life, let alone her death, the Baron announced that although they were both distraught, life had to go on. He needed a replacement and fast. What better candidate than the mother's daughter? If one partner was gone, best not to shed too many tears, for here was someone younger and more eager to please than her predecessor—and, it turned out, possessed of powers even stronger than those of her mother.

What's more, as time went on it became apparent the daughter had more appetite for the family business than her mother ever did. All in all, the Baron decided, a very smooth transition indeed. If anything, business was better than ever.

Or at least it was for a time. That is the trouble with the confidence game, you see. In addition to the facts and common sense, time is also an enemy. And time eventually defeats even the most brilliant confidence artist.

The gospel according to Mrs. Nevermore.

* * *

"So time defeated your father?" I asked.

"My father died a number of years ago," she stated in a formal voice.

"Leaving you with the house and the family business?"

"Let us say, he left me with many unhappy creditors, a good deal of debt, and a house in need of a new roof."

"And now the daughter requires a partner, just as her father needed one, and so here I am to carry on the proud family tradition. What's more—and again this is very much in the family tradition—I even possess the power of the Strange, although nothing like your powers, right Mrs. Nevermore? Nothing like the power of the sorcière."

Did I sound slightly bitter when I said these words? Perhaps I did at that.

"I don't need a partner, Ned," she said evenly. "But you do need a roof over your head. That is what I am providing."

"The roof leaks," I said.

"Not for much longer."

The envelope containing the Savoy documents popped out of my coat pocket. It hovered in the air and then shot across into Mrs. Nevermore's upraised hand.

"You did well, Ned," she said after checking the envelope. "Just as I knew you would."

A compliment. A form of love, I suppose.

Part IV

The Power of the Strange

THIRTY-NINE

Peregrine balanced motionless on his tree branch at number 52, and merely cocked his head inquisitively as Mrs. Nevermore and I marched across the courtyard. I glanced at him out of the corner of my eye, but otherwise was at pains to ignore him, still angry over his betrayal.

Inside the house, on being informed of my triumph recovering the Savoy documents, Gamelle scowled. Told that I had also dispatched the evil Corbeau, sending him down a black hole, the scowl turned dubious. "That is not the same as killing him," Gamelle said. "Unless I can personally cut his heart out and eat it, then I do not believe he is dead."

With no hearts to munch on, Gamelle contented himself grumbling about the one hundred thousand francs we had given up in return for a few pieces of paper. We were broke. There was nothing to eat. If I could find documents so easily, and kill off the Edmond Corbeaus of the world, why could I not be turned into the streets to scrounge for food?

Mrs. Nevermore sent a note around to the Hotel Ritz. There was no reply. Gamelle became more belligerent. Tragic mistakes had been made. Mobs of creditors howled at the gates with pitchforks. The world was about to end. Mrs. Nevermore remained calm.

On the second night we were home, I lay wide awake in my bed when I heard a familiar tapping at the window. At first I was going to ignore it, but I was feeling so miserable I wanted company, any company. I got up and went to the window and sure enough, there was Peregrine on the sill.

I opened the window and said, "I shouldn't be talking to you."

"What does that mean?" inquired Peregrine. "Does that mean you shouldn't talk to me but you will? Or you shouldn't talk to me and so won't?"

"It means I am still mad at you."

"I believe you missed me when you were in London and Vienna," he said.

"If you believe that, you're crazy."

"I also believe you are worried."

"Well, I have every reason to be, don't you think? I am trapped with people who believe they can convince governments of canals that don't exist, and sell the Eiffel Tower. I have witnessed murder, taken things that don't belong to me, and perhaps have done worse, although I can't talk about that."

"Oh, dear," said Peregrine.

"What's more, no one tells me the truth about anything, and I can't talk to anyone except a bird. Who would not be worried under those circumstances?"

"Falcon, I'm a falcon."

"I'm sorry. I talk to a falcon."

"You can count on me as a friend," he said.

"No, I don't think I can. After all, you betrayed me, Peregrine."

"I certainly did not." He sounded indignant.

"That's the amazing thing. Everyone tells me they did not lie to me even as they tell me lies. There is no such thing in this world as truth. It's been lost along with honesty and loyalty."

"I'm loyal to you," insisted Peregrine. "It may not seem so, Ned, but I am looking out for your best interests."

"I don't believe it. I don't believe I can count on you or anyone."

"I'm sorry you feel that way, but the fact is, you can count on me. One of these days you'll see that for yourself."

"I have certainly not seen it so far," I said. "What's more, I don't expect to see it any time soon."

"Well, I'm glad you're back. I wanted to tell you, that's all."

I thought I detected a note of sadness in his voice. But that was impossible. Falcons couldn't be sad for they are only falcons.

He rose up off the sill, spreading those tapered wings, and flew away into the night.

I was sorry to see him go. It was good to be talking to him again. Maybe I liked Peregrine more than I chose to let on. Perhaps I shouldn't have spoken to him the way I did.

Feeling more despondent than ever, I went back to bed and tried to fall asleep.

* * *

Another day went by.

Smiling Jack Dozen arrived. He was not smiling. "This is not going to work, Laura," I heard him say to Mrs. Nevermore. "You've gone after too big a fish this time. He's slipped the hook."

Mrs. Nevermore said nothing.

The following day a breathless messenger arrived at the door. He handed Gamelle an envelope. Inside was a dinner invitation to the Ritz. Mrs. Nevermore smiled. Jack shrugged.

"Of course they want you for dinner," he said. "They are anxious to have their precious documents back, that's all. But don't expect Prince Edward to be there. Why should he? They've got what they want—for free!"

Mrs. Nevermore did not argue the point. Instead, she went about the business of preparing herself.

"Ned," she said to me. "I want you to put on your best suit."

"Why would you want me to do that?"

"Because you are coming with me."

I was unsure whether to cheer or despair.

Arriving at the Ritz that evening, we were immediately led back to the kitchen by none other than the formidable Olivier Dabescat, the maître d'hôtel.

A steamy tropical heat rose in the Ritz kitchen so that one could barely breathe. The young men in their toques and white aprons sweated even more than the last time we visited as they chopped and cut with dedicated fury.

An *annonceur* called dinner orders as waiters marched through the rising steam bearing plates, everything overseen by a sharp-tongued *saucier* who acted as platoon sergeant, mustering his troops for battle. It should be said that the chaos here was a *controlled* chaos. Escoffier disliked the yelling and the screaming that were the hallmarks of the typical French kitchen. What's more, he frowned upon the consumption of spirits during meal preparation and instead urged his staff to drink barley water from a nearby cauldron as a way of relieving the intense heat.

The man himself stood—calmly—with the *patissier* overseeing the preparation of various deserts. As soon as he saw us, he nodded and led us into his glass-enclosed office, wiping absently at the folds of his apron. He closed the door. Quiet descended. The tumult of the kitchen was reduced to background murmur.

Escoffier smoothed his hair and gazed anxiously at us. Mrs. Nevermore reached into her purse and pulled out that all-important white envelope. She gave it to Escoffier at the very moment César Ritz stepped in, closing the door carefully behind him. His face was tense, no sign now of the carefree overseer of the rich and famous. Escoffier did not acknowledge his partner's arrival but concentrated on tearing open the envelope. Ritz eagerly plucked out the Savoy Hotel documents and together the two men apprehensively scanned their contents.

"Devastating," pronounced Escoffier without taking his eyes from the pages.

"Lies!" cried Ritz, angrily grabbing at the report and ripping it in two. "Lies! Lies! Lies!"

Escoffier stood back saying nothing as Ritz tore at the papers, reducing them to confetti-like bits fluttering to the floor. He suddenly became aware of what he was doing, and how this uncharacteristic show of anger must look to those inhabiting the other side of the glass. He quickly straightened himself around.

"Mrs. Nevermore has saved us and now we have destroyed the evidence. That's the end of it."

He took Mrs. Nevermore's hand in his. "We don't know how to thank you, madame, we truly do not. But let us at least try."

Mrs. Nevermore shook her head. "I told you before, monsieur. I don't want your money."

"Then let us return to the dining room. Auguste is preparing a wonderful meal, and I do believe, Mrs. Nevermore, we have a pleasant surprise in store for you this evening."

Whatever the surprises, they did not include our fellow dinner guests. Present once again was Marcel Proust, the arrogant Parisian who claimed to be that most questionable of all things, a novelist, a claim unsupported by anything like an actual novel.

Beside him, the well-known Brazilian dirigible flyer and adventurer, Senor Alberto Santos Dumont, tapped his fork lightly against his folded linen napkin.

There was, however, no sign of the Prince of Wales.

Mrs. Nevermore froze briefly when she saw the two men. A faint cloud crossed that otherwise perfectly unperturbed face. Whatever she was expecting this evening, this was not part of it.

She allowed herself to be seated beside Santos Dumont. The usual greetings were exchanged. Mrs. Nevermore's smile appeared to have been glued in place. Ritz, oblivious to his guest's unhappiness, bounced about making sure wine was poured, napkins unfolded.

Proust's uninterested gaze fell upon me.

"The young man uncertain of his sexuality," he observed.

"I'm not certain I would put it that way," I said.

"Then how would you put it?"

"I would say unknowing."

"To be crossing uncharted territory without knowing, that is very dangerous."

"Yes, I suppose it is," I agreed.

A flurry of excitement erupted around the entrance. Olivier stiffened, adjusted his monocle several times, and cleared his throat.

The Prince of Wales, done in rich chocolate shades, burst into the room. His face lit up when he saw Olivier. *"Mon ami!"* He pumped the maître d's hand. "I just saw Pilly Baker at Dunrobin. He said to say hello."

"I remember him," said Olivier, grinning.

The prince lowered his voice. "He doesn't look as bad in a kilt as they say."

"Glad to hear it," said Olivier.

The prince dashed toward Ritz who was on his feet, rushing to greet his old friend from the Savoy Hotel. "My brother sends his regards," said the prince.

"The Duke of Connaught," Ritz said. "Charming fellow."

"At the end of the month he goes to Plymouth to begin a long cruise. Two years I should think."

"Two years," said Ritz. "My. My."

The prince swirled around to our table. His rosy face lit like a Christmas tree. "Mrs. Nevermore! Jolly good!"

The prince hurried over and kissed her hand. He did not smell of cigars this evening.

"Delightful to have you back in Paris, Your Highness," she stated formally.

"Do you know the Grosvenors?"

"Of London?" Mrs. Nevermore looked vaguely surprised.

"Southampton. I spent four days in the Reay Forest with them."

"You don't say," said Mrs. Nevermore.

"Shot four stags," said the prince.

"Impressive," Mrs. Nevermore said brightly.

"Twenty-one killed altogether. A lovely weekend, really. I also shoot in Windsor and Richmond. Next month I'm to shoot with General Hall in Newmarket."

"You're so busy," she said.

Ritz introduced the prince to the others seated at the table.

"Are you interested in flight, Your Highness?" asked Santos Dumont.

"Oh, no dear boy, I'm a member of the Royal Family, you see. We're not allowed to fight. We have to be nice to everyone."

"No, no, I said flight."

"Flying? Good Lord, no. Baccarat. Grouse hunting. And the horses, of course. Those are my interests. Why on earth would I be interested in flying?"

If only to escape Senor Dumont, the prince's gaze lighted upon me. "And what of you, young man? Ned, is it not?"

"It is indeed, Your Highness," I replied. "I believe in hard work and honesty."

The prince seemed taken aback. "Admirable qualities, I must say."

"And morality," I added. "Especially a moral life dedicated to honest achievement."

"Mrs. Nevermore, you've certainly managed to keep this young man on the straight and narrow."

"Oh, he manages the straight and the narrow all by himself," said Mrs. Nevermore.

"Most admirable," the prince said amiably.

Mrs. Nevermore shifted uncomfortably in her seat. Auguste Escoffier hurried into view, harried and distracted as usual. "Ah, and here is our beloved Auguste," exclaimed Ritz. The prince broke into another smile and rose to shake the chef's hand. Escoffier looked even more flustered.

"Auguste, please describe the particulars of the work of genius you have created tonight in honor of His Highness."

The Prince of Wales beamed. Escoffier, even though he had been through the same ritual dozens of times, still managed to give off a combination of surprise and horror at being the object of such attention. Sole Alice would follow the cream of carrot soup, he announced.

Edward looked pleased. "Named after Princess Alice, Countess of Athlone." He smiled at Proust. "My niece. A delightful young thing. English.

Obviously it will be the hit of our dinner."

"English sole in a French dining room," said Proust with disgust. "Only a chef of Monsieur Escoffier's greatness could possibly bring off what would otherwise be a culinary travesty."

FORTY

The newspaper reporter Georges Duroy arrived. Mrs. Nevermore looked even more discomfited. Instead of an intimate evening with the future head of the British Empire, she now had to share the prince with the gossip-spouting, wine-swilling Duroy.

Ritz by contrast could not have been happier. He enthusiastically welcomed Duroy while a waiter quickly filled his wine glass. He then introduced the Prince of Wales. If Duroy understood he was shaking hands with the future King of England, he gave no sign, but then he was French, and what self-respecting Frenchman would admit to knowing anything about the English, let alone who their next King might be?

"Georges brings us the most delicious gossip in Paris," announced Ritz in gleeful tones. "Give us a name, Georges. Tantalize us with a name!"

Duroy slurped down the wine and smacked his lips. He sat back so as to allow the waiter to refill his glass. "A name everyone in Paris knows," pronounced Duroy.

"Captain Dreyfus!" declared Ritz with glee.

"Ah but this is gossip, not travesty," said Duroy.

"Then what other name in France is known by all of France?"

"Gustave Eiffel," Duroy announced.

Silence descended. Ritz's face fell into gloom. "Gustave Eiffel? The tower builder? The well known Parisian bore?"

The disappointment in Ritz's voice caused the hovering waiter to pause, the wine bottle held at an angle in mid-air, as though uncertain whether to continue, given Duroy's abruptly uncertain status at the table.

"He has fallen from favor with the government." Duroy spoke at an uncharacteristically speedy clip, as though attempting to outrun his audience's fading attention.

"Thus, finally there is a move afoot to rid Paris of his dreadful iron eyesore."

"The Eiffel Tower is an eyesore?" Edward's tone sounded incredulous.

"You believe it isn't?" This from Proust.

"Well," sputtered the prince, "I rather like it."

"As do I," added Santos Dumont. "In fact it is my ambition to circle the tower in a dirigible."

"My God," said Proust with a melodramatic groan. "Reason enough right there to tear it down."

"Which is precisely what is to happen!" interjected Duroy in an explosion of wine-scented words.

Duroy's blurted revelation reduced Ritz's guests to a distracted murmur. Pleased with the effect he had created, Duroy smacked his lips and polished off the second glass of wine. The waiter quickly poured a third.

"It is all highly confidential, of course," Duroy continued. "No one is supposed to know."

The prince inclined toward Duroy. "But they really intend to tear it down?"

"Indeed."

"How is that possible?"

"It is not as outrageous as it may seem," said Duroy in the calmly authoritative voice of a man who knows he has the facts at his command. "Quite simply, the tower is ten years old. It was never intended to stand forever. The only reason it has survived this long is because that arrogant sot Eiffel lobbied so hard to keep it up. Well, as I said, Eiffel no longer carries much weight with the government. Also, the tower is in need of expensive repairs, and no one wants to spend the money. Easier to go ahead with the original plan and get rid of it as soon as l'Exposition Universelle is finished."

"Who is going to do this?" demanded Edward. "Who will rid France of her Eiffel Tower?"

"Well, that is the question is it not? A very large and important question, I might add. Whoever is chosen, the demolition will be worth millions. What makes it all the more interesting is that the fate of the project has been entrusted to a single man."

"A Frenchman, I trust," said Proust.

"In fact, Mrs. Nevermore, I believe you know the person in question."

"I?" said Mrs. Nevermore in a surprised voice. "I'm afraid my association with the Eiffel Tower is like that of every Parisian—something that cannot be avoided each time one steps outside."

"Are you not familiar with Monsieur Arnaud Poisson?"

"My rather peculiar brother-in-law?"

"The deputy director general of the Ministère des postes et télégraphes. Correct?"

"A dull government bureaucrat, I fear."

"He will decide the fate of the tower!"

"Evidence of just how dull he is," said Mrs. Nevermore.

There was general laughter at the table. Duroy's flushed face drooped with seriousness.

"As long as he does not allow the project to fall into the clutches of the Jew financiers who daily jeopardize the welfare, honor, and security of France."

"There is a possibility of that happening?" asked the prince.

"Of course it is possible," declared Duroy. "Jews destroying the Eiffel Tower? Very possible indeed. That is why I have it on the best authority that Monsieur Poisson will go to any lengths in order to prevent that from happening even if it means assigning the task to foreigners. There will be no shortage of applicants. After all, the profits for anyone charged with the contract to dismantle the tower will be enormous."

Mrs. Nevermore, other than to address questions about her brother-in-law, had remained silent throughout this exchange. I had been so engrossed in what was being said, so devastated at the news the tower might be destroyed, that I had failed to keep an eye on her—until she unexpectedly rose from the table.

"I'm afraid, gentlemen, you will have to excuse me." She turned to me. "Come along, Ned."

I stumbled to my feet, as did everyone else. Ritz recovered enough to say, "My dear woman is everything all right?"

"I'm afraid I have another appointment."

"But that's impossible!" the prince exclaimed. "We've not had an opportunity to talk."

"I do look forward to seeing you again soon, Your Highness."

And before anyone could object further, Mrs. Nevermore sailed out of the dining room. I followed her through the esplanade into the lobby.

"What are you about?" I demanded. "You do not have another appointment."

"Don't I? I would have sworn I did."

"I am hungry and therefore was looking forward to Monsieur Escoffier's cooking."

"You must learn that the time to make an exit has nothing to do with your stomach."

"Did you not hear what was being said about the Eiffel Tower? They are going to tear it down. That's dreadful news."

"Terrible."

"It puts an end to your plans," I said.

"So it would seem," she agreed.

"That's why you should have allowed Escoffier to pay us. Now we have nothing."

"Ned, when will you ever learn? In order to make a lot of money, it is sometimes necessary to make it look as though you do not need a little money."

"But surely now that the city plans to tear down the tower, you cannot possibly sell it." I came to a stop. "That is true, is it not? The city does plan to destroy the tower. Doesn't it?"

"Monsieur Duroy is a reputable reporter. I presume he knows what he is talking about."

Outside, she started across place Vendôme. I hurried to catch up.

"So there is no grift?"

She did not answer. "Did you hear me, Mrs. Nevermore?"

"It's a pleasant enough evening," she announced. "We will walk home."

"Walk home? But I am tired and hungry. Can't we take a carriage?"

"Alas, for the moment, a carriage is not in our budget."

And so we walked away from the Ritz, the Prince of Wales, a lot of money, and a good meal. After all we had been through, we had nothing to show for it. For the life of me I could not understand this woman.

FORTY-ONE

I felt terrible. My mouth was dry and my head throbbed, as though the weight of all that I had to contend with was simply too much for one boy's brain.

What was I to do if they destroy my beloved tower? That would be the end of me would it not?

My head continued its drum-like banging. My mouth felt even drier. My body ached. I needed air, some time to think.

Finishing dressing, I debated whether to take my sketchbook and pencils, decided against it, and went out the door into the courtyard. No sign of Peregrine. Just as well. I didn't want to deal with him this morning.

Each step was an effort, as though heavy weights had attached themselves to my legs overnight. My breathing came in sharp, short rasps. I pushed myself forward.

The day was already warming, the sun shaking itself free from low-level clouds as I came along the river via the Quai d'Orsay, the tower looming into view. I reached the Champ de Mars. The tower was a glistening iron anchor before me.

Feeling weaker than ever, I made my way beneath the tower's maze of girders, ignoring the morning crowds swirling past me. I stumbled and fell to my knees, unable to move further.

I didn't have to.

An energy charge surged through my body. The tiredness began to fade, the dryness in my mouth disappeared. I felt strong again. It was as if a terrible beast had been lifted off me.

Still on my knees, I looked up into the genial face of Inspector Cecil Ribblesdale of the London Metropolitan Police.

"So how have you been, Ned?" the inspector inquired good-naturedly.

The Sûreté's Anton Ganimard lingered nearby. They were like two black crows in bowler hats blotting the sun.

"Pleasant trip abroad was it? London weather not so bad, and Vienna lovely, of course, as it always is this time of year."

Ganimard stepped forward to peer down at me. "What are you doing on the ground like that? Are you sick?"

"Now, now, that's enough, Anton," admonished Ribblesdale. "The boy seems a trifle pale is all."

He settled onto his haunches so that his cheery English face was inches from mine. "Tell you what, Ned. You do look as though you could use something to eat. Why not come along with us and we'll treat you to a bite while we have a talk?"

"Talk about what?"

"Life and love, son; your recent travels, views on the **Dreyfus** affair. Up to you. You like sticky buns? Of course you do. Who **can resist these** wonderful Parisian pastries? Put the English to shame, they do."

"Everything about France puts the English to shame," **said** Ganimard.

Ribblesdale slapped his hands against his knees to signal **he** was straightening. "Except we run the world, Anton. You get up in the morning and make those delicious pastries. We get up and run the world."

Ribblesdale addressed me. "What say you, Ned? I know just the place. Shall we be off?"

He spoke to me like a child, but that was fine. The less they thought of me, the more I gained. Had I learned that from Mrs. Nevermore? More likely recent events caused me to figure it out for myself.

Ribblesdale helped me to my feet.

* * *

Ribblesdale and Ganimard took me to a pâtisserie on a tiny jewel of a square called place de Furstenberg. The interior was paneled in wood-framed gilt. I soon found myself gorging on a pain au raisin while the two policemen stared across the table as though I was a science experiment gone horribly wrong.

Ribblesdale nattered on about being a lover of French pâtisseries in general and in particular the chocolate delicacies contained in this little shop. Here, according to Ribblesdale, was offered only the best Madeleine, the most incredible Gateau Opera, the finest Baba au rhum, not to mention a creamy Paris-Brest worth dying for.

Finally, after the sort of grave consideration that goes into peace treaties, Ribblesdale allowed himself a pain au chocolat, a rather uninspired and deflating choice, I thought, after all the fussing and negotiating and contemplating. But Ribblesdale munched happily away, a glaze of crumbs comically set at the corners of his mouth.

Ganimard, meanwhile, ate nothing and sat stone-faced as though determined to demonstrate Gallic discipline in the face of British excess. Ribblesdale took no notice. "I wonder if I should have another pain au chocolat?" he said, looking around, as though expecting someone to insist upon it.

Ganimard looked irritated.

"Perhaps instead of stuffing our faces, Inspector, we should get down to business."

Ribblesdale brushed at the crumbs. "Anton is the one for business, I'm afraid. Not that I blame him. That's what we're here for, after all."

"What kind of business?" I said.

"The business we spoke of earlier in London. The business of bringing the notorious Mrs. Nevermore to justice. That's the business we're about here, Ned. We've been patient, allowing you to go off to Vienna and all that, but now you're back and it's time to deliver. We need Mrs. Nevermore in custody and we require your help to ensure that you don't end up in the same bad spot she's in."

"Yes, I understand that," I said, finishing the pain au raisin, and feeling rather nauseous. Was it the pastry or the police? Hard to say. "What I'm not at all certain about is how I can help you."

Ganimard poked his narrow face close to mine. "You can help us, monsieur, by telling us what you know about the crime she is currently involved in committing."

"A crime that I daresay involves the Prince of Wales," chimed in Ribblesdale.

"Well, when I was in London, I thought she was up to something," I said. "But now I'm not sure."

Ribblesdale looked perplexed. "What do you mean you're not sure?"

"Just that. I am not sure what she is up to. I am not sure if she can be up to anything at this point."

"I don't understand," said Ribblesdale. "There is always the ability to commit a crime. That is never in doubt. It is merely a question of what crime is to be committed, and that's where you come in."

"I'm not certain she has committed any crime. She came to the aid of a troubled chef. But I don't see how that was a crime."

I did not add that if there was a criminal in the vicinity, it was probably me, the murderer of Edmond Corbeau.

Silence at the table except for the sound of me licking the sugar off my fingers.

"She helped a chef?" The question came from Ganimard. "Who was that? Monsieur Escoffier?"

"That's right," I said.

"In Vienna?"

"We went to Vienna, yes."

"What happened there?"

As best I could, without revealing that I may have been responsible for the demise of Edmond Corbeau, I related events involving the Savoy documents. What had happened to those documents? Ganimard wanted to know. I told him they had been returned to Ritz and Escoffier the night before. "The Prince of Wales told Mrs. Nevermore she saved the entire British Empire."

The detectives looked disappointed.

"I'm afraid you are going to have to do better than that, Ned," said Ribblesdale.

"Better than saving the entire British Empire?"

Ribblesdale's face darkened. His voice took on a nasty edge. "Enough, son. I don't want to hear more nonsense. We need evidence of a crime. You must provide it to us. It's as simple as that. We will meet back here tomorrow. At that time, you give us something on Mrs. Nevermore, understand? Something we can make use of. Otherwise we will be forced to take action that will be unpleasant for all of us, you in particular."

Ribblesdale reached out a meaty finger and gently swiped at the side of my mouth. "Sugar, lad," he said. "Don't want to send you home covered in sugar."

FORTY-TWO

I walked the short distance from the square back to rue des Saints-Pères numb with fear, torn about what to do next. If Mrs. Nevermore was not going to commit a crime, I would have to make one up for her. But how could I do that? I was the criminal after all, the killer. What did she do but save the British Empire by retrieving the Savoy documents? Even if she wanted to, it did not look as though she could sell the Eiffel Tower. And even if she could, I was not so certain that was a crime.

I entered the house and went up the stairs to the drawing room where I found Mrs. Nevermore. I expected sharp questioning. Suspicious glances. Explosions from Gamelle. Instead, she looked surprised. "What are you doing here?"

"When I left this morning, I lived here," I said. "Or has that changed?"

The doorbell rang. Mrs. Nevermore looked up sharply.

"Who could that be?" I wondered.

"I believe that is the Prince of Wales," she said.

"The Prince of Wales is coming here?" I could not shake the note of disbelief out of my voice.

"He is not coming here; he *is* here," amended Mrs. Nevermore. "Gamelle was supposed to wait outside and stop you before you came in."

The doorbell sounded again, reminding me of how little I knew about the ways of men or princes where women were concerned.

"What are we to do?" A further note of panic.

"Go into the other room," she ordered. "And stay very quiet."

A third time the bell rang, signaling royalty's impatience.

"Ned, get out of here. Now."

Mrs. Nevermore glided down the stairs. I stepped out into the corridor.

Below, I could hear the door open and Mrs. Nevermore say gaily, "Your Highness. Right on time."

"I've just come from the Duchess of Cumberland," I heard the prince say. "She's in town. Did you know that?"

There was a silence before Mrs. Nevermore replied, "No, I'm afraid I didn't."

"The papers have her in Copenhagen. She won't be there until July. Goes to show, you cannot pin your faith on the press."

"Apparently not," Mrs. Nevermore agreed.

"But she's doing as well as can be expected under the circumstances."

"I'm so glad to hear that," said Mrs. Nevermore, who sounded as though she did not have the faintest idea what circumstances the duchess was doing well under.

I stood against the wall as Mrs. Nevermore led the prince up the stairs. Bright eyed and rosy-cheeked, outfitted in a canary yellow waistcoat, he appeared alert and rested, positively shining with the anticipation of being alone with a beautiful woman. Except they were not quite alone. If he had but glanced around, he would have spotted me. Thankfully, he could not keep his eyes off Mrs. Nevermore.

They disappeared into the drawing room and I heard Mrs. Nevermore say, "You have caught me totally unprepared, Your Highness."

"Have I indeed, Mrs. Nevermore?" The prince sounded pleased by the notion.

"The servants are gone for the afternoon, so I'm afraid we're on our own. Can I offer you tea?"

"I detest tea, if you must know."

"You? Of all people."

"It is something I admit only in Paris," he said. "You must help me keep my secret, Mrs. Nevermore."

"It is safe with me, Your Highness."

"I was sorry that you left so hurriedly last night," he said.

"Another engagement, alas."

"I'm told you are a very clever woman, Mrs. Nevermore."

"You must call me Laura."

"A woman who walks away at just the right intriguing moment. A woman to be watched carefully, I would say."

"I'm not so sure whether that's good or bad."

"We shall have to see, won't we?"

Silence. A slight rustling of clothing. "Your Highness," I heard Mrs. Nevermore say. More silence. A sharp intake of air. "Highness."

The prince coughed and sputtered. "I've just been in touch with London. Apparently my head gardener at Sandringham has diphtheria."

"My goodness," I heard Mrs. Nevermore say.

More silence. Again Mrs. Nevermore said, "Your Highness."

"Jackson," murmured the prince.

"Jackson?"

"The head gardener."

"With diphtheria."

"Indeed."

"Please, Your Highness. You must stop."

"You must call me Bertie."

More rustling of clothing. I heard Mrs. Nevermore clear her throat. The prince let loose a contented sigh.

"It is good to be away from trade delegations and boring princes from countries I didn't know existed, claiming they are relatives of mine."

"The trials of Royalty," sympathized Mrs. Nevermore.

"Indeed, indeed," said the prince. "Very pleasant to finally have you all to myself in my favorite city in the world."

"Paris? Is it really your favorite?"

"I am of a family filled with grim Germans. There was no hope for me until I arrived here in 1855, young and impressionable, and immediately in love. London was swathed in gray. Paris was strung with lights. Napoleon III was on the throne, and the delightful Empress Eugenie, so incredibly beautiful. And he was a fascinating man, Napoleon, lived for pleasure and made no excuses for it. Rated anyone who didn't as a fool. I must say I have come to agree with him. A life lived without pleasure is no life at all."

"Well, I couldn't agree more, Your Highness," said Mrs. Nevermore.

"You must call me Bertie," he said.

The doorbell sounded.

"Who the devil could that be?" The prince, suddenly irritable.

"Let me see," said Mrs. Nevermore.

The prince uttered another sigh, this one less contented. Mrs. Nevermore charged down to the door and I retreated along the hall so as not to be seen by this new arrival.

Presently, I heard a familiar voice. Jack Dozen came up the staircase, resplendent in the Bon Marché suit. He disappeared into the drawing room, followed by Mrs. Nevermore.

"Your Highness, I'm pleased to introduce my brother-in-law, Monsieur Arnaud Poisson, the deputy director at the Ministère des postes et télégraphes. Arnaud, allow me to introduce my very good friend, Edward, the Prince of Wales."

The penny dropped, then. Mrs. Nevermore had found her mark. She found him back in London, in fact, in Lord Goring's study, if not before that. It was never to have been Sir Robert Chiltern. He was merely the means to a much bigger end. The grift was under way. What a fool I was for ever thinking it might be otherwise.

FORTY-THREE

It is an honor, Your Highness," said Jack in his most admiring voice. "I am so sorry to barge in like this."

"Not at all," said the prince. "Not at all. Mrs. Nevermore and I were just having a chat. I was about to tell her about Cherbourg."

"Cherbourg?"

"Interesting. I was there with mama. She was in a foul mood, dreadful headache, and all that. The beastly heat. Must have been in the eighties. Princess Eugenie arrived and she was out of sorts as was the emperor. Awful visit. Awful. And of course Cherbourg. Not one of my favorite places, I'm afraid."

"You look pale, Arnaud," I heard Mrs. Nevermore say. "Is everything all right?"

"Please, I don't wish to bother you. If I had known you had company —and such distinguished company, I would never . . ."

"You really don't look well, old fellow," the prince said. "Come, sit down, please. Can we get you a drink or something?"

I heard a tormented gasp that must have come from Jack.

"Arnaud," cried Mrs. Nevermore. "What's wrong? You must tell us."

"I'm so sorry, I don't mean to . . ."

"I say old fellow, you do seem in a state."

"It's little Marie," he sobbed.

"Marie?" The prince sounded confused.

Mrs. Nevermore interjected: "Arnaud's eight-year-old daughter. Arnaud, is she all right?"

"Why I hurried over here unannounced. I knew you would want to hear the news."

"What news? Good?"

"Not so good, I'm afraid," Jack said in a voice draped in funeral crêpe. "She needs the operation, that's for certain."

"Oh no, Arnaud."

"I do apologize for this, Your Highness," Jack said in his most plaintive voice. "I shouldn't burden you both with my problems."

"No, no. Quite all right. Quite all right."

"All is not lost," Jack hastened to add. "The doctors believe they can save her. I do not know where I am going to find the money, but find it I must. Her life hangs in the balance."

"My word," said the prince. "It does sound as though you've got problems, old man."

"There are many troubles for a Frenchman forced to care for a large family and a sickly daughter on a civil servant's salary," said Jack dolefully. "The price you pay, I suppose."

"Yes, well, I wish you all the luck in the world, my good man," the prince said brusquely.

He made the noises that accompanied a large man rising.

"Must you go?" Mrs. Nevermore sounded disappointed.

"Great Early arrives this afternoon," the prince said. "You know him?"

"No, I'm afraid not," Mrs. Nevermore said.

"Always in great force, Early. Wish we'd had him at Cherbourg. Might have saved the weekend."

"What a shame," said Mrs. Nevermore.

"Red face. A sun burn. Don't know how he does it. But it has been most pleasant seeing you again, Mrs. Nevermore." He seemed to remember Jack was still present. "A pleasure, monsieur."

"An honor, monsieur."

"Let me see you to the door, Your Highness," Mrs. Nevermore said.

"No, no, stay with your brother-in-law. He needs you right now. I can find my own way out."

"It's no trouble, I assure you."

Everyone sounded formal and awkward. I couldn't see him but from the sound of things, the prince practically charged down the stairs in his haste to leave.

I stepped into the drawing room. Jack sat very still. Below me I heard the door open and close.

"Good God in Heaven but that went badly," breathed Jack.

* * *

"It's finished, I tell you," stated an irate Jack Dozen. "He didn't buy one word of that sorry spectacle this afternoon."

By now Gamelle had returned, having failed miserably in his mission to keep me away from number 52. He tried to make up for it by aiming an extra strong glower in Jack's direction. "You give up too easily, as always. The first sign of trouble, you want to run like the rat you are!"

"The first sign of trouble? For God's sake, it didn't play!" Jack shrieked. "I was there. You weren't. This isn't just another mark. It's the bloody Prince of bloody Wales. He's liable to send the police around to pinch the lot of us!"

Gamelle's gaze turned toward Mrs. Nevermore. So did mine. She sat in a window seat, staring down at the darkened courtyard.

"We tried something that didn't work," Jack continued in a calmer tone. "It happens. So now let's lick our wounds, close down the tent and steal away into the night. Right?"

"Everything stays in play," said Mrs. Nevermore.

"Are you serious? The prince will not remain in play. He will not be back, mark my words."

"I will mark your words, Jack," she said. "Now mark mine: he won't go anywhere."

"The dying daughter of a poor French civil servant? My God. The man practically tripped over himself getting out of here. He never even mentioned the bloody tower. He wants news of the races at Ascot and who's going to be at Sandringham next weekend and what the shooting's like at Knowsley. Not bloody civil servants who can't pay the doctors' bills! We're finished, I tell you."

Mrs. Nevermore was on her feet confronting Jack. "What do you want to do? Slink back to Les Halles, drown yourself in absinthe, and then when you're good and drunk, come stumbling back here swearing words of undying love? Is that what you want? Then do it Jack, and be gone with you!"

Jack said nothing.

"I'm disappointed, too, but as you have said, this is no ordinary mark. It's the Prince of Wales, a boor of the first order, but certainly no innocent. He's been in enough trouble to know he must be careful. But that doesn't mean we've lost him. So let's play it out. I ask you yet again, Jack. Are you in or out?"

Jack paused a long time before he said, "It won't work, I tell you. I've seen enough of these things to know. It won't work."

"In or out?" she said sharply.

He threw his hands in the air. "All right, damn it. Let's see if he comes back. I guess we can give it that much."

Mrs. Nevermore rose majestically and that was the end of the arguing. Jack left, accompanied by more heavy sighs. Gamelle disappeared into his kitchen. Mrs. Nevermore straightened the drawing room, plumping the pillows on a love seat, adjusting a throw rug. Finished, she sank into a chair, her eyes watching me with a certain glittery energy.

"Where were you today?" she said.

"At the tower."

"What were you doing there?"

"I was feeling weak and out of sorts."

"The tower will do nothing for you."

"I believe it does," I said.

"Were you alone?"

I hesitated too long before I said that I was. Her eyes gleamed with even more suspicion.

"How else would I go to the tower?"

Nothing from Mrs. Nevermore.

"Also I went to a pâtisserie. For a pain au raisin."

"You like pain aux raisins?"

"I do."

"I didn't know that, Ned. I'll keep it in mind. Still alone?"

"Yes, alone."

"A trip to the tower, certainly I can see doing that alone. But a pain au raisin. Well, a pain au raisin is no fun alone is it?"

"I didn't know you liked pain aux raisins," I said.

"Oh, but I do, Ned. A pain au raisin, yes indeed."

"The next time I go for one, I shall ask you along."

"Please do."

I wondered what she knew or didn't know. Could the sorcière see into the depths of my treacherous soul? I suspected she could.

"This is a terrible thing you do," I said.

"Asking questions about your pain au raisin consumption?"

"Attempting to defraud the next King of England. It can come to no good. What's more, I suspect that you will destroy the Eiffel Tower."

Her face lit with amazement. "I? Destroy the Eiffel Tower? Whatever would lead you to believe such a preposterous thing?"

"I believe there is no end to what you would do, the lengths to which you would go in order to have your way."

"My goodness, you certainly have me down on the debit side of the ledger, don't you?"

"You said it yourself, Mrs. Nevermore. Nothing stops you."

"You think too much of me, Ned. Or too little. In any event, it is late, and I am tired. Go to bed."

"I'm going to stop you," I said.

"If nothing stops me, how will you?"

"I will figure the way."

She said nothing in reply, just smiled enigmatically, and then rose and left the room.

* * *

I climbed up to my little loft and sat on the bed for a time, contemplating what had just happened and what I had said. I was wrong, of course, as I always seemed to be wrong where Mrs. Nevermore was concerned. A crime was indeed in progress and Mrs. Nevermore was its chief architect. She had to be stopped or else I would be implicated, too, and end up on Devil's Island with Captain Dreyfus.

Or worse, beneath the guillotine's blade.

But how would I accomplish such a thing? The woman was a witch. Could anyone stop a witch, let alone a boy? Admittedly I was possessed of the power of the Strange, but a weak power at best. Certainly no match for her.

I undressed and got into my nightgown. I turned off the gas lamp, plunging the room into a darkness lit only by the uncertain glow from without. I went over to the window, wondering if Peregrine might be there. An almost-full moon shone over Paris, bathing the street beyond number 52 in an unnatural bright light that outlined the lingering figure in black.

He turned and a sliver of moonlight found its way beneath the floppy black hat he wore illuminating the white line of the scar along his cheek.

Corbeau.

It couldn't be. The man began walking along the street. Not so much walking as limping, and I now saw that he leaned hard on a cane. Someone who was stabbed in the leg and fell down a hole in the Staatsoper might limp like that.

FORTY-FOUR

Paris the following morning shivered in a rainy gray mist, befitting my mood. It should not have been so black, considering I would no longer go to the guillotine for the simple reason that Edmond Corbeau, the man I thought I had killed, was not dead. However, because he was not, there was every reason to fear Monsieur Corbeau would kill me.

Thus my gloomy state.

Mrs. Nevermore, as always, seemed totally unaffected by anything as inconsequential as inclement weather. Radiant in shades of summery brown and pale ivory, she strode purposefully along the Champ de Mars, ignoring the jostling throngs, parasol at the ready should the rains return. I hurried to keep up with her.

"What are we doing here?"

Mrs. Nevermore came to an abrupt stop. "Sometimes I do get the impression, Ned, that you are not telling me the whole truth about a number of things."

"You are reading my mind," I said in an accusatory voice.

"What makes you think I can read minds?"

"Because you are a sorcière and sorcières can do such things."

"They can? Very well. Remind me of what you are thinking."

"I think a great deal about Edmond Corbeau."

"What about him?"

"I saw him last night."

The glare in her eyes receded, replaced for an instant by what could have been concern. "Are you certain?"

"In the moonlight on the street outside my window. Limping."

"Perhaps you were dreaming."

"Not a dream, a nightmare. But real enough, I fear."

"There you are!"

We turned in unison to see lumbering toward us His Royal Highness Edward the Prince of Wales.

How could she have known he would be here? If the mark was properly chosen then the mark could be read and his moves plotted in advance—the gospel according to Mrs. Nevermore.

"Your Highness, what a pleasant surprise." She snapped on a welcoming smile so fast it scared the nearby starlings.

I was not so quick; unable to quite stuff away the resentment I was feeling towards her and the entire adult population, princes included. Not that it made the slightest difference. The prince did not so much as glance in my direction. His red-rimmed eyes were for Mrs. Nevermore only.

"I've just come from breakfast with Great Early," reported the prince happily. "In the neighborhood, so to speak. Your man Gamelle said you were off for a stroll with the lad here. Thought I'd take the opportunity and pop around for a visit. Hadn't been here since the opening."

The point of his walking stick jabbed at the tower, its upper reaches lost in the mist. "When you really look at the thing, you see it for what it is—an eyesore, don't you think?."

"How is the Great Early?"

"Weekending at Dunrobin with the Sandwiches. Sorry I can't be there, but there's no choice. I must listen to the nattering of the Paris trade delegations."

"Ned and I like to walk here in the mornings," said Mrs. Nevermore. "It's good exercise for the boy."

The prince's reddened eyes fell reluctantly upon me. "You do so much that is good, young Ned. Tell me, do you possess any vices at all?"

"I am occasionally forced to socialize with people I dislike," I shot back.

The prince looked vaguely surprised and then laughed. "Aren't we all, young man! Beware the long-legged guardsmen and the fluttering Reggies, I say! The Eton scugs in particular. Can't be too careful!"

Still chuckling, he took Mrs. Nevermore's arm and led her forward. "Notes from London first thing this morning, had to be up dashed early."

"The affairs of state," said Mrs. Nevermore in her most sympathetic voice.

"Apparently my sister, Princess Louise, has caused a bit of a stir at court.

Turned up in a dress with a train consisting of a fringe of real violets."

"Goodness gracious," said Mrs. Nevermore.

"No one's been able to stop talking about it."

"I can imagine."

He steered Mrs. Nevermore to one side, indicating he wished to speak of a matter not for the ears of children. Of course I strained to overhear every word.

"Such a great pleasure seeing you yesterday," the prince murmured.

"I'm only sorry you had to leave so unexpectedly, Your Highness."

"We all leave unexpectedly on occasion."

Mrs. Nevermore issued a low, knowing laugh. "Yes, I suppose we do."

So that was it, a little tit for tat; not a man failing to buy into a grift but a prince playing the games of love and seduction.

"You are quite a cunning woman, Mrs. Nevermore."

"You must call me Laura," she said.

"Sir Robert says I should be careful around you."

"Does he?"

"Advises me to stay as far away as I can."

"How quickly Sir Robert forgets recent history," said Mrs. Nevermore.

"Exactly what I told him. Without your help, who knows what sort of difficulties the two of us might be facing."

"I was glad to be of service, Your Highness.

"You must call me Bertie."

They walked on a few yards in silence before he cleared his throat and said, "If I asked you to take me to your brother-in-law, could you do it?"

"I suppose so," she said. "No doubt he's at his office."

"Would you take me there now?"

"If you wish," Mrs. Nevermore said in an uncertain voice. "But why would you want to see him?"

"Be so kind as to humor me."

"Of course."

The prince turned and raised his walking stick. Immediately a coupé with red-rimmed wheels and shiny brass coach lights swung into view, pulled by an impressive black horse. The coach came to a stop, the passenger door opened, and out stepped a large fellow in a bowler.

It was Cecil Ribblesdale.

"Inspector Ribblesdale of Scotland Yard," said the prince. "He looks after my protection when I'm abroad." With a smile: "Keeps an eye on me.

Discreetly, of course. Isn't that so, Inspector?"

"Do my best, Your Highness," Ribblesdale said.

"Mrs. Nevermore, can you please give him the address of your brother-in-law's office?"

Ribblesdale doffed his bowler and bowed slightly as he helped Mrs. Nevermore into the carriage before turning to me. "Here you are, young sir. Need a hand, do you?"

"No, I'm quite capable on my own," I said.

"I can see that," replied the inspector.

He closed the door behind us.

FORTY-FIVE

The prince settled back against the cushions as the coupé started off. His bulk seemed to fill the carriage. The silk topper sat straight upon his large head. He gripped his walking stick as though he expected to hit someone with it.

"You can imagine, Mrs. Nevermore, it is not always easy for a man in my position."

"Please, do call me Laura."

"Yes, Laura, well, the demands of my office, the expenses, all enormous. And the royal coffers, believe it or not, fail to cover everything. As a result of this lamentable state of affairs, a group of private investors works behind the scenes promoting my interests by providing capital for various ventures I steer in their direction. The proceeds from these ventures not only produce extra income for the office of the Prince of Wales, but also enable the syndicate to realize a small profit for itself."

"And I'm sure the investors are left with the good feeling that comes from serving the Royal Family and by extension, Britain herself," said Mrs. Nevermore.

"Quite right," agreed the prince. He fell silent, as though discussion of anything but the number of stags taken at the weekend was too much for him.

We crossed the Pont Neuf. One of those stone fortresses the French devote to their bureaucracy rose up before us, the River Seine on one side, a lovely little park lined with chestnut trees on the other.

"Here we are at Arnaud's offices," Mrs. Nevermore said. She gently laid her hand on his sleeve. "If I may make a suggestion, Your Highness."

"By all means."

"Given your high profile with all the peoples of the world, perhaps under the circumstances it would not be the best idea to go marching into a French bureaucrat's office. That might produce the sort of gossip I suspect neither you nor Arnaud particularly wants."

"Yes, you make a good point." The prince thumped his walking stick up and down, a signal perhaps that he was fighting to come to grips with this dilemma.

"Why don't we send Ned in to get Arnaud? That way the two of you can have a nice chat out here."

The prince looked at me in a way that suggested I might disappear entirely once I escaped his coach. He thumped the walking stick one more time and said, "Very well. Why don't we do that?"

I got out of the coach, and crossed the street. It had more or less stopped raining. A vaporous murk saturated the city, the same color as the stone gargoyles that attached themselves to the building. They glared down with sightless eyes opening twisted mouths in soundless shrieks as I came along the walk.

Ahead, I could see Jack Dozen, once again resplendent in his Bonne Marché suit, coming down the steps. He was accompanied by a handsome dark-haired man with a mustache turned up at the ends. Jack did not see me, preoccupied as he was with shaking hands with the gentleman. He watched him go off down the street and only then turned to me.

"The Prince of Wales is waiting," I told him.

"There's a sentence I never expected to hear," Jack said. He looked across the street to where the coupé waited. "Well, then, let's be off to greet His Highness."

He strolled across the street and as he went, he transformed before my eyes so that by the time he reached the coach he had become the slightly nervous *fonctionnaire* with a hesitant, shuffling walk, a serving man about to meet his betters.

"That wasn't young Bruce Ismay I saw you with just now?" I heard the prince say as I clambered into the coach behind Jack.

Jack, settling uneasily against the cushions, looked surprised. "Why yes, as a matter of fact it was. You know him, Your Highness?"

"Only slightly. He failed to turn up at the Duke of Sutherland's in the Highlands for the grouse hunt. Threw everything out. The duchess was in a fine frazzle what with the dinner settings, and not knowing for certain whether he would show."

"Most unfortunate," said Jack.

"Knew his father better. Tommy Ismay. Much more dependable than the son, if you want to know the truth. He died earlier this year."

"That's right," said Jack. "Bruce has now taken over his father's firm, Ismay, Imrie and Company. They own the White Star Line, passenger ships."

"Indeed, indeed," said His Highness. "Young fellow is said to have a head for business, even if he can't show up when he's supposed to."

"He seems impressive enough, no question," Jack agreed.

"Do you mind if I ask what he is doing in Paris? Don't tell me he wishes to purchase your Eiffel Tower."

The prince chuckled at the notion. Jack did not. He glanced at Mrs. Nevermore.

"Don't worry, Arnaud. I believe anything you tell His Highness will be treated in the strictest of confidence."

"Naturally," the prince said.

Jack leaned toward the prince, as though what he had to say was for his ears only. "Of course he's heard all the rumors floating around about the tower."

"That it's to be torn down," said His Highness.

Jack touched a finger to his lips.

"So he wants to buy the tower, is that it?" The prince actually sounded a trifle anxious.

"It's not that he wants to *buy* the tower. What he wants is the iron in the tower."

His Highness looked confused. "I'm not sure I follow."

"It's quite brilliant when you think about it. The tower weighs seven thousand tons, contains eighteen thousand steel pieces."

"Not to mention more than two million rivets," I added.

Everyone looked at me. "Exactly," Jack said.

"And the point being?" The prince, impatient.

"The point being, as far as Monsieur Ismay is concerned, a great deal of metal and steel will soon become available. He has a dream, you see, to build two great liners, the biggest in the world, titanic ships. He reckons to take on the Cunard Line which, I understand, is his main competition."

"Indeed," agreed the prince.

"He will need enormous amounts of iron for the plating required for the hulls of these behemoths. Well, here it is, waiting for him. All he would have to do is haul it away to his Belfast shipyards."

"And he is willing to pay for this, I imagine."

"He is willing to pay a great deal to whomever wins the contract to dismantle the tower. Thus in addition to the huge amounts the government will pay, there will be further income from men like Monsieur Ismay, anxious to pick up what they consider to be a bargain."

The prince seemed to consider this at length. Then he once again thumped his cane against the floor. "It would be an enormous undertaking, tearing the thing down."

"Indeed, Your Highness, and one that must be undertaken quickly and with a great deal of secrecy and cunning."

"Oh? Why so?"

Jack paused for dramatic effect and then said, "The Syndicate." He whispered the words as though it was dangerous even to utter them.

The prince leaned further forward. "The Syndicate?"

"A subterranean fellowship of Jews; the very incarnation of evil. It is believed The Syndicate supplies the financing for the defense of Captain Dreyfus, the Jew army officer who spied for the Germans."

"You don't say," said the prince.

"I have received information that The Syndicate knows of the government's plan to dismantle the tower and will stop at nothing to get the contract. Money will be no object to them. They will spend what is necessary."

"But to what end?"demanded the prince.

Jack moved closer so that he was practically speaking into the prince's ear. "Jewish bankers, along with the Germans, of course, fund The Syndicate in order to undermine not only the army but all French institutions. Can you imagine what would happen should they get hold of the Eiffel Tower?"

The prince paused as though attempting to conjure what might happen. Then he sat back and said, "I'm not sure I can."

"Catastrophic," pronounced Jack. "Under no circumstances can it be allowed to happen. These are my marching orders, so to speak. My superiors are most adamant."

No one said a thing inside the coach. Finally, it was Mrs. Nevermore who broke the silence. "Arnaud, I believe His Highness wanted to make sure you were all right. After meeting you the other day, he was concerned about your little daughter."

"Indeed, indeed," said the prince, seemingly thankful the subject had changed. "How is the little girl doing?"

"As well as can be expected, Your Highness," Jack said in a funereal voice.

"Thank you for asking. It is most kind of you to drop around like this."

"Well, I hope we haven't interrupted your working day, my good fellow. But Mrs. Nevermore is right, I was concerned. If there is anything I can do, you must let me know. I'm in Paris for a few more days."

"I hardly know what to say, monsieur. I am left speechless by your thoughtfulness."

The two men gravely shook hands. Jack departed the coach. The prince drove us back to number 52. He went on about Sargent's painting of Lady Elcho and her two beautiful sisters. He spoke of a museum he opened, a hospital he visited, a cattle show attended, artillery inspected.

He never said another word about Arnaud Poisson, Jewish cabals, or the Eiffel Tower.

FORTY-SIX

J ack came in the back way, irritating Mrs. Nevermore who feared the prince's
detective, the inestimable Inspector Ribblesdale, might be lurking about.

I said nothing of my association with Ribblesdale, of course, uncertain
of a number of things, including why he would not immediately betray Mrs.
Nevermore and her intentions to his employer.

What was he playing at?

In the fading afternoon light, Mrs. Nevermore rather than celebrating
her triumph on the Champ de Mars, appeared drawn and tense sitting at her
usual spot in the kitchen.

Jack slumped into a nearby chair while Gamelle fussed in the background,
clattering a pot here, running a dust cloth there, every so often throwing off
an explosive growl, unintelligible to anyone but himself, a smoldering vol-
cano coming to angry life.

Mrs. Nevermore ignored him, calming herself with a cigar, unusual for
this time of day and as indicative as anything of the strain she was feeling. Jack had loosened his tie and sat watching the blue cigar smoke curling
around her, drumming his fingers against the table's surface.

"Jack, don't do that," commanded Mrs. Nevermore. He stopped drumming.

"I still don't think he's buying any of it," Jack said. "I'm not even sure he
knows he's supposed to buy. He sees Bruce Ismay and it's the grouse hunting
he missed at the Duke of Sutherland's in the Highlands. I've met those too
smart to fall for a grift but damned if this isn't the first time I've encountered
anyone too stupid."

"How did you get Ismay to appear with you?" I asked.

Jack allowed one of his Smiling Jack smiles. "You don't get a Bruce Ismay.

You get someone who from a distance looks like Bruce Ismay. Or some other member of the British aristocracy that might give His Highness comfort."

"He knew enough to insist on going around to your offices so he's not to be under-estimated," said Mrs. Nevermore. "He's smarter than you think or at least he possesses a certain native cunning when it comes to smelling out trouble. The Ismay thing was a nice touch, incidentally."

Jack looked suitably pleased.

Mrs. Nevermore sat back and carefully placed her cigar on the edge of a nearby ashtray. "He says he has a syndicate of people who make investments for him. Why would he tell me that? Why would we get beyond grouse-hunting weekends if he didn't have something else in mind? Let's be patient and see what he does next."

"So we wait for him to make the move?"

"Jack, you know as well as I it's always better when the mark acts. That's when you know you have him."

"We may be waiting for a long time," he grumbled.

She turned and looked over at Gamelle. "Right now, let's think of what to do about Corbeau."

"Corbeau?" Jack looked alarmed. "I thought he was dead."

"Apparently not," said Mrs. Nevermore.

"Good God."

Gamelle came over and placed a knife on the table. He fumbled beneath the folds of his apron and somehow came up with a small black gun. He placed it on the table beside the knife. "This is what we do about him."

"Careful Gamelle," Jack said. "You don't want to arrive on the French throne with blood on your hands."

"We either take care of this man or this man takes care of us!" thundered Gamelle.

Mrs. Nevermore picked up the cigar and took a final draw on it before dousing its remnants into the ashtray. She exhaled more blue smoke, somehow lending the gesture a world-weary elegance. For the life of me, I could not imagine what she was thinking.

Or what she planned to do next.

FORTY-SEVEN

"Ned. Ned, wake up. It's time."

Mrs. Nevermore's pale face was a lovely sheen in the darkness. I couldn't decide whether I was dreaming or if she was actually in my room.

"Come along," she said. "You must hurry."

I was not dreaming.

I struggled to sit up. "What is it?" I gurgled.

"Get dressed," she ordered.

I sat in my nightshirt on the edge of the bed, trying to keep my eyes open. I said in a cross voice, "I don't understand. What's going on?"

"Do as you're told," she commanded. "Dress."

She was gone as suddenly as she arrived. I struggled into my clothes and went downstairs and found Gamelle in the kitchen. He was dressed in a long cape and a topper, in the process of hiding the knife beneath his cape.

"What are you doing?" I said to him.

"Silence, boy!" Gamelle snapped. "The last thing I need this morning is your wheedling and questioning."

He roughly grabbed me. I struggled against him. He tossed me across the room like the sack of the potatoes I occasionally had to drag up from the cellar. I landed against the wall, seeing stars. I expected Mrs. Nevermore to arrive issuing sharp orders for Gamelle to leave me alone. But she made no appearance. Gamelle wrestled me through the back door and down the stairs to the coach.

He got the door open and threw me inside.

"There, take it easy lad." Smiling Jack Dozen's voice came out of the shadows. He leaned forward and put a restraining hand on me as I struggled to sit up. "Just sit quiet."

"What's going on, Jack?" I slumped back on the seat, trying to clear my head. Vaguely I was aware of the coach moving forward and out the front gate.

"Sit back, enjoy the ride."

"It's the middle of the night," I protested.

"Indeed it is, lad. Indeed it is."

* * *

We moved through silent Paris streets, the *clop clop* of the horses' hooves rebounding off the dark facades of passing apartment blocks. Finally, the coach came to a stop. Jack leaned forward. "Now don't get upset, Ned. I'm going to take hold of you, rough-like. You can fight me, but not too much. Just enough to make it look as though you're being taken against your will."

"I am being taken against my will," I said.

Jack flashed a smile. "That's the spirit."

With that, he thrust me out of the coach. I hit the cobblestones and rolled onto my back. Jack came out and jerked me to my feet and tossed me down a flight of stone steps. A bolted door was at the bottom. Jack opened it and pushed me through into darkness.

"Good work, lad." Jack's whispered voice came out of the void. The next thing a lantern flared to life, held high by Jack. Yellowish light threw itself across damp walls; the suggestion of a cavern descending into the depths. A terrible odor rose up.

"Come on, then," he said and started off.

I followed after him. "Where are we?"

"Beneath the Quai d'Orsay, running along the Seine. *Les egouts*. The sewers of Paris, lad. The sewers of Paris."

We followed a glistening stone passageway past the outlines of a large basin and a footbridge with the hulks of wooden boats nearby.

I heard something in the distance and stopped. "What was that?"

"Nothing, lad," said Jack. "Come along."

Just beyond the bridge, the lantern light showed the passage forking into two tunnels. A narrow catwalk ran along each side of the tunnel above a shining stream.

I heard the sound again—a scratching emerging from the darkness, growing louder. The louder it became, the more terrible it sounded.

I snatched the lantern out of Jack's grasp and shone it behind us. I could see a black tide swallowing the stream as it raced forward. Jack grabbed the lantern back.

"Run for it, lad!" He cried before leaping onto the catwalk. I followed him, glancing behind me. The black tide had expanded, rising up into the catwalk, their panicky chatter filling the air.

I picked up speed, passing lumbering Jack, not at all constructed for this.

Rats as big as cats came abreast of me, fangs bared in the uncertain lantern light. Behind me, Jack screamed. I turned to see the vermin scaling his legs and back. He fell against the side of the tunnel. One of the beasts clawed up his chest, tearing at his face. He dropped the lantern.

Everything fell into blackness.

The creatures engulfed me. My nostrils filled with the foul sewer smell of them. I felt the awful dampness of their bristling fur, the tiny claws digging into my body as they scurried up to my face.

I concentrated as hard as I could. A split second later, the rats went flying away off me. The herd paused as one, and, as though sensing an enemy in their midst who was too much for them, turned away, disappearing back down the tunnel.

I groped over to where I could hear Jack calling out, his voice echoing in rising panic.

"Jack!" I cried.

Behind me, I could see another light bobbing through the blackness illuminating Jack covered head to foot with rats. I concentrated again and the rats began popping off him as though blown away by tiny explosions. In the oncoming light, Jack collapsed to the landing.

As quickly as they appeared, the rat tide was gone. A bent figure draped in black, his lantern raised high, approached, hovering three or four feet above the sewer floor. I glimpsed an unshaven face beneath a floppy hat. A pole was thrown across a bony shoulder, the corpses of rats strung from it.

The fellow slowed as he passed, glaring at me with mad, red-rimmed eyes. "You shouldn't be here," he hissed.

He veered toward us and I concentrated again, and he felt my power, and that brought him quickly to a halt. "A fellow traveler," he said. "Best be careful, lad. The Strange won't do you much good down here. Nothing does, you see. Nothing does."

Then he was gone, extinguished by the blackness. All returned to echoing silence except for Jack's great sobbing explosions of breath.

"God almighty, lad," he exclaimed. "I thought we were finished for sure."

I fumbled around in the darkness, found the lantern on the floor, and handed it to Jack, who managed to get it relit. His face was covered in bloody scratches.

"Are you all right?" I said.

"I'll be fine." Jack leaned against the railing. His clothes were chewed and torn, as were mine, I noticed.

"Fine pair we are," I said.

"Come on," Jack said. "We'd better be moving on."

* * *

A maze of cavities like intestines branched off in a multitude of directions. Slivers of light seeped through manhole covers above us, hinting at an over world unseen down here. To the left, the vast sewers of the Platriere, a sort of Chinese puzzle thrusting out as far as the Seine.

To the right lay the mouth of the rue du Cadran with its three openings like black teeth turning into blind courts. I followed Jack to the left through a larger artery that zigzagged haphazardly until it emptied into a grand crypt, the outlet of the Louvre. Here, a breathless Jack came to a stop.

He held the lantern so that it transformed his face in a ghastly combination of shadow and light; the devil's gatekeeper.

"This is it, Ned. We stay put here. And we stay quiet. Understand?"

I didn't understand at all. "Something's not right," I said.

"It'll be fine." Jack's voice had an edge to it.

"Those rats attacked us."

"They're rats, lad. That's what they do."

"And that rat catcher. He possessed the Strange."

"What do you expect of a fellow lugging dead rats around? Not like you encounter normal gents down here this time of night. Now pipe down, Ned, and let's just wait this out."

"Wait what out, Jack?"

Instead of answering, he extinguished the lantern. The inside of your coffin could not be so black. The silence was the silence of death.

I stood there listening to Jack's raspy breathing for what seemed an eternity.

Then the silence was broken by the scuff of boot steps coming toward us. I tensed, but said nothing. Beside me in the dark, Jack also remained silent, but he shifted around, and he too became tense.

I had the sense of a figure's outline and then suddenly I understood the game being played out. I was the bait, the gazelle staked out by the watering hole. Now here was the hunting lion to take the gazelle.

A voice rang out: "Corbeau!"

Another figure materialized out of the blackness and melded with the first, transforming into a beast with two backs writhing awkwardly, as though trying to perform dance steps.

The beast moved slowly through its paces, emitting low grunts and growls, this grappling together being hard, demanding labor.

Suddenly, the two-backed beast cried out, and began making a terrible gurgling sound and, like liquid parting, the beast divided, part of it dropping to the floor.

I caught the flash of a knife blade and then heard a pistol shot, followed by a second shot.

Jack lunged forward, lighting his lantern. I followed wavering light until it encountered a heap on the damp stone floor. Jack thrust the lantern into my hands and bent down to Prince Gamelle, the self-proclaimed heir to the French throne.

For once he did not scowl when he saw me. He did not do anything. His mouth yawned open as though trying to call out and his eyes held no life.

Mrs. Nevermore arrived in the sputtering circle of yellow light. I was surprised to see she wore a man's clothes, complete with a worker's cloth cap pulled low on her forehead. I almost said something to her about it but then I saw the pistol in her hand and realized she was the one who had fired the shots, fired them at Corbeau—one last desperate attempt to kill him after he killed Gamelle. I decided to keep my mouth shut.

FORTY-EIGHT

Back at number 52, badly shaken, Mrs. Nevermore dabbed at our cuts and scratches with stinging iodine and then poured brandy. Jack downed his at a single gulp and grabbed the bottle; Mrs. Nevermore sipped hers; I stared at mine, my stomach in knots, unable to take advantage of this unexpected acceptance into adulthood.

"We shouldn't have left him there." Jack poured more brandy.

"What should we have done? Dragged him out of the sewers and through the streets of Paris? And then what?" Mrs. Nevermore took another sip. "Gamelle would understand."

"He was to be the bloody king of France!" Jack glared at her.

Mrs. Nevermore said nothing. I noticed her hand shook as she raised the glass to her lips. Could something finally have gotten to our Mrs. Nevermore? Friends dying in Paris sewers? Would that do it?

"Doesn't seem right, somehow." Silence. Jack drank more. "Not bloody right at all."

She noticed me staring at my glass, not touching it. "Problem, Ned?"

"My face hurts. Rats chewed on it. You used me—again."

She looked more irritated than impatient. "I'm sorry about your face and the rats."

"They were driven by a rat catcher who possessed the Strange. Would you know anything about that, Mrs. Nevermore?"

"Unfortunately, I number few rat catchers among my acquaintances. As for using you, well, I did not use you, any more than I used Gamelle or Jack here. Edmond Corbeau, whatever powers you may or may not attribute to him, is a terrible danger. You only have to ask Gamelle. He threatens us all. Therefore, we all have to work to end that threat. It's as simple as that."

"Except we haven't ended anything," Jack said. "All we did was get a man killed. He'll be coming for us, mark my words."

"Tell me what to do, Jack." She appeared on the verge of tears. "Run to Corbeau—and Natalia, too—waving a white flag? I don't think that's going to do the trick. You're wonderful at pointing out what I do wrong. All right, then. You solve this. What do we do, Jack? Tell me what to do."

What Jack did was pour more brandy. Mrs. Nevermore sat back watching him with ill-disguised repugnance. She knew Jack would never get us out of this and so did I. No, it would be left to her and right now, in the dead of night, with Gamelle's corpse lying on a damp sewer floor beneath the Louvre, she seemed as hesitant and uncertain as I had seen her. She had moved against Corbeau and, by extension, Natalia, and the move failed. Now what?

The doorbell rang.

Mrs. Nevermore looked up sharply. The doorbell rang again.

"Who the devil could that be?" Jack said.

I immediately thought: Corbeau.

She looked at me. "If it was, I doubt he would ring the bell."

I was more convinced than ever: the woman could read my mind.

"Answer it, Ned. Find out who it is."

When I stood up, she grabbed my wrist. Her eyes looked tired and haunted. "Careful," she said.

* * *

I went down the stairs, took a deep breath and threw open the door.

"The Great Early has canceled the hunt at Balmoral."

Topper firmly planted on his large head, face the color of an open blast furnace, gleaming pinprick eyes swimming in rosé, the Prince of Wales swayed in the doorway, held fast by a firmly planted walking stick that he gripped for dear life as though caught in the eye of a hurricane.

"Mrs. Nevermore will wish to know immediately." He spoke in carefully articulated cadences as though each word had to be unwrapped from tissue paper.

"Should I tell her, Your Highness? Or would you prefer to do it yourself?"

"Better do it myself."

The prince proceeded inside at a stately pace, the walking stick marching before him, testing the solidity of the terrain, ensuring his safe passage up the stairs. I did not think he would make it to the top and feared what he would encounter if he did. The civil servant Arnaud Poisson? At this time of night? Would that not require elaborate explanations that even in the prince's obviously pickled state might raise suspicions?

Reaching the top of the stairs, he paused to catch his breath, leaning even harder on his walking stick. "Whatever are you looking at young man?"

"I am looking at you, sir."

"Why would you do that?"

"I have never seen a drunken prince before," I said.

"Nor have you spotted one tonight," said the prince. "Princes never get drunk. It is not allowed."

"I didn't know that," I said.

"Now you do. Keep it in mind."

He continued into the drawing room. Neither Mrs. Nevermore nor Jack Dozen was anywhere in sight. I offered to help the prince to a seat but he shook me off, nearly losing his balance in the process. He righted himself and at the same time also managed to straighten his topper, a not inconsiderable feat.

Mrs. Nevermore appeared then, plastering on a welcoming smile as she twisted at the cord of the robe she had just wrapped around her, no sign of the men's clothing she had been wearing. "Your Highness," she said as though it was the most natural thing for the future King to appear at her door at two in the morning.

"Great Early," the prince solemnly intoned. "I thought you should know."

"Why don't you sit down?"

He allowed her to guide him over to the settee. She glanced back at me. "Ned, best get some sleep. It's late."

The prince in the meantime lowered himself to the settee, his topper still in place, his body rigid as though he was about to review the regiment. Leaving the room, I heard Mrs. Nevermore say, "Wouldn't you like to take off your hat, Your Highness?"

"I insist you call me Bertie."

I went into the hall and nearly tripped over Jack. He touched his finger to his lips. From my vantage point beside him, I could see the glow from the drawing room but not Mrs. Nevermore and her late-night visitor. However, I could certainly hear them clearly enough.

"I can understand the Great Early," I heard the prince say. "Who in their right mind would want to spend the weekend at Balmoral? Certainly not I. The Queen is the most boring woman in Britain. I cannot imagine how she is my mother. But she likes Early and she dislikes me completely."

He heaved a great sigh. "That does not make life easy, Laura. One has great difficulty when one's mother is boring and also hates her own son."

A murmur of sympathy rose from Mrs. Nevermore.

"Oh, but it is, Mrs. Nevermore, and when I've had some drinks, I think about it, and that's not good for a man like myself, a fellow normally of sanguine temperament."

A long silence ensued. Jack and I traded worried glances: what was happening in there? Finally, another sigh exploded out of the prince. "So tonight I am quite sad, for my mother and the Great Early, and for myself when it comes down to it. I thought I might drop around so that you could cheer me up with a kiss."

"But do you think I should be kissing you, Your Highness?"

"Not if you keep calling me 'Your Highness.' However, if you would call me Bertie, I believe a kiss would be fine."

"Very well, Bertie. But only a kiss."

More silence followed, interrupted by rustling clothing and a sharp intake of air. "Your Highness."

"Bertie."

"Enough."

Then, as though following up on another conversation entirely, one that no one else had been privy to, the prince said, "The French government's plan to tear down this tower, that is precisely the sort of investment in which I believe my backers would be interested."

Mrs. Nevermore seemed confused. "I beg your pardon?"

"The largest venture my people have yet undertaken, no question. Nonetheless, should the circumstances prove right, I believe it would be of great interest."

The prince fell silent. I could hear his raspy breathing, as though he had run a long way. He said, "What they would need in deciding to enter into such an investment is assurance that their offer would be successful."

"My goodness," said Mrs. Nevermore with a flutter. "I am so naïve about business. I really should pay more attention. For example, I have no idea what sort of assurance you might require."

"You shouldn't have to worry your head about such matters, for you are a woman and you have other concerns."

The prince paused again and when he next spoke, it was as though a wonderful idea had just occurred. He did not sound so drunk. "Why, it might be the sort of assurance that your brother-in-law could provide."

"I see."

"Yes, yes, he could be most helpful," the prince continued in such a way as to suggest this idea was now gathering momentum in his head. "In order to gain these assurances, I believe you would find my backers exceedingly generous. Arnaud would not have to worry about his beloved daughter's operation, for example."

"You have no idea how happy that would make him," Mrs. Nevermore said.

"Anyway, just an idea," the prince said after another pause. His voice sounded slurry again. "A passing thought late at night. I have them often. Not always to be taken too seriously."

"The musings of a great mind," Mrs. Nevermore said.

The doorbell rang. That elicited another deep sigh from the prince. "My minders, I'm afraid. They have grown impatient. Perhaps it's just as well. I've drunk a great deal, stayed too late, and perhaps talked too much."

"You can never be too late here," said Mrs. Nevermore magnanimously. "And what you have to say is always fascinating."

"When I get to the subject of Great Early, my mother, and weekends at Balmoral, I'm not so certain."

I heard the prince lumber to his feet, punctuated by the crack of the walking stick as it struck the floor to provide much needed balance for our future King. "But I mustn't complain, Laura. Oh, no. This is the life to which I was born and these, these are the burdens I carry."

"Steady, Your Highness," I heard Mrs. Nevermore say.

"Really, I insist you call me Bertie."

Mrs. Nevermore escorted the prince down the stairs. I slipped past Jack and went through the sitting room over to the windows. Pulling one of the drapes to one side, I could see down into the courtyard and the gate beyond where the prince's coupé waited.

He emerged unsteadily on the arm of the individual who rang the doorbell. I expected that it was Inspector Ribblesdale. But then the moonlight caught the round face of Lord Goring. He helped the prince to his coach.

Jack was at my elbow and he too spotted Goring. "What the devil is he doing here?" he said.

FORTY-NINE

The next morning I came down at my usual time to collect the coal. I brought it into the kitchen and then sat waiting.

No coffee brewed on the stove. Breakfast smells did not assault my nostrils. Gamelle's apron dangled untouched from its hook by the cold oven.

I should have been overjoyed at his absence. He thought nothing of me. If it had been up to him, I would have been tossed into the street.

I felt terrible.

Eventually, I got tired of sitting there. I rose and fired up the stove the way I had seen Gamelle do it. Then I prepared coffee. Mrs. Nevermore came in wearing the pale lavender nainsook with trimmed ruffles. She sat at the kitchen table. Wordlessly, I brought her a cigar, and, keeping in mind how Gamelle had done it so many times, used his knife to cut off the tip. I found the matches and helped her light the cigar. She sat back exhaling smoke. I served her coffee.

"Liane de Poguy has tried to commit suicide."

I stared at her.

"She drank a bottle of veronal because Dr. Robin, her favored lover, apparently refused to marry her. Liane would not permit him to speak of his home life. If he referred to his wife and child, he was required to address them as 'The Monster' and 'The Little Monster.'"

She drew delicately on her cigar and was lost in a cloud of smoke.

"The veronal put her to sleep for forty-eight hours. When she came around, she vomited several times. That cleared her system. Apparently she is lovelier than ever."

A tear ran down her cheek.

"However," she continued, her voice choking, "Dr. Robin still will not leave his monster and his little monster. There is talk Mademoiselle de Poguy will enter a convent. I am told that's where many of the horizontals end up."

A stream of tears followed. She turned her face from me. I wanted to say something, but could think of nothing except to ask if she wanted more coffee. She shook her head, rose, and left the kitchen.

The cigar remained smoldering in the ashtray. I sat at the table and stared at it for a while before snuffing it out. The silence in the house was broken only by the ticking of the big kitchen clock.

Vaguely, I heard footsteps coming down the stairs and thought it was Mrs. Nevermore returning. But instead of coming into the kitchen, she went down the front stairs.

The door opened and closed. She should not have gone out, I thought. Not with Edmond Corbeau lurking about. I shouldn't go out either, but I was supposed to meet my two detectives and I feared what they might do if I did not keep the appointment.

I placed the remnants of the cigar into the garbage, washed the ashtray in the sink along with Mrs. Nevermore's coffee cup. Then I wiped my hands, put on my coat, and went out the door.

In the courtyard, Peregrine flew down from his tree and landed on the cobblestones in front of me. "I understand there has been tragedy," he said.

"Yes, Gamelle is dead."

"I never much liked him," Peregrine said. "I think he would just as soon have had me for dinner."

"I believe he felt the same way about me if it's any consolation."

"Nonetheless, he's gone, and that is sad."

"Yes, it is," I agreed. "Mrs. Nevermore is devastated. I've never seen her like this."

"What is she to do now?"

"I have no idea," I said. "But I don't imagine the grift will continue. How can it without Gamelle?"

"That should make you happy."

"Well, I don't like what she is doing, that's for sure. I should be in school."

"I don't know why anyone would want to be in school when you could be out there in the world," said Peregrine.

"That's because you're a bird. What do you know about it?"

"I am a falcon," he said.

I stepped around him. "I don't have time for this."

"Where are you going?"

That was the last thing I wanted Peregrine to know. "It's none of your business," I stated. "And I don't want you following me. Understand?"

"You could be in danger," he said. "You might need my help."

"I will not be in danger, and I don't need any help."

"Have it your way," he said in a huffy voice. "But you just might be sorry you didn't take me along."

Maybe he was right at that.

* * *

I sped around to the pâtisserie on place de Furstenberg. Detective Anton Ganimard was already there, nibbling on a pain au chocolat with surprising daintiness. I sat across from him. He asked me if I wanted anything. I longed for a pastry—not having eaten anything since yesterday—but that seemed childish under the circumstances; the good police detective buying the kid a nice dessert while he spilled the beans.

"Where is Inspector Ribblesdale?"

"He won't be here today." Ganimard put his pain au chocolat to one side.

"Because he is with the Prince of Wales?"

"I don't know where he is." Ganimard did not seem particularly concerned that I knew of Ribblesdale's association with the prince.

"What I don't understand is why you need me to inform you of Mrs. Nevermore's criminal conduct since you already have firsthand knowledge of it."

"Never mind about that," said Ganimard dismissively. "Just tell me what you know."

Well, what did I know? Better to ask what I didn't know. Endless volumes could be produced on that particular subject. Still, I had little choice but to confess something and so I said, "The Eiffel Tower."

He looked at me. "What about it?"

"Mrs. Nevermore plans to sell the tower."

Ganimard actually shook his head slightly as though not certain he had heard correctly. "She plans to what?"

"To sell it. Sell the Eiffel Tower."

"To whom?"

"You must know this. She is attempting to sell it to the Prince of Wales."

Ganimard shook his head again. "I know no such thing. How would I know this?"

"Ribblesdale is with the prince. He must have some idea of what is going on."

The French detective rearranged himself in his chair so that he sat up straighter, the pain au chocolat forgotten. I longed to take a bite of it.

"Let me understand this, monsieur. You believe Mrs. Nevermore conspires to sell the Eiffel Tower, yes?"

"In a manner of speaking," I agreed.

"In a manner of speaking. And she plans to sell the tower to the Prince of Wales?"

"That is if he is interested. It's hard for me to tell whether he is or he isn't—interested I mean."

"But she does not own the Eiffel Tower," Detective Ganimard stated. "The tower belongs to the people of France. So how could the Prince of Wales possibly purchase it?"

"That is the point," I said impatiently. "The prince believes he can."

"But he cannot."

"No, of course not."

Ganimard's face was like stone. "We have been patient with you, Arnheim, more patient than I would have allowed. But this is too much. What do you take me for, a complete fool?"

"I'm telling you the truth," I protested. "Or the truth as I know it."

"Do not further try my patience," he snarled.

"If you don't believe me, ask Ribblesdale," I insisted.

"I will speak to Inspector Ribblesdale. You and I will meet back here tomorrow. If he does not confirm your highly doubtful tale, then I shall arrest you on the spot unless you decide in the meantime to be more honest with me. Do you understand what I am telling you?"

"I understand."

More head shaking occurred as he rose from his chair, as though I was a lost soul and there was no use wasting more time on me. He turned and started from the pâtisserie. For one glorious moment I thought he might leave behind the pain au chocolat. But then he wheeled and came back to the table.

Without so much as a glance at me, he swept up the pastry and strolled out.

* * *

I came out onto the square and stood by one of the columns trying to convince myself I had done the right thing by telling Ganimard about the tower, even if he didn't believe me.

Doing the right thing, I decided, always made one feel better. So then why did I continue to feel so miserable? Because I was betraying Mrs. Nevermore? But then she was doing something that was terribly wrong. What's more, it would get me into a sea of trouble, too. She had at least lived a life. I had not. Yet as a result of this my entire life could be ruined.

Ruined!

I turned to cross the street and that's when I noticed one of the posters pasted to the column. Sketched in charcoal by the great Toulouse Lautrec, an ethereally beautiful woman with a black eye patch in a crimson gown held high a magic wand. Natalia the Magnificent had returned to Paris for an engagement at the Étoile Palace. Not only was Corbeau not far away but Natalia was with him. More trouble I didn't need.

An instant later I found myself being lifted off my feet and yanked backward.

"What do you think you're up to, you little bugger?"

FIFTY

Jack Dozen, glittery, suspicious eyes driving away any semblance of Smiling Jack amiability, shoved me against a wall.

"Did you hear me?" he demanded in a rough, scary voice. "What do you think you're doing?"

"I'm not doing anything," was all I could manage.

"What were you doing at the pâtisserie?"

"Eating a pain au chocolat."

"I saw you with someone."

I found my voice. "Did you, Jack? That's curious because I've got no one to be seen with. I have no friends. I jump when Mrs. Nevermore tells me to jump. What are you doing here, anyway? Do you need another decoy? That's about the only time anyone gives a damn about me."

"Lad, if you're looking for someone to be shedding tears for you, you're talking to the wrong gent."

"No tears, Jack. None expected. Here I am. How high do you want me to jump? Just don't accuse me of talking to anyone. That's a real laugh, that one. Thanks to you and Mrs. Nevermore, you don't have to worry about that."

"You do like to yammer on, for God's sake." Jack let go of me. "We've got enough problems so right now, you don't go missing, no matter how sorry for yourself you feel. Get my drift?"

"Sure, Jack."

"For the life of me, I don't know what to make of you."

"Don't you?"

"You're Flix Arnheim's orphan kid, so I suppose Laura thinks she owes you something. And you did save my skin down there in the sewers, whatever hocus pocus you employed, and I do appreciate that. Still, you seem a little shifty to me, playing out something I don't quite understand, and ill-suited to this business."

"I don't want to be in this business, maybe that has something to do with it."

"See, there's my point in a nutshell. You're in possession of the one thing you should never have in our trade, and that's morality. Right versus wrong and all that nonsense. Not that there's much of a distinction. As long as you got that going against you, might as well tie both hands behind your back for all the good you are."

"Perhaps I might be better at the things that don't require so much lying and cheating."

"You're too bloody naïve, Ned. You think the world is out there telling the truth. Well, grow up, lad. The world lies. Mrs. Nevermore and myself, we're just part of the world is all."

"Convenient for you, isn't it, Jack? That kind of world. Everyone's dishonest anyway, so you can sell boxes that print money and tear down the Eiffel Tower with a clear conscience."

"My God, your morality comes easy enough, squirt. Nothing on the line so there's no cost. Mrs. Nevermore puts the roof over your head and food on the table. You can hold your nose in the air and proclaim your purity. Well, for the rest of us, it's not so simple."

"There's only one reason Mrs. Nevermore feeds me or puts a roof over my head."

"Yeah? What's that?"

"Because she can make use of me."

"Just how is it she does that?"

"Against Natalia. She wants to be my mother, you see."

"Natalia wants to be your mother?"

"Motherhood makes Natalia vulnerable. Or so Mrs. Nevermore thinks. Otherwise, I'm out on my ear."

His eyes narrowed. "You think Natalia is your mother?"

"That's what she told me in Vienna," I said. "That's how she sees herself."

"Laura's sister told you this?"

It was my turn to stare at him. "Natalia is Mrs. Nevermore's sister?"

Jack's mouth was moving but nothing was coming out. You could see his eyes brighten as though the machinery inside his head was going at full speed trying to come up with something that would get him out of this. But the machinery wasn't working very well.

"Tell me. Is she Mrs. Nevermore's sister or not?"

His face darkened and the light in his eyes went out just before he seized me again.

"Keep quiet about that, understand? Not a peep to anyone. I mean it."

I said breathlessly, "I don't believe it."

Jack released me. "Well, then don't. Forget I said anything."

"But you're pretty sure, aren't you Jack? You know them both. You know about these things. Don't you, Jack? Don't you know?"

"What'd she tell you about herself, eh? She tell you about her poor misspent English childhood, did she?"

He saw the look on my face and smiled maliciously.

"Right. She must have dragged out that dog-eared photograph, supposedly of her mother. Said she never showed it to another living soul, right?"

I stared at him.

"Oh, God, lad. Not the bloody photograph! Waved it under your nose, I'm sure, and told you how her mom was a witch about to be burned at the stake or some such nonsense; dad an international confidence man saving the witch from the pitch fork-waving mob."

I didn't say anything, but then I didn't have to. All he had to do was read the look on my face. The malicious smile drooped. The voice became gentler. In victory our Jack could be magnanimous.

"As far as I know—and that's not so far at all—our Mrs. Nevermore was born in a village called Saint Alban in the southwest of France. Her father was no confidence man. He was the village simpleton. He thought his wife was the local witch, and I guess she never gave him much reason to believe otherwise. As it turned out little Laura and her sister Natalia were just like their mother. They began creating all kinds of myths and fantasies at an early age. Kept themselves entertained putting on the locals with far-fetched tales —the witch daughters of the sorcière mother."

"So then she is a witch. Natalia, too."

"Are they? Or were the tales of witchcraft merely part of the con, the illusion, an extension of their fantasy world?"

"But Mrs. Nevermore has the power of the Strange," I countered.

Jack did not seem impressed. "Does she? You say so and maybe you're right. But I'm not so certain. An artist of the first rank when it comes to sleight of hand? Undeniably. But witchcraft? That I'm less certain of. But then I am uncertain of most things where those two are concerned."

"She has the Strange," I said. "I know this because I have it, too."

"Maybe you do, maybe you don't. Maybe you're as much illusion as they are. How am I to know? Only thing I know for certain, I'm human. Flesh and blood, and every time I try to see the truth, corner it, stare it down, it scampers away from me.

"I've learned that if you look at this so-called truth a certain way, it's the one thing. You look at it another, it's something else entirely. You learn there's no such thing as truth when it comes to a Mrs. Nevermore or the Eiffel Tower. If there was such a thing, I wouldn't be in business. It doesn't exist. Truth is just more sleight of hand, that's all."

* * *

We passed Les Deux Magots. Jack said it might be a good idea to have a drink, to calm our nerves. I said I'd better get home. He insisted. I agreed to meet him inside, but first I wanted to get a newspaper and see if there was anything about Gamelle's death.

I reached the corner of the boulevard and rue des Saints-Pères just as a familiar red-wheeled coupé with the distinctive brass coach lamps disappeared through the gate at number 52. The prince returning to the scene of last night's crime.

If I went in the front I would be quickly ushered away, none the wiser about what was transpiring. Therefore, I marched around to the back and came up the rear stairs into the kitchen. No Gamelle lurking about, of course. I crept along the corridor. Voices rose from the drawing room.

"I must say I find young Ned's presence rather reassuring," I heard the Prince of Wales say.

"Do you indeed?" Mrs. Nevermore said. "I'm delighted to hear it."

"He is so utterly unhappy with what we are doing."

"Ned is so young and thus untried in the ways of the world."

"You have imbued him with an admirable sense of morality, I must say."

"It is so difficult properly raising children today."

"My parents worried and fretted over me. Mother never allowed me to be alone with other boys. She thought them a bad influence. She failed to understand that I was more than capable of discovering bad influences on my own. I did not need the least bit of encouragement from my contemporaries."

They chuckled together. Mrs. Nevermore said, "Ned is far too serious a boy to find himself on the wrong path, no matter what those around him might have to say about the matter."

"We will have him Archbishop of Canterbury before we're through."

More tittering. Weren't they having a wonderful time sending up the serious, moralistic young fellow hanging on their every word? Perhaps not so moral as they would like to think.

The prince was saying, "I would prefer not to be present."

"I understand, Your Highness. But in this one instance it would be reassuring to Arnaud if you came yourself. Then he knows for certain this is a serious proposition that has your personal backing and that you really do wish to help."

The prince sighed. "Honestly, the effect you members of the fairer sex have on men."

"Ah, but the truly strong men such as yourself are able to resist temptation, are they not?" Mrs. Nevermore's voice had taken on an insinuating quality.

"On occasion I am able to resist," said the prince. "Alas, this does not seem to be one of those occasions."

"I'm sure you're mistaken," Mrs. Nevermore said.

"I don't think so," replied the prince.

The silence took on a certain tension. There came the sound of rustling silk. Mrs. Nevermore murmured, "Your Highness."

"You must call me Bertie," the prince said.

FIFTY-ONE

Sterling silver gleamed in candlelight. Mrs. Nevermore entered the dining room wearing a gala evening gown, crimson and lacy and off the shoulder, with the hint of permissible after dark cleavage. The seductress? And what was I? The dinner guest to be seduced? Or the mark to be fleeced?

Hard to say. Or maybe not so hard at all. The world was to be taken in her reckoning of things, and I was part of that world, one of the suckers.

After the prince departed and I had retreated to my loft, she appeared briefly, her face showing nothing, and told me to dress for dinner. How could I say no?

"I do hope you like cold duck," she said, placing a plate in front of me. Sure enough, there was a breast of duck. Nothing else occupied the plate, just the duck—the limits, presumably, of Mrs. Nevermore's culinary skills in the wake of the departure of the increasingly missed Prince Gamelle.

And no wine, I noticed, not even a glass for her. Was the cupboard that bare? Or were we missing Gamelle that much? Or maybe she merely wished to keep her wits about her tonight.

"The Prince of Wales dropped around this afternoon."

"I saw him as he left."

"You haven't touched your duck," said Mrs. Nevermore.

"I'm not hungry," I said.

"It is perfectly good duck. Now eat it, please."

I lifted up my fork and poked at the glistening, unappetizing breast. Her cold duck; my cold heart. They went well together.

"The prince this afternoon generously offered assistance that will enable the lovely young daughter of my poor brother-in-law Arnaud Poisson to have the operation she desperately requires."

"How much will he pay?" I asked.

"Two hundred and fifty thousand francs will aid Arnaud in his time of trial."

"A big score, I presume. Your biggest? Or have you in the past managed to steal larger amounts?"

I did not attempt to keep the sneer out of my voice. She ignored it.

"Later, when formal contracts are signed, and the syndicate secretly controlled by the prince takes ownership of the tower, a further five hundred thousand francs will be paid."

"But that's impossible, is it not? How can such a contract ever be signed?"

"We will see about that. One step at a time."

"Yes, greed is endless isn't it? Who knows how much you can take the mark for? Before it is over, this could be bigger than Flix Arnheim's canal scheme. But wait. That didn't quite work out, did it?"

The muscles around her mouth tightened. "The prince likes you and your keen sense of morality, Ned. He finds your presence reassuring."

"I do not like him," I said.

"Tomorrow, the prince will appear at the offices of the Ministère des postes et télégraphes with a valise containing the money."

"You should not do this," I said to her. "It is wrong."

"Don't be ridiculous," Mrs. Nevermore said with a dismissive flutter of her hands. "You are a child, Ned. I am an adult. I know what is best. For both of us. Therefore, tomorrow morning you will accompany me."

"I was a child when you met me," I said. "But I am no longer a child, thanks to you."

She peered over at me as though seeing something unexpected and not particularly pleasant. "Remind me how I would have anything to do with your emergence from childhood."

"You force me to confront myself, I believe; to understand what I don't want to be and therefore help to mould what I am."

"Perhaps I should be flattered."

"No, probably not since I am that which you would not want me to be, an honest man."

"I am all for honest men," she said. "I've waited a lifetime to meet one."

"Then you're in luck," I said. "He has finally arrived."

The muscles around her mouth became even tighter, a sign of bad things to come.

"You will be there tomorrow," she said in a decisive voice. "You will remain here tonight."

"You cannot stop me."

The double doors into the outer hall stood open. Mrs. Nevermore glanced over at them. Abruptly they slammed shut. She turned to me, smiling sadly.

"I do worry about what is to become of you."

"I already know what will become of me," I said defiantly. I focused on the doors until they crashed open again.

Mrs. Nevermore did not react. Or seemed not to. However, a moment later the doors hurtled shut.

"I will go to school, I will become an engineer, I will marry and settle down, and raise children, and live a happy life, respecting my wife and playing fair with those around me."

I opened the doors with a force that rattled the house.

"Ah, yes. I almost forgot. You will be good and obey all the rules."

"Except I will not have a mistress."

By now I was standing. Mrs. Nevermore also rose to her feet.

"You still don't understand, do you?"

She directed her gaze at the open doors. They slid silently, gracefully closed.

"*They won't let you play.* You're a Jew, you see, and that ruling class to which you aspire? They don't want you."

"I will make them want me," I said.

I focused on the doors. This time they refused to budge.

"You think you can do anything, Ned. Well, you can't."

I willed the doors to open but they remained steadfastly closed.

"They hate you, that is why they will stop you. Everything is changing before their eyes, the old order is disappearing. What caused it? The Jews, of course."

I concentrated my mind, clearing everything else out, bearing down on those doors. They shook furiously in their frames, but otherwise did not stir.

"The Jews are responsible for all terrible things, so why not change as well?" Mrs. Nevermore continued. "They're afraid you're going to take what is theirs, and so no matter how hard you try, they will still keep you from doing that."

I gave up, exhausted, and slumped down onto my chair. Then the notion struck me and as soon as it did, the question was out of my mouth: "You're Jewish, aren't you?"

She paused before she said, "It's like I told you before. I am what they want me to be. I am whatever it takes to make them believe. Right now, they believe in a Mrs. Nevermore. So that is what I am."

"But what are you really?"

She came around the table, abruptly transformed into an even more daunting—dare I say, dangerous?—figure. Her gaze was once again on those dining room doors. They slid open for her.

"I will see you in the morning."

She started into the hall.

I could not stop myself. "Is Natalia really your sister?"

She spun around in a fury. Behind her, the doors slammed shut with such a resounding crash, one of the panels splintered.

"Who told you such a thing?"

"How did sisters become such enemies?"

The doors crashed open and she swept into the hall and disappeared.

No sooner was she gone than Jack Dozen came into the room. "What's all the ruckus about?"

He looked completely sober and it struck me that perhaps he did not stop off for that drink after all. He stared down at our neglected plates.

"Duck?" he said. "That's it? Just duck?"

FIFTY-TWO

I lay in darkness for what seemed an eternity. Gradually, the house around me grew quiet, a great coffin of a thing settling into silence. Except the coffin never truly quieted. It emitted an unending series of groans and sighs, as though agitated, trying, I imagined, to shake off the evil it contained, unsettled in its misery.

I rose and dressed, holding my breath as I did so. Creeping over to the window, I undid the latch intending to push it open, and drop myself down into the courtyard below.

Except the windows refused to open. I pushed at them again. They held firm. I stepped back, concentrating hard.

Nothing. The windows remained firmly in place. Unless I used a chair to smash the glass, I was not leaving by that way tonight.

Mrs. Nevermore anticipating my every move again. Damn her, anyway.

I went over to the door and turned the latch. The door protested loudly at being so unexpectedly disturbed at this late hour, but at least it opened. Floorboards and stairs under my feet announced their dissatisfaction with a noisy creaking that suggested an entire army on the move.

I reached the bottom of the stairs. Before me lay an endless track of dark frontier that had to be crossed if I was to make my escape. In the distant nether regions, a penumbra of uncertain yellow light glowed. Someone was still awake.

I started along the hall. Each footfall produced a sound like cannon fire. I reached the sitting room and there, propped on the sofa, was Jack Dozen. Our night watchman. The fellow charged with ensuring the young snipe upstairs remained tucked in his bed. He was not making much of a job of it. He emitted a loud snore followed by a series of smacking sounds as though tasting his snore's magnificence. I started past him.

Another snore. More smacking sounds. But he remained sound asleep, undisturbed by the cacophony of his own noise. I reached the main stairs and started down. The entrance door was locked of course; a series of locks and bolts, each louder than the last. But finally, to my relief, the door swung open. No cries went up, no gunshots erupted, no bullets whined through the air toward my pathetic form disappearing outside.

I raced across the courtyard, taking reviving gulps of night air. Reaching the gate, I discovered it locked. Damn!

I lifted myself to the top of the wall. Clumps of stone and concrete fell away as I poised uncertainly, staring down into the street below.

Peregrine settled beside me, gracefully folding his wings against his torso.

"So here you are sitting on a wall in the middle of the night," he said.

"You find that peculiar?"

"I do worry about you, Ned. Your state of mind. The decisions you are making."

"I worry that at times of tension and stress I find myself talking to a falcon."

"What? You don't believe I am real?"

"You're a talking falcon. I could be forgiven for being suspicious."

"I told you when we first met, this is your world now: the power of the Strange exists, the unreal is real, and the falcons occasionally have something to say for themselves."

"The falcons have far too much to say as far as I'm concerned."

"If more people listened to the falcons, the world would be a much better place. Perhaps they would not make the kind of mistakes you seem bound to make tonight."

"I don't want you following me," I said.

"Out there? Tonight? Even falcons, as brave as we are, would think twice about that."

I lowered myself down to the street. Peregrine's fine black head followed my progress.

"Stay here, Ned." There was an apprehensive note in Peregrine's voice. "Don't go out there. Not tonight."

"Tonight's no different from other nights," I called up.

"That's where you're mistaken," he said.

But I was past listening.

* * *

The churning sky faded behind the face of a nearly full moon emerging from scattering clouds. The moonlight turned the city into a ghost land of dangerous shadows.

A black rat scampered past as I hurried along. A lone dog, its rib cage outlined by the moon, regarded me with a baleful gaze. I would like to help you, my friend, I thought. But I can barely help myself.

I crossed a square where an old man played a soundless violin. I stopped to watch. Why was there no sound? I asked. He ignored me, concentrating his bow on those silent strings. Was any of this happening? Or was I imagining everything?

For the life of me, I could not tell.

Uneasily I continued on, crossing the Seine via the recently completed Pont Alexandre III. A light shone through the mist and a barge appeared, slipping beneath the bridge. A cry broke the soundless night, coming from the barge—quickly snuffed out.

I struggled forward.

The two palais under construction on the far side of the bridge were like ghostly toys the children had failed to put together. The skeletal ironwork carapace upon which was to be mounted the vast glass roof of the Grand Palais gleamed in the moonlight. I wondered how they could ever be completed in time for the exposition. But that was not my concern. Who cared about these bloated travesties of iron and stone and glass? They represented no century in which I was interested. But what a dreadful century it would be without the Eiffel Tower!

I picked up speed. I was not far from my destination.

FIFTY-THREE

Avenue Matignon ran off the Champs Élysées all but lost in the mist, as was the palatial townhouse on the corner of the avenue and rue Rabelais, its façade done in Second Empire style, even more severe and foreboding than I remembered.

Across the street stood the Jockey Club, the *gratin* shrine wherein members played polo, drank whiskey, and ran the world. At least that is what I imagined.

The thought of it made me despair. If I really was a Jew, did that mean I could never enter? Could anyone, Jew or Gentile, who played even a minor part in the demise of the Eiffel Tower? I would be *black-boulé*, as they said at the club. Unwanted, a gold bug, one of the bastards of humanity. No! I would not allow that to happen. Somehow I would be different.

Redoubling my resolve to make things right with the tower, I shoved aside as best I could whatever fear I was experiencing. If I was to act before it was too late, I must go beyond fear.

To my surprise, I found the gate to the townhouse wide open. I marched through as though I'd done this many times before, trying not to listen to the sound of my ridiculously beating heart. Crossing a graveled courtyard, I passed half a dozen impressive-looking automobiles and mounted the stairway leading to an ornate entrance. I pounded on one of the glass panels.

And waited. And then pounded again.

Finally, a light flared against the glass. Someone stirred on the other side. There came the rattle of locks and bolts before the door swung open to reveal an elderly gentleman with a white goatee, wearing a silk dressing gown over his pajamas.

It wasn't one of the servants as I expected, but Gustave Eiffel himself.

"I'm sorry to bother you," I said.

"I should hope so, it's late," said Eiffel. "Well, don't just stand there. Come in. Come in."

I stepped into a small anteroom. "My name is Ned Arnheim, monsieur, and I must have a word with you."

Large, sleepy eyes looked me up and down—some would mistakenly call those eyes arrogant and callous—before shaking a fine imperial head full of spiky white hair erupting everywhere as though an explosion had occurred deep within its recesses.

From somewhere inside came a woman's voice: "Gustave, who is it?"

"A young man who must have a word with me," said Eiffel.

"Paris is full of young men who must have words with you," the voice came back. "Tell him it's late, Gustave. Tell him even the great Eiffel needs his sleep."

Eiffel gave a helpless shrug. "I'm afraid my wife dislikes me staying up at all hours discussing—what are we discussing, anyway?"

"I'm sorry, monsieur," I said. "But it has to do with the fate of the Eiffel Tower itself."

He called out, "It has to do with the fate of the tower itself, dear."

"It's always the fate of the tower," his wife retorted in a weary voice.

Eiffel addressed me. "Come with me young man so we won't disturb my poor wife."

"Don't stay up all night bragging about yourself," his wife called.

"I'm going to do my best to ignore that," Eiffel replied.

He led me into a grand foyer with a staircase running up one side, and then down a long hall past a magnificent sitting room done in crimson shades, and a dining room featuring a mahogany table the size of a small country. We reached an empty room at the back of the house. He came to a stop and studied me up and down.

"Ned Arnheim, yes?"

"Yes, monsieur," I said.

"Very well, Ned, let us see if what I think is true of you, really is. I'm about to take a great chance and invite you into my office."

"That is very kind of you," I said. "Is your office nearby?"

"It is right here," came the reply. "At least it is if you are who I think you are."

"And if I am not?"

"Then even though it is very close, my office will always be too far away for you to enter."

"But we are in an empty room," I said.

"Are we now? Are we indeed?"

With that, he gave a little hop that launched him to the ceiling.

"Not you!" I exclaimed.

He gazed down at me. "Why not? The question is—are you, as well?"

He reached out and touched something and a section of the ceiling slid away and he disappeared through the opening. "Come along Ned," he called down.

Dazed, not sure of what I had just seen or what to make of it, but delighted at having so unexpectedly encountered a kindred spirit, I lifted myself toward the aperture into which Monsieur Eiffel had just vanished.

I came up into a vast attic that stretched across the house, dominated by a brass telescope on a podium aimed at a concave ceiling. A dozen statues of Buddha were interspersed among work tables filled with maps and drawings. The surrounding walls were covered with books, including, I noticed, the complete works of Voltaire, as well as Hugo, Zola and even Guy de Maupassant, who was critical of the tower.

"But what is this place?" I said.

"Well, I suppose you could say it is a combination laboratory, observatory, library, and office—my secret hideout!" Eiffel seemed both pleased and surprised by his description. "Yes, that's what it is, exactly. This is where I am able to relax and pursue my interests to my heart's content."

"Those interests being astronomy, physiology, and meteorology," I said.

Eiffel looked impressed. "I am also thinking about building a tunnel under *La Manche* or the English Channel as the British in their arrogance insist on calling it. I am not certain whether I will do this before or after I construct a subway beneath Paris. Also, I am considering the idea of placing that telescope over there at the top of Mont Blanc."

"The highest mountain in Europe," I interjected.

"Indeed," said Eiffel. "And of course, I am continuing with my study of the airfoils that will soon allow man to fly. Did you know that much more lift is produced by air flowing over a cambered wing than from air flowing beneath it?"

"I had no idea," I said.

"These things, are they by any chance interests of yours, Ned?"

"They are indeed, although I can't imagine a tunnel beneath the Channel or a subway under Paris."

"But then who could have imagined an iron tower, the tallest in the world, in the midst of Paris?"

"Nobody but you, monsieur,"

Eiffel positively preened. Then his face became melancholy. "I have all these dreams and plans. They crowd my brain constantly. I can't sleep for all the projects. Except none of it is taken very seriously, I'm afraid."

"But monsieur," I protested, "that can't be true."

"Ah, but it is. The tower is regarded as such a frivolous thing. It doesn't make me very popular in scientific circles or within the government. It's frustrating, let me tell you."

"But you possess the power of the Strange."

He smiled and brushed the top of a nearby Buddha's bald head. "Not very useful when it comes to astronomy or airfoils—or just about anything else. Is the power blessing or curse? There are days when I cannot decide. But each day it is a burden, no question."

"Just the exercise of hiding it from the world is frightening and tiring," I said.

"Yes, yes," agreed Eiffel. "We want to be different, don't we? But not too different. And does the Strange really help any of us in this life? Certainly it does not get a tower built or a tunnel underneath the English Channel. But there you go. We don't have a choice in the matter. We can only make what we can of it, and learn to adapt."

"I'm afraid it can't prevent the destruction of the tower, either," I said. "I've discovered that sad fact for myself. That's why I have come here, monsieur, and disturbed you at this late hour."

"The destruction of the tower, you say?"

"Yes."

"Well, it wouldn't be the first time that's been suggested. It is the favorite subject of penny-pinching bureaucrats in our government. They are out to ruin me, no doubt about it. "

I gazed at Monsieur Eiffel, the great creator himself, his hair firing every which way, those sleepy eyes filling with unexpected understanding, even sympathy, and I was overwhelmed. Here was the opportunity I had been waiting for, my chance to finally reveal all. And yet words would not come out.

"What's wrong?" Eiffel asked.

"I just want to do what's right, that's all."

He appeared taken aback. "Why, yes of course."

"When I look at your tower, monsieur, I can see precisely what is right. It soars before my eyes and there is no doubt what it is. You overcame tremendous odds to create what you believed in, and you stuck by it when everyone sneered and criticized. That is how I wish to live my life."

"Then that is how you must live it," said Eiffel.

"But it seems everywhere I turn, someone tries to steer me onto the wrong path. I am so confused . . ."

"There is no confusion, Ned, and what's more, I think you know it. You have found the right path, so take it. Believe me, I did no more than that. I just took the right path."

"It seems so easy to say."

"It is easy and at the same time it is the hardest thing a man will ever do in his life. But the mere fact that you ask the question at this god-awful hour tells me you are capable of succeeding. This is a funny world on the brink of a new century. I look through that telescope every night and I shake my head in amazement. We are such a small speck in the cosmos. There is so much more than what we are and it endures so much longer. We are gone in an instant in terms of the universe. At the end we are left only with ourselves, and what we have become. So if we cannot be honest what is the point of living? It is honesty that gives us form and substance, nothing else.

"If you can find your own truth, Ned, and you don't allow that truth to be corrupted or compromised, it is amazing what you can accomplish. If you have any doubt, well, you said it yourself, you have only to look at that tower."

"Yes," I said.

"Now go home and get some rest." He began to guide me across the room. "If the fate of the Eiffel Tower indeed rests on your shoulders, you will need strength for whatever it is you must confront."

"But I don't have the strength," I exclaimed. "I just don't." Unexpectedly, my eyes filled with tears. Damn me, and my endless uncertainty, anyway. I needed to look strong and resolute. Instead, I was reduced to the state of a blubbering child.

He regarded me sadly. "It's all right, Ned. Come along. I'll walk you out to the front."

Before I quite knew it we were outside again, and he was leading me down the steps to the gate. "Thank you for coming, my young friend. And thank you for taking care of my tower."

"But I haven't taken care of anything," I said. "I was hoping by warning you tonight that you might be able to do something."

"Ned, I believe you are capable. You have to push yourself a little harder, that's all." He leaned forward and whispered in my ear. "The top of the tower, Ned. That's where you will find what you need."

"No," I protested. "I cannot go up there. I've tried. I can't do it. It will destroy me."

"It will not destroy you. It will save you."

The gate closed. The light in the house went out. Gustave Eiffel stepped off the tiny stage of my life.

It will not destroy you. It will save you.

How could that possibly be? And how could I save the tower if its very creator was unwilling to help? He said I was capable, but I was not capable at all.

In fact as I stumbled along the street, feeling defeated, I had never felt more incapable in my life.

Then it struck me.

Of course. Why had I not thought of it before? I could not save the tower all by myself. But there was someone who might be willing to help. I understood then what I had to do.

And who I would have to involve.

FIFTY-FOUR

The glorious façade of the Étoile Palace stood dark and uninviting at this time of night. But that did not stop me. By now I was a man of the world you see, intimately familiar with such places.

I went around to the alley and once again found the side door open. The big empty hall, without the shifting skirts of the cancan girls or the distraction of one-eyed magicians, sank into a gloom reeking of stale beer and sweat. Nothing about it seemed glamorous now, except that on stage, illuminated by a single light, there stood a replica of the Eiffel Tower.

As I watched, the tower burst into phosphorescent light. There was movement and Natalia Boyer, eye patch in place, wearing a diaphanous gown, her crimson hair tinged with gold and tumbling to her shoulders, stepped out. Abruptly the light disappeared. Then the Eiffel Tower replica vanished, leaving Natalia alone on stage.

"Part of my new act," she called to me. "What do you think, Ned? If I can make the Eiffel Tower disappear, will I cause a sensation?"

"Everyone wants to make the tower disappear," I said sadly.

Natalia came over to the edge of the stage. She seemed not at all surprised or perturbed to see me.

"You are a bit of a magician yourself, Neddie."

"Do you think?"

"Conjuring the knowledge that I was here. Or does your power of the Strange allow you to read minds as well?"

"Posters by Lautrec and death by Corbeau," I said.

She smiled. "He is very effective."

"Lautrec or Corbeau?"

"Toulouse. All Paris knows I have returned. It will be a glorious engagement."

"Yes, but are you here for magic or revenge?"

"For my son. Perhaps I've come back to Paris for him. Even though he deceives and betrays me, I still love him, and wish to protect him from very bad things."

"I don't know who to believe," I said. "You say Mrs. Nevermore. Mrs. Nevermore says you. The lies blur on my brain. They become a single piercing howl. I can no longer distinguish one from another."

She came down off the stage, that one good eye never leaving me.

"But you have come back to me, Neddie."

"Corbeau said that to discover my father's killer, I need look no further than the occupants at number 52 rue des Saints-Pères. I have come to believe he is correct."

"Yes, you are a very wise young man. A young man who has learned a great deal this past while."

"But I can't do what I have to do alone," I went on. "I need help. I believe that because you want revenge and your money back that you will agree to help me."

"The money that you stole from me."

"That you in turn took from Monsieur Escoffier. Do you see what I mean? Lies mounted upon lies. An endless parade. So my suggestion is this: we forget the past. We move on together, the two of us. Just as you wanted. Do that and in addition to retrieving what is yours, you gain another one hundred and fifty thousand francs, and, perhaps most important of all, you defeat your worst enemy, your sister."

Natalia flashed with an anger that was quickly extinguished, like the phosphorescence around the Eiffel Tower replica. "They always said I was the sorcière."

"But it wasn't you at all. She possessed the power of the Strange. She was the witch."

"So now you know her evil, Neddie. You also know how difficult it will be to defeat that evil."

"What did she do to hurt you?" I asked. "How did you become such enemies?"

She did not immediately respond. Then her fingers lifted the patch and I saw the milky blue nothing where her right eye should have been. She lightly tapped at the area below that opaqueness before replacing the patch.

Those same fingers reached out and gently touched at the edges of my face. "Laura used to say you could make too much of your childhood. We disagreed about everything, even that. I believe you cannot possibly make enough."

"I agree," I said.

"Tell me what you want me to do."

"You must keep Corbeau in check," I said.

"He doesn't have the same feelings for you that I do, Neddie, particularly after what you've done to him. He's very angry, feeling betrayed."

"Nonetheless, I need him out of the way for what I have in mind. Otherwise, it won't work."

"I will do my best," she said. And so we sat together on the lip of the stage in the enveloping darkness of the Étoile Palace, amid wisps of smoke from a disappearing Eiffel Tower and I told her of her sister's latest grift, and how she would help me put an end to it.

FIFTY-FIVE

Mrs. Nevermore, beatific in a brilliant white morning dress I had not seen, fluttered above me like a descending angel.

"Hurry," she said quietly. "We don't have a lot of time."

No, we most certainly don't, I thought, sitting up in bed, still half asleep. What with all the traps I'd set into motion, the clever plans I'd conjured over the course of the night, I'd barely slept.

She paused at the door, caught in the morning light, positively shimmering, as though she had descended from heaven—highly unlikely.

"Are you all right, Ned?"

"Yes, of course I am," I said testily. "Why would I not be?"

"Slept all right?"

"I slept fine," I said. A lie. Already I was ignoring Monsieur Eiffel's admonitions about truth-telling. But then he had not met Mrs. Nevermore, had he?

She nodded and disappeared out the door, the angel deserting my room.

Struggling out of bed, trying to shake off exhaustion, I went through my morning dress ritual as quickly as I could, putting on my best suit for the occasion. No matter what transpired this day, I would at least look good for it.

I had arrived back at the house just before dawn, drained and exhausted from my nocturnal rambles and not a little fearful about what I might encounter. I went inside, my heart thumping away. However, this time Jack did not shake the drawing room with his snoring and lip-smacking. I wondered if he had checked my loft before retiring. If he had, he certainly would have been waiting for me on my return. Wouldn't he? Perhaps not. It was no longer a world in which anything could be counted on.

* * *

Mrs. Nevermore was already in the kitchen offering croissants and café au lait when I arrived. Where did they come from? I wondered. Had Mrs. Nevermore been up at dawn baking and preparing coffee?

She sipped at her coffee and daintily gnawed at a croissant. There was no cigar today. Or gossip. She kept her eyes on me as though she knew what I'd been up to the night before—or knew I was the traitor in her house. Or knew something.

"What's wrong?" I demanded.

"Why should anything be wrong?"

"The way you keep looking at me might have something to do with it."

"You're tired," she said. "I don't think you slept well."

She was right, I was not feeling great. My head ached and my mouth was dry, and my body hurt the way it did when it was time for a visit to the tower. But there was no time for that this morning.

"Let's get going," I said.

Mrs. Nevermore finished the croissant and placed her dish on the counter, dusting the crumbs from her fingers. She then proceeded into the hall where she checked her hair, spent some time attaching a large hat with an oversize brim, cocked at an angle so as to shadow half her face and lend further to the sense of mystery that always enveloped her.

"Very well," she said, swirling around to me. "All set?"

I supposed I was. Feeling more sick than ever, I trailed my white angel in her wide-brimmed hat across the yard, glancing over at the tree. Peregrine was not on his limb this morning.

Out in the street, Mrs. Nevermore hailed a cab.

* * *

We crossed the Pont Neuf and once again turned along the Quai du Louvre to that gray stone Gothic shrine built to worship and support the Ministère des postes et télégraphes.

Not far from the entrance, adjacent to the small park, stood the prince's carriage with none other than Inspector Cecil Ribblesdale hunched on the driver's box. I couldn't believe it. The prince had actually arrived early. I glanced at Mrs. Nevermore. The part of her face I could see showed no emotion. She leaned forward and tapped the window. The cab came to a stop at the curb and Mrs. Nevermore waited until I helped her out.

The door to the prince's carriage opened and out lumbered Edward, lugging an oversized valise, a spectacle I could never have imagined—the Prince of Wales himself weighted down by a bag full of money, eager to take part in a monumental larceny, watched over by a London police inspector.

Was there no limit to the deceit of men? Well, I had been learning the answer to that question, had I not?

Mrs. Nevermore wrapped the prince in one of her beaming smiles. He glowed in return, pink-faced and well scrubbed, a little puffiness around the eyes the only sign that the previous night might have ended at a late hour.

"I heard from mother this morning," he said cheerfully. "She has arrived at Victoria Wharf in Dublin. Lord and Lady Cadogan were there to greet her."

"Isn't that wonderful," said Mrs. Nevermore.

"Crowds were most enthusiastic. She had her bonnet and parasol embroidered with real shamrocks, so that might have helped."

The prince noticed me frowning. "And you, young man. Are you not delighted that the Irish have received my mother with open arms?"

"I could not be happier," I said.

"Well, my mother was thrilled, apparently."

Jack Dozen, in the guise of Monsieur Arnaud Poisson, appeared at the top of the steps. When he saw us, he dashed down to bow and pump the prince's hand.

"Your Highness, right on time."

"I'm very punctual when it comes to those in need," the prince said with a knowing smile.

"Your generosity will save a little girl's life," said Jack in his gravest, most sincere voice.

"That is all a man in my position can ask for, to do a little good in his life."

"You should not do this," I said to the prince.

"I'm sorry," said His Highness, cocking his head slightly. "What did you say?"

"I said, you should not go through with this, sir. No matter how hard you try to pretend otherwise, it is not right."

Mrs. Nevermore's smile lost some of its radiance. "Ned, that's enough."

Jack just stared as though not sure how to react. The prince also was looking at me. "Not right?" he said, as though he had never before heard such words.

"Your Highness, you are to be King of England. People look up to you as an example of what is good and virtuous and yet here you are first thing in the morning, sneaking about with a suitcase full of money, willing to trade it for unfair gain."

"Ned." Mrs. Nevermore's voice had taken on an uncharacteristic sharpness. "I said that's enough."

But I plunged ahead. "I know you have convinced yourself that you are doing good, but you are not. You know that, sir. I should not have to tell it to you. I ask you to take the right path today and not the wrong one."

Was that my voice breaking in desperation as I pleaded these things? I believe it was.

The prince remained silent and unmoving as though posing for the statue to be erected in his honor in the little park across the street.

Finally, his opaque blue eyes rested on the valise he was holding. He muttered, "Mother's in Dublin. Enthusiastic crowds, she says. Of course, she would not admit they were anything else. I find it very difficult to talk to her. She's at me all the time."

"Your Highness." Mrs. Nevermore's voice sounded unnaturally bright. "Let us conclude our business, shall we?"

"She worries about what will happen after she has gone," the prince said distractedly. "She thinks me frivolous and irresponsible and wonders if her son has what it takes to run the family business. There are days when I wonder myself."

"Then do better, sir," I said in a beseeching voice.

His eyes briefly met mine and he smiled. "I do like you, Ned. Your voice has become my conscience." He addressed Mrs. Nevermore. "Well, I suppose the boy is something of a conscience for us all, isn't he?"

No one answered. Jack's fierce glare suggested I had yet to become his conscience. Mrs. Nevermore's face remained a blank slate upon which no emotion dared attach itself.

The prince hefted the valise as if to gauge the weight of it.

"We are all greedy and avaricious, I suppose, fumbling around trying to cover our shortcomings with the odd good deed."

He lowered the valise, having apparently found the weight satisfactory. "But business is business, and a good deed, no matter what its underlying reasons, is still a good deed. So, Monsieur Poisson, let us conclude our business and pretend it really is for your daughter and nothing else."

Jack smiled and stepped forward to take the valise. I focused on the prince. Abruptly, the valise flew from his hand and landed on the ground. The prince looked astonished.

"What the devil," he said.

"Ned, do not do this." Mrs. Nevermore pushed each word out between clenched teeth.

"That's all right. I've got it." Jack reached down to pick up the bag. I made it skitter away along the ground.

Mrs. Nevermore glowered at me. "Ned, this is childish. Stop it!"

"What's the boy doing?" demanded the prince, anxiously.

I was counting on the fact that Mrs. Nevermore would not use her powers in front of the Prince of Wales and thus start the sort of tongue-wagging that would ruin her.

The prince stepped over and with a speed and grace I would not have expected, reached down and retrieved the valise.

It was then that Natalia Boyer, her face obscured by the fine black lace of a widow's veil, strode up to the prince and pointed the small pistol she held straight at his head. "Your Highness, be so kind as to give me that bag," she said in a firm voice.

The prince gaped at her. "Who the devil are you?"

Natalia said, "Don't make me ask you again. Give me the bag."

Instead, the prince turned and thrust the valise into my hands. "Here Ned, you take it. You're our moral voice. You decide what's to be done."

I stood there, staring down at the bag. This was the last thing I expected.

Meantime, Mrs. Nevermore, undaunted by the presence of a gun, moved toward Natalia. They made a startling contrast, the white against the black. But who was correctly attired? That was the question, wasn't it?

"Have you completely taken leave of your senses?" demanded Mrs. Nevermore.

"I warned you to stay away from me, Laura. Advice you should have heeded."

Natalia kept her one good eye firmly on the prince. The gun never wavered.

"Neddie, there's a carriage in the street. Go along to it."

"Ned, stay where you are," ordered Mrs. Nevermore.

"Neddie!" Natalia snapped. "Take the valise and go to the carriage. Do it now."

"I insist on knowing what is going on here!" thundered the prince. "Mrs. Nevermore. Who is this woman?"

"Ned, don't move," said Mrs. Nevermore quietly. "Whatever you may think of me, this woman is not the answer. Believe me when I say this."

"Don't, Neddie," advised Natalia. "Believe nothing she says!"

I looked imploringly at the prince. He just shook his head. "Do not look at me, young man. I've got no clue what's going on here. Most damned irregular!"

My eyes darted from one woman to the other. Black or white, Ned? I thought to myself. Which is it to be?

Natalia was supposed to take the money; that was the plan. So why could I not give it to her? What had changed from the previous night? Nothing, except I held the money, not Natalia. And perhaps because I did, I could not bring myself to finally betray Mrs. Nevermore.

The next thing Detective Anton Ganimard of La Sûreté Nationale appeared and jerked the gun out of surprised Natalia's hand. Promptly, uniformed police officers rushed across the street coming out from the cover provided by the park. Officers pounced upon Jack and surrounded the Prince of Wales.

"You are all under arrest!" Ganimard announced.

FIFTY-SIX

More uniformed officers appeared, burly fellows, officious and determined. They unceremoniously handcuffed Natalia while at the same time other officers clapped handcuffs on apoplectic Jack, protesting loudly that he was a government official and could not be treated in this manner. The officers, apparently used to such protests from malignant officials, paid no attention and bundled him away to one of two police wagons that had materialized on the river side of the street.

Mrs. Nevermore retained an icy calm that nonetheless spoke to the tense situation in which she now found herself. Natalia appeared stricken and confused as officers hustled her away. She cast a longing glance in my direction, as though looking for reassurance. I could only stare helplessly.

Cecil Ribblesdale remained near the prince's coupé and made no move to come to his master's aid. The prince, after initially seeming as confused as Natalia and—no other word for it—plain scared, recovered sufficiently to puff himself up and insist that a terrible mistake had been made. How dare the French police treat him in such a manner. Did they not know who he was? They must know and therefore they must also know he was to be accorded the utmost respect due his high office.

Ganimard, as befitted a true Frenchman, was unimpressed. "I see no princes here this morning. I see only a foreigner involved in an attempt to bribe a corrupt government official and that, monsieur, is going to land you in prison."

"Monsieur, I am British Royalty," stated the prince. "British Royalty does not go to a French prison."

"Well, we will see about that," said Ganimard with a confidence God made available only to the French.

The prince suddenly looked drained and defeated. His show of imperial force having come to naught, the sputtering protests abruptly ceased and he stood silent, his eyes fixed on the pavement, pretending he was a long, long way from here—at Balmoral perhaps, grouse hunting with the Great Early, surrounded by people who did as they were told and did not threaten him with prison.

Ribblesdale finally moved away from the coach and proceeded across the street, motioning to Ganimard. The French detective went over to him and the two huddled together. Then they went inside the building.

A few minutes later they re-emerged. Ribblesdale came down the steps and crossed the street where he once again took up his station beside the carriage.

Ganimard, meanwhile, came over to the prince.

"I have just spoken to the Ministry of Justice. The minister himself has taken an interest in this matter. My orders are to release you."

The prince's face betrayed nothing. He continued to stare at the sidewalk. "That is most kind," he said eventually, as though the waiter had just refilled his glass.

"Nothing to do with kindness. You are who you are. Therefore, you are allowed to walk away." He addressed Mrs. Nevermore. "Get him out of my sight, the boy, too."

Mrs. Nevermore went over to the prince. He seemed uncertain on his feet, as though he had grown weak and too exhausted to move.

"My bag," the prince said in a barely audible voice.

Ganimard cocked his head questioningly.

"The bag I brought here today. I wish to have it back."

Ganimard regarded the prince with disdain. "Whatever was taken at this crime scene is to be used in the case against Monsieur Poisson," he said.

The prince appeared to mull this over. His eyes finally lifted from the pavement, filling with desperation as he addressed Ganimard. "People I know, friends of mine, they will be ruined if I do not return with that bag and its contents."

"You should have thought of that before you involved yourself in this matter," said Ganimard coldly.

The prince turned and walked away at a slow, formal clip, as if he were leading a funeral procession. Inspector Ganimard called out to him. The prince hesitated, and then turned.

"One more thing, Your Highness. Don't come back to Paris any time soon. This is no longer your personal playground. If you do return, then I shall endeavor to make life very difficult for you. Is that understood?"

The prince had gone pale. It was difficult to imagine anyone in his entire life had ever spoken to him like that. To my surprise, he managed a slight nod. At that, the French detective turned and walked away. The prince restarted for his carriage. Mrs. Nevermore followed. I kept my eyes averted, lest any contact with Ribblesdale reveal me as the traitor I was.

With every step, the prince seemed to regain some of his lost composure, raising his head and straightening his shoulders, the consummate actor returning to his stage.

"Bertie," Mrs. Nevermore said.

He stopped. "The Queen will open the new Royal Convalescent Home in Bristol. I shall be there at her side of course, as is her wish."

"Listen to me," Mrs. Nevermore said.

"She believes it may well be her last visit to the provinces. Who knows? She is eighty now, so how much time does she have left? One likes to believe she will go on forever, but everything reaches its end. There is no escaping it."

"Bertie," Mrs. Nevermore repeated.

He abruptly seemed to realize she was right there in front of him. "Madam, I am the Prince of Wales," he stated in cold, clipped tones. "You will address me as 'Your Highness.' You will not refer to me as anything else."

He climbed into his carriage without waiting for Ribblesdale to open the door and huddled in a shadowy corner as though light would melt him. He did not move even as the coach started away down the street, an ink smudge against a graying day.

"We must find a cab," said Mrs. Nevermore briskly.

I busied myself hailing a cab for the two of us. The skies became leaden. A cab came along. I held the door for Mrs. Nevermore and then climbed in behind her.

FIFTY-SEVEN

The rain began as we rode in silence back to number 52 rue des Saints-Pères. I listened to the thud of raindrops against the coach roof, feeling dizzy and feverish, wanting to say something.

But what, precisely?

I suppose I could gloat, having defeated Mrs. Nevermore and her plot against the Eiffel Tower. But if it was defeat, did Mrs. Nevermore understand that I was probably its inadvertent architect? If she did, why wasn't she angrily accusing me? And if I had won, why did I not feel victorious?

When we reached the house, I held an umbrella while Mrs. Nevermore paid the driver, and then led the way in the rain through the arched entrance and across the courtyard. Peregrine was mounted on his tree branch. He did not seem at all perturbed by the rain.

I followed Mrs. Nevermore up the stairs, shaking out the umbrella, folding it, growing more apprehensive. What was wrong with her? Why did she not speak?

We entered the drawing room as thunder cracked outside and the rain produced an uncertain radiance through the tall windows, giving a milky hue to Jack Dozen, without handcuffs, holding up a fluted glass while Georges Duroy, surrounded by laughing police officers, poured champagne into it. Not far away, a couple of more policemen stood with the Bruce Ismay look-alike admiring the prince's valise mounted like a trophy on a side table.

Spying Mrs. Nevermore, Jack called out, "Bravo! Bravo!" He put his glass to one side and began to clap. Then Duroy and everyone else present started applauding and shouting, "Bravo, bravo."

Mrs. Nevermore acknowledged the applause with the trace of a smile, and said, "Please, please. You all did your jobs spectacularly." She turned to me and her smile grew wider. "Even you, Ned."

Anton Ganimard made his second unexpected entrance of the day, accompanied by more applause, slaps on the back, and renewed cries of "Bravo, bravo!"

Mrs. Nevermore embraced him and kissed his cheeks and complimented his brilliant performance. Jack came over laughing and said that when Ganimard arrived, he was half convinced the jig was up and he really had been arrested. Ganimard grinned—the first time I'd seen him smile—and said he would go to his grave with the memory of the look on the prince's face.

And what of Natalia Boyer? Jack crowed. The moment Ganimard handcuffed her and the other officers led her away. Priceless!

A roar of laughter.

Rain rattled the tall windows. Georges Duroy handed Mrs. Nevermore a glass of champagne. Jack strolled over. "It's like I said, lad, the truth is a shifting, evolving thing."

"I wonder if there is any truth at all, Jack. Around here, I don't think there is."

"The truth is Laura feared your righteousness might take you to the police."

I glanced over at the woman so concerned about my righteousness. Her back was to me.

"So she enlisted Ganimard and Ribblesdale to keep me busy, is that it?"

"That's it, exactly. None of us thought you'd bring Natalia to the party, though. That was an unexpected touch, I must say. But it worked out fine and ended up solving another problem."

"What problem is that, Jack?"

"Well, we don't have to worry about Natalia and Corbeau, now do we?"

I wondered about that but said nothing. No one was in a mood to listen to anything I had to say, anyway.

Jack grinned. "You did just fine, lad. You stuck by your beliefs, like you were supposed to, and that was no end of help to us." He slapped me on the back. "You've got real spirit, Ned. No hard feelings, right?"

More thunder exploded, ignored by the smug, self-satisfied revelers in Mrs. Nevermore's drawing room. I gazed around. Everything moved slowly in a blur, voices a cacophonous din echoing far away. Jack looked at me curiously, but I paid no attention. A wind rose in my head, its shriek cutting off all other sounds.

Mrs. Nevermore stood talking to Ganimard and Georges Duroy. Her back was still to me. I started forward with what seemed exquisite slowness, as though wading through quicksand. It took forever to cross the room. When I got close enough to the door, I concentrated on the valise.

It lifted off the pedestal and shot straight into my hand.

Before anyone realized what I had done or could move to stop me, I was out of the room.

FIFTY-EIGHT

Darkness descended along with a hazy rain as I ran along boulevard Saint-Germain onto rue du Bac. I turned west on rue de Grenelle, approaching the sprawling mass of the École Militaire, and the rain turned to snow.

I paused to catch my breath, even weaker now, anxious to reach the tower before it was too late. I glanced behind me and that's when I saw the figure astride the white horse, barely visible through the falling snow. I knew immediately who it was.

Edmond Corbeau was coming for me.

Rounding the college onto avenue Bourdonnayne, the few pedestrians out at this hour looked up in surprise at the unexpected flakes, stopping in the street and lowering their umbrellas for a better view.

I sped through a grand entranceway like a sparkling necklace laid out in an invisible jewel box and then stood on its end between tall columns. Fiendish Moors in the midst of an Arabian Nights delirium erected it for l'Exposition Universelle and the beginning of that glorious new century everyone kept talking about.

Ahead of me, the fair grounds burst into light, encased in mist and snow. The Eiffel Tower stood out in a watery radiance against the soupy grays and blacks churning across the night sky. The light atop the tower twisted round and round, my beacon in the darkness, the anchor I had to reach.

Not far away, the Ferris wheel came to life in a glowing ring. Uncertain music crossed the parkland and reached my ears, soon drowned out by the crack of thunder. The tower seemed to jump on its pedestals, hit by two jagged lightning streaks that simultaneously struck the pinnacle.

Suddenly, I felt so weak my legs gave out. I tumbled to the ground. Through the drizzle, the charging horse and its rider were outlined in another lightning streak.

Pounding toward me.

I got to my knees just before Corbeau, straining out of his saddle and bending low to the ground with a movement that was almost beautiful in its graceful athleticism, snatched up the valise.

He shot past me. I caught a glimpse of him straightening in the saddle and at the same time bringing his horse around.

Peregrine dropped through the air like a bullet, the way he would attack his prey, black tipped wings spreading wide. His talons raked across Corbeau's face. He screamed in anger and pain, blood pouring out of deep incisions. To my amazement, he not only kept to his rearing horse, but also held onto the valise.

I got to my feet as Peregrine swooped around and came in on Corbeau again, fearless.

Somehow, he misjudged his trajectory or Corbeau moved in an unexpected way. Whatever happened, the falcon smashed into Corbeau in a blurring thud of feathers and human flesh, sending him flying out of his saddle.

His neck at an odd angle, Peregrine tried to gain altitude, couldn't, and sank to the snowy ground, not far from where Corbeau landed. The horse whinnied loudly before galloping off into the descending darkness.

The ground around Peregrine was speckled with blood. I bent down to him. I called his name. His beak opened once, and briefly there was a gleam in his eye. I called to him again, reaching out to brush his feathers. Then the beak did not move any more and the light went out in his eye.

"Peregrine," I said.

But there was no answer. Finally, the falcon could not talk.

Not far away, Corbeau, bleeding profusely into the snow, stirred briefly, and then did not move. Was he dead? He certainly looked dead. But there was no time to find out for certain. Soon there would be no strength at all left in me.

Crawling around in the darkness, I managed to find the valise. I struggled unsteadily to my feet, feeling sick with grief and anger, not able to look any more at Peregrine's twisted remains.

I headed toward the tower, determined to reach the one place left on my human map where strength and right intersected, where the world became an understandable assembly of solid parts forming a larger imposing truth; the place where, if Gustave Eiffel was right, I might find my true self.

Or die trying.

FIFTY-NINE

By the time I arrived beneath the tower's reviving girders, the fog in my brain had become thicker than the falling snow. My legs were attached to buckets of cement. My bones felt as though they were breaking inside me.

I waited for the surge of energy that would make me right again. But there was nothing except pain. I felt weaker than ever.

The top of the tower, Ned. That's where you will find what you need.

Gustave Eiffel's words echoed in my head. But I could not go up there. I had tried so often and had never been able to do it.

It will not destroy you. It will save you.

The first gargoyle blew out of the darkness, hunched low, ashen against the white of the snow, wing-like protuberances erupting from its gnarled and hunched back. Furious yellow eyes blazed above a twisted mouth opening into a crimson snarl. Sinewy forearms propelled it forward.

I stumbled away as the gargoyle was joined by others. By the time I reached the red cabins that would take me to the first level, there must have been a dozen of them. With a chorus of obscene shrieks they bounded toward me, wings flapping, driving forward at a frightful speed.

I got into the cabin and started to close the doors. A human-like claw reached through the narrow opening, clutching at me. I slammed the doors as hard as I could. The arm disappeared. The creatures pounced upon the roof, thudding against it, shaking the entire structure like I was inside a cigar box.

Deep whirring and clanking sounds accompanied unseen hands starting the machinery into motion. The cabin began to move, rising up the tower's curving pier. The gargoyles regrouped and began to throw themselves against the window glass, their terrible mouths yawning open. A glass pane cracked like a gunshot.

But that was as far as it went, for as the combination of water-powered hydraulics, ropes and gears pulled the cabin higher and higher, the things vanished. The Champ de Mars dropped away beneath me, lost in snow and darkness.

I seated myself on a bench, panting for air, the valise perched on my lap, so weak I could barely remain upright.

* * *

The cabin came to a stop with an hydraulic sigh. Eerie silence, save for the whistle of the night wind. I got up and threw open the door.

The silence was replaced by thunder that shook the air as I stood on the promenade. Nearby was Brébant, said to be one of the finest restaurants in Paris. Opposite Brébant was a bistro devoted to the cuisine of Alsace-Lorraine. They were both closed up tight for the night.

I leaned against the wall, feeling faint. Pain pounded my body. Reaching this level had done nothing at all to improve my condition.

Gathering what little strength I had left, I staggered across to the second elevator that would take me to the very top of the tower. This was a more conventional French construction acting as a cylinder gently pushing me upward. In the darkness, the elevator cage rattled and shook. I held onto the railing for support.

Finally, the elevator clanged to a stop. The doors clattered open and I stepped out. Up this high, the wind drove the snow sideways. More thunder and lightning stitched across the sky, momentarily illuminating the spreading, endless glory of Paris far below.

I felt rather than saw them coming through the darkness. They must have come up the side of the tower. Before I could do anything, one of the creatures sprang on my back with a terrible howl, his clawed appendages digging into my throat. I could smell his hot, rancid breath, the rough, dry weight of his leathery body pressing against me.

More gargoyles engulfed me, pulling me to the floor. I tried to concentrate, tried to use my power, but there was nothing. Vise-like arms twisted around my neck, choking me.

Over the creatures' dreadful shrieks, I heard the thunder renewing itself. The wind grew in intensity. I kicked at one of the creatures as it bent to me, jaws thrust wide. I could not breathe. I struck out blindly, trying to get free.

Couldn't.

An instant later there was a tremendous crash as though the entire city had exploded. The tower burst with a searing white light. Life-giving energy poured through my body, driving off the gargoyles. I focused on the nearest and it started to shake, skin rippling, slowly at first, and then faster and faster. Long strands of flesh began to pull away from its body, catching fire. A cry of pain escaped its twisted jaws, cut off an instant later when it exploded into a fire ball.

I focused on another gargoyle. It flew up, trying to escape into the girders, evaporating suddenly in flames. A third gargoyle and then a fourth were turned into shooting fire balls.

The pain dissolved from my body. The lightning ceased. The fierce wind died away. The snow fell gently. I found myself alone on the tower summit, somehow still holding on to the valise.

Eiffel was right. The tower would not destroy me. It indeed saved me. Here I was then, still in one piece, feeling stronger than I had ever felt, ready to perform the act that would serve as final redemption and purification.

I made my way over to the railing. Hoisting the valise onto the railing I loosened the latch straps.

"Ned," a voice called.

SIXTY

Mrs. Nevermore materialized out of the darkness, a hooded black cloak framing the beauty of Danae. Zeus might seduce her in a shower of gold but the gods this night preferred her swathed in swirling snow.

"Peregrine is dead," I blurted.

"Yes, I know," she said, her face etched with sadness.

"And there are monsters out there," I said plaintively. "You sent them. You sent the monsters."

"There are no monsters," she said. "Only children with vivid imaginations."

"When I ran away with the money, you sent them after me, and when that didn't work, well, here you are—the sorcière."

"Ned, I want you to come home with me and forget this nonsense."

She fluttered elegantly like a black flag on a pirate ship waving in—what? —surrender? Hardly. She would never surrender, not our Mrs. Nevermore. No, she would never give up or give in or change. She would not stop lying. I would do what I came here to do.

"You deceived me and you murdered my father," I said.

"I loved your father," she said calmly. "I would never have hurt him."

"I don't believe you," I said. "I don't believe anything you say."

"If that were true, you would have given the valise over to Natalia as you planned, and you would have gone off with her."

I wasn't listening. I was through trying to figure the right from the wrong of it all. What Smiling Jack said was so true. The truth where Mrs. Nevermore was concerned was an ever evolving thing, a work in constant progress, never to be completed.

I turned, lifting the bag over the railing, holding it against the wind, tearing at its flaps and flipping it upside down.

The contents emptied into the air, the wind catching them in its updraft so that they floated out into black space where they were lost in the thickening snow.

There were a few franc notes. Someone must have laid them across the top to give the impression the valise was full of money. Mostly though, the bag contained bundles of newspaper cut to the shape of franc notes, hundreds of them, quickly lost to the blowing snow.

Mrs. Nevermore gently pried the valise from my stiff fingers and set it down.

"You look pale, Ned," she said. "You need rest. You've had a trying time."

"You switched the contents," I said.

"Mrs. Nevermore did no such thing," announced a voice. I turned to see Lord Goring in a Homburg and a camel hair coat with an upturned fur collar. Cecil Ribblesdale was not far behind.

"If you must blame anyone for all this, Ned, blame me. There was never any money in the bag."

"I don't understand," I said.

"Why I thought I'd best come along so I could explain things to you," Lord Goring said. "Mrs. Nevermore has done a tremendous service today, saving a future monarch from the worst enemy he will ever encounter—himself. And you, young Ned, you have played an invaluable part in helping to bring this about."

I stood there lost in a confused labyrinth of conflicting thoughts, trying to sort my way through the maze. Dimly I heard Lord Goring explain that the Queen had become increasingly concerned about her son's erratic behavior. So, too, had his friends, and even his minders, chief among them Inspector Ribblesdale. It was a matter of time, they all feared, before yet another scandal destroyed the prince's reputation once and for all, and perhaps ended the monarchy in the bargain.

The revelation of the existence of the Savoy documents, Natalia's attempts to blackmail both Sir Robert and the prince, only increased the level of consternation. Something had to be done. The prince had to be brought to his senses. But how to do this? He would not listen to anyone, and seemed bound to pursue a self-destructive course.

"It was Mrs. Nevermore's inspiration to teach Bertie a lesson he would not soon forget," Lord Goring explained. "We met in Paris just before the two of you embarked for London. She proposed a plan to use the blackmail threat against him to convince the Prince of Wales once and for all he was on the wrong track with his life."

"A plan?" I said. "What sort of plan?"

"Simple but quite brilliant: make Bertie face up to actions, force him to see that they can have terrible consequences both for himself and for his country. I think we have succeeded today." He beamed at Mrs. Nevermore. "Thanks to you, Laura."

"You mean, all this was to the good?" The words practically choked in my throat.

"It was indeed. This woman standing beside you is a heroine of the first order. A grateful nation should celebrate her deeds, but alas, these are the sort of deeds that must be celebrated quietly and with utmost discretion."

Lord Goring reached into his inside pocket and brought out a thick envelope. He presented it to Mrs. Nevermore. "A very small attempt at thanks from a grateful nation. Also, Her Majesty the Queen wants you to know how pleased and thankful she is."

"That's very kind of Her Majesty, and of you, Lord Goring," Mrs. Nevermore said.

Inspector Ribblesdale's hand was on my shoulder. "Sorry about all the confusion, lad. But you held up your end of it very well indeed. You have become a fine young gentleman, and the world is a better place for it."

I could not for the life of me think of what to say. I turned to Mrs. Nevermore.

"At the end of it all, you did good."

"I most certainly did not." Her voice was adamant. She held up the envelope. "I did business." She nodded at Lord Goring and Inspector Ribblesdale. "Very good business with these gentlemen. The sort of business that satisfies everyone and puts money into our pockets."

"By providing the confidence that allows one to believe," I said.

"Exactly. Done just right, it can even allow a young man to finally believe in himself."

That was when Edmond Corbeau came striding along. He appeared to be in a great hurry. His face was smeared with blood running from Peregrine's gashes. His clothing was covered with mud and snow. A gun glinted in his hand. His black eyes gleamed with hatred. Without thinking about it, fearing for Mrs. Nevermore, I stepped forward, franticly trying to concentrate, shouting at Corbeau.

The gun went off—a sharp little crack barely heard over the wind.

I felt a hard thump as though someone had knocked against me. I fell to the ground. Corbeau pivoted and shot Inspector Ribblesdale who had drawn his pistol. Ribblesdale dropped the gun and sank to his knees.

Lord Goring stepped back. His hat blew off his head. Everything seemed to move so slowly: Ribblesdale down on his knees holding his stomach, Mrs. Nevermore frozen in place, Lord Goring's stricken face.

Corbeau pointed the gun at Mrs. Nevermore. His finger tightened on the trigger. Vaguely, I wondered why she did not use her power against him. Why did she just stand there like that, head back, as though defying him to pull that trigger?

The rage poured through me, the power heaving wildly, aimed in the direction of Edmond Corbeau. It enveloped him, shaking his body like an angry little boy furiously shakes his sister's rag doll. A moment later, Corbeau exploded in flame.

He screeched horribly and turned, a fiery thing stumbling mechanically away toward the railing. The flames licking around him, he lifted off the ground and was flung backwards, striking one of the tower's cross-beams. His body twisted against the beam before careening out into the Paris night, a shooting star abruptly snuffed out.

I lay on the iron floor, the anger draining away like water retreating, fighting to hold onto consciousness. Mrs. Nevermore hovered in an anxious blur. She called my name like a song. I heard Mrs. Nevermore's high, frightened voice singing to me through the falling snow, the Eiffel Tower wrapping me in its embrace. My hand grasped her hand.

"My son," she said. *"My son."*

EPILOGUE

At the end, someone observed, all you have left is a story. That's certainly true of me. I've no family; any money I ever made is long gone. Nothing remains but my story.

But oh, what a story.

I sit in the residence and I spin it out, not everything all at once, bits and pieces usually, highlights if you will.

Everyone listens politely. No one ever accuses me of being full of hot air, but no one goes out of their way to congratulate me on the veracity of my tales, either. That's all right. Truth, as Smiling Jack Dozen used to say, is an evolving thing.

My listeners don't like to be left hanging, even if they have heard the story before. They want to know how it ends, and therefore I always say that one year later Queen Victoria died and the Prince of Wales became Edward VII, King of England. The regular visits to his favorite city ceased, and, although the new King quietly maintained a mistress, there were no more scandals. The prince had become a king, no small thanks to Mrs. Nevermore, I always believed.

Sir Robert Chiltern never did become prime minister. A few months after the events surrounding the recovery of the Savoy Hotel documents, he disappeared from London, deserting his wife and two small children and causing a scandal that reverberated for months as the London and Paris press sought to discover his whereabouts.

Eventually, he turned up in South Africa involved with various mining interests. He was said to be with a one-eyed beauty, a magician of some note named Natalia Boyer. I have since learned that love is the strangest and most mysterious enterprise in which human beings engage, the endless grift as it were. The most unlikely people find one another and end up together. There is no explaining it, any more than you can explain why someone would believe a wooden box could manufacture endless amounts of money. Or how a person with no money whatsoever could be mistaken for someone with all sorts of it.

Or how a boy could possess the power of the Strange.

Or how a beautiful, enigmatic woman could convince the future King of England to buy the Eiffel Tower.

We hope always for the best in everything, and thus end up believing in almost anything.

Even love.

* * *

The newspapers for a time were full of news of the Eiffel Tower shootings. In the midst of a rare Paris snowstorm, according to the accounts of the day, an unknown assailant had shot a fourteen-year-old American boy named Ned Arnheim on the tower's upper level. A quick-thinking Scotland Yard detective, Inspector Cecil Ribblesdale, a visitor to the tower, had dispatched the assailant but not before suffering a gunshot wound himself.

The assailant's body was found at the bottom of the tower, so charred and crushed by the fall that the police had been unable to identify him. How he had caught on fire was the subject of much speculation. It was argued that such was the speed of his fall that it had caused him to ignite. There were calls for more research into falling bodies.

Officers interviewed Ned at length from his room at the L'Hôpital des Enfants-Malades at 149, rue de Sèvres, but the boy seemed confused by events and proved of little help.

Recovering from the gunshot wound to his shoulder, young Ned was visited by none other than Gustave Eiffel, anxious to dispel any notion that one could easily be shot while visiting his tower.

They spent several hours together, Monsieur Eiffel recounting his meteorological experiments and his attempts to popularize the science of weather forecasting.

He pronounced himself delighted with the visit saying the boy was the sort of young gentleman who would put France in the forefront of the new and shining century, even if he was an American.

By the time I left the hospital, the Eiffel Tower shootings had been all but forgotten. That was fine with me. I wanted to get on with the things that a boy my age wants to get on with—like school.

Mrs. Nevermore had other ideas.

"The Comtesse Anna de Noailles is throwing a fête next week," she said as we strolled onto the Champs de Mars for the first time since the unlikely events that recently had transpired there. The sun was out. The Eiffel Tower gleamed before us. No gargoyles interrupted our progress. That was a relief, I must say.

"But honestly," continued Mrs. Nevermore, "she floats through these affairs dressed in white, reading terrible poetry, insisting her guests only talk about her. I think we should go to Morocco instead."

"What is in Morocco?"

"What is anywhere? A change of scenery, a new mark, an irresistible opportunity to become what you are not."

"But you are my mother," I said. "No matter where you go, you cannot escape that."

"Your mother? Now who told you that?"

"You did."

"A moment of weakness."

"Most mothers would not consider that a weakness."

"I am not like most mothers."

"You certainly are not," I said. "All this time I thought I killed my mother."

"You did no such thing," she said. "How could you ever think like that?"

"You should not have deserted me," I said.

"Ned, I am many things, none of them perfect, I'm afraid."

"I've had a great deal of time to think about all this," I said. "You came to Père-Lachaise that day out of a sense of guilt I expect."

"That's not true at all," she said vehemently. "I am immune to such petty emotions as guilt."

"Everything since then has been in your own curious way an attempt to make up for what happened. At least that is what I tell myself."

"As I've told you before, we can all make too much of our childhoods."

"And I have said that I wonder about that. For better or worse, this is what I make of mine."

"The Prince de Sagan has a box at the opera Saturday, so that could delay a Morocco trip, although I now hear the man is a notorious pederast and not to be trusted."

"I do not think you killed him, incidentally."

"Killed who?"

"My father. Natalia was wrong. Or she lied. I'm not sure which."

"If it came out of Natalia's mouth it was a lie."

"In any event, you are not my father's murderer."

She studied me before she said, "That's a relief."

"I believe Gamelle is, however."

"Gamelle?"

"He found out Flix Arnheim betrayed you. Flix had fallen in love with Natalia. She told me the truth about that. They were about to go off together, and she really did expect to become my stepmother. My father was on his way to meet me when he encountered not you, but an angry, vengeful Gamelle."

Another long silence. "No man ever loved me more than Gamelle," she said finally. "Loved too much I'm afraid. I believe it was because I took seriously his claim to the French throne. He always appreciated that. In return for his love I overlooked a number of his shortcomings. Perhaps I should not have. Anyway, it's too late for recriminations. Besides, I hate recriminations."

She heaved a sigh. "I miss him."

"Gamelle or my father?"

"Your father, of course. But Gamelle, too. He was angry and impetuous and unpredictable, but I miss him."

We walked in silence for a time.

"Peregrine could talk."

"There is also the prospect of Geneviève Straus's salon, the best in Paris for my money, although, honestly, since the Dreyfus affair it has become something of a bore."

"Did you hear me? I said Peregrine could talk."

"Falcons cannot talk, she said. "No, I think it's Morocco for us."

"I do not want to go to Morocco. I want to go to school."

"You want to go to Morocco. As yet you are unaware of the fact, that's all. I understand the air there is very good for orphans."

I reminded her that I was no longer an orphan. "If I am your son, then you must do what's best for me."

"There are wonderful schools in Morocco."

"I want to go to school here," I said. "I want to be an engineer."

"Honestly, Ned, I don't know what's to become of you."

"Whatever becomes of me, it will not occur in Morocco," I said adamantly.

There was a longish pause before she said, "Geneviève has been after me to attend her salon. Perhaps I shall give it one more try. Morocco will be there for some time to come."

I smiled, feeling oddly elated. It was suddenly very good indeed to be alive. I took her hand. It felt wonderful, somehow reassuring.

She frowned. "Do not get any ideas about changing me or making me a better person or any of that other nonsense you fill your head with, Ned. I am who I am, someone who makes others believe, and nothing will change that, certainly not you."

But she did not take her hand away and we continued on like that, the Eiffel Tower looming out of the distant haze, enduring.

* * *

Esther my caregiver finishes undressing me for the night, laughing, wanting to know if that's truly the end of the story. Of course not, I tell her. It's just the beginning, really. There were so many more adventures after that. But it must be the end for today because I am tired and yearn for the sleep that brings on the dreams wherein I am young again, and life spreads in front of me as endless as Paris itself.

Esther is my most avid audience, even though she keeps shaking her head and making clucking sounds, as if she does not believe a word. Ah, but I tell her, it's true, it's all true.

Even the part about the falcon? she asks.

The falcon talked, I say. I swear.

ACKNOWLEDGEMENTS

Writing *The Strange* was very much a love affair involving friends and family, and a city whose power to seduce remains, after nearly thirty years, impossible to resist. Steve Rubin and Frances Hanna read early versions of this book, didn't like them, and that forced me to do what every writer must do—rewrite!

My incredible wife, Katherine Lenhoff, not only read numerous drafts and made invaluable suggestions but also inspired me to see Paris in ways I had never seen it before.

My daughter, the remarkable Erin Ruddy, saved my hide any number of times editing the manuscript, and did it while patiently and lovingly caring for two very young children. Alexandra Lenhoff, as she has on previous books, came in at the end of the process bringing insight and rigor to the final line edit. Thanks also to Anne Stambouli and family, Bill Hanna, Bob Johnston, Victor Gordon, Jean Base, Lynda Schwalm, Kim Hunter, Dick Lowry, Jonathan Dorval-Lenhoff, and Joel Ruddy.

The talented Caroline Versteeg created the book's unusual cover design and put up with the finicky demands of an uncertain author.

My brother, Ric Base, worked overtime from Florida to get the manuscript into shape for publication. This is the second book project I could not have completed without him.

Finally, heartfelt thanks to Brian Vallée, publisher and author extraordinaire. I have known Brian all my adult life. This book is an anniversary salute to forty years of enduring friendship.

Printed in the United States
147956LV00001B/11/P